PRAISE FOR KEIIC

"Hirano's English-language debut is [...] thriller . . . As back-alley gritty and entertaining as a Raymond Chandler novel, the book asks what it means to be 'you' and suggests that the answer means nothing at all. Hirano's stylish, suspenseful noir should earn him a stateside audience."

—*Publishers Weekly*

"Keiichiro Hirano's *A Man* has all the trappings of a gripping detective story: a bereaved wife, a dead man whose name belongs to someone else, mysterious coded letters, a lawyer intent on uncovering the truth. Together with a willfully understated title, however, these features belie a deeply thoughtful novel whose mystery premise gives way to an examination of the most profound questions of identity and artistic creation. In a work so rooted in Japanese cultural history, the questions posed by the author become distinctly literary, moving ultimately to address the very practice of novel writing."

—The Arts Desk

"A riveting examination of desire and identity, *A Man* patiently unpicks the nature of unfulfilled aspirations. Keiichiro Hirano has written a multilayered tale of human reinvention, at once eminently readable and deeply moving."

—Tash Aw, author of *The Harmony Silk Factory* and *Five Star Billionaire*

"There is no doubt that Keiichiro Hirano is an author with an extremely pioneering and modern spirit. His works have opened up a very imaginative space in analyzing and exploring the spiritual world of humanity."

—Sheng Keyi, author of *Northern Girls* and *Death Fugue*

"Hirano has continued to grapple with new themes ever since his debut. In this work, he has arrived at the primal question of what validates human existence."

—Yōko Ogawa, author of *The Memory Police*

AT THE

END

OF THE

MATINEE

ALSO BY KEIICHIRO HIRANO

A Man

AT THE
END
OF THE
MATINEE

KEIICHIRO
HIRANO

Translated by Juliet Winters Carpenter

Text copyright © 2016 by Keiichiro Hirano
Translation copyright © 2021 by Juliet Winters Carpenter
All rights reserved.

Previously published as マチネの終わりに (*Matinee no owarini*) in the Minichi Newspapers in 2015 originally and a book published by 毎日新聞出版株式会社 Mainichi Shinbun Publishing Inc. in Japan in 2016. A paperback version was published by Bungeishunju 文藝春秋 in 2019. Translated from Japanese by Juliet Winters Carpenter. First published in English by Amazon Crossing in 2021. English translation rights under the license granted by Cork, Inc., and Media Do International, Inc.

Published by Amazon Crossing, Seattle

www.apub.com

Amazon, the Amazon logo, and Amazon Crossing are trademarks of Amazon.com, Inc., or its affiliates.

ISBN-13: 9781542005180 (paperback)
ISBN-10: 1542005183 (paperback)

ISBN-13: 9781542005203 (hardcover)
ISBN-10: 1542005205 (hardcover)

Cover design by David Drummond

Printed in the United States of America

First Edition

AT THE
END
OF THE
MATINEE

PROLOGUE

This is the story of two people whom I call Satoshi Makino and Yoko Komine. To protect their privacy, I have altered various details: their names, to begin with, as well as the organizations they belong to, the chronology of events, and so forth.

If I were to be absolutely faithful to the truth, I myself would have to make an appearance in certain scenes, but no such person exists in the novel.

My purpose in writing their story was not to lay their lives bare. Realizing that the story is not completely "true" may lessen its interest for some readers. But while fiction makes it possible to refrain from revealing some secrets, it is the only way to reveal others. I wished, while guarding the outer details of my friends' lives, to write freely about their inner emotional lives by presenting them as fictional characters.

When Satoshi and Yoko first met, they were, to borrow from Dante's *Divine Comedy*, "midway in the journey of our life," losing sight of "the straight way." Both were around forty, an age of peculiarly delicate anxiety. Whether they envisioned the bright hustle and bustle of their lives continuing or coming to an end, they felt dispirited. And just as in those opening lines, though it was "a hard thing to speak of," they found themselves lost in that "dark wood."

What name should I give the feeling that my friends had for each other? Was it friendship? Was it love? They maintained a strong relationship of trust that brought equal parts suffering and healing, and, at times, even a semblance of hatred; but investigating only the outer aspect of that relationship would tell us nothing.

I came to know Satoshi first, and later, Yoko. I was therefore in a position to fully sense why the two of them were so drawn to each other.

Brilliance and desolation appear intermittently in the record of their lives. Joy and sadness play tug-of-war. This is all the more reason why the alignment of their souls possesses a quality that is rare in today's world—a quality that I shall call, if I may, beauty.

I sympathized with them, grew disgusted with them sometimes, and yet I admired them. Nothing is as tedious as the romance of others, but in their case it was different. Why? Over the course of a few years, I experienced several enormous disappointments, and pondering their romance in spare moments offered a brief escape.

From the first, theirs were lives I was incapable of leading, yet even now I often wonder what I would have done if those things had happened to me.

Their lives contain riddles, some of which I never did fathom. They were such distant figures, even for me, that the reader should beware of hurrying to feel a direct sympathy for them, lest they elude the reader altogether.

As time went on, my desire to write about them grew, and when the time felt right, I picked up my pen.

1

The Long Night of the First Encounter

In 2006, classical guitarist Satoshi Makino turned thirty-eight. To celebrate the twentieth anniversary of his professional debut, he gave an extraordinary number of concerts that year—thirty-five in his home country of Japan, fifty-one overseas.

Tonight was the crowning event of a hugely successful tour. The autumn leaves in the vicinity of Tokyo's Suntory Hall were just then at their peak, and the trees, lit up by champagne-colored lights, shone brilliantly. A cold wind was blowing, sometimes strong enough to whirl the leaves, but this only kindled greater excitement in the hearts of the people standing outside, bundled in coats, tickets in hand.

Makino's performance that evening was talked about long afterward.

The main item on the program was *Concierto de Aranjuez*, which he performed with the New Japan Philharmonic orchestra; for his three encores he played Lauro's "Seis por derecho," then his own arrangement of Brahms's Intermezzo no. 2 in A Major, and finally a Toru Takemitsu arrangement of the Beatles' "Yesterday." The instrument he played on was for once not his beloved Fleta but a Greg Smallman guitar.

Ever since his storied debut at eighteen, when he'd taken first prize in the Paris International Guitar Competition, Makino's performances had always been sure-footed and trouble-free. The past twenty years had demonstrated not only that he possessed talent, but that of the many talents out there, his was singularly fine.

Makino's listeners frequently forgot to breathe. His stylistic perfection made it impossible to half listen, critics often said, and this wasn't entirely a compliment—the wry implication was that listening to Makino perform was a bit exhausting.

From the first, he was so excessively good at whatever he played, in any genre, that some thought he lacked commitment and was merely toying with his talent. Others found him thoughtful, partly because of the look of brooding concentration he wore while playing, like a chess player staring at the board.

That night, he showed an insightful understanding of the music with startlingly original interpretations that won listeners over: "Yes, yes, of course!" Even in the third movement of the *Concierto de Aranjuez*, the music was articulated in such fine-honed and loving detail that every nuance came alive, leading some critics to raise an eyebrow, surprised to discover that a piece so infamously difficult—it seldom sounded impressive, no matter who the performer was—should turn out to possess such charm. In short, the music was so persuasively rendered that, regardless of one's personal likes and dislikes, it was impossible to find fault with any of it.

At the encore, as if on cue, the audience rose in a standing ovation. While clapping, people leaned backward slightly and thrust their arms forward as far as they could in hopes of getting him to hear them. The height of clapping hands rises in direct proportion to the degree the applauder is moved; this was another thing the audience discovered that evening.

With every curtain call, Makino gave a refined bow of a slightly different flavor. He showed how satisfied and moved he was, not hiding his fatigue. The shy smile on his face, so different from the solemn expression of moments before, radiated the exhilaration he often displayed on television talk shows.

After the concert, the lobby was in an uproar, creating a synergy that convinced people their private impression was right: the performance had been stupendous. People who had come without a companion quickly began sharing their excitement online, standing stock still and causing others to bump into them with annoyance.

The recording of the concert, released afterward as a CD, went on to win that year's Record Academy Award and sold extremely well for an album of classical music—classical guitar, no less. It was reviewed widely, covered not just in specialty magazines and newspapers but also on television, giving even those with no interest in music the vague notion that that fellow Makino must really be something, all right.

The value of having attended that concert subsequently rose even higher, as Satoshi Makino's solo performances came to an abrupt halt, ushering in a period of long silence.

Looking back, there was one incident that might have been an omen. After the concert, more people than usual flocked backstage to see Makino, but he kept them waiting for nearly forty minutes. Suspicion mounted that he might have collapsed in his dressing room, but his manager, Sanae Mitani, adamantly refused to let anyone open the door.

Mitani, who had been in her position at Kinoshita Music for a year or so, had recently turned thirty with a resigned sigh. She had a round, pink-cheeked face, short brown hair parted on one side, and black-framed glasses. Her appearance inclined people to treat her like a child, but she was a woman of spirit. Older men in particular tended to fall into one of two camps, either lavishing affection on her or bristling with displeasure.

Before going into his dressing room, Makino had left instructions that no one was to knock on the door. Why he'd said this, Mitani didn't know, but she faithfully carried out his wishes. Finally, he emerged, apologizing in a droll way: "Sorry to keep you waiting, folks. I don't know, I just ran out of steam. I guess that's what happens when you're coming up on forty." He twisted his head from side to side to loosen the tendons in his neck.

He had changed into a white shirt subtly embroidered with tiny white stars, a black jacket, and narrow-leg cargo pants in dark moss green. His face looked refreshed and his hair was combed. He was smiling, but his glance darted from face to face as if he were unsure where to look.

His staff was relieved, judging from his expression that he was all right. Afterward, they all remembered seeing a 750-milliliter bottle of Evian water lying empty on the floor. When one of them brought it up, the others chimed in: "Yes, right! That struck me as odd too." Though what it might have meant, none of them knew.

During the forty minutes he was hidden away, unavailable, most of those waiting had given up and gone home. He exchanged friendly, gracious greetings with the few who had stuck it out. At the end of the line was Keiko Korenaga, his contact at Jupiter, chatting with a woman with pretty hair.

Long before the two women's turn came up, Makino was aware of them, glancing their way more than once. More precisely, it wasn't "them" he checked out but rather Korenaga's unknown companion. From the stage he had noticed her, having spotted her sitting in the orchestra section. His gaze, searching for Korenaga, had been drawn to the woman at her side and lingered there, his interest piqued by the small, fair face whose features he couldn't quite make out.

Lustrous black hair fell to her slightly square shoulders and crossed in front, the way a woman crosses her ankles. Her nose was well defined, eyes not deep set, eyebrows a pair of serene arcs. Her large eyes turned down slightly at the corners and crinkled when she smiled, giving her the air of a mischief-loving boy. Wound around her slender, pale neck was a scarf with a design of flowers scattered on a checkered background of black and pale green. Her lightly distressed jeans looked good on her long, straight legs.

Makino ended up studying her longer than was prudent. Then, when it was finally their turn and she stood before him, he hastily slid his gaze over to Korenaga at her side. After speaking words of praise and appreciation, Korenaga introduced the woman. "This is Yoko Komine. She's a reporter for the French news agency RFP."

Smiling, Yoko said, "Congratulations," and shook his hand.

The word sounded to him like a direct translation from a foreign language. Westerners often greeted him with "Congratulations!" or *"Félicitations!"* after a concert. Her makeup was applied with a light touch, unlike that of many young Japanese women; her name was Japanese, but her features suggested she might be part Japanese and part something else.

"That Brahms you played for an encore is a favorite of mine," she said. "The arrangement was marvelous."

Makino's eyes widened in pure pleasure. She was the first to speak of that piece instead of the *Aranjuez*, and moreover, it was the only performance he'd been satisfied with tonight.

"Thank you. It's not an easy piece to play."

"I was entranced." She laid a hand on her breast and smiled without exaggeration. Her voice was low and resonant—a cultivated voice, he thought. "It was as if the music were taking me to some far-off place, urging me to come along, leading me gently by the hand."

Makino held out his arms smoothly, as if inviting her to dance. "Actually, that was me, issuing you a personal invitation from the stage."

She looked surprised at this forwardness, perhaps put off.

"Watch out, Yoko," said Korenaga. "Makino is a bit of a ladies' man, and he's stayed single all his life. A word to the wise."

"Come on, don't say such slanderous things about me. Is that really what you think?"

"What everybody thinks. But I've got news for you: Yoko has a fiancé. Somebody she met in college—an economist, your polar opposite. And he's an American."

Makino withdrew his hands, as if he had just been cautioned against touching a work of art. "That *is* too bad. What do you mean,

7

'He's an American'?" He glanced down at Yoko's left hand, where a platinum ring sparkled on the fourth finger.

Listening to their banter, Yoko evidently decided not to be standoffish. "Anyway, I always liked Glenn Gould's rendition of that Brahms, but from now on I'll listen to Satoshi Makino's version on guitar." Her expression softened.

"I like the Glenn Gould recording a lot too. If you do listen again, I'm pretty sure you'll decide it's better after all, so do me a favor and stay away from it." He grinned. "I'm joking, of course. He's a total genius, far above me, but we do have one thing in common."

"Oh? What's that? Are you sensitive to cold too?"

"Could be, now that you mention it. But no, actually, I hate giving live concerts."

Yoko took this in. "Then tonight you did a brilliant job of enduring us 'spectators at a bullfight.'" She locked eyes with him for several seconds.

A bit shaken by her gaze, at once probing and profoundly understanding, he felt his social smile slip and struggled to retrieve it.

His manager, Mitani, standing to one side with Makino's guitar case in her arms, frowned. She had apparently mistaken "spectators at a bullfight" for Yoko's own phrasing, not realizing it was a Glenn Gould quotation. Meanwhile, Korenaga, assuming from the look on Makino's face that Yoko had incurred his displeasure, rushed to continue her introduction.

"Yoko's father is the director of that movie you like so much, Makino-san. *Coins of Happiness*."

"Really? Jerko Solich?" He turned to Yoko in astonishment.

"Yes, I'm the daughter of his second wife, who's Japanese. They were already divorced by the time I was old enough to notice, and I hardly lived with him at all, but we are in touch now."

"Is that right! That movie is the reason I fell in love with the guitar in the first place. I can't tell you how many times I've seen it, ever since

I was a kid!" He paused. "Well, well, well. I have the greatest respect for your father. I really do."

"Thank you. I actually knew you admired his work. As a matter of fact, this is the second time I've heard you play. After you won the Paris International Guitar Competition, my mother and I went to see you. We were so excited that a Japanese person had won! It was at the Salle Pleyel, wasn't it?"

"What? Are you serious? Good lord. I mean, I'm honored, but . . . back then I was still pretty bad."

"Not at all. Your playing was so wonderful, I was madly jealous. To think that a high school boy two years younger than me could play the theme music from my father's film so brilliantly and be showered with accolades—it was unforgivable! I was quite put out about it." Her nose wrinkled when she laughed.

She laughs like a child, he thought.

Mitani had stepped out to make a phone call, and when she came back, she urged Makino to move along to the after-party.

Yoko glanced at her Omega watch. "Goodness, look at the time! I'm so sorry to keep you when you must be exhausted." She made as if to leave.

Swiftly, Makino said, "If you don't mind, would you come along to the party? I'd love to talk some more."

Korenaga seconded the invitation, taking her by the arm. "Yes, do come!"

Yoko hesitated, glancing again at her watch before agreeing: "All right, if you're sure I won't be in the way."

They rode in separate taxis to a Spanish restaurant nearby. By then it was going on eleven o'clock.

The dimly lit restaurant was full, except for their reserved seats. Flamenco music was playing, and the white walls by the register were decorated with visitors' autographs. Yoko slipped off her coat and studied the signature of Paco de Lucía, whose guitar music was just then filling the room.

Makino hadn't noticed a resemblance when looking at her straight on, but now, viewing her in profile, he definitely saw a touch of her father. Or maybe it was something in the way she was engaged just then in looking, feeling, and thinking.

Becoming aware of Makino's gaze on her, Yoko turned toward him, indicating the autograph. Since they had ridden in separate taxis, this was only the second time their eyes had met. Apparently at ease talking to artists, she offered him her full impression of the concert and then unself-consciously joined the circle of guests. Makino realized that he was in slight awe of her, instead of the other way around. She seemed a little unapproachable, intellectual, but there was something friendly about her at the same time, he thought, something warm and appealing.

Eight of them sat at a table and drank a toast with cava. Dish after dish was carried in, and they passed them around the table, sharing everything without ceremony.

Makino was his usual talkative self. One of his staff brought up S, Japan's leading photographer, and Makino joined in with an anecdote from his ride back from Kyoto on the bullet train toward the end of his tour.

"When I got on board, there he was in the row right in front of me, across the aisle. S can be difficult when he wants to be, so I wasn't going to say anything, but then our eyes happened to meet. After that I couldn't very well ignore him, so I went over to say hello. 'Hi, it's been a while. I'm Makino.' Then—you know that way he has—he just flicked a glance at me. Cut me dead."

"No!" someone said. "That's awful."

"I didn't know what to do. I figured he might have forgotten who I was, even though we'd worked together. Just in case, I tried again. 'Satoshi Makino, the guitarist.' Even then, he just looked at me like, 'Who is this guy?' He was starting to piss me off."

"Right."

"'Remember?' I said. 'We were on that TV talk show together once, and then later on we bumped into each other in Aizuwakamatsu and went out drinking.' And so on. I brought up one encounter after another, trying to get him to react. What do you think he said? 'I'm afraid you are mistaken.'"

"Did you get on his wrong side somehow? Or was he just in a bad mood?"

"Well, when he said that, it kind of jolted me. So I took another look, and lo and behold, it wasn't him after all."

"What?"

"Yeah, the guy was a total stranger. Once I got a good look at him, I could see he was someone else. Why the *hell* I ever thought he was S in the first place, I have no idea."

Everybody had been listening blankly; now they all burst out laughing.

"I was so embarrassed. I felt like sinking into the ground and disappearing. It wasn't just him—everybody around was looking at me too."

"What did you do?"

"I was in too deep to come out and say I was wrong, so I acted angry: 'All right, *be* that way! Never mind!'"

"You didn't apologize?"

"Couldn't. I went back to my seat in a huff and slept."

"You slept?"

"Pretended to. How could I sleep after all that? But I was too cowardly to open my eyes, so I stayed like that the whole rest of the way to Tokyo. Even though I had piles of work to do!"

Once again the table convulsed with laughter. As he told the story, Makino glanced at Yoko from time to time. Their eyes met more than once. She was leaning back in her chair, holding a lightly cupped hand to her mouth, shoulders shaking with mirth. "Hilarious!" she murmured, and wiped a tear from her lower eyelid with her middle finger. He felt accepted, and glad of it.

While Makino talked, Mitani had been making sure the others were served. Now, passing a dish, she said, "When you're telling stories, Makino, you turn into someone else. Listening to you speak, it's hard to imagine you're the same person who gave that phenomenal performance tonight. When I first took this job, it was a continual shock."

"That's how most people are. People like S who get on their high horse and stay there are the exception."

"Give the poor man a break. It wasn't even him, for God's sake!" said someone else, sending a new wave of laughter around the table.

Yoko, sitting across from Makino, heaped her plate with vegetables.

"Are you a vegetarian?" he asked.

"No, but now and then I concentrate on vegetables by choice. It helps me stay fit. And this is a pretty late dinner."

Makino looked at her in some surprise. Choosing now and then to "concentrate on vegetables," as she put it, sounded easy, but how many people managed to pull it off? He'd never met anyone with such intelligent eating habits. He felt he had glimpsed the freedom, and discipline, with which she arranged her life.

"Besides, I'm leaving soon for Iraq."

"Iraq?"

"I went there once last year too. Sorry, I never did give you one of my business cards, did I?" She pulled out a card from a gold-colored holder, and he reached over and took it.

"How long will you be there?"

"Six weeks, then two weeks off. I'll do that twice—so four months in all."

"Is it safe? I saw the news about Hussein's death sentence the other day."

"Now is the most dangerous time since the invasion. But I'll be all right. We have permanent staff there, and security is tight. What worries me more than anything is the scarcity of good, fresh vegetables. That's another reason I need to eat them now."

"Ah, so that's it! Go on, stuff yourself while you can."

She smiled and sipped her wine. "Before leaving for Baghdad, I wanted to surround myself with beauty. That's why I came to your concert tonight. And I'm so glad I did."

"After you return from Iraq, please come hear me play again. I'll send you an invitation. Where are you based?"

"Paris. Yes, thank you, that would be so nice. I'll go anywhere. And while I'm gone, I'll listen to your music on my iPod."

Here, Mitani spoke up. "Let me know, and I'll be happy to reserve a seat for you anytime." She and Yoko exchanged business cards.

"Thank you."

"Have you lived in Paris long?" Mitani asked. "Makino-san lived there for a while once."

"Oh really? I've lived there ever since I took this job. About ten years now, I guess. I grew up in Geneva."

"You graduated from Columbia, right?"

Yoko looked at her with some surprise.

"I checked your father's Wikipedia page before, in the taxi," Mitani explained.

"Oh! I didn't realize there was information about me on there. I studied literature at Oxford, and then I went to Columbia for graduate school."

"Super elite! Amazing."

"Hardly. There are a lot of people out there far more amazing than I'll ever be. I owe a lot to my mother. She's the one who brought me up and made it all possible. She wanted to prove something to my father,

I suppose. Her existence is wiped clean from his personal history, and he never mentions her in public. How anything about me got on his Wikipedia page I have no idea. That's the trouble with the internet, don't you think?" Yoko sounded casual, but her words sent a hush over the table.

Mitani tactfully changed the subject. "So, Yoko, how many languages do you speak?"

"Basically Japanese, French, and English, and some German I picked up in college, because I was studying German wartime literature. Rilke especially. Also I can read Latin, and I know a smattering of a few other languages, Romanian for one, but carrying on a conversation is difficult. So when people ask me how many languages I speak, I never know quite what to say."

"Whoa."

"I would really like to learn Croatian, my father's native language. When I was little, I didn't know any English, so when I saw him, we couldn't talk. And that's what my mother spoke to him in, so I could never understand what they were saying. I remember bursting into tears and wondering who my real parents were. When the chance came, I studied English for all I was worth. Still, it's neither my mother tongue nor his." She paused. "However many languages I might speak, it's sad not to know my father's."

Yoko explained this difficult situation without a trace of sentimentality, even smiling now and then. Makino, listening respectfully, paused with a forkful of omelet in midair as the realization struck him that there were parents and children in the world who didn't share a common language. He pictured Yoko as a little girl sitting across from her father, unable to do anything but smile. What might she have looked like? Had she always resembled him the way she did now? After living so long with her mother, did she discover on one of his visits that she looked like him? Solich must have seen it right away. But even if

14

they'd both made the same discovery, they would have had no way to share it with each other.

Makino's background was just the opposite. He'd been brought up from early childhood to fulfill the dreams of his guitar-loving father. By the time he was in kindergarten, they already shared the same language—guitar. Rather than playing music, Makino had had fun making his guitar "talk." Though his aging father had slowly lost the ability to comprehend what Makino's guitar was saying . . .

Mitani and Yoko went on chatting, letting the sad anecdote slide without further comment. "My one linguistic claim to fame," Mitani was saying, "is knowing Hakata dialect. My English never gets any better, sadly."

"So you're from Fukuoka?"

"Born and bred!"

Makino spoke up teasingly. "Every day, I am made acutely aware of how strong Kyushu women are."

"My mother's roots are in Nagasaki," said Yoko.

"No! You're from Kyushu?" Mitani said this in a voice so loud that every head at the table turned.

"Yes. In summer and winter we used to vacation at my grand-mother's house. I went swimming in the sea."

"How about that! I feel a real bond with you now. You're Japanese after all!"

"I think I am pretty Japanese inside, actually. Everyone says so. My father's roots are a bit more complicated. He identifies much more strongly as Yugoslavian than Croatian. Plus he has some Austrian blood. My mother's family history is much simpler. I learned to speak Nagasaki dialect from my grandmother. That gave me a fondness for Japanese dialects. Hakata dialect spoken by a woman is really charming. Very attractive. And not too different from Nagasaki dialect, either."

"See, Makino?" said Mitani, using her native dialect. "Yoko thinks so too!" Then she asked Yoko if she ever got back to Nagasaki.

15

"Yes, but unfortunately, my grandmother died the year before last."

"Oh, I'm sorry."

"No, it's all right. She was ninety. My mother lived in Europe from the time she was a young woman, but in the end she went back to live with Grandma, just over ten years ago. Not that Grandma needed looking after; she was really healthy and alert. She never did get sick, either—she fell."

"How sad. Nowadays people stay healthy well into old age, so falls are what's really dangerous."

"It's true. I never knew my paternal grandparents, so my Japanese grandma meant a lot to me." After a brief pause, she said, "When she fell, she hit her head on a stone in the garden. A natural stone, about yea big. When I was a little girl, I used to play house there with my cousin, using the stone as a table and setting out red berries and leaves on it. Never dreaming that, one day, that same stone would take my grandmother's life . . ."

Paella arrived, and Mitani scooped some onto a plate for Yoko. "Well, at that age a fatal fall can happen anywhere," she said comfortingly. "It was just one of those things."

"Yes, but you see, it was the very stone where I used to play," Yoko repeated as she took the plate.

Mitani looked dubious. "Well, yeah, I suppose if you'd known ahead of time you could have done something about it, but what? Was it in a dangerous place?"

"No, that's not what I was trying to say. I just meant that as a child I played innocently at the very place that years later would take my grandmother's life. That's all."

"Okay . . . but you know what, the world's a dangerous place for old folks. Don't blame yourself."

"I *don't* blame myself. I mean, how could I? It's just that . . ." Yoko paused, uncertain whether to continue, not having expected to encounter such difficulty in getting her point across. People at the other half

16

of the table, finding the large mound of late-night paella somewhat daunting, were discussing which Italian restaurant in Tokyo was the best. Yoko glanced over as if debating whether to join their discussion instead.

Makino poured red wine into Yoko's and Mitani's glasses, then his own, and waited for a moment before addressing Mitani. "I think Yoko is talking about memory."

Both women directed their gaze at him.

"Because her grandmother died at that stone, her memory of playing there as a child will never be the same. Isn't that right? In her mind, the two stones are one and the same. And as a result, that childhood memory has now become painful."

Yoko looked steadily at Makino, who was speaking quietly now, without his former ebullience. Her eyes shone with the pleasure of knowing someone understood.

But to Mitani, his explanation merely sowed new seeds of confusion. "Wouldn't her childhood memory be just that, a memory, with no connection to the future? At the time, it was just an ordinary stone. For her to play there without knowing what was going to happen years later was only natural."

"Yes, at the time. But after the loss of her grandmother, memories of playing at that stone would give rise to mixed feelings."

"Well, I don't get it. Yoko, is that what you meant?"

"I just realized it myself for the first time, listening to him explain."

Makino looked briefly at Yoko and then lowered his eyes.

Mitani was unsatisfied. "Yeah, but . . . I mean . . . What's the point? Sorry, it makes no sense to me."

"It's nothing. I'm sorry I brought up such a weird topic anyway." Yoko, realizing that Mitani was tipsy, tried to smooth things over. Makino, however, wasn't ready to let it go.

"It's not at all weird," he said. "Music is like that too. After you follow a musical theme to the end, looking back, what do you see? Beethoven's

17

diary contains a mysterious line: 'Ascertain all in the evening.' I forget offhand what the original German is. Yoko, you could probably help me there. Anyway, I think he meant something similar. Listening to a musical theme develop, you come to see that it contained a certain potentiality all along. Once you follow it to the end, the theme never sounds the same again. A bud that you look at knowing nothing of the flower to come isn't the same as the bud you look back on in memory with the flower before you. Music doesn't just progress forward in a straight line but works backward into the past as well. Without understanding that, you would never appreciate the fascination of the fugue."

He paused slightly before going on. "People think that only the future can be changed, but in fact, the future is continually changing the past. The past can and does change. It's exquisitely sensitive and delicately balanced."

Yoko was nodding as she listened, one hand pressing her long black hair against her neck. "This moment is no exception," she said. "From the vantage point of the future, it's exactly that, exquisitely sensitive and delicately balanced." After a pause, she said, "But I'm not sure how helpful this way of thinking really is. It's a little frightening to me, actually. Tonight has been so enjoyable. I wish it could go on forever."

Makino didn't reply, but his expression showed he agreed. The pleasure of having someone understand sank deep inside him, made him ecstatic. This was not something he was used to by any means.

Mitani, apparently still unconvinced, turned her attention woozily to the conversation at the other end of the table. From then until the restaurant closed at two thirty, Makino and Yoko were absorbed in a private conversation.

She looked into the flame of the candle on the table. "You did apologize, didn't you? To the man on the bullet train, I mean."

Makino stared. Then, thinking once again—how many times now?—how much he was enjoying this evening, he smiled. "Well, sure. Who wouldn't? But it makes a better story to say I got angry."

18

"I thought so."

"How did you know?"

"I don't know . . . I just did." She smiled too.

Still smiling, Makino looked down, then raised his head again. "There's one other thing that only you caught."

"What's that?"

Tonight's concert was a dud, he started to say, but then thought better of it. He had expected to spend the night with the bitter aftertaste of disappointment, but thanks to her, that had changed. No need to spoil the evening now.

"Never mind. Sorry. It's okay—it's nothing."

"What is it?"

"Just . . . something unimportant."

She seemed to have some notion of what he meant. Her face expressed her dissatisfaction, but she didn't press the issue.

More than once they surreptitiously checked their watches, realizing how late it was getting but pretending otherwise, prolonging the evening all they could. Finally, the others began suggesting it was time to leave. Mitani was asleep in her chair.

"She must be exhausted, after the strain of the concert. I hope she didn't mind what I said." Yoko looked at her, concerned.

"It's all right. When she gets an idea in her head, she won't let it go, but her stubbornness helps me. She's a really solid person."

Promising to keep in touch, they drifted out of the restaurant with the others. After helping Yoko into a taxi, Makino watched through the window as she gave instructions to the driver, his eyes on her profile. The daughter of Jerko Solich. Someone who for twenty years had never forgotten a concert he'd given at age eighteen . . .

Then she turned and looked back at him.

Impossible as it seemed at the time, afterward they each felt separately that they could have spent the remainder of the night together, that the option had been real. As their relationship developed, the long night of their first encounter came back to them frequently in memory as something special. The moment of that lingering last look was indeed "exquisitely sensitive and delicately balanced." Amid the swirling rapids of time's ceaseless rush downstream to the past, it shone with a soft and lonely light—while beyond lay the vast ocean of oblivion. Every time they were wounded in the future, again and again they would return in memory to look into each other's eyes, embraced by the darkness of that night.

2

Silence and Noise

One cold day in February, in a café near Shibuya Station, Makino spent two hours talking with Korenaga from Jupiter. Mitani was also present.

Since the end of December, Makino had been busy arranging and recording the music for his new album, *What a Wonderful World: Beautiful American Songs,* for which the promotional line was "Old standards made new with classical guitar." The four finished numbers, including Simon and Garfunkel's "Bridge over Troubled Water" and Stevie Wonder's "Visions," were hits with Jupiter employees in other departments who never listened to classical guitar.

In addition to concerts, planning was underway for various publicity ventures, including television and radio appearances. The project had come from the recording company's desire to put out "music that will sell," combined with the intent to introduce Makino in the uncharted territory of North America. Makino himself was convinced of the project's value and had been deeply involved in the song selection. Korenaga, while impressed by Makino's extensive knowledge of popular music, had argued heatedly in favor of another, more famous Stevie Wonder song, backed by someone from the Western music division. The age bracket of the album's projected listenership was slightly too high for "Visions," she felt.

Yet today, Makino had suddenly announced he wanted out. He gave only one reason, over and over: he'd lost interest.

Having failed to win him over, Korenaga accompanied him to the first floor of the building, said a grim-faced goodbye, and left. She had predicted during the course of their conversation that she would be replaced as his contact in the company, and she was probably right.

Makino looked up at the darkening sky and recalled Korenaga's mention of coming snow. They'd had several days of balmy, springlike weather, and then this morning the chill had suddenly set in again, as if some untouched stock of cold air had turned up. He wanted to get something to eat before going home, and when Mitani said she had a meeting scheduled with people from Orchard Hall at Bunkamura, he decided to go to the café there. The wind was nippy, and he felt his body stiffen.

A dump truck roared by, passing under the station viaduct. A taxi made a sudden stop to let off a fare, and the car behind took offense and honked as if clucking in exasperation; the fuzzy chord, a slightly low A and C, rang deep in his ears. Swirling in his brain was Roberta Flack's husky, somehow innocent voice singing "Killing Me Softly with His Song," a song he had begun to arrange and then abandoned.

Before long, Makino, whose poor sense of direction people always found appalling, turned a corner with the intention of taking a short-cut and soon had no idea where he was. He stopped at the crosswalk of a narrow street and waited for a car to go by. As he was looking up at the building signs, a voice at his side said, "Something's funny." He turned in surprise, having all but forgotten that Mitani was walking beside him.

"Yeah, I must've gotten us turned around."

"No, I mean the discussion just now. If a musician says he doesn't want to do something, why can't she respect that? If you want to do something else, that's just too bad for the label, isn't it?"

Makino looked wordlessly into her eyes for a moment. Then he reached out protectively and pulled her out of the way of an oblivious passerby. He found a safe place beside the entrance to a multitenant building before facing her again. He had impulsively grabbed her upper arm to steer her, and even after releasing her arm he remained a little bothered by its unexpected softness through her coat.

There wasn't a trace of flattery in Mitani's tone. She was genuinely angry at Korenaga, the way you get angry at someone who cuts in line.

"It's my fault, really," he said. "I backed out of an agreement. No wonder she was ticked off."

"But you're a musical genius!" Her voice was shrill. "Why should someone who has fans all over the world, a revered artist, be treated like an average person?"

"Calm down, we don't want to make a scene." He held out his hands, palms facing her. "Sure, life would be easy if I could put myself on a pedestal and get away with it. But I never could. I'm pretty humble, believe it or not."

"I have to disagree there."

"All right, maybe I've got my share of ego, what can I say. I tell you what, it's freezing, jabbering with my manager like this. The day's cold enough as it is." He pulled his coat collar together and shivered.

Mitani looked at him blankly, the way she did when she wasn't sure what he was getting at. "Korenaga only thinks about herself. I've always thought so."

"Really? I thought you two got along." He paused. "Anyway, don't be too hard on her. We're all looking out for ourselves, aren't we?"

"All I want is for you to create wonderful music."

Makino let a beat go by before responding. "I'm glad you feel that way. But when it comes down to it, that's for your own benefit, isn't it?"

"No."

"I'm not being critical. Just realistic."

"No! I'm merely another fan who wants to hear what you create. All right, in that sense, it *is* for my benefit. How can I help make that happen? That's all I ever think about. That's why I'm telling you what I think right now."

Makino faltered at the intensity of her tone, half-afraid she was going to burst into tears. Over the past year he'd become familiar with her odd ways, had thought he understood her, but this outburst left him bewildered. Passersby hastened past them. Did it look like a lovers' quarrel? A manager so naively devoted to her client only spelled trouble. What was she thinking? At the same time, her frankness touched him. That she had confessed this way, unable to contain herself, signaled that he didn't know her as well as he'd thought.

"I understand what you're saying," Makino said unhappily, "but look, this is business. I shouldn't have to tell you that. Our roles are getting reversed here."

"Of course it's my job to see that you can carry on with your work smoothly! I understand that. And I am well aware that I'm no artist. I haven't got a big head that way, and I take my responsibilities seriously."

"Okay, then. Realistically speaking, we just have to figure out how to get along. I rely on you, Mitani—on the company you represent—to handle the things that are beyond me."

"I know. So leave all the messy stuff to us, and just concentrate on your music. If you walk away from this album and your tour, that puts us in a difficult position. We'll have to go around and cancel all the concert venues. We'll suffer a far greater loss than Jupiter will. Even now, the thought of it makes me queasy. But if that's what you want, I believe that's what we should do."

Makino started to say something, but no words came out. He only nodded in silence and started walking again, biting his lip.

"Makino-san."

This time he couldn't control his impatience. "What?"

"Bunkamura, right?"

"Yes!"

"It's this way."

He looked skeptically in the direction she pointed, then glanced back at the way he'd been headed. His flare-up only made the error more embarrassing, and without meeting her eyes, he strode briskly forward.

Ж

First thing the next morning, Makino received a call from Jupiter. Another meeting was soon scheduled, this time not with Korenaga but with her boss, Okajima.

Snow had begun falling late the night before, and by dawn the streets were buried.

After hanging up, Makino opened the curtains, thinking listlessly that it was February. February 2007. Only a little more than ten months left in the year. Thirty-odd more times around the sun and he would be dead. His mother had died in her sixties, his father in his seventies, so he didn't expect to live particularly long. Knowing that the number thirty would steadily shrink made his remaining time seem neither abstract nor abundant.

He sat down by the window, coffee mug in hand, and stared outside.

After his father died, Makino had combined his savings with his modest inheritance and made a down payment on an old four-story building in Yoyogi that was now both home and office. The first floor was a garage; the second, a practice studio; the third, storage space; and the fourth, his residence. He had kept the decor as simple as possible, putting everything superfluous on the third floor. His furniture consisted of antiques he had picked up on tour, judiciously mixed with contemporary pieces. For a sofa, he used an orange foam Ligne Roset Togo one-seater. It was pulled up by the window now, just far enough back to fend off the cold.

The building was adjacent to Yoyogi Park, the view from his window partially blocked by tall Himalayan cedars. Their dark branches bent under snow that had piled up adroitly all the way to the tips.

The snow falling soundlessly at a fixed tempo against a grayish-white sky gradually caused him to lose all sense of time. Even on such a day, sounds of construction reverberated faintly in the distance. Otherwise, all he could hear was the whir of the heater and sounds emanating from his own body—the slight rustle when he shifted his legs, little sighs, saliva gurgling in his teeth. The area was always quiet, today unusually so.

Silence. Makino felt again how deeply pleasant it was. "Music is born in opposition to the beauty of silence; the creation of music lies in the attempt to use sound to bring about new beauty that contrasts with the beauty of silence." Conductor Yasushi Akutagawa's book *Fundamentals of Music* had given him his first understanding of music in conceptual terms when he was just a boy. This definition that he had read with his father was imprinted on his memory. He ruminated on it now, his head slightly cocked.

A half century ago, had Tokyo been so quiet? Not just Tokyo . . . Had the world known such silence?

What was he fighting against now? The beauty of silence? Had he not spent years fighting its polar opposite, noise? But oh, the perfect beauty of this moment! Music had to offer something that made you willing to listen, even at the sacrifice of such beauty. "New beauty." Back when he used to perform seeking only that, hadn't his guitar playing sounded better than it did now? It wasn't just him. These days, musicians of every sort, and audiences too, were denied the experience of this rich silence. At any rate, there wasn't enough time to simply lose oneself in it.

Makino felt thirsty. Last year after that concert at Suntory Hall, alone backstage, he had gulped down a huge quantity of water, as if to rid himself of an uncomfortable feeling that seemed somehow ominous.

At last he gave in and admitted to himself that he was fed up. Yes, fed up. He had cautiously avoided that awareness, but yesterday's conversation with Mitani had finally persuaded him.

"I'm fed up." He said the words to himself again, savoring their bitterness. What physical effect might they have on him? he wondered, growing anxious. The beginning of a slump might well feel something like this.

He looked down at the fingertips of his left hand. Opened and closed them. Made the motions of a fast melody, as if fingering the fretboard. And somehow felt, in that left hand carrying out his will with such apparent submissiveness, a falsity. No matter how submissive those fingers might seem ordinarily, when playing music, they were different. All of a sudden, bothered by a phrase, they might start to tremble or take off on their own. Over the years, he had learned to cope with the almost childish sensitivity of his flesh. So familiar had it become that he had begun to feel that, at this point, any change could mean only alienation.

He folded his hands and kneaded them, testing the sensation. He wound his fingers together so tightly that the bones creaked, seeking through the pain the truth of his flesh, to reestablish oneness with it. Then he felt it was pointless, and after clasping his hands firmly together a final time, he relaxed and let them slide onto his lap.

In exchange for the privilege of life, individuals in the modern world put up with ceaseless clamor. Not only noises but images, smells, tastes, perhaps even the warmth of others . . . all of it rushing at them in a mad free-for-all, each bit screaming its presence. And society, still unsatisfied, crammed in yet more, until one's very sense of time was destroyed. It was unbearable, human exhaustion. Surely this was a historic, decisive change, wasn't it? From now on, people would forevermore be creatures of exhaustion, distinguished from other animals by their continual state of fatigue. Caught up in the tempo of machines and computers, their senses buffeted by constant noise, people griped about daily life with piteous intensity before entering the complete silence obtainable only by death. For years, Makino had felt these things every time he went onstage.

The ideal venue for a classical guitar concert was one where the performer's awareness was able to extend to every corner of the audience. Therein lay the instrument's special, intimate nature. It was also the reason he felt the guitar suited him.

Most of his listeners were fans of classical music and seasoned devotees of the guitar; a fair number of others had encountered him through his television appearances and covers of pop songs. Some followed him enthusiastically, turning up at every venue, and others were lured by his reputation as a "genius," as they would inform him meaningfully after a performance.

What Akutagawa described as "opposition to the beauty of silence" was, in part, the sensation of anyone who stood onstage. A concert hall, before it held music, was a place enclosing sheer silence within its walls. A refuge for silence found nowhere else in society, nor in the natural world. Last year Makino himself had gone up against the beauty of silence no fewer than eighty-six times. He had felt the silence like the blade of a sword, waiting till its cold point touched his breast before striking his first note.

On that tour, he'd had a troubling experience. At rehearsal on opening day, after tuning up, he played an A on the open fifth string. Immediately, a shiver ran through the tip of his shoulder, spread to his back, and shot all the way to his fingertips, leaving behind an unpleasant sensation. It was different from pre-performance jitters, which he seldom had anyway. When he was young, he used to see other performers backstage who were frozen with fear and feel sorry for them, his pride flattered by his own serenity. But the shiver he had felt last year had been an omen unlike anything in his experience.

From then on, to get to the bottom of it, he would do the same thing at every rehearsal—release a plain A that swiftly vanished into the walls of the empty theater. He listened for its last tremor, along with the fading vibration of the body of the guitar, with a lingering sense that he was poking his nose into a nearly inaudible dispute.

The notes all wanted to be released into stillness. As he played with eyes closed, that agonizing ardor would sweep over him all of a sudden. When it flashed and glittered like gold leaf, once again the shiver would run through his shoulder.

But in that very moment, music should confront the beauty of silence—of death—should it not? The life force! The joy of being alive: Beyond that, what more did music even need? But the life he was now seeking to refine, amid the clamor of the everyday world, was gasping for breath.

At noon he had a simple lunch of soup and salad, and then, before starting to practice, he checked his email. However, of the seven new emails in his inbox, none were from Yoko Komine.

He had heard about the suicide bombing of Baghdad's Murjana Hotel a few days earlier, and he knew that was the building where Yoko worked.

She had sent him several emails from Baghdad, one with a photo attached showing his Bach CD in her room. She could easily have listened to the music on her iPod, but she'd gone to the trouble of taking the CD with her.

Plenty of overseas media agencies had offices in that building, and hers, RFP, had rented out the entire seventh floor. Newspaper accounts indicated that the bomb had been detonated in the first-floor lobby, killing or wounding more than thirty people, including a local tribal sheikh there for a meeting, police, and members of the foreign press.

Anxious to know if Yoko was safe, he quickly sent off an email. The next day he wrote again for good measure, but again there was no response. Until then she had always written back on the same day, explaining that "going out is impossible." Thoughts chased each other in his head, wearing him out as he first imagined the worst and then swiftly denied the possibility. He was in a state of emotional paralysis, filled with dull anxiety.

Several times, he tried to write a third email, but he had already said all there was to say. If he reiterated the same content, he feared that his words—as with the previous two emails—would fail to reach her. In a few days or weeks, a flood of greetings would appear in a computer opened not by Yoko herself but by someone else. He would simply be adding one more to the deluge of too-late messages.

Of course, even if she was safe, the situation was probably still chaotic. In addition to her work, she would have to answer all those emails one by one, and his would by no means be a top priority. Her moral support would come from family and old friends, and, above all, from that American fiancé. As messages flew back and forth between the two of them, a third email from him would be a rude interruption. Imagining her dry look when she saw it, he hung back.

Then he opened his drafts folder, cut out everything except his hopes for her safety, and pushed the Send button. He couldn't help himself. Right now, all that bound them together was that email.

As Yoko had said the first time they met, after the 2003 invasion of Iraq, that country's security was at an all-time low. Later, with the 2005 parliamentary election, the strife after the fall of Baghdad had escalated into civil war, and the number of civilian fatalities rose sharply. Last October, just before Yoko had gone to Iraq, the monthly casualty toll had reached an all-time high of 3,709. As was his habit, Makino thought of that number in terms of seating capacity. Suntory Hall had seating for 2,006. He imagined it filled with bodies in a shocking state, and another 1,700 stacked high outside. A hellish vision.

Time and again, he recalled her smile as she talked to him. What had gone through her mind when she saw the terrorists? Or would she have been incapable of thought? How would a woman of her intelligence come to grips with her fate in such a moment?

He combed the internet for information, and the more he found out, the more amazed he was that she had put herself in a place of such danger. He reread her last email, dated a week ago:

> *My father told me I suffer from Death in Venice Syndrome, a disease he made up. It supposedly means "Growing suddenly tired of conforming to society at the onset of middle or old age and taking self-destructive actions with the intent of returning to one's original self." That's me in a nutshell. lol.*
>
> *Over and over he told me to come back alive. With his words in mind, I try at all times to stay safe.*
>
> *I am very grateful for your concern. Thank you.*

The words "tired of conforming to society" struck a chord with him. Perhaps she had sensed similar feelings in him that night they met, and she was expressing empathy by sharing this now. What if these were her last words to him? They would weigh on his life more heavily than a curse.

The email had already affected Makino's thinking and actions over the past few days. Besides canceling the recording of *What a Wonderful World*, he had begun to think he would prefer to tackle Bach again—an idea likely stemming from "the intent of returning to [his] original self," even if it were not an especially "self-destructive action." Or was he simply naive? Gustav von Aschenbach, the main character in *Death*

31

in Venice, maintained a balance between his art and his private life through incessant mental effort—and had his heart stolen by Tadzio, a boy of supreme beauty, like a work of Greek sculpture. He followed the boy around, abandoning his normal life and ending in ruin. But in the beginning, he would have had no way of knowing what lay in store.

Did Thomas Mann's work contain more clues? Makino, familiar only with the film by Luchino Visconti, had hurriedly ordered a paperback copy.

He wanted to talk to Yoko about *Death in Venice*. Or about anything at all. Wanted more than anything to hear her voice. To spend more time with her, alone next time, utterly at ease while enjoying the intellectual stimulation of her company and, above all, her ceaseless smile. There was no one like her.

Am I overidealizing that evening? But oh, if she were to die at forty in Iraq . . .

Other members of their generation were ending their lives in Iraq. Imagining them clouded Makino's vision as he sought to discern his own fate. He did not feel in those impending deaths the same sense of unfinished lives cut tragically short as he did when younger people died from illness or accidents. Their lives might be ending too soon, but they had attained a measure of completion. As had Yoko. The thought weighed heavily, painfully, on him.

He and Yoko had met only once. What if someone asked him whether he knew her? He wasn't even sure he was entitled to call her a friend. And yet his admiration for her and his sense of closeness to her were stronger than ever. That evening, she had smiled teasingly as she said, "You did apologize, didn't you? To the man on the bullet train." He couldn't forget the look on her face then. If she had suffered an injury that would require lifelong care, he even thought he could devote himself to her. But it was crazy to let his emotions run away like this, he told himself, shaking his head.

To banish ill-omened thoughts, he reached finally for the recording of that year-end concert. Korenaga had written several times asking him to please check it out, but he could never bring himself to listen to it until now. People were unanimous in their praise of the concert. He put no faith in critical acclaim, never had, but at this stage of the game, he felt inclined to do so—to hope that, just maybe, the praise was deserved. If he listened to the recording, he might be able to breathe again.

He pressed the Play button, swallowed hard, and listened to the *Concierto de Aranjuez*. Every detail came back to him. He listened through to the end with an occasional scowl and then fast-forwarded past the thunderous applause to the encores. Not bothering with the Takemitsu arrangement of "Yesterday," he stopped the CD and flung himself back on the sofa in gloom.

The Brahms that Yoko had liked was tolerable. Overall, the performance might not have been as bad as he had pessimistically assumed. The Smallman he had used for the first time onstage, though lacking a bit in tonal depth, was definitely a nice guitar. Anyone playing it would get a good sound.

Musical depth and breadth. Richness that rewarded repeated hearings and a sudden radiance that captivated listeners the very first time. Relief from humankind's most pressing psychological afflictions and a friendly invitation to capriciousness. Spiritual liberation and day-to-day solace. Maintaining these contradictory impulses, an obsession of contemporary musicians, was a task that Makino had set himself over the past few years. In that regard he was achieving more than any other guitarist. His pride accepted this, and yet he felt an obscure, overpowering anxiety.

The performance couldn't be faulted—not because it was faultless, but more likely because he simply couldn't discern its faults. It had almost everything. The one thing it lacked was exactly what he now wanted with every fiber of his being: a future. It lacked the thing that until now had characterized all his performances at every stage of his career: the suggestion of newer, fresher music already putting out sprouts, scarcely able to wait for the completion of that moment. Or rather, the music that had now begun to sprout was disillusioning.

He still had faith that he could reach the next level in his development as a musician. But despite that faith, he suspected that the mountain he was now climbing was less challenging than those in his past. And perhaps it wasn't only him. Perhaps others heard the difference as well.

Feeling alone, he got up from the sofa. He didn't want anyone to know about his situation, and at the same time, he wanted to be understood. These conflicting feelings were something he had never experienced as a musician. Painfully aware of approaching forty, he recalled Yoko's face in the taxi that night as they had looked at each other in parting.

3

Death in Venice Syndrome

On the afternoon of February 21, Yoko was in the lobby of the Murjana Hotel to cover a meeting of local sheikhs. Besides members of the press from various countries, the hotel accommodated diplomats as well, and high officials from the new Iraqi government paid frequent calls. The location was near the Green Zone occupied by US troops on the west bank of the Tigris, so there was very little in the way of fighting or terrorist incidents.

As Yoko finished her work and started toward her office on the seventh floor, she noticed three men coming in through the main entrance.

No one else was in the elevator. Before the doors closed, as one of the men swept the lobby with his gaze, his eyes locked on hers. Or perhaps she only imagined it.

Just before it reached the seventh floor, the shock of an explosion brought the elevator to a halt. Yoko slammed into the wall, arms out to brace herself. Then came silence. After a moment, screams rose from somewhere far below, and the entire building was thrown into an uproar. An alarm went off, and voices in many different languages shouted, "Run!"

She knew immediately that it was a bomb. She pricked up her ears to hear what was going on outside the elevator, but all she could catch were fragments of panicky speech and footsteps running down the emergency stairs. Armed insurgents must have been trying to take over the building. Only recently there'd been a simulation of just such an attack. If you were late making your escape, you'd be taken hostage. The distress she had felt changed to frantic terror. Searching her memory for the escape protocols, she called her boss, Philip.

"Are you all right, Yoko? Are you okay?" He explained that it was a suicide bombing, and that no subsequent wave of terrorists had stormed the building. He offered words of encouragement, and she felt better, but then the line was cut off. Communication with the outside world became impossible.

Yoko sat in a corner of the elevator, letting the walls on either side support her. She covered her face with both hands and shut her eyes, taking refuge in darkness. Only in the darkness did she feel a little bit safe. Out of the depths of her apprehension, she offered fervent prayers. Since she lacked religious faith, she thought first of her mother and father and silently called to them for help. Then she prayed to a nameless greater power after all.

Why had she come back to Iraq? After her first assignment here, she had gone safely home. Then why? Memories came flooding back, but which to choose, where to linger, she had no idea. Amid her confusion, she remembered the conversation she'd had with Makino in Tokyo. "People think that only the future can be changed, but in fact, the future is continually changing the past. The past can and does change. It's exquisitely sensitive and delicately balanced."

The words had a cruel ring now that they hadn't had that night. Would she never see him again? The thought made the brief, wonderfully pleasant time they had spent together seem infinitely precious.

She took out her reporter's notebook and began making a record of her plight. She had returned to Iraq of her own free will, she thought, and yet if the outcome were to prove disastrous, then perhaps fate had brought her here to fulfill its own dark ends.

The future scared her. When the elevator doors opened at last, would she see Philip and other rescuers, or armed men?

\)\(

"Are you all right, Yoko? Are you okay?"

A voice came from right beside her, and the view outside the window was restored to her mistrustful eyes. The winter sky, hazy with sand particles, was touched by the faint light of the afternoon sun. It was not the gray of a lightly overcast day, but a color formed from the ocher of the sand and the blue of the sky. A plume of black smoke rose in the air.

I'm in Baghdad, thought Yoko. She was in the Murjana Hotel on Haifa Street, on the west bank of the Tigris. Ten days earlier, she had barely escaped from a suicide bombing in the lobby below. Even now, somewhere in the distance, there was the sound of a blast. A car bomb, probably. She raised a hand to stop her imagination from racing to the scene, the body parts scattered about. The deafening boom was softened by distance.

Here in the seventh-floor office, six RFP overseas representatives were working alongside a dozen or so local staff. Some of them had probably failed to notice the blast, and of those who did, several didn't bother looking up from their computer monitors. A few glanced out the window as if they'd just momentarily lost their train of thought. Only Yoko kept staring out the window, unable to look away.

In 2005, upon being posted to Baghdad, she had experienced for the first time the desert climate she'd studied in school long ago. Though she never would have imagined it, Baghdad was a windy city. Unlike the irritable winds that pummeled Tokyo high-rises, these were dry, billowing gusts that had blown across desolate, uninhabited lands. Day after day, they cleared away the smoke with the practiced air of a janitor. But today, the scale of the explosions must have been greater than usual, for the smoke did not die down. It was as if someone from the underworld kept dribbling the black ink of death onto the town.

"You okay?"

Yoko turned and looked up. Philip, the scar across one cheek covered by a stubbly brown beard, was standing by her desk looking concerned.

"Yes, I'm fine. Thanks. Totally fine. What is it?" She smiled and, as he made no move to return to his own desk, stood up. "Feel like a cup of coffee?"

"Sure, thanks. I'll make it. Let's go in the next room and have a chat."

"No, let me. I could use a breather. I'll bring you a cup."

As she waited for the coffeemaker by the window to heat up, Yoko looked down distractedly at the palm trees around the three intersecting circular pools. The layout of a typical luxury resort hotel. Beside the pool, exposed to the elements, stood a decaying white bench. Between the tiles on the ground, dark-green weeds grew tall, as if they owned the place.

Time gone feral, a flock of hours separated from its masters. This area had once been filled with people reading suspense novels and sipping piña coladas as they worked on their tans.

"The easiest way for security companies to make money is to tell us it's not safe and keep us locked in here," Philip had opined. "Of course it's not safe. But if we listen to them, we can't do our job. To find out what things are like for the people living here, we need to go out and hear what they've got to say. Without that, all our political analyses will miss the mark."

Most of the expat staff, Yoko included, were neither Mideast experts nor full-time war correspondents but were stationed here temporarily from branches all over. Philip was different. A veteran reporter who had long covered African hotspots, he'd been in and out of Iraq ever since the American invasion in 2003 and had witnessed the famous toppling of Hussein's statue. If asked, he would occasionally tell inside stories about the incident. The relatively stable work rotation of six weeks on, two weeks off, was his innovation.

Some of the other foreign press in the hotel left all reporting to their local staff. After the fall of the Hussein regime, with security plummeting, that approach could by no means be faulted as too conservative. But RFP, under Philip's direction, was continuing to send reporters out to gather information on the streets of Baghdad whenever the chance arose. Yoko herself had gone out several times, experiencing the strain of such assignments.

Needless to say, this was possible only under the heavy guard of the US military.

In a car on the way to her destination, she would look out the window at heaps of rubble and walls pockmarked with bullets. Administrative services were at a halt, so everyone burned their overflowing garbage in the streets. She tried to gain a sense of people's everyday lives from the smell.

If only she could have walked freely about and spoken with the local people, she could have gathered so much information. But unlike uniformed soldiers, terrorists blended invisibly into the populace, beyond her power to detect.

Listening to the coffee drip down into the stainless steel pot, she gratefully inhaled the faint aroma. The design of this German coffeemaker kept most of the scent enclosed in the pot. She missed the old machine with a glass carafe that used to fill the room with fragrance. Especially here, where coffee was indispensable.

She glanced up at the window, saw someone's reflection behind her, and spun around defensively. The staff member, a local woman, gave a little shriek of surprise and almost jumped in the air. Yoko recovered, one hand on her breast to calm herself. "Jalila—what is it?" She smiled and bent her head slightly to one side.

"I wanted you to check these photos."

"Oh—right. The angle here isn't very good, is it? The trees on the opposite side of the street need to be included, or you can't get a real sense of the place. Oh, use this one. Trim it a bit here."

39

"You're right. I'll tell the photographer."

Jalila was a graduate of the University of Baghdad and an aspiring filmmaker who currently worked in their office helping with the editing of photographs and video. She and Yoko were the only women on staff, and during breaks they often liked to chat about music and movies. Jalila could do a dead-on imitation of Britney Spears; just the other day she'd made everyone crack up with a parody of the "Toxic" video. It was the first good laugh they'd had since the bombing in the lobby.

Jalila looked up to Yoko almost like an older sister. She thought Yoko's looks and her intellectual approach to her work were "cool," and she was also fascinated by talk that Yoko's father was a famous film director who had won an award at the Cannes Film Festival. She hadn't seen his work, but she was certain that he must be an outstanding director if he was Yoko's father, just as Yoko was outstanding precisely because she was his daughter. Her admiration only grew.

Yoko carried the coffee into the room they used for meetings.

"Jalila's worried you might leave here early," Philip confided.

"Oh—that explains it." Yoko nodded. "Just now, she was standing behind me, staring. Caught me by surprise."

"How many more days now?"

"Till . . . ?"

"Till you go back to Paris."

"About . . . two weeks?"

Philip took a drag on his cigarette and crinkled his eyes. "Less than that. Today's March 2, right? Won't be long now. Everyone gets worn out in their fifth week. Not only you, Yoko. You had requested an extension to come back for a third rotation after your time off, starting April 1, but the main office agrees that's unreasonable. Your on-site reporting in Iraq is over. No more god-awful English cake for breakfast, either."

Yoko listened silently to this simple announcement, and, after a long moment, she accepted it. The news wasn't entirely unexpected. She felt a blend of relief and helplessness.

"I don't think I'll ever forget the flavor of that pound cake."

"You should jot down the recipe and take it with you in case you start to miss it."

"I'll pass. You know, when I went back to Paris for two weeks, I never really relaxed. I kept watching the news, and writing articles too. After I came back here, I realized I'd made a mistake. I wasn't sure I'd last another six weeks. Then there was the suicide bombing . . . If I'd been in the lobby one more minute, I'd be dead. One more minute, that's all. I feel fear, but more than that, it's just a mystery to me why I'm alive in this moment."

"Why was I in that particular place at that particular time—that's what every soldier asks on the battlefield."

"I actually had one more question for the sheikh. I was going to ask him what lies ahead for Iraq. But he had already basically answered the question, so I decided to let it go. He was eager to wrap up the interview anyway. If I hadn't held him up, he might be alive today."

"He chose to stay. The others did too. You've got to believe in your luck. You weren't meant to die here."

She knew Philip was just saying this to ease her mind, but she found comfort in the thought. "That's right." She nodded. "'Truly our times resemble in strangeness all others that history mentions, in tradition sacred or profane. In times like these, whoever has lived yesterday and today encounters so many events piled together that he has already lived years.' Those are the words of a refugee patriarch during the French Revolution, from *Hermann and Dorothea*. It's absolutely true. I've lost all sense of time."

Philip blew smoke toward the ceiling and laughed. "I've been a war correspondent for years, and that's the first time anyone ever quoted Goethe to me at the front."

"I'm too bookish, I know. Not a desirable quality in a woman."

"Way sexier than a woman who doesn't know her Goethe."

"Few men would agree with you there," Yoko countered, brushing off his flirtation.

"Coming from a young woman, it'd be even better."

"Thanks a lot!"

"After a certain age, when a man goes to bed with a woman who has no intellect, he feels rotten the morning after." He paused and smiled sheepishly. "Anyway, Yoko, it's time for you to go home. Although really, after seeing your work over the past three months, I'm more convinced than ever that we need reporters like you here. Your articles get deep into the minds of the Iraqi people, from a variety of angles, and your explanations of the historical background are terrific. You gave a dispassionate analysis of people's expectations and opposition to the buildup of American forces. You're good, incredibly good."

Coffee cup in hand, Yoko looked down and shook her head. "That does wonders for my ego, but you flatter me. I've given a lot of thought to how to mediate between the reality of Iraq today and the minds of Europeans living their ordinary lives. I've never felt that I got very far. Take the buildup of American forces. I've never worked it out from the perspective of the past—that the war was wrong to begin with—never mind the future, what to do now that it's come to this."

"Nobody has. War and police action to preserve the peace are getting harder and harder to distinguish in this so-called war on terror."

"I can't say I feel as if coming back for another six weeks would give me any more insight, to tell the truth. I shouldn't think of you as superhuman, Philip, but I'm not in your league. You've lost so many friends, and you've come close to death more than once yourself, and yet you stay so strong."

"My sense of death has gotten lazy. It doesn't hit me unless I meet it halfway. Not just on the battleground, but in Paris too. When I hear news that they've given up hope on someone, my face flushes and I feel faint. If I can stop it there, I can stave off the reality. My emotions have gone numb, and that's part of what keeps me going."

"I think I resist numbness, but not very effectively. If I'm not in decent shape myself, I can't report on people who are suffering. That much I know. But when I feel like I've reached the end of my rope, what can I do?"

"As a journalist, sensitivity can be a problem, but as a human being, it increases your charm. And it's my job to watch over my staff, so I feel responsible. Maybe you should move your departure up. Have you gotten counseling over Skype?"

"Several times. Thank you."

"For me, the numbness is . . . Listen, I don't see this job as just a duty. It suits me. It's exciting to know I'm a witness to world history, in the center of the action." He smiled, then looked around. "Do you mind if I ask you a personal question?"

"Be my guest."

"Did you ever think of making movies?"

"Never. Not even once. I don't have any talent along those lines. I'm better at reporting facts than inventing fiction."

"You mentioned Death in Venice Syndrome. Does that mean reexamining your role as a journalist? Or something more private, like your relationship with your father?"

"What's the connection? You lost me."

"Your father's images are magically beautiful, but at his core he's a socially aware artist. *Coins of Happiness*, his masterful war movie, is a prime example. You're like him. You probably don't want to hear this, but when I look at you, I see Solich's daughter. It's there in the directions you give your photographer. It occurred to me that for you to sort out your relationship with your father, you might need to accept the fact that you've surpassed him in a different arena—news reporting."

"You're imagining things. It's not like that. You're way off." She denied it with a flustered smile. "I have a good relationship with my father now because there's adequate distance between us. I respect him as a director. Objectively speaking, I mean, like anybody does. The pain of not being recognized as his child is behind me now. I'm too old for that."

"All the more reason. You're older now, and you came to Baghdad in search of your Tadzio, didn't you?"

"Oh, come on, Philip. My Tadzio?"

"Whenever I pass by your room, I hear the theme song from *Coins of Happiness*."

"Oh, so that's it!" Yoko smiled broadly. "You're mistaken. It's the guitarist I like. He's a Japanese artist named Satoshi Makino. Have you heard of him?"

"Can't say I have. I don't listen to classical guitar."

"Careful. No woman wants to take an uncultured man to bed."

Philip laughed and emitted a wavy stream of smoke.

"He's a genius, pure and simple," Yoko said. "Just before coming here, I went to a concert of his and we were introduced. I first heard him play at the Salle Pleyel after he won the Paris International Guitar Competition at eighteen. It was such a shock. To see genius like that—it was depressing in a way. Knowing there could be somebody like him. I lost track of him after that, but it just so happened that a friend of mine in Tokyo works for his record label, and she took me backstage after the concert."

"Is he young?"

"Not so much. Two years younger than me." Yoko thought for a moment, turning her eyes out the window. "His gift is like . . . a paper airplane that God folded and let fly just for fun. It appeared high in the heavens one day and just keeps on going, flying and flying and never falling to earth. The line it traces is a thing of beauty."

"Don't tell that to your fiancé."

"Why not?"

"He'll figure out that you're in love."

Yoko brushed the words away in annoyance, taking them as just more teasing. Her ears burned. "I'm a fan, that's all. An ordinary fan.

44

Although he is really fun to be with. Someone like that probably sees no need to become deeply involved with one woman. There's probably a whole parade of them."

"None like you, I'm sure."

"More flattery to cheer me up?"

"A little bit."

"Thanks. Maybe I do take after my mother, being drawn to an artist, especially since I have no artistic talent myself. But I'm not after Satoshi Makino. Richard loves me. And I love him. We've been talking about getting married as soon as I get back."

On top of her regular daily reporting, Yoko spent the final week and a half of her posting writing three feature articles, making Philip shake his head. She was particularly concerned about the issue of arms control by the state. In the sixteen years since the Gulf War, Iraq had undergone extreme militarization. Large numbers of small arms had spread not only among the armed forces but also among the general populace, thanks to the draft system and the mustering of militias. In May 2003, after the disbanding of Iraq's armed forces and the security organizations that supported Saddam Hussein's regime, 400,000 armed soldiers roamed the streets, 4.2 million stockpiled weapons were dispersed, and public order rapidly deteriorated. Yoko wrote about the particulars, comparing the situation to ethnic cleansing in the Bosnian War, which had been aided not only by smuggled arms but by military stockpiling all around town as Yugoslavians braced for a possible Soviet attack.

These features evoked a strong response even back in France.

Yoko finally wrapped up her work just three days before it was time to go home. Then one night, taking a break from packing, she went out to linger on the balcony, coffee cup in hand.

Baghdad nights were the most complete silence she had ever known in her life.

Curfew had been moved up to eight o'clock. After that, there was no sign of life in the streets, no traffic sounds. Given the climate, there were never any chirping insects, just the whoosh of a strong wind sweeping sand into the air and, now and again, the distant blare of a siren. Sometimes she would overhear the voices of reporters from other countries distracting themselves with a party, but not today. Probably she would never again experience a hush so profound. Surely something of it would remain inside her, return with her to everyday life.

She thought of the half-ruined city, covered night after night by darkness. In a few hours, the world of rubble heaps inside walls would reappear with the morning sun. Meanwhile, in the depths of this dark, deathlike silence, people imprisoned by violence carried on their lives with bated breath.

She thought about the Skype conversation she'd just had with Richard.

When she told him she wouldn't be returning to Iraq after this rotation, he had jumped out of his chair with joy, so that all she could see on the screen were his hips doing a happy dance.

Then, still smiling, he had protested, "Why didn't you tell me sooner?" His eyes were serious. "Let's move the wedding date up. The honeymoon'll be just the thing for you to recuperate. Did you look at the photos of the villa in Cancún? My friend says we can use it for as long as we want. Of all the resorts on the Caribbean, it's far and away the best. Blue sky, shining sea! The lapping of waves will heal your spirit, wounded by the desert and that gruesome war. When you're tired of being embraced by the sun, we'll stay in our room, and then it'll be my turn to hold you! We'll make love again and again. I know we'll make a baby in no time. Our child! The thought of it makes me dizzy. Dizzy with happiness! I'm waiting for you, darling, going crazy with worry. I want you in my arms right now, so bad I could dive right into the screen! But no, I won't. I need to get you over here instead. Back to the civilized world."

"I'm sorry, I haven't looked at the photos yet."

"No? Oh, okay." A beat. "Sorry. I kind of got ahead of myself. I just want you to get well."

"Thanks. I know, and it means a lot."

Richard's smile faded. "I've respected your wishes all this time as much as I possibly could. But listen to one man's opinion, would you? You're too hard on yourself. You've done more than anyone could ever ask. If one of your colleagues said they'd never been to Iraq, would you think worse of them? Of course not. And yet you're still over there. Worried that there's something more you could have done. Overestimating not just *your* ability but human ability. After all, human beings evolved in an environment where they could migrate on foot. Having the entire earth linked up in real time this way goes beyond human potential. Individual human potential. All you can do is choose the best environment to live out your life in peace and make that your world. Seek happiness there. Right? Believe me, you aren't shutting your eyes to the world's misery. But you've done more than your share. Not everybody could do what you've done. Now it's time to let others take over."

She went back to her room and lay down on the bed, wondering why she had ever come to Baghdad. After the American invasion, so many people in the agency had requested a Baghdad assignment that there'd been competition. Later, as journalists began dying in the field—RFP journalists included—and those who returned suffered from post-traumatic stress disorder, applications dwindled.

Yoko's turn had finally come in 2005. And only a year later, she had surprised her colleagues by requesting a second posting. "That's Yoko for you," they had murmured with a respect leavened by ironic smiles suggesting she must not be quite right in the head.

That first posting had come just after the fall of Saddam Hussein's regime, when Ibrahim al-Jaafari's transitional government was formed and the electorate voted in a referendum on whether or not to ratify the new constitution. After that, another parliamentary election was held, and in May 2006, Prime Minister Nouri al-Maliki was inaugurated.

Now, the Bush administration stressed its nation-building efforts, but the fighting just kept intensifying and no one could see a way out. How many times had Yoko heard the phrase "out of control" since coming back here?

Under the circumstances, the buildup of US forces was predicted to have a positive effect, and indeed, the number of civilian deaths had gone down over the past two weeks. However, Yoko's reporting on the development had earned the wrath of close friends of hers who consistently opposed this war that was founded on lies about the existence of weapons of mass destruction. She herself was concerned that the nation-building program was haphazard and shortsighted, the buildup a mere stopgap. But regardless, she had no choice but to report the facts. She was well aware of how, during the Yugoslav Wars, the media had fanned the flames of ethnic conflict and manipulated public opinion around the world. In that sense, perhaps Philip was right that her Yugoslavian father was one reason she was here.

At first, she had intended to request an extension of her tour, but before Philip could protest and before the main office had ruled out that possibility, her therapist had given the idea a firm thumbs-down: "You yourself will get 'out of control.' The reality is, you're already showing signs of post-traumatic stress disorder. Please don't underestimate that. As it is, I think it's crazy that you're still there in Baghdad. Is it because you're from the country of *karoshi*, death by overwork? Are you prepared to burn out completely, not be able to work for years?"

Yoko calmly looked back on her sky-high expectations for a second trip to Baghdad. Now that her time here was ending, she felt an obscure dread of the future. As a journalist, what should she do next? What she'd accomplished here would surely merit a promotion, but she couldn't work up any excitement at the prospect.

That day, if she had asked just one more question, she would have died in the bombing. Just one question, that's all. Why was she still alive?

What if Aschenbach had gone home without dying in Venice? What then? Keeping his mind trained on the beauty of the boy Tadzio, whom he had seen by the beach, as a "health measure" akin to the impulse to travel that periodically came over him, would he have returned quietly to his workplace, "the humdrum scene of his cold, inflexible, and passionate duty"?

Yoko sat up and tapped the remote by the bed, turning on the CD. It was a performance from Makino's late twenties of Bach's unaccompanied Cello Suite no. 3. The prelude opened lightly with a high G followed by a rapidly descending scale that shot a ray of pure light into her breast. For a while, as the music played, that light was hers alone.

For the guitar arrangement, the suite had been transposed from C major to G major. That alone created quite a different impression.

Casals, Rostropovich, Fournier, Maisky . . . In the past she had listened to records by the master cellist of each successive age, but she had come to love this particular piece only by listening to Makino's guitar rendition here in this city of death. The sublimity of cello reverberations was too much for her just now.

The towering beauty of Bach's music was far beyond everyday human emotions. Makino's performance, recorded when he was still young and reveling in a honeymoon with his gift, took unchallenged possession of her heart. If she could just become one with his music, freed from all else. She longed to melt into the flowing beauty where time and melody combined in perfect measure.

She remembered the way he'd smiled as they looked at each other across the table.

What if, instead of getting in that taxi, she'd told him she wanted to be with him all night? What would have happened? The bold suggestion set her heart pounding. If, before returning to Baghdad, she had done more than surround herself with beauty—if she'd lain in his arms—how different would her life be now?

I want to see him again. Yet his three emails expressing concern about her welfare remained unanswered. In her desire to write back properly, she'd let day after day go by. She needed to let him know that she was safe. And thank him. She wanted him to know how much his music meant to her. Somewhere inside, she knew she wanted to write more than that. "You're in love," Philip had said. That one uncalled-for remark was working on her emotions, propelling them in a direction from which there could be no turning back.

She curled into a fetal position and thought again about her conversation with Richard. Was she really going to go home and marry him? Have his child? Doing so would mark a new chapter in her life, beyond all doubt. There was her age to think of. Another six months and she would be forty-one. *Time is short.* That knowledge was a stone weighing on her heart.

4

Reunion

It was the end of March, and even though Yoko must have been back in France by then, Makino had had no word from her. Once the bombing had been properly investigated, there'd been reports that no RFP members were among the dead.

He continued to worry about her safety, but the gnawing anxiety was easing with the passage of time. Looking back over their email exchanges, he found his own discordant cheeriness depressing. Encouraged by her remark that "fun emails are a nice distraction," he had always picked out an amusing story to include. She wrote back to let him know she appreciated these efforts. "I tried to tell your story to my staff, but I just couldn't stop laughing!" He imagined the wrinkles on the bridge of her nose as she laughed like a beautiful boy, and smiled at his computer screen.

But with a brutal bloodbath taking place around her day in and day out, what had she really felt as she read his silly emails? He couldn't be sure. Maybe she had been forcing herself to go along with them. She might have enjoyed the stories at first, but he could well imagine that after the bombing at her hotel, they might have been too frivolous for her.

She had probably stopped listening to his music too. After all, with Baghdad deep in civil war, what possible meaning could there be in classical guitar renditions of Bach? Makino asked himself this between sessions in his studio, unable to concentrate even for a mere five hours of practice.

In deciding to give up on any hope of a relationship with Yoko, Makino made the contrary discovery that he had already begun to fall in love with her. That was the most important change wrought by her nearly six weeks of silence. With no way to know how much of a hold he might have on her heart, he was forced to accept the lonely reality that they lived in different worlds.

Just as he was reaching that conclusion, Yoko's "long, long email" arrived.

He was startled by its inordinate length. The thumb of the scroll bar was as tiny as a grain of rice. He had never received an email this long from anyone, and at first, he was more worried than pleased.

But after reading ten lines, he was drawn in by the extremely compact sentences. Despite the length of the email, there wasn't one place where she rambled. It was as pleasurable to read as a short essay, and once again it occurred to him that here was someone truly out of the ordinary. Moreover, it seemed safe to conclude that he was someone special to her.

She first apologized for her long silence and then told him how delighted she had been to receive his three emails. She had wanted to write back, but just couldn't, she said.

There is no way to pull myself together except to put everything into words, and yet I am struck more than ever by the difficulty of writing about myself to myself. I wrote this imagining you were listening, picturing you the way you were that night when we sat across from each other in the Spanish restaurant. When I did that, the sentences came flowing out. I don't know why. Perhaps it's because when I was in Baghdad, I listened constantly to your music. In that world of despair, your music was my moral support.

Originally, I had no intention of showing this to you; I was just going to leave you as my imaginary listener. But after finishing it, I reconsidered. I decided I wanted you to know.

She began with her narrow escape from the suicide bombing and then set down as rationally as possible the emotional ups and downs she had experienced thereafter. Her resolute, quiet style moved Makino.

If I had asked just one more question, I would have died. Whatever I do, time rewinds to that moment. Why didn't I die then? Why am I alive now? For the first time in my life, I am grateful that time moves second by second in a progression that is even, silent, and straight. Until now, that progression seemed pitiless, but it would be intolerable if time were overly considerate of my feelings. Now I am glad to let time carry me forward as it will.

Then she wrote about her concern for the people still living in miserable conditions in Iraq and mentioned that she had seen her father's film *Coins of Happiness* again after returning to Paris and also that she'd reread the Rilke poem quoted in it, an excerpt from the *Duino Elegies*.

After two weeks off, she was now back in her office in Paris.

Not a word about her fiancé or getting married. She ended by writing that, if Makino was still free in June, she would like to see him in Paris and have another enjoyable conversation.

Makino had been invited to a June 2 festival in Madrid, commemorating the twentieth anniversary of the death of Andrés Segovia, the father of the modern classical guitar, and after that, he was scheduled to teach a master class at the Paris conservatory where he had studied. On the last day of class, students would join in a matinee performance in the school auditorium. In his New Year's email, Makino had invited Yoko to attend. At the end of that matinee, he intended to perform the theme from *Coins of Happiness* for her.

He answered her right away. He rejoiced that she was safe and expressed gratitude that she had chosen him as the recipient of her "long, long email." And he added that his schedule in Paris was unchanged, and of course he would like very much to have dinner and continue their conversation.

Her response came the same day. The simple words "I'm glad" made him glad too.

He had no doubt now that he wanted her to love him. Deep within him, a light shone as bright as day, a brightness that he found blinding.

Perhaps she loved him too. Every time he found a sign that she might, he felt the anguish of love, yet when he reconsidered and thought he must be wrong, he was in anguish again. He tried to consider rationally whether he was worthy of her love, but that had the opposite effect.

Such were the humbling effects of love. As they grew older, people distanced themselves from love not so much from a diminishing of passion, the desire to love, as from a dulling of the clear and anguished self-awareness of adolescence, the fear that they were not lovable. The value of work and hobbies was the easy comfort they provided to lonely people who suffered from not being loved because they were not beautiful or lively. But such people forgot to dream fervently of becoming beautiful or lively in order to be loved. What was love if it failed to inspire the desire to be worthy of the one you cherished?

Makino had begun falling in love with Yoko the first time they met. Looking back on that night, he could come to no other conclusion. The respect and admiration he felt put her at a remove, creating a distance that he must now bridge. While she was still in Baghdad, his emotions had necessarily been held in check. Now that she was back home, he felt the urgent need to make a drastic choice between two alternatives.

Thinking of what must be accomplished at his reunion with Yoko in Paris—the first time they would ever be alone together—he was pessimistic. He had stayed out of the love game for some time now. But what about Yoko? After meeting him only twice, she would have to love him enough to call off her marriage. Given that she was already forty, Makino imagined that would be tantamount to choosing to marry him instead.

For the first time in his life, Makino gave serious thought to marriage, and felt his lifelong indifference melt away.

If, when they met again, they merely reaffirmed the friendly feelings they had established the first time, then forever after they would each be "someone I met a couple of times," and nothing more. Makino knew that possibility was far more likely.

Unable to contain himself, he altered his itinerary so that instead of merely passing through Paris, he would remain there several days. He didn't tell Yoko he was changing his plans for her sake, but simply said that something had come up. Every romance has one or two such feigned coincidences. And often, the beloved dimly suspects the truth.

She responded:

> *Then of course I'll free up the end of May too. But are you sure it's all right, letting me monopolize you for two full days? We'll be able to have an extra-long conversation, won't we—part one and part two. Let's talk about each other's lives, one day for each. lol But with the Madrid festival coming up, you mustn't wear yourself out. If you have to cancel at the last minute, I'll understand.*

Makino read and reread the email, three times. While relieved that she had promised to spend the time with him, he told himself he might need to cool off a bit.

As Yoko had said, he was actually not at all sure he could afford to take time off just then. A lineup of masters from all over the world would be on the Madrid program, and there was talk of livestreaming the event as well. And Makino knew he was at a difficult juncture as a musician.

The rumor that he'd canceled the *What a Wonderful World* album had spread, and at every joint concert he participated in till the end of April, industry folks wanted to know what lay behind his decision. He was taken aback, feeling it was a private matter; the reason for their interest later became clear.

Among those who wanted to know was Seiichi Sofue, with whom Makino had studied as a teen. Sofue was born before the war, when it was possible to actually take lessons from Segovia, and had introduced Western guitar techniques to Japan. He had also dedicated himself to training the next generation. Makino was fond of declaring how much he owed to Sofue.

Sofue was a man of great rectitude and a Christian, but his austere recordings of Bach's lute suites were regarded in Europe as "Bach in the spirit of Zen." He was known for observing the niceties of polite behavior and for addressing his former pupils with the same respectful language they used with him; he followed this practice even now, when some of them were young enough to be his grandchildren.

When Makino was still in elementary school, his father had taken him to a class taught by Sofue. The master had been astonished at his talent and called him a "boy genius." From then until Makino won the Paris International Guitar Competition, Sofue had been his enthusiastic mentor. Makino had taken the train alone from his home in Okayama all the way to Tokyo for lessons, staying overnight at the Sofue home and enjoying Mrs. Sofue's home cooking. An only child, he had played with the two Sofue children as if they were his brother and sister. Sofue was a warmhearted man but a cool-headed judge of talent, and among his many pupils he regarded Makino as his special favorite, taking him under his wing and looking after him.

Once he'd struck out on his own, Makino was surprised to learn how much Sofue had spoken of him to others, not only in Japan but overseas. "Sofue used to complain that teaching you made him sick. 'How can a mere child understand things it took me decades to figure out?' he'd say." Every time he heard something along those lines, Makino would smile and wave a hand in self-deprecation, not out of false humility but because he doubted it could be true. Then he would reminisce about those days and wonder what the master had truly thought as he trained him.

Back then, Sofue would have been around forty, roughly Makino's age now. Around that time, he had started taking on private pupils, something that had seemed perfectly natural to Makino at the time but in retrospect was hard to understand. Sofue's own musical activities must have been deeply fulfilling, so why take such an interest in teaching? Makino tried to picture himself as a boy through Sofue's eyes, tried to hear his boyish playing through Sofue's ears. What if a "boy genius" were to appear before him, Makino, now? Someone who would study commendably hard, looking up to him, but who might sometimes wear an expression that said he suspected himself the better guitarist. Unpardonable conceit. And if the boy turned out to be not so gifted after all, what would it take for Makino to keep on finding time in his busy schedule to teach him? Perhaps there had been financial considerations. Or could his beloved teacher have been going through his own crisis as a musician?

Reunited for the first time in a long while, Makino and Sofue performed Fernando Sor's Fantasy for Two Guitars op. 54, but Sofue never said a word about the performance. Backstage afterward, he casually asked about the cancellation of *What a Wonderful World*.

"Oh, that?" Makino responded with an embarrassed half smile. "Well, it was just . . . I couldn't go through with it."

"Remarkable. So such things happen even to you, do they?" Sofue said in the same quiet, grave tone as always. "If there is some external circumstance, then fine; but if the reason is internal, then make sure you use this unexpected free time to your best advantage and don't brood too much. Although, knowing you, I'm sure you must have a great deal on your mind. Anyway, a bit of friendly advice."

No other words were necessary. Sofue must have grasped the entire situation from their performance onstage.

Whenever he came out with a new album, Makino always sent Sofue a CD. The man must have received an enormous number from around the world every day, but he never failed to listen and send a handwritten note of thanks. Makino admired his teacher's unfailing propriety, a trait he felt was beyond him. It concerned him that, over the past few years, Sofue's comments gradually had taken longer to arrive and had become more restrained. The once-euphoric words of praise had cooled considerably, and between the lines, Makino sensed he was struggling to understand. The change dated from around the time Makino had begun seeking a wider audience.

But Sofue was virtually the only one who connected Makino's cancellation of *What a Wonderful World* with his problems as a performer. Others made a surprising conjecture, the "external circumstance" Sofue had referred to. Makino didn't bother to correct the rumor, embracing it as a convenient cover.

In his meeting with Okajima from Jupiter, Makino had learned of an unexpected development: the head office in Britain had agreed to a buyout by Globe Music. The musicians he'd run into subsequently had spoken of little else. People weren't sure exactly why Makino had canceled his album, but they assumed there was some connection.

Like other classical musicians, Makino was not tied exclusively to Jupiter. However, beginning with his debut album, most of his recordings had been with them, and they sold better on average than other companies'.

According to Okajima, rumors of a buyout had been around for a while, and from management's perspective, the time was ripe. To most employees, however, it didn't seem real. "They were caught unawares," he said. A memo had gone out saying, "For now, there will be no dismissals." Everyone's attention had focused not on the assurance of "no dismissals" but on the ominous "for now." Downsizing after the acquisition was bound to affect not only employees but contracted musicians, which explained the buzz among Makino's fellow performers.

Knowing that Okajima was famous for gossiping in obsessive detail about everything from the hiring of overseas conductors to orchestra members' gripes and soloists' financial hardships, Makino couldn't hold back the snide observation that if employees had been "caught unawares" by the buyout, it was a disgrace. He said it in a joking way, but deep down, he was appalled.

But Okajima was ready with an explanation. News of the buyout had only become widely known the morning that Makino met with Korenaga in Shibuya. Okajima, however, had already been tipped off and was probably the only one in the company with advance knowledge. Since the news hadn't been verified, he'd been unable to share it with Makino, for which he apologized. Makino's CDs sold fairly well for classical recordings, but times were hard, and there was no telling what Globe Music would decide to do. Sales departments dealt solely in numbers, and even at Jupiter, every time Makino came out with a new album, Okajima had had to fight for a big release. He'd really championed Makino, more than the guitarist knew. He had decided that a commercially successful crossover like *What a Wonderful World* would benefit not only Makino but everyone in the classical music division. Korenaga hadn't known about the bigger picture, but had agreed it would benefit Makino. His sudden cancellation of the project had upset her, Okajima said, and led her to suspect that he must have known about the pending acquisition at the time.

Repelled by Okajima's suggestive tone, Makino grew depressed. Was any of what the man said even true? Korenaga had long pushed the idea of him covering popular songs, and he had finally gotten on board. Potential themes for the album had ranged from movie music to Japanese pop, until finally, after Mitani got involved, they had settled on "beautiful American songs." None of this necessarily went against what Okajima had said, but it didn't fit smoothly with it, either. Okajima hadn't involved himself in those discussions.

Even if it were true, Makino didn't like the idea of Okajima taking it upon himself to worry about his future in that fashion. Nor did he care what the sales department might think of him. Who did this guy think he was, going on and on so smugly?

Twenty years as a guitarist and it's come to this, he thought gloomily.

"As far as that goes," Okajima went on, "I've devoted myself to classical music all this time, so nobody's more frustrated than me. It can't end here. No, sir! I'm determined to push classical music onto center stage. To do that, I've got to have your help, Makino-san. Won't you reconsider your decision on *What a Wonderful World?*"

Makino put off giving an answer.

The head of the classical division at Globe Music had been urging him to put out a record with them. Makino had turned down offers from Globe in the past, prioritizing his longstanding relationship with

Jupiter, but Globe was twice as big. If a buyout was in the works, then there was nothing to worry about. Although he could do without working with Okajima in the future, thank you. He hadn't noticed it before, but the guy had a real talent for rubbing people the wrong way. He told himself this with a wry inner chuckle, and let it go.

Okajima wanted to meet again before he left for Paris, but Makino didn't respond to that request. Instead he decided to meet with the Globe representative after he came back and asked Mitani to set it up.

When Mitani heard that Makino wanted to rearrange his Madrid schedule to stop in Paris both coming and going, she had no doubt: he was going to see Yoko.

Normally she had little knowledge of his relations with the opposite sex, despite being constantly at his side, but with Yoko it was easy to tell. Ever since meeting her, Makino would always tell people that he'd been introduced to Jerko Solich's daughter. You might think only a hardcore film buff would recognize the name, but in the music industry, mention of the director of *Coins of Happiness* always drew appreciative murmurs. "What's she like?" someone would say, and Makino would lean forward eagerly as if he'd been waiting for the question.

"She works for the RFP news agency, and, boy, she's pretty. Not just pretty, either. Speaks all kinds of languages, French and German and who knows what. She's got degrees from Oxford and Columbia, so she's smart as a whip. And she's got a sense of humor to go along with it, plus she's nice . . ."

"There are people like that?"

"One, anyway. And as you might expect, seeing who her father is, she's a great student of art with a poetic sensibility. Studied Rilke in college."

Mitani had never seen him talk about anyone with such excitement. He wasn't overstating it, probably, but to Mitani the word "pretty" seemed a bit off. Yoko had distinctive features. But that was hard to explain, so perhaps "pretty" was good enough. Another woman would understand, she thought.

Yes, Yoko was a fine, upstanding person, but not someone she could ever get along with. No doubt Yoko felt the same way, perhaps even more so, though if Mitani ever said such a thing to her face she would surely look at her with those all-seeing, gently understanding eyes of hers and shake her head.

Makino soon stopped mentioning Yoko altogether. Mitani took this as a sign not that he had lost interest, but that his feelings were no longer something he could easily expose to others. She picked up on this shift by marking first his distress at the time of the terrorist incident in Yoko's hotel, then his outburst of joy when, after more than a month of silence, they learned she was safe.

Makino enjoyed making others laugh, but he seldom let loose himself. Especially since last year, he could be joking around with someone and then all of a sudden get a faraway look on his face for no apparent reason.

Having been dimly aware of and concerned about his distress over his music, Mitani had rejoiced to see him smile again. But, deeply attracted to him herself, she struggled to extinguish the flames of emotions that had no apparent chance of ever being requited.

Makino would see Yoko in Paris. As Mitani emailed back and forth with him, arranging plane tickets, she pictured their reunion and felt a vague anxiety in the back of her mind begin to coalesce.

"Are you going to see Yoko?" She had meant the probe to sound teasing, but it came out almost like an interrogation.

Seemingly taken aback, he had parried with an air of displeasure: "Well, I have a lot of plans . . ."

Lately she had incurred his displeasure this way more than once. Last year, such a thing had never happened. He might have laughed at her for leaping to conclusions or being stubborn, but he had never seemed put off. When she got into dustups with staff, he'd always backed her.

Now her feelings and actions were at odds with each other, and it made her uncomfortable and upset with herself.

Before she'd purchased his plane tickets, the Madrid office had stressed the special fare and the fact that the dates could not be changed—something Makino knew perfectly well.

Makino told her, "Check again, and if nothing can be done, I'll buy new tickets myself."

"If you won't be using the tickets, how about letting me go to Madrid?" Mitani suggested, feigning nonchalance. "Lots of wonderful guitarists besides you will be performing, and it would be a terrific learning experience."

Normally Makino would have laughed off the request, but this time he let an awkward moment pass before saying, "Can you do that, change the passenger's name? If the airline allows it, I don't mind. You'd learn a lot, that's for sure."

In the end, Makino used his frequent flyer miles to get a seat on the outbound flight to Paris. In Madrid, he was scheduled to perform the Guitar Concerto no. 1 in D Major, which composer Mario Castelnuovo-Tedesco had dedicated to Segovia. On the plane, he suddenly got worried and, though slightly befuddled by wine, went over the score to make sure of a few passages.

It'd be his first time performing this piece onstage, and for the last month or so, he had practiced it fairly intensively. He was a little nervous about performing with the local orchestra, but at this point, that was easier to contemplate than performing solo.

He had also brought on board with him two DVDs—*Coins of Happiness* and *Morning Sun in Dalmatia*, an earlier war movie of Solich's—and a new translation of Rilke's *Duino Elegies* that he had found recently in a bookstore. Despite his love for *Coins of Happiness*, Makino had seen few of Solich's other works, so he'd recently taken a look at Solich's filmography and ordered as many as he could, including the films Solich had made in the eighties after going to Hollywood.

Morning Sun in Dalmatia he intended to watch before he saw Yoko again, partly because it was made in 1966, the year she was born. It was a "partisan film," one of many such Yugoslavian films from that era. As a genre, they glorified the brave exploits of the partisans who had fought against the Axis powers in World War II under the leadership of the victorious "hero" Tito. He had expected something along those lines, but Solich's film was evidently of a different mold. The package stated, "A masterful war movie now being reevaluated! The story of a Croatian youth who throws himself into the cauldron of appalling ethnic conflict, set against the scenic background of the Adriatic Sea and told with penetrating nihilism."

The film was short, barely ninety minutes. Makino leaned his seat halfway back, wrapped himself in a blanket, and watched it, figuring if he fell asleep, no harm done. With the cabin lights turned off, there was a twilight that might have been either day or night, and mixed in with the constant hum of the engines were some impressive snores. The small glowing computer screen allowed him to immerse himself in the story more than when he watched at home, almost as if he were in a movie theater.

The mystical serenity of the main character amid a storm of shelling took his breath away. He was amazed to discover that Solich had filmed a movie like this at such a time. The man was a freaking genius. According to the explanation on the DVD box, he had just turned thirty when he made the film.

The last scene was based on the short story "Four Days" by the Russian novelist Vsevolod Garshin. The sight of the main character's bruised and battered body lying on the Dalmatian soil after battling the Chetniks was overpowering. When he had finished watching and closed his computer, he was shivering so much that he pulled his blanket up around his hunched shoulders. He let out a breath and shook his head, murmuring softly, "Wow."

He had intended to watch *Coins of Happiness* next, but he no longer had the strength.

Yoko was this man's daughter—born to the Solich of that very era. It struck him as extraordinary. He sat like that for a long while, a jumble of thoughts tumbling through his mind amid the lingering reverberations of the film.

The commentary on the DVD box had indicated a nine-year gap between *Morning Sun in Dalmatia* and *Coins of Happiness*, a time when Solich's whereabouts were unknown. Makino couldn't get this out of his mind. Why hadn't someone with so much talent quickly followed this film with another? Had something prevented him? Where had he been and what had he been doing? Only now did it occur to Makino that *Coins of Happiness* must have been filmed considerably after Solich's divorce from Yoko's mother.

Solich had experienced World War II as a child. In Yugoslavia, he knew from an early age not only the invasion by Axis forces but the brutality of ethnic conflict that had erupted as a consequence; diffused reflections of his war memories were scattered throughout *Coins of Happiness*. The main character, a young Croatian poet fond of Rilke, was probably Solich himself in large part, and the Serbian girl he loved was probably based on a real person as well.

The complicated political background was rendered in abstract terms, and the story of a love that was battered but undying had made the film a worldwide hit, but now, having seen *Morning Sun in Dalmatia*, Makino felt that *Coins* probably contained a multitude of symbolic details that he had failed to understand but that must hold poignant meaning for Yugoslavians, or for Europeans.

Did Yoko understand them?

He felt her become a bit more remote, even as the geographical distance between them steadily shrank, and this disconnect only stirred up his anxious affection for her.

As a boy, Makino had loved the guitar theme from *Coins of Happiness*, but more than that, he had idolized the main character's ultimate love for the heroine. She was played by an unknown actress with clean, sculptured features and the unsophisticated charm of a wildflower.

Seated now in the shadowy interior of a plane bound for Paris, he tried to recall the actress's face, and when he did so, he couldn't help glimpsing Yoko's face overlaid on top. His memory of her seen through the taxi window that night had taken on a dreamlike quality, like a scene in a Solich film.

))(

Back from Baghdad and taking a two-week break from work, Yoko spent the first week in a trance, cleaning her apartment and unpacking. Not until the second week did she begin seeing people.

Just going outside and being able to walk on the streets freely was her greatest pleasure. At the local cafés and boulangeries, they rejoiced over her safe return and gave her special deals.

The weather was still chilly, but she needed to move around, so early in the morning when few people were out, she would leave her apartment on rue du Bac to go jogging as far as the Luxembourg Gardens. As she worked up a sweat and grew short of breath, she took in lungfuls of air so deep that she felt a twinge of pain at the back of her throat. With every thudding heartbeat, the joy of actually being in Paris spread through her being.

When she returned home, she would fill the tub, adding on alternate days some of her favorite bath oil or the cypress bath salts she had bought in Japan. Then she indulged in a long soak, leaving the bathroom door open so she could hear music from the living room.

The smoothness of her return to the everyday world was a bit of an anticlimax; she crossed the threshold with barely any sense of unevenness. She had adapted with surprising ease to life in Baghdad with its lack of this and that, and found less pleasure than she had anticipated in returning to Parisian abundance. She found rather that she needed time to adjust to the excess around her. But being in a place where from sunrise to sunset there was never the sound of bombs quietly eased the lingering tension inside her.

As her own feelings settled, she thought with pain of those she had left behind in Iraq.

The doctor who had been counseling her since her arrival smiled as she told him how she had been getting along. He was glad to hear she was adjusting smoothly but cautioned her not to push herself. She had prescriptions for sleeping pills and sedatives, but in the end she never took either.

In April, she set to work covering the French presidential election, which kept her busy from then until May 6, when Nicolas Sarkozy was elected for the first time. She felt things were finally back to normal, but it couldn't last. Change was inevitable. Richard was back at the university in New York, his sabbatical over, but he showed up in Paris every two weeks or so, eager to move ahead with wedding plans.

Yoko adopted a noncommittal attitude toward him. This only increased her self-loathing.

Richard and she had been friends at Columbia and, until he'd visited Paris the year before, she had never imagined him as a lover. They had each known the other's partners in college and had never been particularly close, but that left room for the relationship to grow. Theirs hadn't been the sort of friendship that would have made the notion of dating seem laughable.

What had triggered the change? For both of them, she thought, it could only have been their age. Young people's hearts were extremely combustible. Once lit, the flame of passion would spread with the abandon of wildfire, out of control. If the combustible portion of the other's heart similarly caught fire, the two had to become lovers, if only to escape their misery. Romantic love thus could not be expected to endure. At some point, the flames of passion had to quiet down into a more lasting warmth. For youth, that sort of love amounted to romance gone flaccid. No matter how blessed a marriage based on such love might be, there would inevitably be a pinch of resignation mixed in.

However, Yoko had met Richard again just as she'd begun to think that, given her age, it was about time to marry. As a liberal professional woman, she had long kept an open mind about the possibility of life with or without children, but with forty looming, she had been leaning toward the desire to give birth. She had arrived at a point in life where she did not necessarily require flaming passion, and she had visualized a peaceful future with Richard. What was important to her at that time was sharing a life with him and finding out whether or not he would make a suitable father.

Richard was a rational thinker, though not overly serious; his emotional life was uncomplicated to an enviable degree. For someone so well educated, he had no understanding of art and made no effort to conceal his cluelessness, showing a lack of pretense that impressed her favorably. In his love for her, he was always a step ahead, and he had a well-mannered passion. He had probably never been called handsome in his life, but he was fairly tall and kept himself in shape by going to the gym.

Certainly, however much you might trust and respect someone, attraction is a very different matter. Some even claim that, in the end, it's the only difference between friendship and love. Fortunately, she and

Richard found an easy physical connection. Richard was openly and winningly delighted at "being with someone so beautiful," and Yoko, while finding him a tad conservative, was content with the amount of pleasure she attained.

Her life was moving forward smoothly. And then came Makino—a flame igniting the heart she'd thought had outgrown passion, engulfing it all at once in a fire that only grew ever more consuming.

Richard treated Yoko with consideration, knowing the stint in Baghdad had taken a lot out of her, but he also let her know, in a joking way, the anguish of being forced to wait, and he embraced her with the insatiable passion of the early days of their relationship. She understood that this intensity arose from his anxiety over her coolness with regard to wedding preparations. Perplexed that at this stage of their relationship he should have to seek proof of being loved, Richard wrote it off to himself and to her as pre-wedding jitters.

Yoko yielded to his importuning, and also hesitantly went along with his desire not to use protection. But after he went back to New York and she was alone again, she thought of Makino with enormous guilt. She even toyed with the idea of ceasing contact with her fiancé, all for the sake of a relationship that had barely begun.

She wrote Makino the "long, long email" and promised to meet him again—after which she didn't once sleep with Richard.

Makino arrived in Paris late in the afternoon and checked into a hotel near the École Normale de Musique de Paris, where he had arranged to borrow a practice room the following day. He showered, took a short rest, and then answered a backlog of work emails. At eight o'clock he headed for the restaurant where Yoko had made reservations. It was a five-minute walk from Madeleine station.

He arrived a bit late and spotted Yoko seated at a table by the window, chatting with a waiter. The decor was minimal, with indirect lighting and countless wine bottles lined up sideways on glass shelves—a stylish accent in the oyster-white-and-dark-brown room. When she saw him, she smiled and waved.

"Good to see you," he said.

"Good to see you too. You look well. No jet lag?"

"I'm all right. I rested on the plane. Coming this way never bothers me much, anyway."

"Same here. It's much worse going back to Japan."

"And the older I get, the longer it takes to recover." He chuckled as he took his seat.

Outdoors, it was not yet completely dark, and pale light the color of dry leaves lit up the cheerful faces of people heading through the narrow alleyway toward dinner somewhere. Makino felt that he was really in Paris now. He tried to grasp the reality that Yoko was here, in front of him. She was wearing a chic dress with large pale-pink flowers on a background of white and moss green. At the end of a platinum chain, a small diamond twinkled on her breast. Her black hair was sleek and lustrous.

"What is it?" she said, smiling. "You didn't expect to see me in a dress?"

"No, I—I was just thinking how pretty you are." The words slipped from his lips. Before he said anything else that might sound flattering or facetious, he added, "I should have dressed up a little more." He clutched the front of his jacket and fingered it.

Yoko shook her head. "That jacket is nice. And this isn't that fancy of a restaurant, anyway. Save your tuxes for Madrid."

"That reminds me. I forgot to take them out of the suitcase." He made a face.

They both felt a bit awkward. This was only the second time they had sat talking face-to-face, yet in emails they had each revealed intimate things, things they had told no one else. The gap left them feeling uncomfortable and stiff. Now they were here in the flesh, able to see and touch one another. They each sought to catch up to the words they had written, words full of exhilaration, on the verge of yielding all to the other; yet they could not abruptly refer to the seriousness of what they had written or the intimations of love that had passed between them. Makino did not fail to notice the engagement ring on her left hand, with secret disappointment. There was nothing to do but pick up where they'd left off on that first night.

Now that he was with her again at last, Makino found Yoko even more beautiful than he remembered, which was surprising, since he'd supposed he had idealized her in the interim. That other time, she hadn't felt any particular emotion upon meeting him, he realized afresh. Tonight, however, she had carefully applied makeup and dressed up for the occasion. With her daily life on track, she was full of animation. She was two years older than him, but he thought she looked years younger.

The restaurant's much-discussed chef specialized in *cuisine moderne*. After listening to the waiter's explanations, they decided to order separate appetizers and main dishes and share them.

Yoko's French was flawless. And after hearing Makino order, she commented, "I knew you spoke some French, but your accent is excellent. I guess being a musician means you have an ear for languages?"

"I don't know about that," he said. "You'll notice he brought me an English menu. A bit of a blow to my ego." He smiled ruefully, but she quickly explained.

"No, that's because the last time I came, I brought a Japanese friend and requested an English menu for her. He must have remembered."

The restaurant was nearly full, the tables close together, but speaking Japanese gave them a space all their own. They drank a champagne toast and then, as he was catching his breath, Makino realized that after

71

longing so deeply for this reunion, he had no idea what to talk about next. They set down their glasses and exchanged nervous smiles.

"This feels so strange somehow," Makino said.

"Doesn't it? We met in Tokyo, and now Paris. I wonder where we'll meet next."

"Paris again. I'm coming back here after Madrid."

"Oh, really . . ."

Makino observed mussels being served at a neighboring table and thought of a story to tell. "I have an old friend who's a television director, and on his staff there's this young woman who's a bit strange."

Yoko was smiling in anticipation. "Uh-huh."

"Not long ago, she went to Lake Shinji to report on harvesting little *shijimi* clams, and she brought back a bag of them to share with her boss. The fisherman had apparently taken a shine to her and given her a lecture about the best way to eat them. The funny thing is, instead of eating them, she started to keep them as pets."

"What? Is that even possible?"

"It's not easy, apparently, but she searched the internet and somehow or other managed to do it. She actually gave them names."

"What a sweet girl she must be."

"'Sweet' is one word for it . . . She took pictures of them with her cellphone and went around showing them to her coworkers, people making guest appearances, and so on. And just last week, my friend the director gave a party at his home and she brought her pet clams along to show everybody. In a Tupperware container."

Yoko nodded, listening closely.

"I happened to be invited too. He'd been trying to get me to come over for dinner for some time, but I was always too busy, so this once I thought I should at least stop by. There must have been, oh, six or seven people there. He was serving Chinese medicinal hotpot. By the time I got there, the meal was nearly over, but they had saved me some. I sat down next to this rather strange young woman. We'd never met, so we

72

said hello, nice to meet you, and all that. Everybody was pretty drunk, and I was wondering how I could catch up, when my friend's wife brought out a platter of food and told me to serve myself. Just turn the heat back on under the hotpot and throw in whatever ingredients you like, she said. Long onions, chicken, whatever. Meanwhile, the strange young woman gets up to bring me a glass of wine. So I start putting this and that in the hotpot, and there right next to me are a bunch of *shijimi* clams in Tupperware."

"You didn't!"

"I hesitated, because they're usually in miso soup, right? But this was an unusual hotpot to begin with, and there they were in Tupperware, so I figured they must be some super-special kind of *shijimi*, and I tossed them in with the other ingredients. Everybody at the table started yelling, and then she came back and let out a scream."

"So what happened?" Yoko pressed a hand to her mouth.

"It was terrible. She panicked. My friend grabbed a ladle and tried to fish the *shijimi* out of the boiling pot, but it didn't go very well. They were wrapped in long onions or buried under chunks of tofu. He finally managed to get them out, and she grabbed hold of the plate with her *shijimi* on it wrapped in long onions, then she turned bright red and burst into tears. Meanwhile, I still had no idea what was going on. At first, I thought they were something she'd been saving to eat herself."

"Of course you did. Anybody would think that."

"My friend the director explained, 'Actually, those were her pets.' I tell you, I was horrified. So of course I apologized, and she said no, it was her fault. But she couldn't stop crying. I felt awful. My friend tried to cheer me up by saying, 'It's pretty impossible to raise *shijimi* at home, so they were probably half-dead already.'"

"I'll bet they were."

"Then somebody else told her, 'Too bad and all, but a minute ago you were eating short-necked clams and enjoying them.' He was fairly drunk and meant it as a joke, but it didn't help. She glared at him and yelled, 'My babies are not short-necked clams!' I didn't know what to do, so I just sat there, flustered."

"I can imagine." Yoko smiled sympathetically. "What happened in the end?"

"She put the *shijimi* remains back in the Tupperware and took off. The whole thing was as awkward as could be. I didn't feel like eating any of the hotpot, and my friend's wife decided if the *shijimi* were spoiled I might get sick, so she cleared the table. As soon as I could, I excused myself and left too, although everybody had been very understanding. Looking back, that was one helluva strange evening."

"It bothers you, doesn't it?"

"More than a little. I mean, I've never killed someone's pets before."

"I don't think you should brood about it."

"Apparently, after I left, they went on talking till late at night. How far is it possible to empathize with different kinds of animals—fish and insects, say? Does giving an animal a name make eating it taboo? That sort of thing. I'm glad I missed it."

"Whether any creature born to die has a name or not makes a huge difference, but why that should be so is a philosophical question. And whether or not that name has a connection to oneself is an especially important point. It's something I'd rather not think about right now, I'm afraid."

The smile never left her face, but Makino sensed that his little story had struck a nerve, perhaps having to do with her Iraq experience. He kicked himself for not having come up with a better topic.

"How'd we ever get started on that anyway? Oh, right—the mussels at the next table. Sorry, let's change the subject."

Yoko watched as he awkwardly finished off the appetizer that had been served midway through his story, thinking to herself that being amusing was his way of smoothing things over. He'd done it the night they'd first met, and also in the spate of emails he'd sent to Baghdad. He was amusing not because he wanted to make people laugh, but rather because he felt uneasy without laughter. She liked that he always caricatured himself, never others. His stories had a pleasantly ironic twist, and while he wasn't very modest or reserved, indecent talk was apparently not to his liking; he was always in good taste. He didn't raise his voice but spoke with considerable cadence and pace, and sometimes his voice would crack in a funny way, like vocal harmonics. Perhaps it was a style of speaking only a guitarist could pull off? His voice was well modulated, with good tempo and a touch of rubato where needed, his stories so neatly constructed that it was hard to believe they were truly off the cuff. The moment he had leaned forward and started to talk tonight, she'd felt a premonition of laughter.

She was afraid to make the comparison, but listening to Makino, she understood why she never found Richard's jokes very funny. Someone like Makino, whose innate talents couldn't help arousing jealousy and envy in others, had to cultivate an easy manner, a surprising approachability, to avoid isolation. In the course of her work, she had interviewed various "geniuses," all of whom possessed similar wit and sociability.

Back in Baghdad, Yoko had more than once relieved the suffocating boredom by googling "Satoshi Makino guitar." Then she would feel as if she were poking around in the drawers of his inner life and finally, unable to endure the sensation, quietly close the pages that came up. Amid the bright, flowery words of every kind of praise imaginable were criticisms and slander, like hidden nails and glass shards—fewer in number, to be sure, but gleaming and keen edged, incised in her memory.

For reasons she could not fathom, several times she opened and closed those drawers. The many encomiums on Makino's music pleased her inordinately, as she was beginning to feel something akin to love for him. She also read, besides reviews that were harsh yet reasonable, some that were mere invective, not averting her eyes but perusing them to the end. Each time she felt horrid, as if dirty hands had gripped the inner workings of her heart. She longed to sweep away those hands in contempt and rush to Makino's defense. Her growing sense that she might be someone who could understand and console him brought a special happiness and even some relief.

At the same time, it was she who was subjecting herself to the touch of those dirty hands. Sadly, she was forced to admit that the stirrings of her love for him contained some negativity regarding the dazzle of his genius. The first time she'd heard him play at eighteen in the Salle Pleyel, hadn't she been put off for that very reason?

Thomas Mann, expounding on "the gulf between greatness and the masses," wrote when Goethe died, "I clearly heard not only the laments of nymphs mourning the death of the great Pan, but also sighs of relief." Not only Goethe but all geniuses must be, to an extent, a source of pressure on the lives of those around them.

Now Yoko couldn't help wondering, What exactly might he find special in her? She was thrilled to think he had gone out of his way to come to Paris to see her, and would do so again. But what if there were other women at various points on his tour? It wouldn't be at all strange. As Korenaga had said, he'd remained a steadfast bachelor all this time. If he did have a string of women in his life, she didn't look down on him for it. She was a grown woman, well able to understand such choices, but as for how his life and hers might intersect, she was not sure.

What if she herself were to become "that sort of woman"? She considered the possibility calmly. Was it something she could bear? That she could even entertain such a thought only showed the importance Makino had taken on in her life. And if she couldn't bear it, then what quality did she possess that could make him love her and her alone? Her thoughts traveled in an anxious circle.

But maybe it was all happening too late. Her circumstances had changed, and now she feared any romance with him was impossible. After seeing him again today and realizing how much she enjoyed being with him, the thought that she might no longer be in a position to accept his love was devastating. The irrepressible love she felt for him was painful.

As darkness fell outside the window, the restaurant became even more sparkling and vibrant. Makino watched as Yoko ordered a glass of Cabernet Sauvignon from Bordeaux to go with her main dish, wondering what would happen between the two of them tonight.

For a while they enjoyed meandering conversation. "In Japan, I watched a Yugoslavian partisan film starring Yul Brynner and Orson Welles called . . . um . . ."

"The Battle of Neretva," she said. "Directed by Veljko Bulajic."

"Right, right. You certainly know your films."

"Don't make fun of me, please." She lifted her chin. "When I was born, I had Yugoslavian citizenship."

"You were born in Yugoslavia?"

"No, in Nagasaki. But Makino-san, I'm surprised you watched that movie. Not even Croatians watch it anymore."

"It's another important Yugoslavian partisan film, and I wanted to know more about Solich's world. *Morning Sun in Dalmatia* must have been made about the time you were born, if I'm not mistaken."

"That's right."

"So . . . I wanted to see *Morning Sun* too."

He looked at her with unmistakable meaning. He'd wanted to know more about her. Yoko understood, but allowed herself only the faintest of smiles.

"I saw it on the airplane."

"They were showing it?"

"No, I had the DVD. It moved me. More than I can say. It's completely different from the other partisan films, isn't it? Your father is amazing. I can't really explain it, but the movie made me feel the loneliness of being. The underlying sadness of life. That final scene gave me goose bumps."

"People have always questioned whether it's right to give such a poetic portrayal of war."

"But he doesn't create a yearning for war. He makes you want to be done with it forever."

"It's hard for me to speak objectively about my father's films, but . . . I suppose you could say their beauty makes the horror acceptable, brings it into focus. Few people can look at horror straight on, unadorned. If they do, they try to forget what they've seen, to expunge it from memory. I saw that many times through my work in Iraq."

With a slight shake of her head, she smiled at the waiter serving her filet mignon and said, *"Merci."* Then she looked at Makino, her eyes shining, and said, "It looks delicious! Would you like to try some? We got so involved in talking, we forgot to try each other's appetizers."

"Oh, right. Okay, you have some of mine too. You're eating meat today?" He cut off a piece of his cod, dipped it in sauce, and set it on her plate, and in return, she gave him a piece of her filet mignon. The waiter's slightly affected parting words, *"Bonne continuation,"* had struck him with special force. He speared the morsel of beef with his fork and popped it in his mouth. "It's really good. You chose well. I should have had the steak too. It's just, the airplane meal was beef, and I wanted something different."

"Have some more. I don't need all this."

"Thanks, I'm fine."

Yoko took a bite each of the steak and the cod, and smiled. "You're right. I think I picked the winner."

Makino sipped some white wine before going back to what they had been saying. "I sometimes think beauty must be worn out from being saddled with such cumbersome tasks all the time."

Yoko took a moment to think before responding. "I suppose it was after Romanticism that beauty became so weighed down by expectation.

Even ugliness has come under its umbrella. But beauty isn't only an agent of expression. It has equal power to enable us to turn our eyes away momentarily from the horrors of this world, doesn't it?"

"Yes, but I'm slightly pessimistic about that too, lately. Beauty is like an aging singer barely managing to continue performing, her popularity fading away."

"Beauty is selective, that's all. Like a performer who can afford to be choosy about the work she does."

"Nicely put." After a slight pause he said, "Reading your emails, I had to wonder what earthly good my music could do in Iraq. In a world where Kalashnikov bullets are flying, what value is there in Bach?"

Yoko shook her head. "I was saved in Baghdad by the beauty of your Bach."

"That's what you wrote, but . . . really?"

"You don't believe me?"

"I'm not saying that. It's just that, when I recorded that music, I never had any such situation in mind. It's hard to imagine."

"Baghdad is a hopeless mess, but while I was there in the center of it all, for the first time in my life, I learned to love Bach. I really felt that, yes, this is music from after the Thirty Years' War."

Hearing her say this without a hint of pedantry, Makino felt a slow welling of profound admiration.

"After that horrific war that they say killed half the German population, externally people had to accept coexistence in conflict, while internally their faith deepened. Living in a world laid waste, they must have found Bach's music a tremendous source of comfort. Not only his church music but his secular music too. It was your performance that made me realize that. Although you seem unconscious of it yourself." She peered into his eyes.

"Well, I—thank you. That's very nice to hear. I was just thinking that maybe it's your European blood that allows you to feel such things so naturally."

"The fringes of Europe, mind you. Between the Ottoman Turks and the Habsburgs."

"Still, that very sense of being a mixture, not pure blooded, strikes me as European. Bach's people came originally from Hungary, you know."

"That's right. So many people here have ancestors who lived someplace completely different, several generations back. Which probably explains the rise of nationalism, to an extent."

"I always wonder, How well do I really understand Bach, the core of European music? When I play a period instrument, I feel it all the more. To reach the understanding you just came to as easily as if you were jumping over a puddle, I'd have to spend years building a bridge over a deep valley. That's what I can't help admiring. That cultural depth, for lack of a better word." He paused. "After nineteenth-century Romanticism, the emotional or sensory aspects of music are more approachable, but so much in Bach transcends Bach the man. The existence of God, the lineage of the Bach family . . ."

"The man who plays Bach so wonderfully thinks that way, does he? You give me too much credit, by the way. When I listen to you perform, I always marvel that you can play music from so many different countries and ages, almost as if you had composed it yourself."

"That's what people say. Critics tend to put a negative spin on it, writing that I lack individuality. But I am a performer, and as such, I think it behooves me to try to grasp the composer's intent, or state of mind, or worldview."

"Can you read people's minds like that?"

"That's an entirely different matter." He chuckled. "To hear my manager tell it, I'm good at self-analysis and utterly obtuse about other people."

"Oh. Mitani-san, you mean?"

"Yes."

"She struck me as wholesome and nice. Would you say her analysis is right?"

"I wonder. What do you think?"

She looked Makino in the eye for several seconds before shaking her head with a wan smile. "I don't know yet. This is only the second time I've ever met you."

Makino felt the laughter drain from his smile.

It was true that they had only met twice. If anything was to come of their relationship, tonight was perhaps their only chance, and yet they were still in the state of "not knowing yet" about each other.

Makino's pulse raced. He took a drink of water and opened his mouth to speak, but the waiter, seeing a pause in their conversation, took that moment to come and take their orders for dessert.

They chose from the desserts he described and then faced one another again, only for Yoko to get a call on her cellphone. Purse in hand, she excused herself and stepped away.

The waiter asked if he could take away her half-full wineglass. Tonight she had drunk one glass of champagne and barely touched her wine.

She was gone for several minutes. When she came back, she said, "It's already eleven! I can't believe how fast the time has gone. Do you have to get up early in the morning?"

"No, I can relax a bit, and then I'll spend the day rehearsing. I have an evening flight."

"Oh, okay. I wish I could hear you play in Madrid. It must be so hard keeping yourself in peak condition."

Minutes before, Makino had been about to take the plunge and say what was in his heart. He still wanted to, but the tide of conversation forced him to digress. "Journalists have it a lot tougher. My life isn't in any danger."

Yoko waited for dessert to be served before speaking again. "This time I did ask myself why I'm doing this of all jobs. Seeing terrorism like that up close . . . It was petrifying."

"Of course it was. Now that you mention it, I've never heard why you became a journalist. I'm sure people ask you that all the time . . ."

"No special reason. It's not something I dreamed of as a little girl."

"No?"

"Not at all. For the longest time, I didn't know what I wanted to be. Like many people. Actually, I think journalism suits me. I get to cover all sorts of world events, meet all kinds of people and hear their stories. People I would never have a chance of meeting on my own open right up to me when I say I'm an RFP reporter, and answer my questions. Talking not to me in particular, of course, but to anonymous readers. Journalism is rather suited to people who aren't overly self-assertive, I think. But all we do is acquire broad superficial knowledge of many things, so I really admire someone like you who pursues one thing deeply and single-mindedly."

"I don't know about that. Is 'broad superficial knowledge of many things' enough to land someone in Baghdad?"

"As long as I'm engaged in this work, it's something that I know I should do, that I want to do. Of course there are risks involved, but the anxiety of not going is painful in and of itself. I was far from the only volunteer. And if I'm going to try to understand the world today, I can't very well just leave Iraq out of the picture, now can I? This is the age of globalism. It may sound funny, but really I landed in Baghdad before I quite knew what was happening. All sorts of things punch holes in our destiny, I think. Without there being anything we can do about it. And sometimes it may be a bullet. That's what it comes down to."

For a moment he looked at her wordlessly. Then he nodded and started to poke at the dessert, a novel concoction of strawberries and rhubarb, before raising his head. "If I ever heard that in some corner of the earth you had died, I would die too."

She appeared for a moment to be wondering if she'd heard right. Then, her eyes turned colder than he had ever seen. "You shouldn't . . .

That's not something you should say, even as a joke. Never mind right and wrong—it makes you sound shallow."

"If you ever killed yourself, Yoko, I'd kill myself too. That I promise you. If you ever have suicidal thoughts, just remember, you would be killing me."

"Are you drunk?"

"Not at all. The idea that someone who's suffering silently would try to end their suffering in that way is . . . scary. Also the idea that someone could do that to make people understand their suffering." He paused. "I read *Death in Venice*. Including the autobiographical afterword. I've been thinking about Thomas Mann. His two younger sisters died by suicide, and his son too. I'm no expert, but I got the feeling that he was able to go on living by having the main character die in his stead."

"Oh, is that what you—? Don't worry, I've never thought of killing myself."

"I was disturbed by what you wrote about Aschenbach going home without dying in Venice. That's why I read the book. So that I could talk to you like this. If I could always be with you, and you always confided in me, I could support you in other ways, but that's not possible. All I could come up with was to say what I said just now. It may sound dumb, but I said it, and I will absolutely keep my word."

"Stop it. Just stop." She finally gave a wry smile, seemingly at a loss.

"Your existence has punched a hole in my life. Or rather, it's embedded deep within me."

Without realizing it, he was clutching the front of his shirt almost hard enough to tear it. In desperation, he clutched it even harder, and then he hastily smoothed out the wrinkles, staring down at his chest and hand as if concerned about the flow of blood from a bayonet wound. In the middle of their conversation, he felt stranded.

Yoko flushed, deeply shaken by his words and actions. Forcing back her yearning for him, she let out a deep breath and gave a little laugh. "I'm getting married soon."

"I came here to stop you." He looked straight at her.

Those were the very words she had been hoping to hear. She'd been anticipating them for a long time now, probably ever since she was in Baghdad. But she felt conflicted and anguished at the misfortune of having to hear them now. For the past three weeks, certain signs had led her to suspect she was pregnant with Richard's child.

If she was really pregnant, she intended to give up her love for Makino and marry Richard. She was prepared to accept that as her destiny. But if she was mistaken, then she wanted to be true to her feelings.

A simple home test had gone against her suspicions, but twice she had been forced to cancel an appointment at the hospital for a more conclusive test, due to unexpected work reporting on the new administration's cabinet. If she was carrying a child, she could not bring herself to say the words "I love you" to any man not the father. She should not do such a thing, nor did she want to. For Yoko, that would have seemed like a form of self-betrayal, since from the time she was a small child she had thought constantly of her own absent father.

As she remained silent, Makino said quietly, "I know it's difficult. But we met. I can't pretend otherwise. A life without Yoko Komine would be surreal for me now. You are part of me, of my reality. And I want you by my side always. I want to be with you every day like this, to sit across from you and talk while we eat . . ."

"Can you think realistically of marrying me and raising a family? Is that the right outcome for our relationship?"

After a pause, he answered in a tone of near resignation, "I love you, Yoko, and that's the reality of my life. The me that doesn't love you no longer exists. He isn't real."

She was silent.

"Of course, that's only my side of it. What I want to know now is how you feel."

In the once-bustling restaurant, the crowd had thinned out. The table to their right was empty, and the people to their left were preparing to leave.

Yoko bit her lip and looked down restlessly, then raised her head and looked at Makino. "You're not involved with anyone now?"

Makino smiled weakly and shook his head. Then he called the waiter and paid with a credit card, laying a dissuading hand on Yoko's arm as she started to open her purse.

"Will you let me think about it until you come back from Madrid?" she asked. "I'll have my head clearer by then."

Makino nodded. "I guess I came on too strong. I got my message across, but I could have done better. This wasn't a very *bonne continuation*, after all."

Yoko shook her head many times, afraid she had pushed him away. She felt a crushing despair, yet there was no way to undo the damage.

"You made me happy. Truly. It's me. I'm sorry . . ."

But Makino, as if he could no longer bear the conversation, stood up and said, "Let's go."

5

Yoko's Decision

In Madrid, Makino performed Castelnuovo-Tedesco's Guitar Concerto no. 1 in D Major. Before going onstage, he was unusually nervous and several times came close to lashing out at the local staff as they mistook the program's starting time, had trouble straightening out the sound system, and otherwise made a mess of things. Finally, the concertmaster came by, put an arm around him, and tried to soothe his nerves: "This is Spain. Things aren't the same as in Japan."

The performance wasn't all that bad, and afterward the conductor and orchestra members were in a good mood, apparently relieved. Other guitarists, old friends of Makino's, bestowed easy, laughing praise. "Satoshi, are you trying to get even *better?*"

Makino, however, was not cheered. Despite the prominence of the program, his performance had attracted little attention. The write-up in the paper was small, and the daily blog by festival staff gave a merely perfunctory report. Knowing that a performance had been less than stellar was more painful to him now than having it panned.

On the second day of the festival, after his performance was over, he went to hear as many of the others as he could. Some that he had been looking forward to failed to live up to his expectations, leaving him at once disappointed and consoled, but other people heaped such praise on them that he wondered if he had somehow lost his ear. While in Madrid, he was also practicing for his Paris concert and going over the pieces that hadn't sounded right to him. It occurred to him that he might be sick of the guitar or of music in general. Thirty-six years had gone by since he first took up the guitar at age three. Who could blame him if he had grown disenchanted? Uncertainty made him afraid.

As his concentration lapsed, he let his thoughts turn to Yoko in Paris. Since coming to Madrid, he hadn't written to her, and there'd been no word from her, either. What was she talking to her fiancé about? Perhaps she had concluded that their "illicit love" was something for her to deal with not on her own but with that fiancé at her side. Every time he imagined the conversations they might be having, he closed his eyes in agony.

Why had his conversation with her that night gone so wrong? First and foremost, he had felt pressed to tell her how he felt. That he loved her. But that was a given. He had planned other, more-specific things he needed to say. She had no idea of basic things like how much he earned, where he planned to live, his health, whether or not he wanted a family. Without mentioning any of that, he had summarily demanded that she scrap her plans to marry Richard. Thinking it over calmly now, he could see that a thoughtful woman like Yoko was hardly likely to make so momentous a decision on the spur of the moment. Her question about his other possible romantic entanglements had been perfectly reasonable, and yet he hadn't reacted rationally. Some devil had gotten into him.

He had faith in the warmth of Yoko's feelings for him. But for that very reason, wouldn't she have wanted to talk over the question of marriage in greater depth? Instead he had blabbered on like a fool about boiling *shijimi* to death.

The festival was a success, but Makino felt left out, sensing that his participation had been a flop. He was skeptical of his own performance and unmoved by those of others. The one exception was the performance on the fourth day of a young Polish guitarist who over the past few years had won every major guitar competition he entered, including the International Guitar Festival J. Rodrigo and the GFA International Concert Artist Competition; already some were hailing him as "the greatest genius of the last quarter century." Makino knew him by reputation but had never seen him perform.

The small theater was sparsely filled that afternoon, and Makino sat by himself, at a distance from his colleagues, listening alone to the performance. The program consisted entirely of pieces connected to Segovia, and two—Cavatina Suite and *Variations on a Theme of Scriabin*, both by the Polish composer Tansman—Makino had previously recorded and knew well.

At first he listened with his competitive spirit aroused. The faces of various masters he had studied with came to mind. Overall, and in certain specific passages, he thought the interpretation resembled his, and he began to think the playing was modeled on his own. But as time went on, all sense of rivalry faded. Struck by the other's talent, he felt uneasy, and indeed vaguely apprehensive. In tone, expressiveness, and even depth of interpretation, the young man was his superior. Or to put it another way, he, Makino, had been superseded—at least as far as those two pieces were concerned.

Then he grew tired of comparisons and was caught up in the music. The composition had the vast sweep of the starry firmament, its melodies the systematic order of constellations, each one distinct and unmistakable. Absorbing the beauty of each successive note brought the satisfaction and thrill of taking in the light of star after star.

With nothing show-offy or pretentious about it, the playing was utterly orthodox, simple, and therefore to Makino's liking; it was also close to his own style. And yet Makino felt that of the two of them, the younger man was the genuine article, the one whose time had come.

Throughout the festival, Makino had been discontented, haunted by a nagging sense that something in his playing wasn't as it should be. Now he felt that the problems he needed to grapple with, problems that could provide him with answers opening the way to new achievements, had already been solved by this young man.

On the stage, quivering along with the guitar strings, was the latest shoot from the thickest part of the guitar's evolutionary tree trunk, poised to sprout further before his eyes. Good looking and tall, the young player had plenty of star power. The audience for this wonderful performance was woefully sparse, but everyone there wore a look of admiration, and the enthusiasm of their applause indicated strong appreciation.

After the performance, Makino rushed backstage, asked to speak to the performer, and offered praise. The young Pole, who was not yet thirty, bowed politely. "The day before yesterday, I skipped practice to go hear your Tedesco," he said cheerfully. He merely related the fact and offered no impression. Makino concluded that he had been underwhelmed. The prodigy seemed uninterested in him as a guitarist and made no mention of having been influenced by him, had probably never even listened to his Tansman recording. If Makino told him their approaches to the music were similar, he might well take offense.

The appearance on the scene of a fresh talent was not necessarily a threat. What felt cruel was to be passed by and ignored. Who did this fellow admire? Whose talent did he see himself springing from? It was painful to be sidelined and painful also to be forced to look on in silence as the younger performer's artistic lineage was described without reference to himself. It was no consolation to tell himself that he had behaved similarly years ago; as long as society felt a new talent was truly new, that's how it would be. In his youth, when confronted by elderly guitarists wrapped in such sad loneliness, he had smiled discreetly at them, perplexed. He remembered his heartlessness all too well.

I've reached that age. The realization hit him as he watched the Polish youth greet another guitarist. Loneliness, when it came down to it, was the awareness of your utter lack of influence in the world—knowing that you could and would have zero influence on either your contemporaries or on future generations. It was the conviction that you could search all you liked and never find any indication that you had influenced the growth of another artist. Yet all this time, Makino had blithely supposed that even if he reached the age when loneliness loomed, he would be somehow immune to disillusionment.

Every night, he began dinner after nine and was back in his hotel around midnight. The regularity of his habits also suggested someone approaching middle age, no longer young. He and the Polish guitarist never crossed paths again, but on the fourth night, a Cuban guitarist who was an old friend of Makino's mentioned the younger man by name, adding, "He was tickled pink that you said nice things about his playing."

Makino scoffed as he removed an olive pit from his mouth. "He couldn't have cared less."

"He must have been nervous around you. He told me you gave him confidence."

"Really?"

"Really. He wanted to talk to you."

"Well, well. A decent fellow after all. Maybe I'll send him some CDs and make my presence felt."

The Cuban chuckled. "Do it. The sheer number will make him sit up and take notice."

They laughed together.

Close in age, the Cuban guitarist and he doubtless faced similar career issues, but neither of them was given to pouring out his troubles. Makino did, however, mention that he was considering pulling up stakes and moving to Paris to be with Yoko.

As he had expected, his friend's response was negative: "Times are tough now in Europe. It's hard for a guitarist to make a living. Someone like you could probably get along by teaching, but performing is another matter. Isn't that why you went back to Japan in the first place? Countries like that, where you can give dozens of concerts a year, are few and far between. Count yourself lucky. I'd like to live there myself."

Makino could only sigh and nod.

Seeing his old guitarist friends married and attending the Madrid festival with their wives and children in tow, Makino couldn't help wishing that Yoko were there with him. If they saw him with someone so beautiful, they were sure to be envious and wonder how on earth he had managed to snag her. But it wasn't only her looks. She would instantly become the center of conversation—after all, she was the daughter of the director of *Coins of Happiness*, the film known to every guitarist. How proud he would be, standing next to her as she answered questions, smiling her amazing smile! Not many people around here could know Baghdad the way she did. Also, the topic of Nicolas Sarkozy, France's new president, had come up several times, and just this past month Yoko had been running around covering his inauguration.

Never before had Makino felt like boasting to others simply about being with someone. Through Yoko, he felt he might reencounter Europe. He wanted to know her opinion on things he had learned before and things he would learn in days to come. Talking to her made him feel hopeful that he himself might change. A future where those things did not happen was not at all the same as one where the two of them had never met. He thought of the night of their first encounter and of her profile as he gave the taxi driver directions, and fresh longing overcame him.

The silence of Satoshi Makino as a performer was widely assumed to have come on suddenly after his brilliant concert at Suntory Hall, but in fact, though few in number, his guest performances and joint concerts continued on into 2007. The misunderstanding came about probably because of the minimal coverage of his activities during that interval. He did stop doing solo recitals, with the lone exception of the June 10 concert he gave in Paris after returning from Madrid. Yet that concert has been erased from the official record, as if it never took place.

Apart from Makino's own evaluation of his playing that June afternoon, those who actually heard him play in the Salle Cortot—the faculty and students of the École Normale as well as regular patrons of the afternoon concerts—were unanimous in their praise. "It was a wonderful performance," they would say, never failing to add, "except for that last piece."

Makino had been lackluster at the Madrid festival, but that day in Paris—until the last piece—his playing was so impeccable you couldn't have found a flaw in it with a magnifying glass. The notes shone like gems polished with white gloves. Students were wide eyed, wondering how on earth he managed to produce such perfect tones. Later they told each other, "With genius like that, no wonder he's not good at teaching beginners." They exchanged wry smiles, remembering Makino's master class, which had been frustrating and hadn't lived up to their expectations.

The concert program was varied, featuring Koshkin's Prelude and Fugue in A Major, Rodrigo's Sonata *Giocosa*, and Berkeley's Sonata for Guitar. Makino had been provoked in part by the young Polish guitarist in Madrid, but in retrospect, his own performance seemed rather the culmination of the style built up throughout his career, a blind alley leading nowhere.

The overall brilliance of the concert caused the abruptness of its ending to leave an indelible mark on listeners' hearts.

As his final piece before the encore, Makino played *The Cathedral* by Barrios, his signature piece ever since his debut. Since Segovia had not admired Barrios, Makino had refrained from playing the piece in Madrid, even though it was the one Barrios composition that Segovia had liked. A professor at the École Normale who had seen a video of the Madrid concert online peeked in on the rehearsal and said with a smile, "You'll play it today, won't you?"

The introspective prelude that formed the first movement of the composition was titled "Saudade" (Nostalgia). Makino found the sentimentality unwieldy and performed it with combined hesitation and impatience, as if stranded in time. The singing notes on the upper part of the arpeggios formed a quiet melody, succeeding one another the way reality and recollection alternate even as, underneath, the present moment melts incessantly into the past.

The second movement, "Andante Religioso," represented the prayers of the faithful during Mass as they reverberated against the high vaulted ceiling and beyond, leading into the third movement, "Allegro Solemne," with its dizzying harmonics. Makino's long fingers played the fast melody with spellbinding accuracy. Whenever he began the allegro, even obstinate highbrow types who kept constant vigil against "transcendent execution" marveled at the sheer lusciousness of perfection—achieved despite human imperfection!—and were enraptured.

As long as they gave themselves over to the music, his listeners were freed from anxiety about every imaginable eventuality.

In the third movement, the composer wished to convey the sense of worshippers leaving the cathedral after Mass, pouring out into the street. Faithful representation would seem to require suggesting not so much the idea of flight as the glimmering of an infinite diversity.

Makino had mentioned this in his master class. But that day onstage, he rushed madly on, seeking to bind and control the audience's sensations with a delicate musical thread. In his teen years, Makino's rendition was often criticized as "too fast and lacking in emotional depth," so he'd slowed the tempo in recent years, but that day he gradually sped up, as if in remembrance of those early performances. As if to shake off all emotion.

His performance told of trying to bring something to an end but unwittingly repeating it, intending to flee something, but realizing that instead you are chasing after it. Yet prayer that brought recovery from suffering was just such a complicated process, was it not? Very likely even for Yoko, who, after her hairbreadth escape from death in Iraq, had returned to Paris.

What took place inside Makino during those moments?

As soon as he went onstage, he realized that Yoko wasn't in the audience. The previous day, when he had sent an email to confirm, she had written back promising to be there. Every time he finished a piece, he glanced at the seat where she should have been sitting, next to the stairs in the left rear of the auditorium. Finally, it hit him: She wasn't coming. Not only here, to this venue—she wasn't going to come to him ever again. His lacerated heart slowly bled. But his pride as a performer would have led him to insist that the hemorrhaging had no effect on his music, that the two were entirely separate.

His music was simply loping through a quiet place. Far off he heard the exquisite strains of a guitar, but whether the music was his or not, he could not be certain. Then he was seized by the odd idea that impending silence was not before him but behind him. Would it catch up? The strange shiver he'd been feeling in rehearsals since the previous year spread across his back and wouldn't go away. The piece was just entering the final stage, the bass line ascending in halftones, about to return to the main theme, when it happened.

Silence suddenly caught up, passed him, and stood before him, blocking his way. In that moment, the music fled from his hands. He heard nothing. All was hushed; time was febrile and bore the clarity of nothingness. The silence was dazzling, like stage lights shining in his eyes. Sweat beaded on his forehead. Like the victim of a purse snatcher in a crowd, he searched frantically for the music. He was left only with violent throbbing and a burning sensation.

The audience was astonished that the performance had abruptly ceased. Makino himself appeared stunned, as if he didn't know what had happened. He tried to pick up where he had left off, but his fingers merely hovered over the fingerboard. He was at a complete loss. With another look of amazement, he stared dubiously at his left hand.

As the audience began to murmur, he stood up and wordlessly bowed. Uncertain how to react, they gave him a smattering of applause. He stared vacantly at one empty seat. Then he left the stage, his expression determined and unsmiling.

Backstage, people worried that his erratic behavior was not the result of his having lost his place in the music but of some disaster with his hands. The students were wide eyed with shock—how could someone like that break off awkwardly midnote with no attempt to cover it up and carry on? Up to that moment, the performance had been of such overwhelming artistry that they felt something untoward must have occurred and looked at Makino's hands with concern, as if witnessing a calamity that could befall any of them.

Their reaction was a surprise to Makino, but he did nothing to dispel such concern, only opening and closing his hands a number of times before finally saying with a faint smile, "I don't know, something just happened. But I'm okay."

He chased everyone out of his room, then sat on the sofa and stared at his guitar for a while. He couldn't sort out his feelings. He sighed, stood up, and before changing, reached for his cellphone. He was afraid to look, but then reminded himself it was already over.

There had been several calls from Yoko and one voice mail. Something sudden had come up, and she couldn't come to the concert. She apologized over and over: "I'm really sorry." She wanted to talk to him, so would he come to her apartment that night? She never said why she couldn't come. As she began describing where she lived, Makino held the phone away from his ear, then changed his mind and listened to the end. The thought crossed his mind that her fiancé might be there with her now. When the message ended, he tossed the phone on the sofa and stood rooted to the spot.

✕

After his concert fiasco, Makino returned to his hotel, still in a stupor, and napped for a couple of hours. His sleep was ragged, as if his jet lag had come back. The tightly fitted sheet felt good, and when the alarm clock went off, he was so comfortable he almost went back to sleep. *Imagine being able to sleep like a baby after such a disaster. Talk about nerves of steel,* he thought as he dressed, doing his best to put on a brave face. He pulled on a jersey top and jeans and left the hotel, carrying his guitar case. He picked up a bottle of Bordeaux at a nearby liquor store and arrived at Yoko's *appartement* on rue du Bac by taxi around seven in the evening.

When he lived in Paris, he had gone past this Ottoman-style building any number of times without giving it a thought. He and Yoko might even have passed each other on the street. If he'd gotten to know her then, he could have spent this evening with her in an altogether different fashion.

If her fiancé was there, he would leave without going inside. Some of the professors at the École Normale, worried about him after the concert, had invited him out to dinner. He had brought his guitar along, expecting to spend the evening with them. He wanted to relax and enjoy playing music together to banish the unpleasant memories of the day. Yoko's American fiancé was probably a fine fellow, since, after all, she had chosen him, but he had no desire to see the man's face, knowing he would never be able to forget it.

Perhaps by having the three of them dine together in a congenial atmosphere, she wanted to set her relationship with him, Makino, back on the rails—to put a damper on feelings that had threatened to get out of hand—by introducing him to her future husband. If someone told him such a story, he might even find it beautiful. It was a perfectly reasonable solution, one that in his younger days would never have occurred to him. He felt the beginnings of a resignation appropriate to his years slowly leaving its mark on him.

Perhaps one of these days he would marry someone else, someone not Yoko, and over the years to come, their two families would get together periodically, and one day he would look back and say, "Imagine that—I used to be in love with you," as if it were a joke. They claimed time had that power. Would the day come when, in a completely natural fashion, he stopped loving her? He spurned the thought with a feeling akin to hatred.

When he stepped out of the elevator, Yoko was waiting for him in the open doorway. She was wearing a plaid shirt with the sleeves rolled up and a long white skirt. She'd been cooking; her hands were wet. She wasn't wearing a ring. When she saw his guitar, she looked up at him and said, "Did you come straight from the theater? I'm so sorry I couldn't come. I was really looking forward to it."

Makino shook his head. "Is someone here?"

"Yes, actually."

As she turned back, he sensed a presence in the living room. He intended to find out who it was before any encounter took place, but he wasn't fast enough. A figure hesitantly stepped out, backed by light from the window. Makino stared—it was not who he'd been expecting.

Until that morning, Yoko had been planning to attend his concert as promised. It was the French parliamentary election, but she had the day off.

After jogging, she had gone home, showered, and had breakfast in her bathrobe. As she was considering what to wear, her cellphone rang. She didn't recognize the number. She answered, but there was no reply. She asked who it was, but again there was silence. She was about to hang up when she heard a faint, shivering voice. A woman was apparently crying into the receiver on the other end.

"Hello? Who is this?"

The woman finally spoke up, asked in English if this was Yoko's number, and gave her name.

"Who?" Yoko blurted out in surprise. It was Jalila, her assistant in Baghdad. "Where are you?"

"The airport. Charles de Gaulle Airport."

Jalila's confused explanation made little sense, but as far as Yoko could make out, she was being held in a temporary detention center for illegal immigrants. She had tried unsuccessfully to seek asylum in Sweden and was under Red Cross protection during the stopover in France. The details were unclear, but knowing no one else in France, she had turned to Yoko for help.

Yoko made it to the airport in about forty minutes. She asked at the information desk and was told how to find the detention center on the third floor. When Jalila came out accompanied by an official, she took one look at Yoko, ran to her in tears, and embraced her. She looked extremely worn out. Yoko hugged her and whispered over and over into her ear, "It's okay now. Everything's going to be okay."

Yoko identified herself to the Red Cross official, handed over a business card, and asked what had happened. It seemed that, from the time Yoko was in Baghdad, Jalila had been receiving threats from an extremist group. When Yoko left, Jalila had wept copiously and not only because she was going to miss her. At first she'd received telephone messages from a stranger asking her to find him work, but in time the messages changed to death threats. She had no idea who they were from. She was the only member of her family under attack, probably because she frequented the Murjana Hotel and worked alongside foreigners.

Arriving home four days ago, she had found an envelope with the words "We kill spies" written in red ink on the front. Inside were three bullets. Just that afternoon, she'd learned that a college friend of hers who worked as an interpreter for the US forces had been shot and killed on his way to work. Two days earlier, they'd talked on the phone, and he'd described receiving similar threats. Jalila made up her mind right then to seek asylum.

For $8,000, she bought a fake passport from a black-market dealer who aided asylum seekers, and then fled by car to Amman, where she boarded a flight for Stockholm by way of Paris. The Paris immigration authorities rejected her passport, there having recently been a spate of cases involving similar forgeries.

Yoko asked Jalila why she hadn't turned to their boss, Philip, for help getting out of the country through normal channels. Frustrated, Jalila explained that it would have taken ages to get an official passport, and that if she'd waited one day more, she'd have been killed like her friend.

There was a strong possibility that she could be turned over to the airport police and immediately deported, but following the instructions she had been given by the black-market dealer, she had requested to be taken to the office of the Red Cross, and luckily, they had complied.

Yoko listened to the whole story, jotting down notes out of professional habit, and then talked with the Red Cross representative about how to deal with the situation. A large woman who seemed to cross her arms as a way of enduring the chronic despondency brought on by her profession, the official told Yoko that her friend's case was by no means unusual. Yoko was unsure how to read the woman's restrained and thoughtful expression. Was she trying to help, or was she saying that her hands were tied?

Yoko said that if Jalila were sent back, she would almost certainly be killed, and explained the dire situation with urgency. Before she knew it, her eyes filled with tears. The Red Cross woman nodded and outlined the next steps to take: First Jalila would have to go downstairs to the police department for questioning and then to summary court for a trial to see if she could receive permission to stay in the country as a refugee. Then, if she wanted asylum, they could begin the process at once. A decision would be made in about half an hour, deciding her fate one way or the other. Deportation was often the outcome, but as an asylum seeker from Iraq, she might receive special consideration. She would also need luck.

Yoko promised Jalila that she would stay with her all day and questioned the Red Cross woman closely about what to be on guard about when testifying before the court, finally gathering from the woman's tone that she was on their side.

Jalila broke down in tears: Why, when others succeeded at this game, was she the only one caught? She could scarcely talk. The $8,000 for the fake passport had been a down payment, with another $10,000 due on arrival in Stockholm. In view of the meager salary she had earned working for the Baghdad bureau to support her family, this was a staggering sum of money, but of course her life was far more precious.

The police interrogation soon ended, and in summary court there were four others seeking asylum. All this was an everyday occurrence.

While they waited for the decision, Yoko finally had a moment to call Makino. By then the concert was underway.

Jalila was granted permission to stay. The applications of the other four, who were all from other countries, were denied. The Red Cross official looked relieved at Jalila's outcome, but made no exaggerated show of pleasure. Jalila was, to her, merely one case out of many; thoughts of all who had come before, successful or otherwise, seemed to crowd her mind. She carefully explained the procedure for gaining asylum in a third country while remaining in France, annotating a pamphlet in red ballpoint pen. She supplied all the needed papers and contact information as well as a list of NGOs that aided asylum seekers.

Finally, the woman told them about a homeless shelter run by a monastery near Gare du Nord station. Yoko shook her head. "Come home with me. Stay as long as you want." She put her hand over Jalila's.

When they said goodbye, the Red Cross worker gave Yoko a long look. "Your friend is lucky, having you with her."

"It was no trouble just to sit there with her."

"I mean she's lucky because you're a reporter. Even if they themselves don't realize why they did it, the police and the judge don't want a bad write-up in the press."

"Really?"

"Neither do I, for that matter." It was hard to tell if she was serious or joking. "If you cover Iraq for RFP, I must have read some of your articles." Finally unfolding her arms, she laid an encouraging hand on Jalila's shoulder before turning again to Yoko. "Take care of yourself as well as her. You've seen some grim reality, but you've still got to enjoy your life."

Yoko put the documents in her purse and looked up, moved by this final demonstration of sympathy. "Thank you. You too." They touched cheeks in farewell.

Ж

Makino heard all these details in Yoko's living room.

"I really wanted to go to the concert, but I was sure you'd understand."

"Of course. A life was at stake. The concert didn't go well anyway. You didn't miss anything." He made a wry face.

Yoko's eyes widened slightly. Then, hesitantly, she asked, "Am I by any chance getting in the way of your music?"

"Absolutely not. It's got nothing to do with you. It's my own problem."

In the awkward pause that followed, he stretched his arms upward and looked over at Jalila. She was sitting vacantly on the sofa, unable to understand Japanese. He'd heard she was a cheerful girl who could do a dead-on imitation of Britney Spears, but right now she seemed dazed.

Yoko's apartment had white walls and an abundance of leafy house-plants; while she was away in Baghdad, she'd entrusted them to a friend. The ceiling had antique wooden beams, irregular in shape, and a chandelier hung from one of them. The walls were entirely covered in books, French titles mostly, but a quarter of them were in Japanese, and many of those were old, familiar editions of books he loved.

On the glass table was a Moroccan tagine stew that Yoko and Jalila had made together after first shopping for the ingredients.

"I see you're a good cook," he said while helping to set the table.

"You haven't tasted it yet!" Yoko laughed.

"No, but of course it's good—just look at it!"

"I hope so. The tagine pot makes all the difference. It was love at first sight. I bought it in Marrakesh and brought it home. It's heavy too. But handy. I can use it for all kinds of cooking."

"As a matter of fact, I've got one too. It's smaller and not as nice. I picked it up in a Paris department store when I lived here. To be honest, I've never used it . . ."

"You cook?"

"Well, yes. More back when I lived here, really. Unlike Tokyo, you don't find many convenience stores in Paris."

They'd switched to English to include Jalila. She didn't drink alcohol, but Yoko opened the bottle of red wine Makino had brought, and the two drank it together.

What did they talk about? Japan, for one thing, which Jalila knew something about from Yoko. Paris attractions that Jalila should make sure to see. Makino's life as a guitarist. And then he started telling funny stories. Little by little, Jalila's expression brightened, and now and then she smiled.

As they talked, Makino's eyes met Yoko's more than once, in a very natural way. She seemed relaxed and a bit tired. Her unself-conscious beauty struck him more than ever. The chandelier over the table, which she had apparently owned for some time, shone on every charming detail of her face, from the wrinkle-free brow and the fine bridge of her nose to the lower eyelids pressing softly against the light reflected in her eyes.

What secrets lay in that gaze turned so gently on him? He had no idea. In the past week, what answer had she prepared for him? What had she told Jalila about him, anyway? Jalila had said that in Baghdad she'd listened to his CD, which she'd borrowed from Yoko. Perhaps she had been told that the friend who played that music just happened to be in town and would be coming over.

In Madrid, Makino had spoken constantly in English or French, but speaking to Yoko in English tonight felt different, as if he were meeting her all over again. In French he could carry on a conversation quite naturally, but in English he couldn't express himself with as much ease. Yoko seemed equally at home in either language; sometimes she would finish a sentence for him. He remembered her describing meeting her father when she was a child, after her parents divorced, and being unable to converse with him because she didn't know English. "When the chance came, I studied English for all I was worth." And

103

now here she was, perfectly fluent. Thinking of this made him feel a little closer to her—until he reminded himself that she had exchanged vows of love in English with her American fiancé.

But today, that was neither here nor there. If the judge had decided differently, this young Iraqi woman would probably have ended up murdered. She would have been nowhere in this world, lost for all time, her name stricken from the roster of humanity that was updated second by second—as had happened to her college friend and countless other Iraqis. She had escaped that fate in the nick of time, and in so doing, had changed the world. Now, instead of losing an Iraqi woman named Jalila, the world would go on as before, with a place for her in it.

As these thoughts sank in, Makino was struck by the reason for his presence there. For unhesitatingly going to Jalila, for standing by her and doing all she could for her, Yoko had gained his utmost respect. She, too, had narrowly escaped being expunged from the world's roster when she was in Iraq.

When he headed to the kitchen to help clean up, Yoko was getting dessert ready. "Can you stay a little longer?" she asked in Japanese. "I know you must be tired after the concert."

"I'd be glad to. I'm fine, but aren't you and Jalila pretty tired?"

"Not me. She'll probably go to bed first." A short pause. "There's something I want to talk to you about."

"Okay."

After coffee and cake on the sofa, Makino eyed his guitar case. Through the slightly open window came the sound of someone walking past, singing drunkenly. He got up to close it.

"Are you cold?" asked Yoko. "Or is it too noisy?"

"Actually, since we're all together here tonight, I thought I'd play something. That's about all I can do for her."

Having spoken in Japanese without thinking, Makino turned to Jalila and repeated what he'd said in English. Jalila had apparently been hoping to hear him play. She thanked him and looked with interest at the guitar, confessing that she had never seen one up close before.

As he tuned up, Makino explained the instrument in brief. A memory of the day's concert crossed his mind, but he pushed it away. He hardly deserved to be put before a firing squad just because he had stopped in the middle of a performance.

Makino studied Jalila, wondering what he ought to play for her. He realized he'd been staring when she looked away in evident embarrassment, flushing and turning to Yoko. He was charmed by her innocence.

Music began to sound in his ears, the way it always did. He settled the guitar against him and played the "Gavotte-Choro" from Villa-Lobos's *Suite Populaire Brésilienne*. It was a short, simple piece about five and a half minutes long, and he played it in a relaxed pose, sitting on the sofa with his legs crossed. A gavotte was a dance in duple meter, but as he played, he envisioned a circle of good friends gathered for an afternoon of leisurely conversation. He had never interpreted the piece that way before.

He felt as if he were smiling along with his guitar as it told a funny story about a recent event. As the story continued, he would register surprise or disbelief, sometimes listening intently and sometimes marveling—just as he had done as a boy, entertaining his parents, his relatives, and adults from the neighborhood by "speaking" through the guitar. Back then, playing had been fun.

In the "Saudade" movement of *The Cathedral*, he rendered the nostalgia with a light touch, as always, but even that slight sentimental tinge seemed to move Jalila, who might never return to her homeland. The warm, tranquil circle he was envisioning as he played must of course include her—Jalila and others who sought asylum, Jalila and her family, whom she might one day see again if all went well. The final note of the third movement, "Allegro Solemne," he played with a

105

deliberately childlike touch, hoping to work magic and bring a smile to her face. When he looked up, she was beaming. She clapped with enthusiasm and laid a hand over her heart as if to quiet its beating, while Yoko looked on in delight.

"That's a really pretty piece," said Jalila. "What's it called?"

Makino borrowed a pen and paper from Yoko and wrote down the title. He recommended the Julian Bream recording. Yoko then asked him if he had ever recorded it.

"Yes, some time ago."

"I don't have that CD, Jalila. Let's go buy it sometime, shall we? There's a big music store in town called Fnac. I'm sure you'd enjoy taking a look around."

Then Makino thought of the arrangements of Louis Armstrong's "What a Wonderful World" and Roberta Flack's "Killing Me Softly with His Song" that he had recorded for the *What a Wonderful World: Beautiful American Songs* album, and he played them through once each. Both Yoko and Jalila perked up, exclaiming, "Oh, I know this!" Their obvious pleasure made him start to reconsider his decision to abandon the project; maybe he ought to see it through after all.

Watching Jalila become more animated reminded Makino of the power of music, the art to which he had devoted his life. Music could bring pleasure even amid the most difficult circumstance. How marvelous, the human capacity to enjoy music! Shining brilliantly in exactly this kind of intimate setting, a guitar could reach people close by and sing to them gently. The instrument was warmed by the heat of his body and also, he felt, by his audience.

To make Jalila smile some more, he played a version of Britney Spears's "Toxic." He wasn't well acquainted with the music, but after reading Yoko's email about Jalila's Britney impression, he had found the song on the internet and played along just for fun. Jalila immediately started moving her body in response, imitating by turns the sexy flight attendant and the alluring, half-naked Britney of the music video, wriggling and moving her tongue suggestively to such comic effect that Makino couldn't stop laughing as he played. Yoko must have seen it before, but she clapped her hands and laughed so hard she had to hold on to her stomach, the bridge of her nose wrinkling.

They kept it up until finally Jalila laughed in embarrassment and broke off. Makino ended the music with a flourish, and all three of them clapped and shook hands. Jalila said with a sparkle that someday she wanted to attend a Britney Spears concert. Then she told Makino that there was one piece above all that she wanted him to play.

"Is it one I know? What is it?"

"Would you play the theme from *Coins of Happiness* for me? Yoko always used to listen to it in Iraq."

"Oh . . . sure. I was going to play it after the matinee today and missed my chance." He said this jokingly and winked at Yoko, but what he meant by that was unclear even to himself. Probably he wanted to signal that he had intended to play the piece specially for her.

"What sort of movie is it?" Jalila had always politely avoided asking Yoko about Solich, but his name had come up several times today.

"You've never seen it? Then we'll have to get you a copy at Fnac. It's a classic."

"I have it," said Yoko, then gave a brief summary of the story.

During World War II, the Croatian fascist party Ustasha had set up a Nazi puppet government and, proclaiming a state for "pure Croatians," imitated Hitler's racist policies by constructing concentration camps and exterminating large numbers of Serbians, Jews, Roma, and Croatians in the opposition. The main character, a young Croatian poet who loved Rilke, protected his Serbian girlfriend and her family and joined the partisans in their fight against the fascist government. An Ustasha general who was in love with the same girl ended up arresting her as she attempted to flee her homeland under the main character's guidance. The movie portrayed the complicated romantic entanglements, continuing up to the partisans' victory in World War II.

"Why is it called *Coins of Happiness*?"

"The phrase comes from Rilke's *Duino Elegies*, which the main character loves to recite. It's from the fifth of ten elegies."

Surmising that Jalila wasn't familiar with Rilke, Yoko went on to explain briefly that he was considered Germany's greatest twentieth-century poet. Coffee cup in hand, she also said that the first elegy had been written in 1912, in Duino Castle, near Trieste in northern Italy— Yoko had once visited the lonely castle perched on cliffs overlooking the Adriatic Sea. Rilke was conscripted and served some eighteen months in the military, although he didn't directly experience the horrors of World War I. After the war he led an unsettled life, completing the elegies ten years after he had begun.

"The fifth elegy comes right in the middle, but actually it was the very last one he wrote, and he finished it a little while after the war ended, in February 1922." She went to the bookshelf, took down a thin, antique-looking book, and flipped through it in search of the fifth elegy. And yet, coming across the famous, dramatic beginning of the first, she couldn't resist taking a moment to read it aloud, translating it into English for their benefit.

Makino listened, entranced, as she read the thrilling lines not in tragic, heroic cadences but in a gentle, aching tone—though without losing any of the passage's lofty style. *She might be reading this way for Jalila,* he thought. Her voice had a deep, mellow resonance, and the bridge of her nose, scrunched up as always with the air of a cherubic little boy, gave her a luminous beauty that was not sexless but angelic, androgynous.

Jalila looked thoughtful as she pondered the difficult lines of poetry.

"How does it sound in German?" Makino asked.

"I can read and write German, but I'm afraid poetry readings are beyond me." Yoko tilted her head modestly, looked down at the text, and took a breath before starting off in a low, musical voice: *"Wer, wenn ich schriee . . ."*

Makino and Jalila were so impressed by her splendid reading that, when she finished, they spontaneously applauded.

Yoko shook her head. "I'm really not very good at it, honestly. Anyway," she said, looking at Makino meaningfully, "weren't we supposed to hear a guitar performance?"

He made a droll face, as if to say, "Oops, forgot," then turned to Jalila. "The fifth elegy is about people gathered in a plaza to watch a crowd of street performers. I can't explain it very well, but this poem is quite a bit different from the others. Where they are deeply interior and contemplative, this one is directed outward. The plaza and the performers could be taken as symbols of this world, maybe? Human beings live by exposing their lives relentlessly and comically to the eyes of others." He paused. "The movie ends as this fifth elegy is read aloud against the backdrop of a village laid waste by war, followed by that beautiful theme on guitar. No matter how many times I see and hear that ending, I get a lump in my throat."

Jalila nodded sympathetically.

Yoko stood up again and fetched a notebook containing her own English translation of the poem, so that she could read it aloud without faltering. She turned to the right page and exchanged glances with Jalila.

"After you read the ending, I'll play the theme," said Makino. "Let's re-create the final scene for Jalila." He was already tuning his guitar.

Yoko grinned. "I'm adding a new line to my resume: 'Performed with Satoshi Makino, June 2007.'"

Jalila clapped her hands in anticipation.

"After everyone watches the acrobats perform, the poem ends like this." Yoko took a deep breath and then read the short passage aloud.

Angel! If somewhere there were a plaza we know nothing of,
there on some indescribable carpet might not a pair of lovers,
who in this world never succeeded in mastering the acrobatics
of love, tremblingly display those high-flying, daring figures,

their towers of rapture having long since lost all support, their ladders propping one another in midair? Surely they would not fail again before the silent spectators ringing them round, the countless dead.

Would not the dead then fling their last, their forever hidden, unknown to us, ever-valid coins of happiness? Would they not throw them to the pair standing on the once-more silent carpet, those lovers wreathed now in true smiles?

Makino looked at Yoko's profile as she followed the printed words, her imagination faintly furrowing her brow, her upper lashes swaying slightly with the movements of her eyes. At the same time, he saw the ruined land of Croatia after World War II, the parched gaze of the main character in the film, and the dauntless Serbian girl with whom he was at last reunited. His imagination stirred, he heard the clink of the old coins flung one after another in the direction of the happy lovers.

After a pause faithful to his memory of the film, he began the quiet arpeggios. He had intended to play this for Yoko today, at the end of the matinee. But perhaps the two of them had been fated to do a joint performance for the sake of this young refugee all along. Perhaps the entire day had been leading up to this performance. A fragment from the beginning of the elegy crossed his mind: "For whose pleasure are they wrung by an insatiable will?" This beautiful evening was drawing to an end. What might lie ahead?

When he finished playing, he opened his eyes, reluctantly letting go of the last dying cadence, and saw that Jalila was silently weeping, her hands covering her face. Yoko closed her book, went over, and sat next to her, embracing her as she gave in to sobs. Yoko was gentle, as if sensing her own helplessness.

Makino was acutely aware that, for the first time in his life, he was seeing the tears of an Iraqi war victim up close. Jalila's cheeks, wet with tears, twitched spasmodically. Was he capable of responding with empathy to an endless succession of cheeks such as these? Unconsciously, he searched within himself. Countless other Iraqi cheeks were being stained with tears even now. Countless more were decaying, never again to be moistened by tears. But in the end, he could only know, only share in, this outpouring from Jalila.

)(

Yoko took Jalila into the bedroom and stayed beside her until she fell asleep. The building was old, and the construction of her apartment rather unusual: a wall had been knocked down between two adjacent residences to create one two-room apartment, with the living room and bedroom connected by a short corridor that had no door.

Makino and Yoko felt each other's invisible presence across the length of that corridor.

After a while she turned out the bedroom light and came back. Makino was standing in front of the bookcase, returning a book he had apparently been looking through: Mitsuharu Inoue's *Tomorrow: August 8, 1945, Nagasaki*. Without comment, he set his glass of Cinzano on the edge of the shelf.

Yoko made no attempt to discuss the book.

Here, too, she turned out the lights, leaving on only the table lamp next to the sofa.

"Sorry it took so long."

"Not at all. Is she all right?"

"She's asleep. She was excited, but really tired. Shall I make a fresh pot of coffee?"

"No, it's all right."

Yoko reached for his now-empty glass, intending to take it to the kitchen, but then, standing before him in the sudden silence, found herself unable to move. Her pulse quickened. Looking up at him, she

111

worked up her nerve and brought out the words she had ruminated over in the bedroom: "While you were in Madrid, I talked to him."

Makino said nothing.

"I told him that I had fallen in love with someone else and wanted to break off our engagement. That I wanted to spend the rest of my life with the other man. I wanted you to know, today."

Makino gasped and froze. He had been steeling himself for the opposite announcement. He felt a rush of emotions.

Yoko was resolute as always, but in her faintly smiling eyes he saw a shadow of anxiety.

For the first time, he felt with pain the price exacted by his strong love for her. Not only had she broken off her engagement, but by doing so, she had made herself fodder for gossip and scorn. She stood erect before him, making herself vulnerable, prepared to make an even greater leap if he but sought it.

His heart quivered at the sight of her standing and waiting, offering her very existence to him. So this was her way of loving a person—of loving *him*. Seeing her transfixed by the leap she had taken, from deep within he felt a surge of swelling happiness and took her in his arms.

⋇

A week earlier, the day after Makino left Paris for Madrid, Yoko's body had stopped playing games and, without a fuss, cleared up the misunderstanding: she got her period. The timing seemed almost meaningful, but all she could do was accept that such things were apt to happen in a woman's life. Just as slow delivery does not alter the contents of a letter, the meaning of her body's message was unmistakable.

Now all she wanted to do was follow her heart. People are spurred to act less by eager dreams of a happy future than by anxiety over the danger, remote or otherwise, of remaining stuck in the status quo. Regret still lay far off, but already the waters of that chill lake were lapping at her feet. She could not simply close her eyes and do nothing. Time and again she repeated to herself what Makino had said, adjusting the words to make them her own. *The Yoko Komine that didn't love him no longer exists. She isn't real.*

She had told Richard over Skype that she was breaking off the engagement, but her feelings were still in turmoil, and the conversation had not gone well. The following day he had canceled his classes at the university and flown from New York to see her. Her heart ached as she watched him become indignant, anguished, and then sentimental, bringing up memory after memory mingled with jokes, only to fall to pieces, crying "Why? Why?" over and over again. But she never wavered. Once or twice she felt herself close to weeping, but that right belonged to him.

Still unpersuaded, Richard flew back to New York, promising to come again the following week. She did not see him off at the airport and intended not to meet with him if he returned. Alone at home, she felt dazed. To wallow in guilt seemed hypocritical, so in desperation, she turned her thoughts to Makino. Richard had done nothing wrong—and yet, undeniably, she felt wounded.

Embraced by Makino, Yoko was now swept away by the desire to grant all that he sought from her in soul and body. To see that no part of him remained unfulfilled, to give herself over to him completely, to let herself be his slave. Never at the beginning of any other romance had she felt anything so absurd. Loving Makino was for her a series of such discoveries.

Certainly, this love had to be fitting compensation for her abandonment of that other love. For that reason, he must not be dissatisfied. If she could be to him all that he wanted, would she perhaps be freed from her sense of guilt toward Richard?

She began to feel as if she had stumbled on a new definition of "wantonness." To be wanton meant not merely to be extravagant but somehow to lose track of one's fundamental being in the joy of complete abandonment to the other—a joy that knew no bounds. She sensed that now perhaps she was being swept into the sensual turmoil of Death in Venice Syndrome.

Hesitant to allow things to follow their natural course, they lost themselves in a kiss seemingly without end. Jalila's presence weighed on them. They knew they ought to hold back because of her, but the knowledge only made them seek all the more intensely to absorb the reality of one another's presence, tightening their arms around each other.

Even so, now and again their self-restraint seemed on the verge of collapse, their bodies dissolving into the deepening night. They looked into each other's eyes and traded tremulous smiles. It happened as they lay back against the sofa for a time, wordlessly probing one another's feelings: all of a sudden from the bedroom they heard Jalila cry out in Arabic, and then for a time there was groaning.

Yoko signaled to Makino with her eyes, and he nodded: *Go to her.* She straightened her disheveled clothing as she headed to the bedroom.

When she came back, they sat for a while and talked about what would become of Jalila. Then they nestled together and talked about themselves. Twice after that, just as their kissing began to deepen into something more, they were interrupted by Jalila's nightmares.

The last time she went into the bedroom to check on Jalila, Yoko finally lay down and went to sleep alongside her. Makino had already said good night. He stretched out on the sofa and gazed in abstraction at the ceiling. He did not know when he fell asleep.

6

Vanishing Point

After Makino returned to Japan, memories of that night when Yoko had told him her decision never left his thoughts, reverberating silently. Yet as always happens with memory, all he saw were flickering scenes, a moment here and a moment there. Even when Yoko's voice or Jalila's laughter came vividly to mind, he could not tell what came next; it was like a video freezing.

And so when he recalled that night, he would search his memory for particular scenes as if rummaging through a disorderly heap of playing cards. He would also linger pleasurably on various fragments on the fringes of his memory.

The hopelessness he had felt when he arrived at her apartment now made for a funny story. He must have been on tenterhooks from dinner until he played the guitar for Jalila, but that brief interval was gradually altering his past out of all recognition, imbuing it with vibrant colors and rich shadows. More than any contest that he had ever won or any concert that had earned rave reviews, those few hours of pleasant dinner conversation followed by relaxed guitar music shed a radiance on his life that felt almost miraculous. They enchanted him, brought a lump to his throat, and never failed to leave him with a vague anxiety.

Why he should feel anxious, he didn't know. The memory was so bright that when he returned to reality, it left a dark afterimage like a shadow. Conventional doubts arose, making him fear that that cluster of delightful hours might be something like a school of sweetfish, able to survive only in clean water and certain to die if swept downstream into the muddy currents of everyday life.

The presence of Jalila might have had something to do with his anxiety. Thanks to her, he and Yoko not only had been able to spend time together but also had been joined in worrying over, consoling, and demonstrating kindness to another human being. Through Jalila, he had been able in a small way to fathom something of Yoko's conflicted feelings and sense of helplessness after narrowly escaping with her life from Baghdad, where, to her colleagues' amazement, she had elected to go not once but thrice. Because of Jalila, that magical evening was invested with something beyond mere beauty. The ten minutes during which Yoko had read aloud from *Duino Elegies* and he had played the theme from *Coins of Happiness* . . . The triangle formed by the three of them was special, allowing him to see deeply into himself while at the same time opening up a greater vista.

Naturally, he often thought back to the pale light of morning that had bathed him when he awoke, short on sleep because they had made up for the impossibility of consummating their love by embracing till all hours on the sofa before finally ending up in separate beds. Patchy sleep had given way to languor, blurring the distinction between his memories of the night before and something resembling dreams.

When Jalila awoke, she'd been surprised to find Makino still in the living room and looked back and forth quizzically at the two of them. He had smiled and shaken his head, winking at Yoko, who had shrugged, a suggestion of a smile playing about her mouth. Jalila had flushed, lowering her eyes.

It was Monday, so Yoko hastily dressed for work, put on makeup, and left with Makino, leaving Jalila behind. Once the manually oper-ated door to the narrow elevator closed, without a word they fell into each other's arms, regretting the shortness of the ride to the ground floor. Fortunately, there were no other passengers. When they finally drew apart and looked at each other, Yoko saw some of her lipstick on the corner of his mouth and tenderly wiped it off with a finger.

That night the three of them had dinner in a nearby restaurant. Makino and Yoko wistfully abandoned plans to steal some time alone. To make up for that loss, they locked eyes, finding passion and warm intimacy in each other's gaze.

At the end of the evening, Makino escorted the two women back to the apartment building, but didn't go up with them. Yoko sent Jalila up first and exchanged final embraces with him in the dark space before the outer gate. They promised to meet again soon. She would go to Tokyo, perhaps as soon as next month.

Makino was happy. From that moment on, the light of love reached into every corner of his life, often surprising him and bringing a smile to his face. Happiness was having someone with whom to share all the everyday experiences of his world. When he was in Yoyogi Park back in Tokyo and saw children playing with toy guns that shot out bubbles, he immediately thought, *I must tell Yoko.*

Once he attended a work luncheon where a doctor of internal medicine, older than him, first apologized for never having heard his guitar playing and then confessed without any sign of embarrassment, indeed with a certain pride, that because he saw music as simply a means of calling up memories, at home he listened exclusively to recordings of the theme songs of cartoon shows and other programs he had loved as a boy. Indulging nostalgia was the single benefit of music in the man's hard-driving life. He had tried listening to Bach and Mozart and dismissed that taste in music as mere snobbism compared to the genuine healing he got from the music he liked. While astonished at the physician's almost vengeful sneer at fine art, Makino had sensed an element of truth in what he said, and again he couldn't wait to tell Yoko. When he did, she, too, was fascinated: "But suppose the protagonist of *In Search of Lost Time* ate a madeleine every day—wouldn't that act of repetition overtake the original memory?"

If the one-yen coin in his change at a convenience store flew out of his hand because the receipt was bent, he wanted to tell Yoko, and if he got up early because of jet lag, went for a walk before dawn, and saw the horizon turn flaming orange, he took a picture of it with his cellphone to show her.

They communicated by Skype as well as by email. There was a seven-hour time difference, so for the first time in twenty years, Makino changed the rhythm of his life, getting up early so that he could talk to her when she'd finished dinner. Yoko, for her part, began staying up a bit later so she could talk to him after Jalila went to bed.

Ever since he first met Yoko, Makino had been communicating with her by email and experiencing the joy of sharing things with her. But unlike those early days, when, to distract her however briefly from the death and destruction all around her in Baghdad, he had sent messages that were as cheerful as he could make them, now he could write about a world that she also might share, far apart though they were. Some sunny Sunday afternoon after the rainy season, she might watch with him in Yoyogi Park as the children ran around with bubble guns, and somewhere they might encounter the internist, who moments before would have been listening tearfully to the theme song of an old cartoon show, so that when Makino introduced him to her, the sight of his teary, reddened eyes would induce a smile.

He realized that for the world to overflow with meaning, it couldn't exist only for oneself. Over the course of his life he had been in love a few times, but this sensation was new. Through Yoko he discovered that the world had to exist not just for him but for the one he loved. Even sources of pent-up anger and sorrow could step in and remind him about love. And only when he was face-to-face with her could he forget the noise that was the source of his ongoing distress.

Naturally, they told each other all about themselves. They were each hungry to know more about the other and piled question upon question. When Skype video wasn't working well, just as the conversation was getting spirited, the screen would dissolve into a block of wavy lines.

Makino asked Yoko about the mysterious nine-year gap between *Morning Sun in Dalmatia* and *Coins of Happiness*. "After making a movie that powerful, what did your father do for the next nine years? His biographies all leave that part out."

Yoko did not answer immediately. She was aware of the hiatus, but had never thought much about it. Makino sensed that his question had touched a chord inside her, but that was nothing to fear. While she turned her focus inward, he sat silently watching her. Even if she couldn't tell him anything, he felt those silent moments would bring them closer together.

He loved the look on Yoko's face when she was thinking hard. He loved the seriousness of her approach to life. That the answers she gave others must always apply equally to herself. He was intensely attracted to her unswerving principles.

"My relationship with my father is fine now, but it was difficult right up to my twenties. Whatever the reason, he left me, after all. During the years when I wanted to ask him about it, I couldn't speak English very well, and then after I learned, I came to think the topic was best left alone. My mother remarried, this time to a Swiss man, and after they moved to Geneva, she and I grew apart. I've only been able to talk with her since I became an adult—these past fifteen years."

"Your mother remarried? I didn't know. Is that why you went to school in Switzerland?"

"Yes. I lived in a dormitory, not at home, so instead of a new father, he seemed more like her new boyfriend. Financially we were better off, but I was never close to him, and then she divorced him too, so we're not in touch."

"I see."

"My real father . . . You want to know what he was doing during those nine years? The next time I see him, I'll ask. Or would you rather ask him yourself? I'll have to introduce you. The sooner the better."

"That would be great. I'd be nervous, though. He'd think I was a jerk if I asked him such a prying question soon after we met."

"He seems intimidating, but he's a softie."

"He would have to be a deeply kindhearted man to make those films."

"He might tell you things he doesn't tell me. You're both artists, and he's very fond of classical guitar. I'm sure you'll hit it off."

"Both my parents are gone, but I'd like to meet yours soon—your mother too."

"That's right—she and I both heard you play in Paris that time, when you were in high school! Do you want to come to Nagasaki with me to visit? She lives alone now. I see her whenever I go back to Japan."

"That would be wonderful."

"She's not an artist, but she's a remarkable person. After all, she traveled throughout Europe as a young woman and married first a Yugoslavian man and then a Swiss."

"Why did she go to Europe?"

"No matter how many times I ask, all she'll say is that she was tired of being in Nagasaki. She was too small when the bomb fell to have any clear memory of it. She was a little to the south of the blast zone, which is why she survived. Even that much she kept hidden from me for a long time. She wouldn't let her own mother talk to me about it. I had to hear about it from my father. I only learned about the atom bomb itself after I grew up, by reading books."

"When I visited your place, I saw you had a book about it, and I thought maybe that was why."

"Yes, I've read widely about the bomb. Books by writers like Kyoko Hayashi, Hiroko Takenishi, Tamiki Hara . . . Not just fiction, either. I needed to understand it for my work. Women survivors in particular had a hard time finding partners, and knowing my mother, I think she probably wanted to be rid of all that baggage."

"Makes sense."

"My father said her guilt about running away kept her from really enjoying life, but at the same time, her uncertainty about the aftereffects of the bombing had the opposite effect, made her feel she had to get all she could out of life. Both were true, he said." She paused. "She was attracted to him for a reason. She wanted him to understand. I've been asking myself why I went back to Iraq, and I think my parents' histories are part of it. Not that I like to admit it."

"I wish you had told me sooner."

"It's hardly a good way to start a relationship. Not very appealing, is it? I have more powerful allures than that."

"Oh, I know. I know all about your allures."

"Thanks, but now I want you to know other things too."

"You're part of my life. I'm listening."

"Thank you. While I'm at it, there's something else. You tend to look for what's European in me, but I don't necessarily see myself that way. Think about how I felt when I used to listen to your Bach in Iraq."

"I remember what you said."

"In war, the question of who did what to whom can't be ignored, but above and beyond that, there's the perspective of humanity, don't you agree? Things that human beings should and shouldn't do, period. Making excuses by comparing yourself with others—I'm not as bad as the other guy; my country's not as bad as theirs—that sort of relativism is just aggressors trading winks. It's ugly. I can't accept it. Victimhood in war is absolute, isn't it? You can't just say, 'The bombing of Nagasaki and the London air raids were both awful, so let's drop the subject.' That can never happen. It mustn't happen. Victims have to be regarded as human beings. Now, you may say that way of thinking is European, and maybe it is, but that argument doesn't much interest me."

"I get that. I do."

"Your music is loved universally. You saw how moved Jalila was, didn't you?"

"That's because the reading beforehand was so good."

"If you think I'm being naive, then what about my father's films? They're based on the belief that barriers of ethnicity and culture and religion can all be overcome. It's not just pie in the sky. That's why so many people have died in Iraq."

Makino listened to her as someone who was going to become his family. The first night they'd met, he had listened in wonderment as she told him about her life, a reality far removed from his, he had thought, but now she was opening up a world he would be intimately connected to. Her ideas about humanity, even if they were something that as a musician he should consider, were too grand for him to deal with. And yet, if he was forced to confront such thinking through Yoko, perhaps he could gain something concrete from it, as a member of her family, something that would have a positive effect on his music.

Makino was truly happy. He well knew that he owed his happiness to the considerable, unspoken price that Yoko had paid, not just in breaking off her engagement but also in sorting out relationships with her ex-fiancé's family and friends, canceling wedding arrangements, and all the rest of it. But even as his happiness grew, his musical stalemate became more and more intolerable.

His lackluster performance at the Madrid festival, and the overwhelming presence of the fresh young talent there, weighed upon him. Then had come his dismal failure at the recital in Paris. The fulfillment of his love for Yoko was some comfort, but the contrast between his professional life and his love life was frustrating. He cursed his misfortune in having lost, just at this particular time, the creative fulfillment he had always taken for granted in life. If he could have had that happiness as a musician as well as the happiness Yoko brought him, what a time of radiant joy this would have been! He knew that he could not live on the latter happiness alone. Music was the foundation of his life and the sole comfort he had to offer himself. It was irreplaceable, matchless. If he went on as he was, ashamed of his feckless performances, he knew the day was coming when he could not enjoy a life filled with his and Yoko's mutual love.

He didn't tell Yoko what he was going through. He didn't necessarily want to deny himself the grace her love might bestow; however, the words of the ancient swordsman Miyamoto Musashi summed up how he felt: "Respect the gods and Buddhas, but do not rely on them." It was unreasonable to look to her for salvation, and the mere thought of her giving him unwanted advice and him responding in anger was painful. In the end, there was nothing to do but go on as he had always done and work through his troubles on his own.

Of course, he did not for a moment think the brick wall he had hit was in any way related to Yoko. Signs that something was off had already been apparent to him on tour the past year, before he ever met her. There was also the pressure of encountering new talent. It was ironic that his love for Yoko made that pressure even harder to bear, but if falling head over heels in love made him a worse guitar player, what in the world was the point of his music?

To his surprise, Mitani, his manager, seemed convinced that Yoko was to blame. She attributed his lackluster performance in Madrid to Yoko's hold on him, and she saw no other reason for the change in him since last year, including his abrupt cancellation of a project already underway. She didn't see his current malaise as a serious slump.

Makino didn't doubt the sincerity of her concern, but the illogic of it nettled him. When she told him ardently that she would take responsibility for everything in his life apart from his music, he had lashed out: In that case, why the hell didn't she clean up the mess surrounding the Jupiter takeover? He had always looked down on musicians who yelled at their staff, so he was upset with himself for taking that tone with her. He had lost his temper several times recently, and always with Mitani. She riled him to a surprising degree. Then, seeing how crestfallen she was, he would repent.

If things between them soured more, it might be better if someone else took over her job. But Korenaga had just been replaced earlier that year, and successive changes to the staff lineup suggested that he was the real problem. He tried to think if there was anyone in the Kinoshita Music office he would rather have as his manager. He couldn't think of anyone more devoted to his music than Mitani.

Makino wanted to clear his schedule and devote himself to practicing in order to rebuild his music from the bottom up, but at the same time, he was skeptical of unreasonable expectations. For twenty years, he had maintained his musical skills amid the frenzied tempo of recitals and recording sessions. The idea that in the absence of such external commitments he could improve dramatically seemed cartoonish, a desperate dream. Wouldn't he more likely feel lost doing nothing and become slipshod? Among musicians his age, pursuing a richer musicality by going into a retreat for a "dialogue with oneself" usually backfired.

Since he had already canceled most of his recitals and called a halt to all recording sessions, his schedule was wide open for the first time in many years. All the white space in his daily planner made him uneasy. He had no shortage of time to practice, but he felt himself falling into a state of paralysis that no herculean efforts could overcome.

✕

The breaking off of Yoko's engagement dragged on and on with no clear end in sight. She didn't want to cut off all communication with her ex, the way people did after quarreling. Richard showed no sign of giving up and continued to send frequent emails, some of which touched her with their fervor.

After a couple of weeks, his initial shock having receded, out of the blue, Richard began saying he would "forgive" her "affair."

Your going to Iraq despite the risk to your life shows what a strong person you are, and yet under those circumstances, anyone would become emotionally unstable. I'm at fault for not being there at your side when you needed me. A betrayal is a betrayal, and it hurt me deeply, but before a wedding, people do get cold feet. They may not talk about it openly, but it happens all the time.

Let's wipe the slate clean and get married. I know you far better than he does. I knew you when you were still a sweet young college student—but bright and sensible, just like now. My love for you has never wavered. It's even stronger than before. I know that for a fact, and I want you to know it too.

Richard's argument that she had not found a new love but rather was having a fleeting affair was perhaps predictable, but it took her by surprise. Never in her life had she cheated on anyone. Richard's tone was straightforward, almost as if he were following a how-to guide. The analogy was a bit outlandish, but she was reminded of late-night television commercials for household gadgets—all-purpose shears, say, or a high-pressure washing machine—and thinking, *Now that could be useful.* His approach could apply in any breakup situation, whatever the particulars.

She didn't want to go back to him, but she did feel as if she no longer knew quite where she stood. After breaking up with him, once free and unattached, she had been able to forgive herself for falling in love with Makino. But in Richard's mind, she still belonged to him and had

125

simply, by some caprice, taken a break, wandering temporarily away. She was naturally repelled by his interpretation, but she sensed that the situation needed delicate handling to avoid leaving an indelible scar on her heart, like carefully removing an accessory caught in the threads of a knit top.

She had a few of Richard's things, and she still had her ring; she had tried to return it the day she first told him she was ending the engagement, but he had gone off without it. She thought of mailing it to New York, but it was so valuable that she held back. Also, guilt made her want to hand him the ring in person. Richard thought that her failure to return the ring showed that she was wavering, and he kept finding excuses to call. Instead of trying insistently to talk her into coming back to him, he acted as if she had never left and hung up after cheerfully relaying his message.

Meanwhile, their mutual friends and his family did their best to change her mind. A letter from his aged parents cut her to the quick. His sister, Claire, whom Yoko actually got along with better than she did Richard and who had been excited about welcoming her into the family, called twice. When Yoko told her about Makino, Claire asked in a sisterly way, "Has he proposed?"

"No, but—"

Claire interrupted gently, as if she had heard enough. "No one in the family blames you. I mean it. So please think again. Richie loves you so much. As his sister, I can tell you he's a kind, good man. He's got brains, and he's financially well off. Right now he's in torment. I've never seen him so stricken. That's no surprise. There'll never be anyone like you for him again. So please take him back. Just forget this ever happened."

Yoko spoke of her coming life with Makino as if it were a given that they would marry, but in fact he had never officially proposed. That night in Paris, their need to embrace had eclipsed all words but "I love you," and with Jalila to worry about, the chance had slipped away. After he returned to Japan, Makino had been concerned about their future, and once during one of their Skype conversations, he had started to propose, until Yoko put him off with a smile.

"Not over Skype, please! I want you to say it in person, when we're close enough to touch. I'll be in Japan next month. If you propose now, I can't run into your arms!"

"Well . . . you're right. I'll save what I was going to say until then. Anyway, that's my intention, and I wanted you to know." Since then, he hadn't broached the subject.

Now she regretted her words. They both were surely agreed on wanting to marry, but as their Tokyo reunion got pushed back from July to late August, the lack of a firm verbal commitment left her feeling a bit forlorn. She had originally planned to vacation with Richard and Claire's family at the end of August. They had decided on a trip to Cancún, and Richard's idea had been to have the ceremony first and make the trip a honeymoon. They could have the wedding reception later, after she moved to New York. But if she didn't like that idea, he'd been willing to take a second honeymoon during winter vacation.

Yoko had requested to move her vacation time from late August to July, but as the company was shorthanded, this did not go over well. At the last minute, they offered her four days at the end of July, but flights were already full, and Makino had a scheduling conflict. He was understanding; August would be fine. Yoko realized there was no other choice, but the monthlong postponement gave her a twinge of anxiety. She felt a disjunction similar to the optical illusion where train tracks stretching into the distance appear to converge at the vanishing point, but as station after station goes by, the view ahead never changes, and the parallel rails of course never meet. What appears in the present moment to be an inevitable convergence is, in the end, only an illusion.

Yoko had applied for a transfer to New York because of her impending marriage to Richard, and her cancellation of the request caused a stir among her coworkers. As a good-looking reporter of Japanese ancestry who had done two stints in Iraq, she stood out; also, though she used a different surname and kept a low profile, her colleagues were well aware of who her father was. New York was a popular assignment, and when Yoko's appointment came through, a woman in another department who had applied for a transfer first complained to everyone that Yoko had stolen it from her.

Now she had changed her mind and was applying for a transfer to Tokyo. She explained to her boss that she'd canceled her wedding; this time, her request was put on hold. There seemed little chance of getting it approved in the next year or two, and she was seriously considering quitting her job.

She was going to marry Makino. No, they weren't promised to each other in so many words, but in real terms, they were engaged.

Weren't they?

They had met only three times so far, and physically, while they had kissed and clung to one another with passion, they had never done much more, merely dancing around the desire to unite. That in itself was undoubtedly unusual. She had told a close friend in Paris about breaking off her engagement and why, but hadn't mentioned that she and Makino were not yet lovers. If she herself had heard of such a case, unless religious scruples were involved, she might well have advised, "Physical compatibility is important too, so why not make sure before you commit?"

Of course, they were mature grown-ups, able to understand that all sorts of exceptional circumstances could arise in the course of a romance and not so shallow as to entertain doubts about the strength of their bond merely because intimacy had been postponed. A man might conceivably be bothered by it more, but Makino had never said a word, and no doubt shared her conviction.

Still, thoughts of Richard nagged at her. Back when her affections were shifting from him to Makino and their bond was starting to fray, he had made love to her with increasing urgency. If he knew that her supposed "affair" was unconsummated, he would undoubtedly conclude jubilantly that it was nonexistent—that nothing at all had happened.

It wasn't that she retained vivid impressions of sleeping with Richard. Rather, she ached to give herself to Makino with total abandon, to dissolve in his arms with a finality that meant she could never, ever go back to Richard. Objectively speaking, her desire to give herself wantonly to Makino seemed to mirror Richard's hunger for her. She clung unconsciously to that secret cruelty.

That year, Paris endured its hottest weather since 2003, when thousands of people had died in a heat wave. At work they were shorthanded during the vacation season, and besides covering the new immigration law then under debate in Parliament, Yoko was also sent to find out what steps medical facilities were taking to deal with the heat. She gave up her morning jog, which had become a habit over the past few months. This time, she had an air conditioner installed, but she couldn't leave it on all night, and sleeping was difficult.

Jalila's stay was lasting longer than expected, so Yoko bought a simple sofa bed for two hundred euros and slept in the living room. Jalila, worried that her nightmares were keeping Yoko awake, tried at first to insist that her hostess take the bedroom.

"It's fine," said Yoko with a smile. "I have things I want to do in the living room at night, and I don't toss and turn, so a smaller bed is no problem."

Jalila knew that at night in the living room, Yoko read books, did work, and chatted with Makino over Skype, so although she felt awkward about it, she did as Yoko suggested and kept the bedroom for herself.

Yoko was relieved when they began sleeping in separate rooms. Maintaining a degree of privacy was beneficial for both of them, and what's more, around that time, Yoko herself began having nightmares. It was always the same—a reenactment of that scene in the Murjana Hotel.

Men came charging into the hotel lobby. In real life, she hadn't definitely had eye contact with any of them—she liked to assure herself that she hadn't—but in her dreams a man glared at her from close by and sometimes addressed her in a garbled language that could have been Arabic. His eyes had the look of someone who had already filed notice of his departure from this world and was moments away from collapsing onto the cold marble floor in the blast. But then, time stopped. The man's eyes shook with the agitation of looming death but remained forever taut with strain, seconds before annihilation. The bright light of the hotel chandelier was reflected in his eyes, and in the man's dark pupils she made out her own figure slipping into the elevator . . .

Sometimes she awoke then, heart pounding, and sometimes she dreamed of seeing the blast, though in real life she had not. Shut inside the elevator, she sat in a corner and waited anxiously for help. She could scarcely breathe. When the door opened, the terror of that moment came rushing in.

She had heard of people being tortured by a recurring dream, and now she was experiencing it firsthand. She had the bizarre sensation that the day she left Baghdad, another Yoko had somehow failed to board the plane and instead remained all this time in the Murjana Hotel, caught up in one terror incident after another.

After chatting enjoyably with Makino on Skype, she would turn out the lights and lie down on the uncomfortable sofa bed, wondering apprehensively if the dream would come back. In Paris, it was not uncommon to hear passing sirens in the middle of the night, and when that happened, the deep silence of Baghdad after curfew would unexpectedly fill her ears.

People could neither dream the dreams they wanted nor avoid those they didn't want.

In the daytime she was free, but at night, all alone, she was thrust back into that far-off world of death. The oppressive heat was debilitating, and perhaps from lack of sleep, she had migraines and couldn't focus on her work. She felt lethargic, and reality seemed at all times a bit distant. Every time she reached out an arm or took a few steps, it receded that much farther.

And when the dreams reached a saturation point, Yoko began having vivid flashbacks in the middle of the day. It happened first aboard the Line 4 subway, heading for Château Rouge on assignment. The temperature had been around one hundred degrees all day, and the passengers were mopping their faces and pulling their sweat-soaked T-shirts away from their chests to let in air.

Paris had emptied out for August vacations, and with few tourists around, the streets were taken over by the rays of the sun. When Yoko descended the subway stairs, the bright fountain that she had scarcely noticed moments before left a surprisingly dark afterimage on her vision. She sat near the door and scanned some work-related papers. The interior of the train smelled sweaty, and the air-conditioning wasn't working well, so behind her someone was opening a window. The rails shrieked in the underground darkness, and another train passed by from the opposite direction with a gust of wind and a jolt that shook the passengers' shoulders. The tourists all got off, and around the Strasbourg-Saint-Denis station, people who lived north of Paris began straggling aboard.

Shortly after the door closed, Yoko had the sensation that someone was watching her. She looked up, and across from her, an Arab-looking young man was casting a meaningful gaze her way. For an instant, the eyes of a terrorist bomber looked out at her, then just as quickly vanished into the recesses of his eyes. She concealed the shaking of her hands as she tucked the papers back into her purse and slowly got up, edging closer to the door. Over the loudspeaker came the announcement of the next station, Château d'Eau. She pushed the button next to the door. It didn't open. She glimpsed herself standing on the other side of the window, outside in the dark. Trapped in her dream, she pushed the button frantically, desperate to open the doors of the Murjana Hotel elevator.

The doors wouldn't open. The other passengers eyed her strangely as she went into a panic. The train finally drew up alongside the platform, the doors opening before it came to a full stop. She rushed out and sat on a bench to wait until she was calm, covering her face with trembling hands. She couldn't look as the doors closed again and the train moved on.

She was disturbed that the sight of an Arab youth had triggered her panic. In fact, she had just written an article that was critical of the sort of Islamophobia that saw every Arab immigrant as a terrorist. That she had exhibited it herself offended her sense of justice. She had a visceral dislike of such prejudice, partly because of her own background, which was racially and culturally far from "pure." She was proud of having been to Iraq, where she had actually experienced terrorism and mingled with Muslim residents who were its victims.

In Iraq, US soldiers' inability to distinguish ordinary people from terrorists sometimes led to fatal errors, provoking violent protests. But such errors were preventable by investigating the situation thoroughly in advance and hiring trustworthy escorts.

How could she of all people, inside a train car where everyone else was bothered only by the heat, have connected the youth in front of her with a terrorist bombing and flown into a panic?

Yoko sensed that she was losing her equilibrium. She felt as if she had been handed a tray too big for her and was struggling to balance a dozen balls on it. When she focused on one, the others would start to wobble, and then she took hasty action that sent them all rolling in the opposite direction, over and over.

She discussed this on Skype with her doctor, whom she had been consulting less frequently of late.

"It's post-traumatic stress disorder," said the doctor. "A mild case."

Yoko talked about her new life with Jalila, and the doctor, after advising her to improve her sleeping conditions, explained that after a traumatic event, symptoms of the disorder often took months to appear. "The essence of PTSD is continual avoidance of stimuli associated with the trauma and an overall inability to react. There is a real possibility that the presence of the Iraqi woman has sharpened your memories of Baghdad that were beginning to fade, and now your body is rejecting them." The doctor paused. "But generalities don't mean very much. What matters is, what does Jalila mean to you, personally?"

As always when she was asked something important, Yoko did not answer right away but thought in silence for a moment. Then, for the sake of her own health, she did her best to convey her genuine feelings. "I love her like family. That's the truth, and it's what I want to be true. That's why in the subway, when I had that Islamophobic reaction just because an Arab man happened to be looking at me, I blamed myself and then thought immediately of her. I thought, *Wait, how can I be a bigot? I'm looking after an Iraqi woman who fled Baghdad to save her life! She'd be the first to say I'm not prejudiced.*"

"I see."

"In many ways, Jalila is my rock. I feel as if something inside me broke while I was in Baghdad. Even after coming back to Paris, I haven't felt the same. When I talk to my coworkers, there's a distance between us. But ever since Jalila came, I feel like there's someone who understands me, and that gives me strength. I can't tell you how many times

I've thanked my stars that she's here. Compared to what she's been through, my experience in Iraq is next to nothing. That's another reason why, even though I might feel distant from my Paris friends, I never make too much of what I went through. But Jalila knows that if I'd been in that hotel lobby one minute more, I'd be dead. She wept for me, and she's always worried about me. If someone here ever said, 'But you were only there for six weeks or so, right? Even if you did go three times, that only adds up to four and a half months total, and it's not as if you were embedded with soldiers in battle—you were sitting comfortably in a hotel!' I know Jalila would stick up for me.

"I'm aware that I came back without accomplishing much of anything. I know my own worthlessness better than anyone. It's arrogant to think that I left the Iraqi people behind when I could have improved their lives, that I abandoned them. But in any case, right now, protecting Jalila is the one concrete thing I can do for Iraq. When I think of the enormous loss of life taking place there now, it's the least I can do—and saving someone's life, or helping to do so, surely that's no small thing? Living with her, I finally understand how much it means. So . . ."

Beginning to fear that the doctor would advise her to find Jalila a new place to live, Yoko went on emphasizing that, as much as Jalila needed her, she needed Jalila more. She adjusted her way of speaking to get the psychiatrist's approval; her words demanded sympathy, but her tone lacked passion and was a near monotone.

"If she is necessary to you now—and if you also feel love for her—then there's no reason why you shouldn't live together. But it's not good for you to downplay what you're going through compared to her and suppress your suffering. You've been to war, you know. To think of that experience as something that you can bear or that a person should normally be able to get over isn't in keeping with what you've learned working in the field as a journalist, is it?"

Startled, Yoko bit her lip. She was surprised to find herself near tears. She took a deep breath and nodded. "You're right. Now I think

I understand why people who are feeling vulnerable tend to blame themselves. Is it out of pride?"

"In part. Maintaining pride and self-respect is important. War is an experience beyond the bounds of human endurance, so you shouldn't feel that you can easily bounce back."

"Why do I keep having the same dream? I've done some reading, and I've thought about it. I have a feeling that if I were able to put into words what that experience was, I would stop reliving it. I don't think it's a message telling me to distance myself from Jalila."

"Troubled dreams are difficult to handle. In part they are surely a warning never to have the same experience again. Your body is on high alert, so even if it's clear that an ordinary Arab immigrant isn't a terrorist, warning bells go off. You shouldn't try to overanalyze things in your current state. The more you tell yourself that nothing so very terrible happened to you, the more your body may be protesting: 'What do you mean? Look at these wounds!' Once the circuit is set to issue that warning, it's hard to undo."

"So all I can do is wait for the dreams to stop?"

"Things will improve if you control your anxiety with medication and stabilize your life. Don't give up hope. You are going to get better. But instead of trying to go back to your old self, you need to shape your new self in a way that you can accept. If you do that, your symptoms will eventually disappear."

"Are you saying that the past can be changed?"

The doctor paused, considering, then nodded. "Yes. Changed by the way you live after this. That's a good way of putting it."

Yoko's face softened. "The person I love best in all the world taught me that."

Not a day went by that she failed to think of him. At night when she couldn't fall asleep, she would lie on the sofa where they had embraced

135

and think only of him. She looked back on herself a year ago, before she had met him, with wonder.

If Korenaga from the record company, whom she had met only a short time before, had not invited her to Makino's concert that day in November, she would still be the Yoko Komine who had never loved him. And if she hadn't decided to leave Richard while Makino was in Madrid, she would now be the Yoko Komine who had relinquished his love. She felt as if she were wandering in a maze with any number of exits. Compared to a maze where every wrong path led to a dead end and forced you to retrace your steps, a maze with no dead ends and only different exits was far crueler.

Along with the desire to lose herself in Makino's love, she felt obliged for the sake of his love to hang on to herself, and, caught between those conflicting desires, she was being slowly torn in two.

The doctor had said it would take at least a year for the symptoms of PTSD to subside. She mustn't be impatient, and must accept that time as being necessary for healing. Still, the shock was great, since Yoko had thought she had landed on her feet in Paris and was leading a normal life.

She got the doctor to recommend several books on the disorder, both for the layman and the specialist. The phrase "out of control," which she had heard so often in Iraq, echoed in her mind.

At work, she was able for now to keep herself in check and avoid sudden outbursts of emotion; none of her colleagues suspected that she was in such a fragile state. But how would she manage around Makino? She prayed every day that by some miracle she might recover, so that by the time she went to Tokyo she would be her normal, healthy self again, the way she had been that night with him in Paris.

Should she put off seeing him? But for how long? To wait a year or more would wreak havoc on their relationship. She couldn't wait that long. She yearned to see him again as soon as possible—to marry him and have his child. The yearning had come over her with urgency: she was forty years old, and this increased her impatience.

One day in the second week of August, Yoko received an email from Korenaga for the first time in a while. After Makino's concert last November and before Yoko went back to France, the two of them had gotten together for dinner and become fast friends. While Yoko was in Baghdad, they had communicated every so often, but lately there had been no word from her.

Korenaga's parents were planning to visit Paris during their summer vacation. Would Yoko recommend a nice restaurant for them? That request seemed to be a mere aside; her real news was that, with the take-over of the record company she worked for, she was planning to quit her job at the end of the summer and join the public relations department for a home appliance maker financed with foreign capital.

Sensing a note of dissatisfaction in her brief account, Yoko contacted her friend on Skype that weekend. Korenaga was glad to hear from her, and they chatted for nearly two hours. Korenaga explained the particulars of her employment change. Yoko had had some idea about the difficulties of the music industry, but on hearing details like the exact number of CDs released, she was shocked by the gravity of the situation.

"Will Makino be all right?" Not yet having told Korenaga about her relationship with him, Yoko asked this with apparent casualness, hoping to work the conversation around so she could make the announcement.

Korenaga did not seem surprised to hear his name brought up. She sighed. "Actually, I'm not in charge of his recordings anymore. I was taken off the account."

"You were? Why?"

Korenaga explained that she and Makino had had a difference of opinion about the *What a Wonderful World* album, and that the company had decided that she should be replaced. She had put a lot of effort into the project and had been treating Makino with great respect, she felt, so the dismissal had come as a shock. That was a major reason why she decided she might not have much more to offer in the industry.

Yoko sympathized, but having heard nothing about this from Makino, she asked another question. "Is he difficult to work with?"

"No, not as artists go. He has common sense, and he's friendly and easygoing, the way he was that night when you met him. He can be extremely thoughtful too. I never had any problems with him, which only increased my shock."

"I wonder what happened."

"Well . . ." She hesitated. "I don't know if I should say this, but I'm afraid he's in a bit of a slump. He's having difficulties as a musician. He hasn't said anything to anybody, but people are talking."

Yoko said nothing.

"When he gave a recital in Paris in June, he broke off right in the middle of a piece. A friend of mine who was there said they worried something might have happened to his hand. I didn't really believe it, but recently I heard him play in Tokyo, and he's completely lost his spark."

"Really . . ."

"I can only imagine how frustrated he must be. Aren't you in touch with him?"

"Oh, well . . ."

"I was sure you would be. Last year after the concert, he was so happy to have met you. He talked about you constantly."

"You told me he was a smooth operator, so I was being careful."

"Oh, that! I was joking. There's a lot of speculation about why he's never married. People say it's because he's popular with women, and he likes his freedom. I don't know anything about his private life. He doesn't say anything, so it's all speculation. I doubt if many women would want to go out with him. He's a genius. I've worked with all sorts of musicians, and regardless of the instrument, there aren't many who make you immediately think, *Ah, here's someone in a class all his own.* Nobody knows how he lives, but sometimes when I see him at a venue looking lost in thought, I think he must have a hard life. Constant practicing, and the nerves before a concert . . . I mean, really. In the end I'll bet he marries someone like Mitani. That's what everyone says."

"Mitani . . . You mean his manager?"

"Yeah. The lively one who got drunk that night and gave you a hard time. You remember her? With all the hassle caused by the buyout of Jupiter, she's the only one fighting for him. I'll never forget something she told me at the beginning of the year."

"What was that?"

"'Everyone thinks they should be the star of their own life, and they suffer to achieve stardom.' She said she used to be the same way, but not anymore. Since becoming Makino's manager, all she wants is to be a supporting actor in his life, and let him be the star."

"She said that?"

"Yes. Not all actors are cut out for the lead, are they? Some are more suited to supporting roles. She said she can't get excited over the thought of playing the lead in her life. 'People are hardly clamoring to see a Sanae Mitani biopic, right?'" Korenaga imitated Mitani's voice. "'But if it were a Satoshi Makino biopic, they'd go for sure. And I'd get to play a crucial role in that picture. Isn't that fantastic?' She says if she can go on being cast in an important supporting role in Makino's life, where he's the star, then her own life will be fulfilling. Just the thought of that makes her excited, and so she's willing to do anything for him. She bowled me over."

"That's one way to think, I guess. It kind of . . . wakes you up, doesn't it?"

"She talked about you too."

"Me?"

"As an example. She mentioned you because you're a career woman. She said a woman like you can shine as the star of her own life, but that she's not like that. I didn't comment on her assessment of herself, but I did agree that you're star quality."

"Heavens no. Any movie about me would be an indie film with a two-week run, tops."

"Not at all. Remember, I'm in public relations! I'd gladly take you on. Anyway, after that conversation, I got to thinking. I decided I'm no star either, that I'm more suited for supporting roles. But I'm not shooting for a best supporting actress Oscar in the story of one person's life, the way she is. I think having juicy side roles in various lives with different lead characters would be enough, and might be really fun too."

"You'd be in high demand."

"I'd happily take a role in your life without pay, Yoko. What do you think? Give me a call anytime. It's a shame I got kicked off the Satoshi Makino picture."

After that conversation, Mitani's view of life haunted Yoko for some time. Nor could she forget that Mitani did indeed play an essential role in Makino's life. When they'd talked, Yoko had felt a bit strange and guilty as Korenaga, unaware that she and Makino were together now, spoke of Mitani as his future life partner. Eventually, whenever she got around to confessing the truth, Korenaga was sure to cry, "No! Why didn't you say so sooner?"

But as she listened to Korenaga, she'd begun to feel that of the two, she herself was the one in the dark. What could she do for Makino? What was the substance of her love for him? When she asked him casually how his playing was going, he only said, "Oh, you know, same as usual." Then, while hinting at unspoken trials, several times he had mentioned how much happiness their Skype conversations brought him. Every time he did this, she felt deep within how much a part of her he was, and her heart overflowed with joy.

Despite being filled with a love so great, she was frustrated by her inability to escape from her experience in Iraq. Her desire to cast all else aside and seek peace of mind in him warred with her desire to be *his* peace of mind. But then, were the two so very different? When they were together, wordlessly sharing each other's warmth, were they not fulfilling both of those roles?

For the first time, Yoko was jealous of Mitani. In the story of Makino's life, starring him, she, Yoko, definitely had also been assigned a part. But where was the director? She felt sudden anxiety, as though she alone among the cast had been handed the wrong script. Like someone flipping hastily through the pages to find her place, she reflected on the present, looked back at the past, and thought ahead to the end of August when they would meet again, telling herself nothing was wrong.

※

Makino and Yoko discussed their vacation plans and agreed to spend the first two days in Tokyo and then visit her mother in Nagasaki. Yoko would only be in Japan for a week. It felt awfully short to him, but he understood her desire not to leave Jalila on her own for long. That concern for others was one of the things he loved about her; yet her actual time off was two weeks long, and it frustrated him to think that he couldn't be with her during the second week, after she returned to Paris.

Yoko, too, felt the shortness of their time together. Her concern for Jalila was real, but on top of that, she was uneasy about the state of her own health.

"Why not just tell him about your PTSD?" Jalila asked time and again, certain that he would be supportive.

But Yoko flatly rejected the idea, finally declaring with an expression of greater severity than Jalila had ever seen that she was to drop the subject. "And if you tell him on your own, I can never trust you

141

again." Afterward, Yoko regretted having spoken so harshly to someone in Jalila's position, but she feared her friend's youthful good intentions.

Jalila knew nothing of the musical difficulties Makino was experiencing or of Yoko's desire to watch over him while he was in distress. Jalila didn't know how terrible Yoko would feel if, at a time when only Mitani was at Makino's side, supporting his career, word of her psychological problems should add to his pain. Still less could she have imagined Yoko's envy of Mitani.

Yoko couldn't get Korenaga's innocent speculation out of her head. The idea of Mitani's presence in Makino's life took root within her, sprouting and producing a succession of bright blossoms like a morning glory in summer, wrapping its tendrils around her emotions. None of the blossoms lasted long, but the number of new buds did not decline. The blossoming looked likely to last all summer—until she saw Makino again.

If he were there with her, he would have spotted the first leaves of suspicion and plucked them from her heart with a puzzled look. "It's all in your imagination," he would say. The enormous distance of ten thousand kilometers weighed on her, not as the distance separating Tokyo and Paris but as the distance separating his skin and hers.

Her condition was worsening, and she suspected that had something to do with her failure to swiftly end her engagement. The breakup dragged on and on, making her even less willing to open up to Makino about her physical and mental condition. He had always wanted her to send Richard packing. She herself didn't want her old fiancé casting a shadow on their new life; around Makino, she didn't want to be the Yoko formerly engaged to Richard.

She tried to believe that they would have a peaceful week together in Japan. She would see him again and they would make their promises for the future; how could she possibly suffer attacks of her Iraq nightmare amid the happiness of just being near him? She wanted to forget everything else and be made brand new, reveling in the knowledge that he was there and so was she. Was that how burdensome her life was now? At the very least, she hoped that her phantom self, the Yoko that had stayed in Baghdad, might at last head for home.

At an August guitar festival in Japan, Makino blanked out once again. This time he covered up adroitly, so few noticed, but overall, his playing was shrill and rushed, without a trace of the finely detailed, clearly structured musicality that was his trademark. Even if he wasn't at the top of his game, his technical prowess was unaffected, and so it came off as a superficial performance involving only his fingers and not his heart.

The program was modest, consisting of a duo for violin and guitar followed by four solos, but Makino was unusually nervous and wandered in and out of his dressing room beforehand. Normally he was unconcerned before a performance, so to calm his nerves he made up rituals like practicing autosuggestion by murmuring the same word over and over or smiling at himself in the mirror. He paid attention to his breathing and tried to trace the piece mentally from the beginning, but found himself impatiently skipping the easy parts. He went over the fingering of difficult passages in a fragmentary way, but unexpected memory blanks seemed more likely to occur in the transitions before and after those passages, so he backtracked and jumped ahead, over and over.

Given his long career as a performer, adjusting to ups and downs in his playing should have come naturally, and slightly subpar performances were nothing new, but he was taken aback to find he had completely forgotten how to deal with them. His recital schedule was still quite light, yet twice now in the space of a few months he had gone blank midperformance: something was wrong. And both times, it had happened with a piece he should have been able to play in his sleep.

Makino's hopes for his new life with Yoko, though still vague, were greater than before. When he was with her, he didn't want to look gloomy. That wasn't likely, though, for the sight of her face on his laptop monitor always brought out a smile. He tried to recapture his state of mind on that evening when he had played for Jalila. Re-creating the same mood onstage might be impossible, but that night, for the first time in a long while, he had enjoyed conversing with his instrument. He kept returning to those ten minutes when Yoko had read aloud and he had played the guitar. The guitar itself had sung tenderly for a girl who had barely managed to slip across the barrier between life and death . . . forgetting, for that brief moment, the question: What is music for?

Makino set about getting his stalled work negotiations back up and running before Yoko came. After he returned from Paris, he had been in contact with Globe Music through Mitani, but there was confusion over who he would be working with there, and as he had no immediate plans to issue a new record, they had temporarily shunted him aside.

He was initially assigned to Okajima, who used to be with Jupiter, but Makino had given him the thumbs-down. Times were hard in the industry, and rumor had it that when Jupiter was bought out, Okajima had been promised a job at Globe in exchange for bringing the company's stable of musicians with him. Apparently, he had been conducting various meetings similar to the one he'd had with Makino. In any case, Makino wasn't eager to work with him again. Okajima did know the industry and prided himself on that knowledge. He would sigh over slumping CD sales and bewail the general decline in artistic sensibility, avidly advocating the need for "a new initiative," but Korenaga used to gripe that whenever she or someone else on his team came up with an idea, he would snap as if offended: "You know we can't do a thing like that!" She felt he was mostly angry that "a thing like that" hadn't already occurred to him. He defended himself by pretending that of course he'd been aware of the possibility all along and had a perfectly reasonable explanation for never having acted on it. He was, in short, proud, incompetent, and unwilling to listen—the worst kind of boss.

Having no desire to get caught between his representative and her boss, Makino had paid little attention to these complaints, treating them only as amusing anecdotes, but once he lost Korenaga as a buffer and had to deal directly with Okajima, her words came back with painful clarity. Since dropping *What a Wonderful World*, he'd had no communication with Korenaga, but recently a mass email announcing her resignation had arrived in his inbox, reminding him of all the work she'd put into the project.

Globe honored Makino's wishes and transferred him to Noda, a young man in his thirties. Originally in music distribution, Noda had been assigned to the classical division in the takeover. He claimed to know little about either classical music or the guitar, which was unsettling, but the company held him in high esteem and was apparently eager for him to somehow shake up this unprofitable arm of the business. He had an unusual background, computer engineering, and when introducing himself he had gone on about media studies and whatnot before getting to the point.

Noda's elaborate presentation boiled down to something like this: Ever since Kant, art had been seen as either beautiful or sublime, but in the latter half of the twentieth century, and especially with the rise of the internet, it had come to be seen instead as "cool" or "awesome." In modern art, for example, people were attracted to the "cool" paintings of Gerhard Richter and the "awesome" photographs of Andreas Gursky. Makino appealed so strongly to his admirers because his music possessed those attributes in addition to being beautiful. Unfortunately, however, his music was still remote to the average person.

Then Noda brought out charts showing how the increased production of electric and acoustic guitars correlated to the number of people forming bands, something that had enjoyed successive waves of popularity since the 1960s; his point was that many people around the world knew a bit about the guitar, regardless of genre. Most of them were no longer in a band; at most they occasionally strummed a guitar at home or, more likely, kept their guitar, case and all, tucked away somewhere in the back of a closet. But basically they liked music and secretly dreamed of how cool it would be if they could play a little something for their friends and family.

"Classical guitar has a huge repertory, right? Pop songs, movie music, you name it. I don't want Satoshi Makino pegged as someone from a distant world. I want to bill you as someone who's a model for everyone who's ever played a guitar. We'll upload sheet music and videos of you performing on an official website, so people can play along with whatever type of guitar they may have on hand. If all the people in the world who've ever played a guitar got involved, the numbers would be huge. It'll work exactly because you play classical guitar. Cello or violin would be a different story."

To make this happen, Noda suggested that Makino finish the *What a Wonderful World* project. He wanted not just to put out an album but also to set up the website he'd described, and broaden Makino's fan base. Getting those fans to move on to his Bach and Rodrigo would be the next step.

Makino could see what Noda was getting at. When he performed on television with rock or jazz guitarists, they showed surprising interest in classical techniques. Whether you played with a pick or plucked the strings with your fingers made a big difference, but if it was a slow piece mostly made up of arpeggios, using the same sheet music was no problem.

Picking up *What a Wonderful World* again would be a chore, but ever since coming up with the idea of dedicating the album to Jalila, he had regained interest in the abandoned project. He couldn't forget the look on her face that night as she listened to him play. More than the praise of any aficionado, however refined, the awareness that his playing had so moved her allowed him to believe in himself and his music.

If she saw her name in the credits—"For Jalila"—she would surely be pleased. It might be worth finishing the project just to make her smile. And not only her: Yoko, who stuck close by Jalila and supported her, would also be sure to approve.

Jalila was a precious person, someone whom he and Yoko had worried about and reached out to together. When he'd heard how short Yoko's time in Japan was going to be, he had asked, "Do you have to go back to Paris so soon?"

She had answered briefly, "Yes, because I'm worried about Jalila."

He was afraid his response hadn't sounded sufficiently sympathetic. He'd been disappointed at not being able to spend more time with Yoko, but wanted her to know that he wasn't in the least resentful of Jalila.

Jalila had received official refugee status and could now live apart from Yoko. In three years, she would be eligible to apply for citizenship. Her original decision to seek asylum in Sweden had been dictated by the illegal agent providing her with assistance, but she was now beginning to think she would like to live permanently in France. Yoko, being familiar with the difficulties experienced by Middle Eastern and African immigrants living in Paris, wasn't sure this was the best plan, but she'd nonetheless begun teaching her French.

More and more, it appeared that they would be based in Tokyo after they were married, at least at first, but Makino knew that Yoko would have trouble leaving Jalila on her own in Paris. He wanted to be with Yoko, but he, too, couldn't bear to think of Jalila being left on her own. This was something else they would have to discuss when Yoko came to Tokyo.

"For Jalila." While he was willing to work again on *What a Wonderful World*, anything beyond that would have to wait until he was satisfied with his playing and in the proper state of mind. He could imagine himself after a mediocre performance, surrounded by adoring fans telling him how "cool" and "awesome" he was, and this made him more depressed than ever.

When they were alone, Makino told Mitani that Noda was a new type of employee who hadn't worked in classical music before, and that he would like to work with him. Would she sound him out?

Mitani was thrilled to feel that Makino needed and trusted her for the first time in a while. She wasn't sure whether Noda's ideas would pan out, but with Okajima out of the picture, it was probably necessary to explore them. She felt herself in competition with Yoko to see who could be of greater service to Makino. Apparently, Yoko was coming to Japan at the end of August to spend time with him.

✕

Yoko was set to arrive at Narita Airport on August 29 at four thirty in the afternoon. Makino had intended to meet her plane, but she called him before leaving Paris to let him know that the flight had been delayed three hours already, and there was still no word on when it might take off. Since her time of arrival was uncertain, she said she would prefer to go straight to his place and would let him know when she had boarded the Narita Express train. This sort of thing happened all the time at Charles de Gaulle Airport, she said. She also told him that she couldn't wait to see him, and Makino said he felt the same way. He would meet her train in Shinjuku to help with the luggage.

Soon thereafter, he got a message from her indicating that she had boarded at last. Anticipating that she'd arrive in Shinjuku sometime around nine, he fortified himself with a sandwich. He would decide later whether to take her out for dinner or bring her straight to his place, depending on how tired she was.

Around six thirty, his home phone rang. It was Kana, the daughter of his old teacher Seiichi Sofue.

"Kana, hi, what's going on? It's been a while."

"Actually, it's . . . Father has had a stroke. He went to the hospital in an ambulance."

"Where are you?"

"I'm at the hospital. The doctor says his chances don't look good, and I should call people who need to know. I thought of you right away." She spoke in a steady tone, but her voice was trembling faintly, as if she were standing barefoot on a cold floor.

Makino asked the name and address of the hospital. He glanced at his watch, said he'd be right there, and hung up. Sofue might die before he got there. Even if he lived, he might never play the guitar again—such thoughts flooded through him, filling him with grief. He looked up the location of the hospital online and rushed out the door.

He had to get in touch with Yoko, but it would probably be better to wait until he had a clearer picture of the situation. In Paris, they had nearly missed seeing each other because of Jalila's sudden arrival. Perhaps at their age, this sort of thing was inevitable, as social obligations proliferated and those close to them grew older. What if the worst happened and there was a funeral—would he be able to go to Nagasaki with her?

Outside, he grabbed a taxi and gave the name of the hospital. The driver, a woman in her fifties, simply said, "I'm sorry, I don't know that part of town at all."

"It's Akabanebashi."

"Hmm. Is that in Kita Ward?"

"No, Akabanebashi in Minato Ward."

149

"I haven't been on the job very long. I usually drive around the Koganei area. I'm sorry, I just don't know my way around there."

"Use the GPS to find it. I'm in a hurry."

"Well, I . . . In that case, sir, I think the best thing would be to take another taxi. I'm sorry." She had started driving, but now she pulled over to the curb and opened the automatic passenger door. Makino started to object, but to avoid wasting time he grudgingly stepped out. The driver apologized weakly again.

Makino waved wildly to stop another taxi. This time, there was no problem. The driver said, "I saw you just get out of that other taxi. Something wrong?" Makino gave a vague answer and looked restlessly out the window.

Would he make it in time? When they'd performed together recently, just a couple of months ago, Sofue had seemed fine. His son, Hibiki, was a violinist based in Canada. Sofue's wife had died two years ago; perhaps lingering fatigue from caring for her had hastened this collapse. Kana had married shortly before her mother's death and now had two children, a toddler and an infant. Sofue's survival was the most crucial matter, but if he did survive, the burden of caregiving would fall most heavily on Kana's shoulders, Makino thought, his mind jumping ahead.

Kana had considered a career as a flutist but abandoned it in favor of teaching music at a junior high school. Sofue had always had high hopes for Hibiki, but Makino sensed that Kana was his favorite. His heart went out to her now, worrying alone in the hospital about what would become of her father. He vowed to do whatever he could for her.

Before they arrived at the hospital, fat drops of rain began to splat against the windshield and then came a sudden downpour. Makino jumped out of the taxi and ran through the automatic doors of the hospital entrance. He reached for his cellphone to call Kana, and it wasn't there.

150

He'd had it in his hand when he left home—or had he? Could he have left it in the taxi? He was wearing loose trousers, so perhaps the phone had slid out of his pocket.

Now he had no way to get in touch with Yoko. But there was still time until he had to be in Shinjuku. For now, he asked for directions at the front desk and hurried to join Kana.

She was sitting alone on a bench waiting for Sofue to come out of surgery. When she saw Makino, she stood up, and tears glistened in her eyes. She looked worn out.

Makino laid a consoling hand on her shoulder. "I'm so sorry," he said.

Since losing his wife, Sofue had been living alone in his house, which also functioned as his private guitar school; he had often tutored Makino there. Kana came by once or twice a week with her children to look in on him. Today she had found him collapsed, having suffered a stroke, and apparently an alarming amount of time had already gone by. There was no telling if the surgery would be successful or not, and even if it was, the doctor had already explained that some paralysis was likely.

Kana had contacted her brother and urged him to fly to Japan as soon as possible, but she hadn't notified anyone else yet. After running tests, they had just started to operate. The surgery was expected to take three hours.

Makino looked at his watch. He realized it wasn't going to be possible to see Yoko tonight. Remembering what had happened with Jalila last time, she would surely understand. Plans sometimes went awry. This was, after all, a matter of life and death. She would be tired after the delay and the long flight, so he hated to make her look for lodging in Shinjuku at nine at night. He wanted her to stay at his place, but how could he arrange it? He must have left his cellphone in the first taxi. He did remember having it in his hand when he left the apartment. He couldn't remember the name of the taxi company. When he got out of the taxi, he thought he had heard the driver say something apologetic—maybe she had actually been telling him he had forgotten his cellphone. Then maybe she had turned it in to the lost and found at the police department . . .

Makino regretted that at the very moment his teacher's life hung in the balance, his thoughts were elsewhere, so that he could neither pray for Sofue's recovery nor indulge in fond memories. Assuming Yoko's flight had gone smoothly, she would be arriving at Narita about now.

"Satoshi, I'm so sorry. You must have had plans for this evening."

"It's fine," he said. "I just need to make a phone call. Be right back." He went off in search of a public telephone.

He purchased a prepaid telephone card and picked up the green receiver, its heaviness bringing back memories of the old days when such phones were all they had. Who should he call? He thought of dialing information, but since he didn't know the name of the taxi company, what good would that do? He could call a friend, but he was so used to using his cellphone, he didn't know anybody's number by heart.

Then he remembered Mitani mentioning the mnemonic device she used to remember her phone number. It consisted of combining two dates from history; the number popped into his head and he dialed it.

When Mitani answered, it sounded like she was having dinner in some lively restaurant.

"What's the matter?" she asked.

"Sorry to bother you during your holiday. The thing is, I left my cellphone in a taxi, and I don't know which company. Yours was the only number I could remember."

"Did you try calling your own number?"

"Oh. Right."

"Isn't that the first thing you're supposed to do? Are you all right, boss?" She laughed teasingly.

"Actually, Sofue had a stroke. He's in Akabanebashi Hospital. It doesn't look good."

Mitani was at first speechless. Then she quickly said, "I'll be right there. I'll do anything I can to help. I'll stay in a corner somewhere, out of Kana's way."

Makino hadn't meant for her to come, but the offer was comforting. If the worst did happen, she could help Kana notify people and so on.

"That would be really helpful. I'm so sorry to bother you."

"It's my job. Shall I go pick up your phone from the taxi company?"

"That would be wonderful. I'll call and find out where it is and let you know."

"Okay. Please let me do anything I can. Don't hesitate to call on me. I'll feel better knowing I can help."

ℵ

Mitani had been dining out in Shinjuku with four female friends, but as soon as Makino called back to report that the Koganei taxi company had his phone, she ran to catch a train. Lately Makino had been looking blue, and he'd been curt with her, although he had become more cheerful since starting to work with Noda at Globe. Apparently, he was starting to see a way forward with his musical career. Mitani strongly believed that his true happiness lay in his music and nowhere else.

She was able to retrieve his cellphone right away. She knew his PIN and was able to verify that the phone was his. In so doing, she saw several messages from Yoko.

When she went back outside, the rain was falling even harder. The ground at her feet was white with spray. While she headed back to Shinjuku on the Chuo Line, swaying in the humid train as passengers took care to keep their wet umbrellas from touching each other, she thought about Makino's plan to spend his vacation with Yoko, starting today. In anguish over his possibly dying teacher, Makino had turned to her, Sanae Mitani, and in her eagerness to be of assistance, she had, to her friends' amazement—"You get summoned to work on a night like this?"—left the restaurant after the pasta course, rushed out into the pouring rain, and jumped on a train. All so he could be with his precious Yoko tonight.

What am I doing with my life? she asked herself. She wanted nothing more than to devote herself to Makino, pure and simple, but he showed no sign of returning her love. And what she was doing now would make that forever impossible.

Yoko had written that she had landed and was aboard the Narita Express. Just as Mitani was thinking about this, Makino's cellphone vibrated in her hand. She didn't check it right away. The train pulled into Shinjuku Station and spewed its passengers, herself included, onto the platform. Borne along in the crowd, she got on the escalator and then opened the message, feeling rather faint.

To her surprise, Yoko said she was right there in Shinjuku Station, waiting for Makino at the south gate. She sounded concerned that there had been no word from him.

It occurred to Mitani that, since leaving the taxi company, she had not once opened her mouth, though this was only natural since she was alone. As she walked along, she felt the heat of the breath coming through her nostrils, and several times pressed a handkerchief to her sweating temples and neck.

Her legs carried her to the south exit. When she came to the ticket gates, there by the Koshu-kaido exit gate, where construction had been going on for years, stood Yoko, looking anxiously up at the threatening sky. She had a large red Globe-Trotter suitcase with leather straps around it. Never before had Mitani seen anyone so naturally suited to carrying such flashy luggage—she might as well have had a greyhound on a leash. She had often wondered if Yoko, whom she had met only once before, was really as much of a beauty as Makino seemed to think.

Mitani would search through her memories, head tilted to one side, considering. Now as Yoko lingered near a large pillar in the Shinjuku throng, something magnetic about her drew people's eyes. Mitani had spotted her instantly, before she had time to wonder if she should even try.

Yoko's love for Makino had made her more beautiful, Mitani sensed, and she was all the more beautiful right now because she was about to see him. Fierce jealousy shook Mitani. She roamed aimlessly by the ticket gates amid the never-ending throng, and several times nearly collided with someone, causing the other person to turn and look back at her as if to say, "Watch where you're going, lady!" She was nervous and irritated. The longer she hung around, the greater the danger that Yoko would see her.

She had never before had as a rival in love a woman nearly ten years older than herself. She was ashamed of herself, thirty years old and acting like a child. Yoko was a perfect match for Makino; the thought was a constant torment, and never had she felt it as intensely as now. Yoko was bright and shining, blessed in every possible way, the star of her own life. She was now cut off from Makino, and Sanae Mitani, a supporting actor in Makino's life, would make their reunion possible by returning his cellphone. That was truly an important role, one that no one but she could take on.

Mitani felt wretched. In a cruel irony, she had taken this role upon herself. Makino had let her know the PIN to his cellphone, never imagining how much it would hurt her to find messages from Yoko on it. He had trusted her.

Getting on the escalator for the Oedo Line, Mitani had only one thought in mind: she didn't want Makino to see Yoko. The thought took strong hold of her, forcing on her the melancholy question of who she really was. On the platform, she sat on a bench and looked at the messages from Yoko as trains incessantly came and went. The sound of passengers' voices above the din made her loneliness all the more acute.

155

She was driven to a peculiar kind of daring, like a boy who sets fire to his house because he doesn't want to go to school. All that mattered was preventing Makino and Yoko from getting together. What message from Makino would be enough to discourage Yoko from ever seeing him again? She focused on that one thought. The problem was not the two of them, but the love they shared. Slowly she lifted her face and told herself that one thing was true: ever since he had met Yoko, Makino's music had gone perilously downhill. She frowned.

She searched for "To Yoko" in his Sent folder to find out how he usually addressed messages to her and then wrote without pausing. She could always worry later about whether she should send it.

Sorry to be late contacting you. And I have to apologize for something else. I have agonized over the decision till the last minute, but I'm afraid I cannot see you. I have been contemplating this for months—it's my own problem as a musician. You've done nothing wrong. But ever since I started seeing you, I've been unable to concentrate on my music. I've tried hard to get over this and haven't mentioned anything to you. But if I continue to gloss over the problem, I would be acting in bad faith. It would be unfair to both of us.

I have always loved you, but I have no confidence that I always will. And so I think it's better to call a halt to things while there is still time. If I see you, I will only lie to myself again and deceive you.

I look forward to the day when we can meet again as friends. But I need time to sort things out. I'm so glad that I had the chance to meet you. Thank you. Goodbye.

Satoshi

As she wrote, Mitani had the strange sensation that her cheeks were at once flushed and cold.

Without sending the message, she got on the next train and headed for Akabanebashi Station. What she'd written was precisely what she wanted Makino to say to Yoko. It was what she thought, and it was also her heart's desire. She had used clichéd phrases that Yoko could not possibly fail to understand.

She sat down in the train and reread the message. She had the illusion that she hadn't written it herself. She could hear Makino's voice through the words on the screen. There were emails that he and Yoko had exchanged, there was work-related email from Mitani herself, and there was this one, like an email he had written and never sent.

For some reason Mitani became extremely sleepy and closed her eyes. She would erase the message before arriving at the station. Reality was reality, and she would accept it. But no one could blame her if, for a brief moment or two, she fantasized that Makino had actually written this to Yoko. After that, guilt stricken, she would resist the impulse, pretend nothing had ever happened, and return the cellphone safely to Makino. Then her own love for him would also be as if it had never happened.

Or what if she sent it? Yoko would disappear from Makino's world. Vanish, poof, never to be seen again. All she had to do was press the Send button with her thumb and it would be so. Just like magic. Anyone in her place would do the same, wouldn't they?

She rubbed her wet shoes together and let out a pained sigh. The light beyond her eyelids was too bright. She recalled Yoko's forlorn appearance in the station and pitied her. She felt a pang, but in time she would surely forget.

Until now Mitani had lived a far more honest life than most. Everyone, no matter who they were, committed sins in the course of their life, and from that perspective, she still had a long way to go before she had used up her allotment. She opened her eyes and regarded the other passengers, many of them evidently tipsy after drinking with their evening meal. They all surely had a dark secret or two.

No one would know. All she had to do was forget about it right away. It was like pricking your finger on a needle—something to fear, but only a moment of pain. She opened the cellphone. With a trembling finger, she pressed Send and then closed her eyes again.

Seconds later she realized she had done something monstrous and hastily looked down at the phone. The screen already bore the words "This message has been sent." She imagined Yoko, still standing in the station, reacting to the signal on her phone at this moment. Naturally she would find it odd and try to contact Makino by email or phone. What Mitani had done would be exposed. Why had she done such a stupid thing? Full of regret, she tried to find a way to recall the email, but there was nothing she could do.

She went ashen from despair and frustration. Makino would never, ever forgive her. He would be enraged, his contempt for her intense. He would banish *her*, not Yoko, from his life, not want anything to do with her ever again! What should she do? Go back to Shinjuku and find Yoko, confess to her and apologize, and beg her never to say anything to Makino. Yoko would be sweetly understanding and forgive her.

Impossible.

Maybe she should take the phone and disappear with it?

But Makino was waiting for her. For *her*, Mitani. More than anyone else in the world, he was waiting for her to come to him. Once Yoko read that message, surely she wouldn't try to contact him again, would she?

The rain showed no sign of stopping. Mitani got off at Akabanebashi Station, opened her umbrella, and started walking. The raindrops beat on her umbrella like drumsticks. Suddenly, she pulled out Makino's cellphone and erased the message to Yoko from his Sent folder. Because she was walking with her eyes on the screen, she stepped right into a huge puddle, getting soaked to the ankles. She stumbled, and in that instant—not on purpose, she would swear to it—she lost her grip on the phone and dropped it in the water.

"Oh no!"

After some hesitation, she plunged her hand into the muddy water. When she retrieved the phone, the screen had gone blank. She wiped it off, but no matter which buttons she pressed, it was dead.

※

By the time Makino finally had his cellphone again, it was after nine thirty. Sofue was still in surgery.

Mitani was soaked through and looked exhausted. Once in front of him, she burst into tears. "What's wrong?" he asked in surprise. She told him only that she had dropped his cellphone in a puddle. When she handed it to him, he pressed the On button and then a random succession of others, but there was no response.

"I'm sorry." She was shivering. Makino was upset, but he couldn't get angry. In fact, his conscience pricked him. Lately he'd been so hard on her that now, when she made a blunder, she shook in fear.

"It's all right," he said. "I'm the one who lost it anyway, and just getting it back is . . . thank you."

He felt that there was something odd about her, but perhaps that was only natural; she had, after all, been forced to go out in a rainstorm to get his stupid cellphone. She might well be coming down with a cold, standing there wet and shivering.

The problem was how to get in touch with Yoko. She must be worn out after her long journey; what would she be doing now? She was too quick witted to stand around forever in the station. He was beside himself with worry, but with Sofue's fate undecided, he couldn't very well go home to contact Yoko from his computer.

Suddenly he remembered that Yoko and Mitani had exchanged business cards at their first meeting. "Do you happen to know how to get in touch with Yoko Komine?"

Mitani's eyes widened. She should have said she didn't know, but the question was so unexpected that the words popped out of her mouth: "I think I have her email address."

"Oh, you do? That's great. I absolutely must contact her. Can I use your phone?"

After a moment's pause, she said, "Yes, of course." Consumed with dread, she called up Yoko's email address and handed him the phone.

"I was supposed to meet her today."

He wrote to tell Yoko that Sofue had collapsed, and he was unable to leave, so she should either stay in a hotel tonight or come to the hospital so he could give her a key to his place. He couldn't possibly ask Mitani to take it to her after all she had already done. He wrote that as soon as he was able, he would write again, and if she would be awake till late, he could go directly to see her when he left the hospital. He apologized repeatedly and then wrote his name. He felt a little awkward pressing the Send button on someone else's phone, so he handed it to Mitani. "Would you send this to her?"

Mitani saw the words without really meaning to and felt her heart would break. She pretended to press the Send button and, holding the device out of Makino's sight, erased the message instead. Then she looked up and nodded, smiling stiffly.

Relieved, Makino said, "Thanks. Would you let me know if she writes back?" He let out a long breath. Then, his expression clouding again, he turned back to Kana, who was sitting motionless on a bench.

Yoko found an empty hotel room in West Shinjuku, and while she was checking in, she felt that she was somewhere entirely different. A high-pitched tone like the one used in hearing tests kept sounding faintly, and everything she saw and touched felt blocked off from her. All she could think was that she needed to get to her room quickly. This sort of numbness to reality was a disturbing sign, which she had experienced several times over the past few months.

She prayed that nothing would happen. She pursed her lips and let out her breath, determined to keep her composure. Her right hand was damp with sweat. She made a fist and rubbed her index finger with her thumb but then stopped, laid her hand on her left arm, which was on the counter, and with downcast eyes tapped her watch repeatedly.

"Sorry to keep you waiting, ma'am. The bellboy will show you to your room."

In the sunken lobby with its gigantic chandelier, many different languages were being spoken all around her. The memory came back to her of finally returning to the Murjana Hotel after reporting on the hopeless anguish at the site of a gun battle.

This was different. It wasn't Baghdad, where bullets could come flying at you from any direction. She was in Tokyo. Safe in Tokyo. Her body's default was always set on high alert now, like an oversensitive sensor, so even small, inconsequential things made her nervous. That was all.

No need to be on her guard here. She'd come back from Baghdad alive and safe.

Back then, the best release from stress had been to go to her room, lock the door, rinse the sand from her body in the shower, and then relax and listen to Makino's Bach CD. She had worried that she might have a panic attack on the flight from Paris, but she hoped that once she was in Tokyo, she could put all that behind her. While fearing that an emotional breakdown might mean the end of their romance, at the same time, she had longed for the comfort and peace of his love.

161

But that email from him had plunged her into a crisis of unforeseen terror. "I have always loved you, but I have no confidence that I always will." The words ran through her mind again and again.

She followed the bellboy into the glass-paned elevator, and as it rose to the twenty-second floor, she looked down on the lobby through the gigantic chandelier. They were moving away from the ground. The glass-paned elevator soon dimmed, and they were wrapped in the rainy night view of the city.

Light flashed before her eyes. Then instantly, with a cracking sound like that of a huge tree splitting in two, she felt the impact of a thunderbolt so powerful that it seemed to announce a catastrophe. The elevator jerked to a sudden stop. She shuddered. Trapped inside, she heard cries from various floors of people running around trying to escape. Others whom she had spoken to only moments before were now lying sprawled on the lobby's marble floor, their blood-spattered bodies covered in dust. The gigantic chandelier was smashed into a thousand pieces, crystal shards everywhere. That's what would have happened to her. Just one more question would have done it. And oh, the eyes of the terrorist watching her board the elevator . . .

Yoko couldn't remember how she got to her room. She felt faint, as if she had anemia, and must have either fallen or crouched down.

The bellboy called a physician, who examined her and prescribed medication. She took the pill, thanked him, and asked to be left alone. It was just after ten thirty. Three thirty in the afternoon, Paris time. When Makino came to Paris, they had first talked about jet lag—how much more difficult it was traveling from Paris to Tokyo than the other way around. If she had seen him tonight, they probably would have begun their conversation there.

When she felt a little better, she wanted to get in touch with him. But what should she say? He had put all there was to say about his change of heart into that email. He was going through a hard time with his music, just as Korenaga had said. Yoko had been worried all along, uncertain whether she was a good influence on him or not.

The email hadn't sounded like his ordinary self. But then, how well did she really know him? "I will only lie to myself again and deceive you." Those words had hurt her the most. The past can change, he had once said. Well, it certainly could. That smile of his while they talked together so happily—had that been an act?

No. She swiftly denied the possibility. And yet tonight's email was now casting a dark shadow over every moment of her memories with him.

Why did she feel like blaming him now? Precisely because this had happened *now*. He had waited till now, when the vague understanding that they would marry needed to be solidified into a promise. He had waited until the last possible minute to choose a different course. If he had told her this before she left Paris, would she have gone along with his decision and meekly given up her trip to Japan? No, she would have come anyway. She would have wanted at least to talk to him one more time.

She couldn't help considering the blow she had dealt Richard. He had been impatient to see her after she'd ended things, had flown directly from New York. Should she take a similar approach with Makino? No, because she knew better than anyone how ineffectual it would be.

She loved Makino. Sometimes a wave of love swept over her so forcefully that it hurt, but at the same time she genuinely *liked* him. When they were chatting face-to-face, just having an ordinary conversation, she often experienced moments where she felt *this* was life's sweetest pleasure. It felt miraculous, mysterious. The world was a livelier and more colorful place when he shared his experiences with her in words than when she experienced it directly herself. She had come to understand his slightly offbeat sensibility, to appreciate it and at times to be amused by it: "There you go again." At such times she felt the age

163

difference between them—though he was a mere two years younger. And above all, she respected and admired him as a musician.

Shouldn't she try to understand him now? Try to understand the decision he had worked his way to after much thought, letting it drag on with the worst possible timing. The conclusion he felt he had to share with her, no matter how it hurt. His honest feeling that, after nine months of knowing her, he had decided she wasn't someone he wanted to spend the rest of his life with. If she could believe that this was the best for him, then simply out of love for him, could she not give up her love?

Yoko was rather surprised that she was able to think this way. Was this another change related to her increasing age? Or was love different from what she had always thought it to be?

She was sad. But she was afraid to give herself over to bottomless, unthinking sadness. Tonight's flashback had been different; she hadn't so much remembered that earlier incident in Iraq as relived it, been swallowed whole by it. For a brief time, she had lost all sense of the here and now. Would that happen again? She was frightened.

Until now she had believed herself to be steadily recovering, but perhaps her health was actually getting worse. A year at the earliest, the doctor had said, before her symptoms were gone—but if she didn't do something, that year might stretch on without end. She had read about chronic PTSD and knew how harrowing it could be.

Even without Makino at her side, she must somehow remain strong while she was in Japan. Pull herself together, for her own sake. At least until she went to Nagasaki to be with her mother.

No more thinking tonight, Yoko told herself sternly. Makino might send a different kind of message in the morning. The chances didn't look good, but neither could she rule out the possibility. Until then, she would just lie down and wait quietly to return to normal.

She wanted music to pass the time, and after putting in her ear-buds, she searched among her albums. Looking for a piece unconnected to him, she finally came up with Anna Moffo singing Rachmaninoff's "Vocalise." The year before, when Moffo died, she had spent some time listening to recordings of the beautiful soprano voice.

Yes, this was a good choice. She could not have borne listening to vocalization that had words, but she didn't want purely instrumental music either—she wanted the closeness of a human voice.

The room lights off, she lay on the bed with her face turned toward the night view of Tokyo spreading to the west. The rain was letting up a little. Rain like this would never fall in Baghdad, she assured herself again. Baghdad nights were never this humid or this bright. This was Tokyo, a safe place.

The tremulous vibrato of the beautiful voice lit her whole being, like flickering candlelight. She was gradually coming back to herself. Why did this voice touch her heartstrings so? It was too charming to call truly sublime. From now on it wouldn't be Makino's music that gave her comfort. If she let her guard down, her thoughts would soon drift to memories of him.

She set the music on repeat, so that when the song finished it would start up again from the beginning. She wanted the song to go on more times than she could count, forever.

Her cellphone rang in the middle of the night, after two thirty. It was the short ringtone. Another email. At some point, the Rachmaninoff had stopped playing, leaving her to lie in the shallows of sleep. Unable to bring herself to reach for the phone immediately, she went into the bathroom to fill the tub with hot water, then turned to face her reflection in the mirror.

The lights were too bright. This was her first view of herself since she had fixed her makeup in the airport restroom, preparing to see him. It seemed ages ago that she had whispered to herself that her constant grin would make her look like a freak.

165

The email was from Makino. Suppressing the throbbing of her heart, Yoko went over to the sofa by the window and read it.

I'm finally home.

Did you read the note I sent you late in the evening? You didn't answer, so I worried.

I'm so sorry this had to happen the very day you arrived, though given the situation, I'm sure you'll understand . . . The rain was coming down something fierce, and difficulties at this end kept me from writing sooner. I'm worried about you.

The situation is just as I described before. It's not going to be easy, but I think somehow the crisis is over. The only thing to do is accept the reality of what's happened and do all I can from now on. I'm feeling my age. I've been remembering everything that's happened from the time I started playing the guitar till now.

Are you in a hotel? With the rain and everything, it must have been awful. I'm so sorry. Rest up, and when you feel up to it, will you call me?

I'll tell you more about tonight when we can talk. I'm going to turn in.

Satoshi

This email bore no resemblance to the tormented message she had read in Shinjuku Station. She thought of the way he always smiled when they were together, but that lightheartedness seemed miles removed from the way he sounded now. She was able to read calmly this time, perhaps because the medication had taken effect.

Had he been somewhere? "Somehow the crisis is over." Could he have been practicing? Perhaps this was the euphoria of a good practice session. In any case, he seemed to think it was all over between them. The reflective tone of this email was more upsetting to her than the first email had been.

He wasn't taking back anything, and he seemed anxious to know her reaction. Somewhere inside, she hadn't fully believed the first email, but his repeated message forced her to accept reality. Her eyes went back again and again to the line, "Given the situation, I'm sure you'll understand." If he said that to her face, she would undoubtedly nod. But she would protest: "What a cruel thing to say."

⋊⋉

The next day, toward noon, there had still been no word from Yoko. Worried, he sent her another short message, but as with the previous two, there was no response. The emails didn't bounce back, so she must have received them. He had replaced his broken cellphone first thing in the morning, but retrieving the data was apparently impossible and he still didn't know her telephone number. He tried to contact her using Skype, but again there was no response.

The operation had saved Sofue's life, but he remained unconscious. Kana had sent Makino home, assuring him that she would call right away if there was any change. She wrote once after that to let him know that all was well for the time being.

At first, Makino attributed Yoko's failure to answer his email to "roaming," whatever that was, or some other technical problem. But it was hard to believe that a journalist with abundant overseas experience couldn't have found a way around such a snafu by now. He wrote asking for her phone number, and again she didn't reply. Finally, he began to think she must be offended. He thought hard about what to do.

With no way to reach her while she was waiting for him in Shinjuku, he'd been distraught, but after explaining the situation using Mitani's phone, he had focused all his thoughts on Sofue's perilous condition. She knew how much Sofue meant to him. She couldn't possibly hold it against him if he broke a date with her while his old teacher hovered between life and death. Back in Paris, she'd explained why she couldn't come to his concert, and he had naturally thought she was right to give Jalila priority. Yes, he had stood her up at Shinjuku Station, but hadn't the email he sent via Mitani cleared that up for her?

Could there have been some special meaning for Yoko in meeting yesterday, rather than today? Or was she mixed up in some unthinkable trouble? An accident? Sudden illness? Some such awful possibility seemed more likely.

Yoko's email arrived just after he finished a late lunch, past two o'clock. Makino, who had been changing the strings on his guitar, frowned when he read it.

I'm sorry to write back so late.

It was all so sudden that I had trouble sorting out my emotions. I did get your emails. It's not as easy as you think for me to understand, but I do see what your situation is. I will spend the rest of the time in Nagasaki with my mother, just the two of us. I need some time to myself.

Yoko

She was going to go to Nagasaki by herself? He read the email over and over. Upset, he dashed off a reply.

Thanks for writing. It's so good to be in touch.

I'm sorry again about yesterday. I'll be home all day today, so I can see you anytime. Even under the circumstances, I'll go with you to Nagasaki. Let me know when and where to meet.

This time her response was instantaneous:

I don't think it's possible for you to come to Nagasaki under the circumstances.

I'm all right, so you needn't worry.

It was true that Sofue's condition could change at any time. It was like her to encourage him to stay with Sofue, but then why did it bother her so much that they couldn't meet yesterday? There was a chilliness in her tone that he had never felt before. Maybe she didn't *want* to see him. If he didn't go with her to Nagasaki, they had only two days together—today and the day of her return. Then why not write to him sooner?

I know I would be a little on edge if I did go to Nagasaki, but at least let's meet and talk about it. Where are you?

There was no response for a while, but it seemed to him the normal amount of time she took when she was thinking. The email she sent, however, left him reeling.

As a matter of fact, I'm already in Nagasaki.

Why? Your flight wasn't until tomorrow!

I'm sorry. I can't go on anymore.

Why?

But there was nothing more.

Even after going to Nagasaki, Yoko wavered. She hadn't made up her mind to never see Makino again—rather, she was considering when and how to see him. Saying that she had left for Nagasaki a day early had been a desperate lie. When he wrote that he wanted to see her, she had felt herself weakening, but as with his comment in the late-night email—"Given the situation, I'm sure you'll understand"—she was not at all confident that she could remain calm. She wanted to sympathize with him in his troubles, but she herself was in a precarious mental state and doubted that she could take on any more sorrow.

What did he really want? She couldn't grasp it. If he thought he was being considerate, well, that only showed how shallow he was. His attitude was insulting, even narcissistic. Until the day before, she had believed she was someone special to him. Now she realized it wasn't so much the content of his first email as the way it was written that had hurt her so much. She was increasingly sympathetic about his long and ongoing struggle. But the tone of that first email had been so vague and cheap, more suited to someone he saw as a mere diversion. Most women, given the curious excuse of "artistic suffering" for breaking a date, would be outraged and end the relationship in short order.

Couldn't he have broken it to her some other way? Why hadn't he used words that didn't have the sound of a form letter, words that wouldn't make anyone recoil? Hadn't they always shared special, intimate conversations? They each understood the other more deeply than anyone and had therefore needed each other, sought each other, loved each other—hadn't they? Or was that belief a mere dreamlike state, a mistaken assumption of the sort that all women who went out with him briefly experienced? Perhaps he, too, always shared that assumption only to wind up disillusioned time and again.

What if he intended to take back his first email, swear his devotion, and ask her to marry him? What then? It seemed hardly likely, but Yoko wasn't yet ready to give up all hope. Even if he did do that, however, she couldn't just heave a sigh of relief and accept his proposal as if nothing had happened.

Pride wasn't the only reason. They needed to have a proper discussion about the problems he was going through and what role she could play in his life. But in her current fragile state, where she seemed likely to fall apart at the slightest provocation, she didn't feel up to it. Above all, she wanted time. She wanted him to wait until she was ready to have that conversation.

At Haneda Airport, her heart leaped with faint hope every time a late passenger came aboard the plane. But at the same time, she felt anxious. When the plane taxied toward the runway with the seat beside her still empty, she was disappointed but told herself it was for the best.

Her mother drove to meet her at the airport. Yoko hadn't warned her ahead of time, so when she saw her emerge alone, she looked puzzled. "Where's the new boyfriend?"

Sensing people behind her, Yoko shook her head and murmured awkwardly, "It's complicated." Her cheeks were red.

Her mother studied her for a moment and then smiled a rueful smile mirroring Yoko's own. "Your life is turning out just as complicated as mine."

"Two of a kind, I guess," said Yoko lightly. Growing up in a "peculiar" single-parent family, she had at times been at odds with her mother, but in recent years had come to look on her as a trusted friend.

She had turned her cellphone off when she boarded the airplane. Now she got it out but left it off. If she was to have rest and recuperation, that would be best.

The house was slightly south of the city center, on a little rise above Glover Street. It was an old-fashioned Japanese-style house with a stone fence and a garden; inside, mementos of her mother's life in Europe were everywhere. The sight of the sieve she used to drain vegetables for salad reminded Yoko of their pleasant life in Geneva.

Her mother seemed well, but Yoko worried about her living alone, especially since her grandmother had died after slipping and falling here in the garden. The house had plenty of rooms, but she and Makino had planned to stay in a resort hotel in Iojima, thirty minutes away by car. Her mother had made the reservation, but since they would be charged a cancellation fee anyway, the two of them decided to spend one night there.

"I wish I had more time to be with you," said her mother, "but I've got a full schedule." This summer, she had volunteered to give intensive lessons in French and English to high school students giving talks as "peace ambassadors" at the United Nations European headquarters in Geneva. They had just returned a few days ago, and she was scheduled to attend a dinner reception for them. "You come too, Yoko. It'll take your mind off things."

Yoko marveled at the change in her mother, who for so long had rejected the idea of ever returning to Nagasaki—or to Japan, for that matter.

In the afternoon the sky clouded over. For the first time in thirty years, Yoko visited historic Glover Garden and Oura Church, Japan's oldest Christian church, before heading to the place where they would have dinner.

It was a small gathering, with fewer than ten people, including Yoko. She was moved to see how attached the children were to her mother, passing her bottles of Swiss white wine as they talked about their adventures overseas. They had been especially impressed by cheese fondue. At that point, Yoko joined in the conversation, describing her childhood years in Switzerland, of watching the Japanese anime *Heidi: A Girl of the Alps* on television and seeing Heidi toast cheese. The students looked at her blankly.

"Yoko," said her mother, "how old do you think these kids are? They were born in 1991."

Yoko's eyes widened. "Then they weren't even born yet!" She couldn't help smiling.

It amused her to hear the children praise her mother's foreign language ability as "real English" and "real French." To Yoko, who had attended high school in Switzerland and college in the UK and the US, and then spent years living in France, her mother's linguistic skills had what she might call "rustic charm"; and yet, in those languages, her mother had loved and been loved by two men, had twice experienced married life. If someone had said, "Isn't that enough?" she would have had to agree that it was. If her mother had spoken less English and been a little more retiring, Yoko herself probably would never have been born.

The only reason Yoko had ever heard her mother give for leaving Nagasaki was that she "got sick of the place." As her father saw it, her mother had hidden the fact of her exposure to the atom bomb out of fear, not just fear that she would face marriage discrimination but that she might never be able to love and be loved as a woman. Even with these high schoolers, she continually slipped in comments like, "Now, I never personally experienced the bombing, mind you . . ."

Life as a single mother in Europe must have had its trials, but not once had Yoko heard her mother say she wanted to go back to Japan. Still, during all her years of life abroad, she had never abandoned the Japanese language, and she had made sure that Yoko's own Japanese was in no way inferior to that of children growing up in Japan. When Yoko was a teenager struggling with ideographs, she had started to think that spending so much time trying to master them might be pointless for her future. Her classmates had asked, "What are you, a masochist?" as she went on taking Greek and Latin on top of Japanese.

When she came home from the dormitory for the first time in a while, her mother, sensing what was happening, had brought out a set of modern Japanese literary works and begun reading them with her. Her mother hadn't necessarily been fond of reading the novels herself, and many of the volumes were previously untouched, their pages stuck together. But from then on, she and Yoko had written back and forth, sharing their opinions of the books they read. Cardboard boxes full of that correspondence—written, of course, in Japanese—were still packed away in a closet somewhere.

Yoko was grateful for that experience. She felt a special affinity for the Japanese language now, and she was grateful that no matter what European café or other corner of the world she might find herself in, she could immerse herself in a private world of just the two of them, mother and daughter. She couldn't speak with her father in his native language, and if she had never learned to be at home with Japanese, she would have lost that opportunity with her mother as well. She didn't necessarily think that would have been a serious impediment to their love for each other, but she still strongly believed that her mother's native Japanese gave greater clues to understanding who she was than what the students called her "real French."

Yoko had thought she had some idea of her mother's complicated feelings toward her home country. But now, seeing her chatting with high school kids as a "slightly eccentric local lady," she realized that her mother's desire to return to Nagasaki had been unexpectedly strong. Her mother had long been a Nagasaki survivor, and now at last she was giving her life a fresh start there. That might be exactly why she was able to talk about the bomb with these young people better than she could with members of her own generation. Her time in Nagasaki had stopped when she was about their age, allowing her to forget the slight guilt she felt toward those who had moved on with their lives in the city.

When her mother went out, leaving her alone at home, Yoko gave herself over to sadness. She put a rattan chair out on the veranda and sipped iced barley tea, listening to the distant hoot of ships and feeling sentimental.

In the garden before her was the stone where her grandmother had fallen and hit her head. The "table" where she had played with her cousin as a child. The stone that had been a topic of conversation between Makino and her that first night, leading her to believe that he truly understood her.

"As if a hole had opened in one's heart." That Japanese expression describing emotional emptiness was dead on, she thought. Talking with Makino had always left a lingering warmth inside her, a sense that for a brief time she had been sunny and bright. When she talked with other people, she was never all smiles, the way she was with him. When she went over their conversations in her mind, she never found a single thing that wasn't exactly what she had wanted to say or hear. She had felt a special attachment to the person she became when she was with Makino, a feeling new to her. She felt she had learned how to live. With Makino she felt more comfortable than with anyone else in the world. Even sitting alone in a room, she would try to conjure his nearness so that she could be at perfect ease. Losing him meant losing that other Yoko Komine, someone who now would exist only in memory. The hole in her heart was filled with unceasing loneliness.

How much longer would it take for her to adjust to life outside Baghdad? To stop hearing thunderclaps as terrorist bombs and seeing menace in every stare, to stop being this absurd, foolish person she had become?

Mixed in with Yoko's despondency at being unable to see Makino was, she discovered, the rather shameful admission that she didn't *want* to see him. She didn't want him seeing her as she was now. She had always felt that he overestimated her; even if she couldn't live up to his exalted ideal, she wanted to appeal to him as a woman. The sense of inferiority brought on by ill health had never hit her as hard as now. The shame she felt was unjustified. If any friend of hers had ever become ill and confessed to such feelings, she would surely have been puzzled and offered ringing words of encouragement: "What do you mean? There's nothing to be ashamed of!" In that previous self, she now perceived the arrogant dazzle of one blessed with good health. She was not experiencing a strong, conscious resistance to or a rejection of his pity; it was simply that she didn't want him to see her losing control, panicking when a fit came on and making a spectacle of herself.

But did a relationship like that truly deserve the name of love? It seemed more likely that the two of them were still far from the goal of real love. How had her mother opened up to her father about having been a victim of the atom bomb? She tried to imagine it. Wouldn't she have been ashamed to admit to the man she loved that her body was "tainted" by exposure to heavy radiation? Yoko herself was perhaps no longer capable of bearing a child. Even if she did give birth, the child might have some abnormality. Try as she might to banish the dark fear, it rose continually in her mind.

Yoko had intended to wait until her physical condition improved and she had regained her equilibrium before seeing Makino again while she was still here. However, now that her peace of mind was returning during this tranquil interlude, she was slowly coming to think it might be better to end things with him altogether.

In the driver's seat on the way to the hotel in Iojima, her mother suddenly said, "Why not go back to Richard?"

Yoko looked at her mother, whose eyes were just visible behind Ray-Ban sunglasses. Unlike so many Japanese who had spent years abroad, she no longer wore heavy eyeliner.

"You didn't break up with him because you didn't like him anymore, did you?"

"I couldn't possibly go back to him, Mom, and I have no intention of doing so. It's over."

"Your Tadzio is gone too, isn't he? Why remain in Venice forever?"

Yoko looked dubiously at her mother's profile. "Did I tell you about that? About Death in Venice Syndrome?"

"I heard about it from your father."

"You're in touch with him?"

"He was worried about you, so he contacted me a little while ago."

"I had no idea. But that wasn't what he meant by Death in Venice Syndrome. He was talking about me being in Iraq. He was saying that doing something self-destructive is no way to regain a sense of oneself."

"And isn't that what's happened in your love life? You shot down a perfectly good chance at happiness—if that isn't self-destructive, I'd like to know what is."

Yoko appreciated her mother's ironic turn of speech, but at the moment, she couldn't come up with a snappy rejoinder.

She had left her cellphone turned off since arriving in Nagasaki. Now she was scared to turn it on again. Once she was back in Paris, settled in her usual life there, with Jalila able to come running from the room next door if anything happened, she could come to terms with her feelings and perhaps be able to send Makino an email. Surely that way, rather than talking to him directly, she would be able to get across exactly what was in her heart. Given her present state, there was no telling how long that would take. Still, rather than settling things by texting with her thumbs, she preferred to sit at a desk and write a deliberate, thoughtful message.

Whether she expected an answer or not, she wasn't sure. All she knew was that, to get on with her life, some such step was necessary. Any talk of seeing him again would have to come after that.

The day before she left Nagasaki, she and her mother stood in the kitchen making breakfast together and then took their time eating, seated across from each other at the table. The menu was simple: green salad, yogurt, and a baguette with ham.

Yoko's mother was lost in thought for a while and then suddenly said, in English, "I hate seeing you like this."

Yoko raised her head and looked at her mother.

Blushing, her mother went on. "I never told you, but when I was young, my health also wasn't very good. Right around your age. I went to the hospital, but they couldn't find anything wrong."

"Was it an aftereffect? Of the bombing, I mean."

Her mother's expression didn't change, as if she had known all along that Yoko had guessed the truth. "I don't know. I never learned the first thing about my health. I talked it over with your father just once, before we were married. I told him that I might not be able to give birth to a healthy child. And not only that, I myself might come down with a serious illness at any time. 'Do you still want to marry me?' I said. I couldn't bear to just say nothing."

"What did he say?" Yoko was echoing her mother's English. Why her mother had switched into that language, she didn't know; perhaps it happened naturally with thoughts of Solich. Or was it that she didn't want to talk in Japanese about her experience with the bomb?

"He said he didn't believe any such thing would happen, but that even if we did have a disabled child, he would love that child his whole life long, and if I got sick, that wouldn't change anything either—how could it?"

"Only none of that was true, unfortunately."

"No, he meant it. And he loves you very much."

"From a distance, yes. I'd rather he had been close by."

"Yoko—you've got it all wrong."

"Never mind. I don't want to get into it after all this time. I was just thinking that it was pretty crummy of him to run out on you after making a promise like that. Fortunately, I'm healthy, but if I'd gotten sick at some point along the way, would he have come back?"

"You mustn't blame him."

"You always say that, but you never tell me why you divorced him, so I'll never understand. I'm on your side. What did he do after leaving you, anyway? Those years in his life are a blank." She asked the question, remembering that Makino had once inquired about that gap in her father's life, but quickly thought better of it. She would soon be out the door; there wasn't time to get into it. To show that she didn't necessarily need an answer, she began clearing the table. Her father was living in Los Angeles now; the question should really have gone to him.

Her mother shook her head. "That's not what I want to talk about now." Her eyes reddened and her lips trembled a little as she said, now reverting to Japanese, "It means the world to me that you are well and strong. You know that, don't you?"

"I'm fine, Mom. I always have been."

"You just never know with this sort of thing, when it can strike."

Yoko was startled to hear her mother insinuating that her poor physical condition was somehow related to her mother's own exposure in infancy to atomic radiation. She herself had never given the idea a moment's thought—but then, her mother had not raised her to think of herself as a "second-generation atomic bomb survivor."

"I'm fine. I'm just tired now because I was in Iraq . . . and because I've had my heart broken."

"Take care of yourself. Whatever you do is up to you, but don't be overconfident. You're not getting any younger, and you do want to be a mother, don't you? In that case . . ."

Yoko shook her head, scoffing. "I know. Thanks, Mom. You take care of yourself too." She got up, went over to where her mother was sitting, and gave her a big hug. Her mother felt small to her. When she was a little girl, her mother had often hugged her this same way.

Yoko changed her plans and decided to stay one more night in Nagasaki. Having heard out her lively but aging mother, she felt she now had to get back to Paris to care for Jalila. She couldn't bear the thought of spending another night alone in Tokyo, where Makino was. She wanted to maintain the peace of mind she had found in Nagasaki, spend a little more time in her mother's company.

Until then, she wouldn't turn on her cellphone.

She had no interest in an ugly, drawn-out farewell. She was, in short, now able to accept the reality that it was over between them.

After several days with no word from Yoko and no way to contact her, Makino could no longer doubt the meaning of her silence. She had no intention of seeing him. He had been hoping she might reach out to him before her return flight to Paris, but as time grew shorter, he was forced to accept the firmness of her resolution.

With Sofue still unconscious, he couldn't help being on edge, but as the days passed with no change, that freak event had been absorbed into everyday life much the way a snake opens its jaws, swallows its food whole, and slowly digests it. The heaviness of the event slowed time to a crawl and weighed on him like a stone.

Rereading her last email, he sensed that she was drifting away from him. But why? Perhaps that night she had sent some reply to his message via Mitani's phone. He contacted Mitani and had her search her junk mail just to be sure, but she said she found nothing.

Sofue's stroke and Makino's failure to show up at the train station were probably unrelated to Yoko's change of heart. However much he apologized, she remained silent, as if shaking her head and repeating, "No, that's not it."

Makino recalled the time when she had given him a dirty look he would never forget. In a Paris restaurant, he had told her that if he ever heard that somewhere on this earth she had died, he would die too. She must already have had feelings for him then, yet she had rejected his impulsive statement with all her might, even looking at him with a tinge of contempt. Makino had loved her for that fierce individuality. And now he could only think that she was rejecting him, not for anything he had done but for who he was. After exchanging emails and conversing on Skype with him over the past nine months, and meeting in person only three times, she had concluded that he was not the man she wanted to marry.

Yet after talking to him in Paris just before her flight took off, how could she have done such an about-face in a single day? He was baffled. Had she meant to tell him something else on the telephone? Had removing the physical distance between Tokyo and Paris somehow given her the jitters? He tried being critical: *In that case, doesn't she owe me an explanation? We're both grown-ups here.* He felt he ought to be angry, but somehow he couldn't be.

He thought more than once about going to Nagasaki to see her. He didn't know where her mother lived, but if he went to the resort hotel where the two of them had planned to stay, he might be able to see her by emailing her from there. He didn't want to do anything that drastic—or rather, he didn't want Yoko to put him in the position of having to do something that drastic. Oddly, he had the painful feeling that going after her would not only make him into a pitiable figure but the fact that she'd made him go might also lower her ever so slightly in his estimation.

After weighing the pros and cons, he finally decided that, on the day she came back to Tokyo, he would go to Haneda Airport to see her. Though prepared to hear her say it was over between them, he wanted at least to talk to her one more time. He might ask her to continue seeing him on a different basis. It might be unmanly to beg, but he wanted desperately for their relationship not to be over; he wanted it to be on pause. A short pause, just until their lives had moved on sufficiently for them to meet calmly again.

In the airport arrival lobby, he held his breath, waiting for her to emerge, intending till the very last minute to tell her all that. He searched for her through the glass enclosing the baggage claim area, but finally the conveyor belt stopped moving and the last person came out, dragging his suitcase behind him, and there was still no sign of Yoko.

He had told her ahead of time that he would meet her plane, which meant she had deliberately avoided him. He worried that something might have happened to her, but he couldn't bear to see in that possibility a reason to hope. He decided that he wouldn't reach out to her again but just wait to hear. If no word came, he would simply have to learn to cope with his shattered emotions.

One afternoon about two weeks later, he received an email from Yoko. Unlike that "long, long email" she had sent him from Baghdad, this one was extremely brief. It said only that she had gone back to Richard and was now married.

7

The Acrobatics of Love

In the summer of 2009, Makino spent a week in Taiwan to serve as a judge in the Taipei International Guitar Competition. Seiichi Sofue had been scheduled to judge the newly inaugurated competition, but he was still undergoing rehabilitation after his stroke two years before, and so it fell naturally to Makino to replace him.

Makino's inclusion on the panel made news, as he'd previously declined to judge any contest, in Japan or abroad. Interviewed by a music magazine, he explained that this time, he couldn't say no, having been asked personally by Sofue. Still, people whispered that not only was his attitude softening with age, he was also strapped for money.

That he should be in financial difficulties was no surprise. After coming out with two albums in 2007, *Concierto de Aranjuez* and *What a Wonderful World: Beautiful American Songs*, he hadn't performed in public at all. The former album, a live recording of his acclaimed concert at Suntory Hall in the fall of 2006, won the Record Academy Award, and the title song of the latter was adopted for use in a whiskey commercial on television, attracting considerable attention. But he gave no promotional concerts and was no longer seen onstage in recitals, guest appearances, or joint performances.

He appeared intermittently on television and radio shows and didn't seem particularly indisposed. His face was a bit puffy, as if he had put on weight, and even when he laughed and told jokes, he didn't have the same animation and sparkle as before. Rumors circulated that he suffered from severe depression or had injured his hand and could no longer play, but it wasn't clear whether such talk had originated with people concerned about him or jealous of him.

The final round of the Taipei competition lasted a full day, from ten in the morning until seven thirty in the evening. After the results were announced and the prizes awarded, the top three winners, including the Finnish guitarist who took first place, joined the judges and others at a reception held in a restaurant that the contest sponsor proudly declared "the third best in Taipei." Fifteen people were seated at a long table. Beer was brought in and they drank a toast, but everyone was worn out.

The conversation turned to trends in free-choice pieces, particularly the selection by both teenage competitors of Rodrigo's fiendishly difficult Toccata. Makino commented that while undoubtedly educational standards had risen, another factor was probably the ready availability on YouTube of world-class performances that students could try to emulate.

Then, after touching lightly on the judging process, a German guitarist whom Makino had never met before declared that he had been impressed by the astuteness of his, Makino's, opinions. He told the winner, "Makino really pushed for you."

As the youngest of the five judges, Makino hadn't said all that much, but the two top finalists were so close that the panel had debated about which one should get the prize, and Makino's clear evaluation had largely influenced the outcome.

Makino shook his head at the German's praise and, more from awkward embarrassment than from modesty, sipped his shark fin soup and wiped his mouth with his napkin. Then, as if remembering something, he turned to talk to the winners, their faces still stiff from exhaustion and tension.

"This morning I had some time," he began, "so I took a little walk around the hotel. Along came a woman so gorgeous she took my breath away. She was like Scarlett Johansson and Lin Chi-ling put together, only twice as good looking."

"What? How could there be anyone that beautiful?" One of the young guitarists across from him laughed, wide eyed.

"I don't know, but she was. Must have been a model or an actress, no one ordinary, that's for sure. And after she passed by, there was the most wonderful fragrance in the air. Enough to make you swoon—as if her own natural fragrance was mixed in with it."

"Didn't you go after her?" asked one of the Spanish judges with a grin.

For some reason, this reasonable, teasing question caught Makino off guard. He started, but quickly recovered and continued.

"Well, you know how it is . . . Anyway, I went on, enveloped in that fragrance, and the funny thing is, as I kept walking, it didn't disappear. I turned around, but by then she was pretty far off. I wondered, if her smell is this strong outdoors, what would it be like to be in the same room with her? But I figured the fragrance of a woman so beautiful probably would always be welcome."

"True."

"And then I realized something strange."

"What was that?"

"When I quickened my pace, instead of tapering off, the smell only grew stronger, as if it were following me. I looked back at her, wondering what kind of perfume it could be, and then when I turned my eyes forward again, I saw that walking just ahead of me, there was a middle-aged man. Damned if it wasn't him all along! *He* was the source of the perfume."

Everyone had been listening intently. Now there was a ripple of laughter as they exchanged puzzled looks.

"He was a perfectly ordinary middle-aged guy, medium height and build with black hair, but bald on top. I sniffed the air again to be sure, and no doubt about it, it was him all right. The perfume was so appealing, and the contrast with his appearance so great, it was weird. How do you explain that?"

"Laundry soap, maybe?" said one of the Spaniards. "There are lots of perfumed detergents on the market now. The other day I sat next to someone like that on the airplane and nearly died. He said his wife did the laundry with it."

"Detergent! That makes sense. Anyway, I'd been breathing the smell in, thinking only of that gorgeous woman, so the sight of the guy's sweat-soaked shirt and flabby body gave me heartburn. I was in a hurry to go off somewhere and get a breath of fresh air, replenish the oxygen in my blood, so at the next light, I crossed the street just to get away from him!"

Everyone smiled politely and nodded.

All too aware of his unimposing record as a guitarist over the past two years, Makino had felt embarrassed and uncomfortable at the praise for his role in the judging. He'd told the silly story to deflect attention from himself and help the winners relax, but perhaps because his English wasn't up to the task, it hadn't gone over terribly well.

Just then, as if someone had been waiting for a break in the conversation, from behind he heard his name called: "Maki-chan!" He turned and saw a thin man wearing a light-blue striped shirt. It was Fumiaki Takechi, a fellow guitarist and old acquaintance.

"Hey there," he replied in Japanese, standing up with a smile. "How long has it been, two years? Did you just get here?"

"No, I was in the audience. Came straight from the airport. I had my luggage with me, so as soon as it was all over, I went to my hotel to check in."

"Thanks for coming on such short notice."

"Not at all. Thanks for inviting me. I don't get to perform overseas all that often, so I'm really looking forward to it. Not at all sure I can fill in for you, though."

"Everyone will be delighted. I'm in such a wretched state, what can I say . . ."

"How've you been doing? I was worried."

"Haven't played in a year and a half now. Haven't touched the guitar, not once."

"What?"

Takechi, always a serious type, flinched as if he'd been shown a nasty scar. Makino wasn't offended, but seeing the shock on his friend's face made him feel isolated, as if he'd been abandoned by the world. The thought occurred to him that some children get hurt easily because every little thing they do tends to evoke surprise in their friends.

Every guitarist knew just three days without playing could seriously affect a player's finger coordination. A gap of eighteen months might well be irrecoverable. Takechi wasn't alone; to one degree or another, the other guitarists he had encountered here in Taiwan had all shown similar concern.

"Have a seat," said Makino. "We've got a lot to talk about." He made room for Takechi at the table and asked the waiter to set a place for him. Then he poured him a beer. After they touched glasses, Takechi was the first to speak.

"Where's Mitani? Oops, I mean Mrs. Makino. It's going to take a while to get used to that. Maybe I should just call her Sanae?"

"Mitani is fine. She still uses that name at work. She sat this one out; there's work to do in Japan too."

"I can't believe she's your wife now, Maki-chan. But who else would be so perfect for you? It had to be her. Everyone says so."

Makino shrugged. "I'm as surprised as anybody, frankly. But you may be right. I owe her an awful lot. You should see how devoted she is to Sofue. Even granting that he's an important figure in my life, she knocks herself out caring for him."

"How is he?"

"Out of the hospital now, but there's still considerable paralysis."

"Can he play?"

"Oh, gosh no. He's in rehab."

"I'm so sorry."

"We tried to get him into a rehab facility, but everywhere you go, there's a waiting list. A therapist comes to the house a couple of times a week, and the rest of the time, Kana looks after him. She's got her hands full with two small children, so I go over as often as I can to help out."

"I heard you were looking after him, hardly leaving his side. Very impressive."

"Well, that's an exaggeration, but I do what I can. There's his school, for one thing. I took over giving lessons for a while. Everyone from little tots to a high school kid who wants to study abroad in France."

"And you with so much else to do."

"But then Kana's boy came down with hand, foot and mouth disease. Ever hear of it?"

"Nope."

"You get red spots on your hands and feet, as well as inside your mouth, and there's a fever. It's a kind of summer cold. Goes away in a week or so. But for some reason it spread through his nursery school in the winter, and since I was looking after him and his sister, I got it too. It's worse if you get it as an adult. Like chicken pox. My mouth was *full* of canker sores. I had a whole galaxy of them running down the back of my throat . . . Hurt like hell. I could hardly swallow."

"I can imagine. Did you lose weight?"

"Quite a bit. The trouble is, after a while, the skin on your hands and feet starts to peel off. See this hand? The skin is completely new. But the worst thing is, your fingernails come off."

"Good God."

"Mine would get loose at the bottom and then gradually loosen toward the top. They'd catch on things and hurt, so I clipped off the loose parts, and in the end the whole thing would just fall right off."

Takechi looked ready to jump out of his chair. "How long does it take for nails to grow back?"

"Took mine six months. I couldn't play at all."

"How scary. I'd better watch out too."

"You can't be too careful. It had me pretty down for a while, but all you can do is face up to it. Make a fresh start. I hadn't been too happy with the way I was playing anyhow."

"And now? Must be tough, getting back into it."

"Still haven't played once. I've asked other people to do the maintenance on my guitars, even. It's not how I ever thought things would go . . ."

Takechi was speechless. To cover up his consternation, he started in on his food, which was getting cold. Makino added ice to his glass of Shaoxing wine and glanced around the table, which was lively with conversation.

After a pause, Takechi looked at the nails on Makino's right hand, which looked well cared for, and asked solemnly, "So no more guitar?"

Makino shook his head. "Now and then I make up my mind and walk over to the guitar case, but all I can do is look at it. My hand just won't reach out."

"Oh . . . It won't be easy, but one day you'll play again."

Makino had been talking without emotion, but at this, his eyes blurred, and for a while he stared at the ice in his glass. Then he smiled wanly. "Sorry to spoil our get-together with a sob story."

"Not at all."

"I've got to do something. I keep telling myself that. I need to make a living, for one thing. I'm getting sick of making cheesy television appearances."

"Can't you teach?"

"How? I'd need to be able to play. Anyway, someone else is covering Sofue's students now. Kana feels responsible for my getting sick, and

190

I hate to see her that way. I don't blame her or her little boy for what happened, not one bit."

"It must have killed her to see the skin on your hands peel off, though, and your fingernails too."

"The one good thing was that it happened just *after* I finished the recording for *What a Wonderful World.*"

"You know, I really liked the way they promoted that album by running an online contest for people to record their own covers. Great idea! I thought I might participate anonymously, submit my version of one piece."

"They'd know it was you in a minute. The guy in charge at the recording company—a young fellow named Noda, know him?—he wanted to expand it more, but then I couldn't participate, and it all fell apart. Still, they managed to get the website up and running, using old video footage and whatnot." Makino sighed and looked up. "How are things with you? Seems like lately you haven't been sending me copies of your new CDs. What's up with that? Here I send you all mine!"

"Haven't made any to send. Mine never did sell, you know, and I don't think I'll be making any more. I suggested a new one to my agency, but they nixed the idea. Haven't got any concerts scheduled, either. That's why I was so glad for this chance. I figure probably a slew of people turned it down before my name ever came up, but still." He shook with laughter.

Makino was of course aware that times were tough in the music industry, but he'd had no idea that Takechi's career was so badly stalled.

"It's been especially rough since the Lehman shock last year," said Takechi.

"Oh?" Makino said vaguely.

"When you make your comeback, you'll be able to give concerts right away and put out CDs too! You're a lucky son of a gun, Maki-chan."

"I doubt it. Who knows if there'll even be a comeback?"

"A waste if there's not—that's my point of view."

Sensing a slight barb in Takechi's tone, Makino said only, "Who knows?" and couldn't think of how to go on.

Then, as platter after platter of food was brought to the table, inspiring wide-eyed cries of "Don't tell me there's *more*!" they joined in the general conversation in English.

As Makino got tipsier, the question someone had asked earlier, as he was telling the anecdote about the fragrance in the air, kept going through his head: "Didn't you go after her?" All of a sudden, he thought of Yoko. It had been two years. What might she be doing now?

Was there something more he could have done to hold on to her love? Every time such thoughts threatened to trip him up, he would shake his head and force himself to focus on the future. He had tried to get himself to hate her, and when he'd had a drink or two, he used to say negative things about her in a humorous way, telling the story of "a girl I used to date." But such efforts only made him miserable. Acquaintances who laughed at his story of the anonymous "girl" aroused secret enmity in him.

Had they really been dating? They'd only been together three times. What they had shared hardly deserved to be called love, and so in the end, he didn't have the heart to blame her. He tried not to think of her, hoping in time to forget. Why she had turned against him like that, he had no idea. That "Why?" still affected him after all this time, but he couldn't allow it to harm his marriage to Sanae. What mattered now was not that Yoko didn't love him, but that Sanae did.

He was frustrated by the unexpected halt to his performing career and saw no way out. Perhaps a comeback was beyond him now. That anxiety caused him no end of suffering, but the one and only solution— to pick up his guitar and play it—felt an eternity away. The memories of Yoko that had come back to him just now made his situation seem all the more unbearable.

Makino watched for a moment when Takechi wasn't engaged in conversation and then addressed him again in Japanese: "If you want, we could do something together. It'd be better for me to have a clear goal. I'll practice hard so I'm not dead weight."

At this unexpectedly serious, yet somehow weak invitation, Takechi swallowed a mouthful of fried rice and nodded immediately. "Yes, let's do it! I've hardly ever performed with you. If we teamed up, I'm sure the record company would agree to an album." He smiled without a trace of his earlier irony.

Makino thanked him. Looking into Takechi's friendly eyes, he thought, *What a nice guy he is.* "I can't guarantee it'll come to a recording deal, but I'll see what I can do. It won't be easy, I know. If you have any ideas, speak up, okay? I trust you."

)(

At a party in a Tribeca penthouse, Yoko left her unfinished, now room-temperature martini on the table and went over to the couch. Richard noticed when she got up but made no move to follow her.

She sat down on a streamlined silver sofa designed by Zaha Hadid to suggest the moon. So spacious and luxurious was the apartment overlooking the Hudson River that even that exorbitant piece of furniture attracted no attention. The DJ's music was raucous, and the abstract Christopher Wool painting on the wall stood out like a giant smear. The room was crowded with a gathering of the very rich.

In the dim light given off by the room's elegant fixtures, Yoko surreptitiously checked her watch. It was only a little past ten—just half an hour since she had last looked. She had finally managed to escape from the apartment owner, a real estate magnate in his midforties who went on and on about how he had purchased a Bugatti Veyron worth $2 million. Apparently, before you could buy such a car, you had to be investigated to prove you were deserving of ownership. Once you passed that hurdle, you were flown first class to the company's Alsatian "castle" for detailed discussions about available options. That was the gist of it— an interesting enough story if told in three minutes, unbearable when it dragged on for over half an hour without anyone else getting a word in. And as soon as that story finished, someone else would jump in to tell their own tedious tale. It happened over and over, like a chain reaction.

In the global financial crisis that had begun two years ago, stock prices had plummeted due to a succession of shocks: the September 2008 failure of Lehman Brothers, the subsequent AIG management crisis, then the rejection of the Emergency Economic Stabilization Act by the House of Representatives. For a time, there'd been talk of world-wide panic. Yet these financiers continued to prosper as if none of that had ever happened. Yoko had anticipated that the party would be this way, but the spectacle still made her ill.

Through political deals struck with an eye to the upcoming presidential election, the congressional act had been speedily amended and passed, resulting in a $700 billion bailout using public funds. That taxpayers had had to provide relief for the Wall Street ringleaders who precipitated the crisis sparked worldwide anger, but the culprits still got off scot-free.

The Dow had bottomed out in March at 6,547.05, and since then, stocks had risen dramatically. This week, the Dow had finally crossed the 10,000-point mark. To celebrate, they were holding a secret "witches' Sabbath," away from the disapproving eyes of the world.

Yoko looked idly out the window. The dark of night spread across the river as far as New Jersey, with the guests reflected on that backdrop. For some reason, she herself was among these people. Without a glass in her hand, she looked as if she did not belong; she regretted having left her drink behind.

"Why do men like to brag so much?"

Yoko turned around. A blonde woman in a red dress that accentuated her bosom stood holding two martini glasses. Yoko gratefully took the one held out to her and slid over to make room on the sofa. This was someone connected with Richard's work; he had introduced them a short time ago.

"About cars, second houses . . . and women."

"Surely not all men do." Yoko smiled. The woman's name was Helen, she recalled. She worked for a bank where Richard was an advisor and had just gone through her second divorce. Earlier, she had made everyone laugh by using the word "greedy," now being bandied about in the media, in an ironically self-referential way.

"Basically all of them. I've never met one who was any different. We girls have to pity them or we'll go crazy."

She might have been drunk; she was looking at Yoko with languid eyes exuding such sympathy that Yoko was taken aback. It felt almost as if Helen was making a pass at her. "Around someone who's as good looking as you and has a career besides," Yoko said tactfully, "men probably feel so inferior, they're desperate to make up for it somehow. I'll bet that's it."

She must be five or six years older than me, Yoko thought as she glanced at the slack skin on the back of Helen's hand. Her face, however, was taut, frozen nearly expressionless by cosmetic surgery and injections. As a college student living in New York, Yoko had never noticed such things, but now that she was older and associating with a certain social stratum, she was constantly surprised by the number of women around her who'd had plastic surgery. A fight against aging that was doomed to fail. The faces putting up all-out resistance did not seem to be faring all that well in their struggle; what must they think of *her* face, where the advance troops of aging were setting up camp so openly?

Helen was indeed good looking, but her cheeks and the corners of her eyes—places that conveyed emotional nuances—were so immobile that you couldn't help wondering if she meant any of what she said. Yoko felt as if her own expressions were becoming slowly boxed in by the corset-like face in front of her.

195

Richard was shooting nervous glances their way. Deep down, was he expecting her to undergo such maintenance surgery too?

"It's got nothing to do with me," said Helen. "That's how men are. They may not all brag about their Bugatti, but they find plenty of other things to brag about, depending on how much money they make, don't you think? Your husband sure brags about you."

Yoko shook her head, deflecting. She couldn't accept Helen's premise. In this environment, it might seem that way, but Yoko did not feel that she had ever been particularly subjected to men's bragging. Her father was not a boastful man, partly because he was taciturn by nature. She had been all ears after he won the Grand Prix at Cannes, but he'd had very little to say, acting almost as if the topic bored him. And what about her colleague Philip, back when she was working in Iraq? The work he did was invaluable, worth more than any amount he might receive in some higher-paying field, but as a fellow journalist, she had never felt he wore his accomplishments on his sleeve. Rather, he was imbued with a kind of chagrined modesty.

Was it because the people here were Americans? Yoko doubted it. She was now raising a one-year-old while teaching French at a language school and working at a gallery near her home in Chelsea, but of the men she encountered in those various settings, none struck her as show-offy in the least.

Then for the first time in a while, she thought of Satoshi Makino. What might he be doing now?

Someone blessed with such talent that it set him apart from others, that it made him stand out whether he liked it or not, longed to be ordinary; this much she had learned during their brief connection. Though far from being a genius herself, she did know what it was like to be unable to relate to others, so she could empathize. And she had always thoroughly enjoyed their conversations. He, too, was a man. Being able to hold up someone like him as a refutation of Helen's remarks flattered her pride.

At the same time, she realized that Makino remained present in her heart and mind, that she still missed him. It had already been two years. *Only two years,* whispered a voice. Memories of him flooded her mind, bringing such pain that she closed her eyes.

Helen seemed dissatisfied with Yoko's vague response. "Bragging is a small pleasure," she said. "When men get together with kindred spirits, if they can't indulge in some boasting, what's the point of living, really? Poor dears. Now, just because they've got money, the whole world thinks they're evil."

"I understand the human desire to brag sometimes, but is it really that rewarding to tell people you're riding around in a luxury car? Even if it is among friends." Yoko immediately worried she had gone too far. She had known she would get in trouble if she got started and had intended to keep quiet. But thoughts of Makino had led her to speak her mind, the way she used to do in Skype conversations with him. Being here was painful, but talking it over with him would have been fun.

"You people must know it was madness to securitize subprime mortgages that anyone could see were headed for delinquency," she continued. "Don't you feel the least bit guilty about getting bailed out with taxpayer money? While so many other people got thrown out on the streets, having lost their homes and jobs."

Helen snorted and finished her martini. "You're an idealist, aren't you, honey, not one of us. You dress the part and act like you're blending in, but you're still a journalist at heart. We took the freedom we were given and used it fully to achieve the lives we lead now. It takes smarts to survive in a competitive society. Sure, we feel sorry for the people forced out into the cold, but at least for a time, our subprime lending made it possible for them to live in houses nicer than they could otherwise have dreamed of. Of course, we wanted them to pay back the loans. That's what they *should* have done, since they're the ones who borrowed from us in the first place. Who's really at fault? It's the people who didn't pay what they owed. We're the victims."

"The banks took everyone for a ride—the borrowers and the people who bought high-risk, supposedly triple-A securities."

"They're all grown-ups who should have known better. Globalization is making the world a more and more complicated place. People have to do their homework. If someone is too lazy to do it, whose fault is that?"

Yoko knew perfectly well that she was goading Helen, but this spiteful remark didn't sit well with her. "Risks in the world we live in are becoming more and more complicated and invisible. At enormous speed. It's true—people with expert knowledge and those without it are in a very asymmetrical relationship. You and the people you work with are knowledgeable about finance because you've devoted time to acquiring that knowledge, and you have a monopoly on it, but are you as informed about genetically modified foods, global warming, and Mideast politics as you expect the average person to be about financial engineering? And even if you do happen to be super informed, a political theory premised on the idea that every member of society ought to be equally informed is doomed from the start, isn't it? If you were talking not in the abstract but face-to-face with an actual person, could you really condemn them for knowing nothing about collateralized debt obligations? Especially when they've been made so complicated and opaque?"

"Well, Yoko, that just shows how little you really understand. We don't set out to complicate the situation to deceive people. We spread the risk. But there are always going to be a number of unforeseeable factors. That's why loans are insured."

"Yes, in principle, but those who issue mortgages and those who sell them have both clearly crossed a line, wouldn't you say? For so many people to default just two months after starting to make payments only shows there was something fishy about the contracts they signed."

Helen laughed out loud as if she found this hilarious. "That's exactly what Richard has been working on, isn't it? The reason we have such complicated financial products and the reason the mortgage bonds are ranked triple-A is precisely because they're backed by strong economic theory. Are you criticizing Richard as an accomplice in this so-called fraud? Is he going against his conscience as an economist? You're feeding your child with money from the bank he advises, and you associate with people from there who are in the 'one percent.' How can I conclude that you alone are pure and uncorrupted? I'm sure it must feel virtuous to say things that are so true no one could possibly object, but when you stop and think about it, it's hard to tell which of us is more shameless. Shall we call it a draw?"

Helen spoke in the tone of an adult trying to educate a naive high school student. Her defiance made Yoko increasingly irate, but she had to admire the way Helen kept from getting emotional. She felt uncomfortable, her own integrity now called into question. And she had no defense for what Helen had said about Richard. This had been the most serious cause of their marital disagreements over the past year.

As if he'd caught the drift of their conversation, Richard looked pale as he came to get Yoko. "Having a good time? We should get going. We told Ken's babysitter we'd be back by eleven."

Yoko stood up and said goodbye to Helen, who saw them off with heavy-lidded eyes. Richard gave her a stiff smile. "You've got nothing to worry about," she told him. "We just had some girl talk, that's all."

He put his arm around Yoko's waist and guided her to the door.

In the short taxi ride home to Chelsea, Richard seemed ill at ease and wanted to know what she and Helen had been talking about.

"Nothing new," she said. "Nothing that would make you happy, either." Then, not wanting to sound mysterious, she added, "She was setting me straight about my misconceptions of the work you do." She detected a relieved look on his face that struck her as odd.

Having argued over the topic time and again, they had lately avoided rehashing it, but now he launched back in. "It's not easy for the average person to understand, but if you talk with people like her, your thinking will change. You'll trust me again, the way you used to. I know you're fair minded. People demonize anyone in the finance industry, but as a matter of fact, the markets are recovering. The problem was only temporary. Things are fluid in this world, so the picture isn't always going to be rosy. What's important is having a system in place to deal with problems when they arise so you can get back to normal."

"Do you really *like* seeing those people? Or do you do it because it's work, because you have to?"

"It's not that simple. You should know better than to ask such a thing. Sure, I don't agree with everything they say. They're buccaneers, and now and then they go off the rails. But fundamentally, they're whip smart, and that's a fact. Way out of my league. I've told you before that you don't have to have anything to do with them if you'd really rather not. It's not even like we socialize with them that often. Anyway, now we have Ken to think about. Isn't it important that our finances have been stable through all this turmoil? After all, I'm only an economist."

Yoko let out a small sigh and gazed at her husband with sad eyes. Then, as if her stare had finally exhausted his patience, he stomped his foot and looked away, annoyed.

That summer two years ago, after Makino had broken up with her by email and she'd stayed with her mother in Nagasaki, Yoko had flown back to Paris. She'd been surprised to be greeted at the airport by Richard and his sister, Claire. Her mother had contacted them, saying she was worried about Yoko and would they go to her?

The financial market was just starting to collapse, and Richard must have been swamped, but he had dropped everything to come pick her up. He greeted her exuberantly, almost as if she were the prodigal son and he the forgiving father. Even after Yoko later found out why they were there, she refrained from blaming her mother.

What happened at that airport encounter? Claire, not Richard, was the first to hug her, and the hug lasted a little too long to be an ordinary greeting. As it went on, Yoko's reserves melted into relief; she wanted only to go on being held. Her strength drained from her until it was all she could do to remain standing. The embrace with Richard that followed, their first in three and a half months, also went on so long that there could be no going back. She had intended to write to Makino again after arriving home in Paris, but then she reconsidered: maybe that wasn't a good idea after all. This was her chance to cut off all ties with him. And after the horrible blow she had dealt Richard, here he was reaching out to her with a generous heart. She took his hand and his heart. She wouldn't, mustn't, let go. She needed to forget what had happened, as if it had been a dream, and marry Richard.

Just as Richard said, it had been a simple case of cold feet, the sort of thing that often happens before marriage, and amounted to nothing in the end. When she looked back, she realized that her PTSD was at its worst during that same period. Vivid flashbacks like the one she had experienced in the elevator of the Shinjuku hotel gradually subsided, but healing did not come spontaneously. Richard's devotion made all the difference, and she was grateful.

When she was in Nagasaki, a number of messages from Makino had arrived while her cellphone was switched off, but to keep herself from backsliding, she erased them, unread. Such drastic action was due in part to her personality, but mostly it had to do with her psychological state. She sent him a single email informing him of her marriage, but there was no reply. Of course, nothing in her message had invited one.

She stopped listening to his music. She shut out not only him but classical guitar itself, and if guitar music happened to be playing, she turned a deaf ear. Such music might summon unpleasant memories of her time in Baghdad. If she listened to it, the sensor inside her, still not entirely disabled, might start setting off alarm bells again.

She moved to New York to be with Richard and also quit her job. Jalila weighed on her mind, but when Philip returned from Baghdad on leave, she talked it over with him, and he arranged for a friend of his to look after her for the time being. Jalila sincerely welcomed the news of Yoko's wedding and urged her to go to New York with an easy conscience. "There's always Skype," she reminded her.

It was hard to forget Makino, but Yoko blamed herself for that. Around the time she became pregnant, she had started thinking of him less and less. That memories of him had suddenly been revived today was a significant action on the part of her unconscious. The party marked a turning point in her marriage.

Since the beginning of spring, she had suspected that Richard was having an affair; she later learned that Helen was his lover. Her conversation with Helen at the party turned out to be their one and only private talk.

Richard found vast comfort, both physical and emotional, in Helen's arms, and his guilt did not detract from that comfort. The pangs of conscience were a surprising and indispensable potion enabling him to believe that reality was beyond his control. The sense of superiority he derived from engaging in secret wrongdoing acted as a corrective and made him humble. Patience generally goes along with calculation; he felt that he had been asked to endure much hardship, and so the guilt of surreptitiously breaking a common taboo had a bracing effect.

When a friend boasted to him about the tender pleasures of marital love, Richard grew depressed, realizing the paucity of what Yoko gave him. But when that same friend went on to say flatly that he had never contemplated cheating on his wife, the knowledge that he, Richard, was indulging in a kind of pleasure his friend knew nothing of brought him a solace accompanied by sweet torment. He still loved Yoko, but being with her somehow wounded his pride. He tried to act cheerful, but couldn't keep up the charade. Alone in his room he would pace irritably. The only times he felt the joys of family life were when he was with Ken, but at the same time he sometimes thought that the trouble in his marriage derived from Ken's too-soon arrival.

Richard hadn't been this way when they were first married. But his confidence waned, and the crux of it seemed to be that he was fixated on Yoko's "affair" during their engagement, a lapse that he had *all too generously* forgiven her for. She was definitely in his debt. He had poured all his passion into the competition with Makino, that rival for her affections who had popped up out of nowhere, and the headiness of victory had left him happily drained for a time. As the fever of that happiness abated, a sense of emptiness lingered and gradually intensified.

He and Yoko had known each other a long time, and as neither of them was young anymore, their married life from the first had lacked the sweetness that melted all troubles. She continued to suffer bouts of ill health, and he, while unsure what to do, stuck gamely by her side as she struggled with post-traumatic stress disorder.

Yoko was grateful, and she could not doubt his love.

Under the ministrations of a skilled ob-gyn, her visits to a popular women's clinic paid off, and with surprising ease, she was soon pregnant with Ken. No words could have described how much joy the pregnancy brought her, or how great her sense of renewal. Richard was thrilled, as were both his family and hers. Their beaming faces made her feel at once happy and slightly under pressure.

Now forty-one, Yoko assumed this was her last chance at mother-hood. She had severe morning sickness, and there was some risk of miscarriage, so marital relations were put on hold. Richard accepted this as a matter of course and made no complaint, but tended to prolong casual, everyday kisses and embraces with heavy passion. Childish ways of coping with sexual desire made him uncomfortable. On nights when sleep wouldn't come, he would hint at a substitute for intercourse, and Yoko would comply. Eventually, however, he grew ashamed and ceased making the requests.

In Richard's defense, never once did such ordinary discomforts associated with pregnancy cause him to feel dissatisfied with Yoko. But just as morning sickness plagued her, the situation wore on him. The trouble was the peculiar way in which his frustration emerged. During their engagement, whenever he worried that perhaps Yoko didn't love him, he would seek to banish his doubts through the intensity of their lovemaking. Then, around the time when Yoko's once-flat abdomen was finally round enough to notice, he suddenly asked, apropos of nothing, "Are you sure you aren't sorry you married me?"

He posed this question at a chic little pizzeria near their home in Chelsea, where they had gone at Yoko's request, once she was able to enjoy rich foods again. Unusually for him, Richard ate only two and a half slices of the house specialty, loaded with mushrooms.

"Why would you ask such a thing? I've never thought that!"

"You don't smile as much as you used to."

"No? Look at me. Don't you think I'm smiling now? Pregnancy isn't easy, you know. Try tying a weight around your stomach and you'll see what I mean. That's the only reason."

"You're not sorry you didn't marry the Japanese guitarist?"

"Really, why rehash old history? Is it because *you're* having regrets?"

"No."

"You put it down to cold feet, didn't you? I don't want to think about it now."

"I'm still jealous of him."

"There was never anything to be jealous of. As I've told you so many times—"

"Artists are a rotten bunch."

"Yes, they are."

"Not your father. He's different."

"No, he's a classic example." Laughing, she laid her hand over Richard's and held it tight. "I love you. I'm happy."

Yoko felt that she was in the midst of a light brighter than she had ever dared imagine for herself. She was sitting in a pizzeria in Chelsea, New York, across from her economist husband, who in three more months would come face-to-face with the child growing inside her. His face now bore an expression of bleak resignation like that of a character in a novel by Michel Houellebecq. But why? She remembered what her friend Korenaga had told her once about people with lead roles and supporting roles in life. Apparently, Mitani, the one who had come up with that view of life, had married Makino and was now continuing to be an "outstanding supporting actor" opposite him in the lead role.

Why?

Did he have a child by now? Did he sit and look into his wife's eyes like this?

When her maternity leave began, Yoko responded to the rising criticism of the financial industry by taking a good look for the first time at Richard's academic writings. Several points made her uneasy. Economic theory was not her area of expertise, and the complicated formulas filling the pages were unclear to her, but it bothered her that Richard was calculating the probability of individual housing loans being unrecoverable based on the rate of banks' bad real estate loans to companies, and making that the basis of the securitization risk. Reasons for indebtedness differed for individuals and corporations, and the circumstances leading to default had to be completely different as well; individuals were far likelier to become victims of lending scams. Now, uncollectible housing loans mixed in with top-grade credit were scattered all around the world like salmonella, causing food poisoning throughout the money market. She had other doubts as well.

When Yoko brought this up, Richard was as indignant as if she had snooped in his private emails. She had been hoping for a straight answer to her questions that would set her mind at ease, so his reaction was disconcerting. She said she was sorry if she had sounded rude, and rephrased the question, but even after Richard calmed down, his response was not to the point:

"I know what you're saying, but we have no data about nonbank private housing loans in default, so the question is moot."

They respected each other's work, but whereas topics in journalism could come up in ordinary conversation, Richard had hardly ever spoken to Yoko about the technical aspects of his job, and she had not inquired. The goodwill she felt toward her husband had almost nothing to do with his occupation. With Makino, it had been different; she had loved his music before she'd ever loved him.

Eventually, Richard explained to Yoko that the new financial commodity he was developing was a highly practical means of using a surplus in the money market to help economically disadvantaged people purchase homes. "Someone like your mother, say, a single mom doing her best to cope, deserves a home of her own where she can focus on raising her child, right? But no one lends someone like her money. They see her standing there with a baby in her arms, and they figure no way is she going to be able to pay them back. The solution is simple: take her out of the picture. Lump all such loans together, increase the interest to sweeten the deal, and then add on more secure loans for good measure. Offer it as a package, and investors will go for it. They can't *see* the single mother, so they feel no anxiety. It's ironic, but this is a new, scientific way for the rich and the poor to achieve mutual trust and work together to achieve happiness, based on mathematical probability. And it unites the poor in solidarity. It's a kind of alchemy that changes rich people's 'greed' to philanthropy. In my own way, I want to make the world a better place too, just like you. You call attention to injustice. I helped create a system to make the world a happy place. What a team we are!"

Yoko was moved, glimpsing as he spoke a new way of doing good through finance, a world about which she knew little. This wasn't something she had stumbled on while searching the internet but a plan that the man who loved her spoke of with passion as his own lifework. She didn't want to believe that it could be a bogus explanation, a way of clothing impurities in fine talk so they didn't show.

But the more she listened, the less likely it seemed to her that Richard could have been unaware of the disconnect between financial engineering in theory and practice. If he was, that would reflect poorly on him as an academic. But if he knew all along and was colluding with the industry, feigning ignorance, that was reprehensible. Then he would be willfully providing a mathematical camouflage to make it seem there was no disconnect. As his wife, how should she react to this reality? She felt conflicted. In the past, she had spoken up strongly against social injustice. Now that her husband was directly involved, how could she simply close her eyes to the problem, pretend it didn't exist?

Ken was born the day after the collapse of Lehman Brothers. Two weeks later, the Dow fell 777 points, the biggest one-day drop in its history.

Richard couldn't be present for the birth, but when he encountered the as-yet-nameless infant lying beside Yoko in the hospital bed, he stood transfixed, overcome by joy. As Yoko looked up, she was touched by the genuineness of the emotions on his tear-streaked face. They smiled at each other and embraced.

They named the baby Kendrick. Yoko called him Ken, picturing the Japanese ideogram for "healthy." As she saw Richard's attitude to fatherhood, she was struck anew by what a loving family he had grown up in. He shared the work of childcare, changing Ken's diapers, feeding him, and above all bathing him in the baby bath, a job he regarded as his own. He was deeply conscious of his duty to protect his family and strained to do so. He seemed determined to re-create the sort of family environment he himself had experienced as a child, and took an almost worshipful view of maternal love. That Yoko might be of a different opinion never crossed his mind. Convinced beyond all doubt that her childhood had been disadvantaged, he was warmly sympathetic.

Richard's oldest friends had often teased him for being a mama's boy, but his mother and his sister, Claire, were both sweet to her, giving her no cause for concern. That day when she returned from Japan, if Richard alone had come to the airport to meet her, she wouldn't have embraced him like that, she thought. Somewhere inside, she couldn't help being drawn to the kind of love that Claire demonstrated for her younger brother. And in the end, the image of family warmth that Richard himself projected had filled her with peace.

The party where Yoko met Helen had taken place a month after Ken's first birthday. From then until New Year's, when Richard confessed his adultery with Helen, Yoko felt more desolate than at any other time in her life. Jay-Z and Alicia Keys's "Empire State of Mind" was then at the top of the charts, and everywhere she went she heard the lines, "There's nothin' you can't do. Now you're in New York." Later, just the sound of that melody was enough to bring back that disconsolate loneliness. She had a knack for blending in, no matter where she lived, but now, in a way that was different from what she had experienced in Iraq, she was deeply aware of being an outsider. While she understood the faint pathos of the melody, frustration at her situation kept her from singing along.

In addition to her work at a language school and a nearby gallery, Yoko had just finished writing an article on Herta Müller, winner of the Nobel Prize in Literature. A friend from her journalist days had requested the piece, which was for a website aimed at book lovers. Afterward, she was surprised to receive a number of requests for similar articles. While happy to immerse herself in literature again, she was feeling energetic and ready to move on to more journalistic work. She needed something she could throw herself into with passion. Richard's reasons for going out struck her as suspect, but she pretended not to notice and took her failure to speak up as a sign of weakness.

Most of her attention was focused on Ken. He grew so fast that later, looking back, her memories were surprisingly vague. She had very few pictures of her own early childhood; in comparison, the first few years of Ken's life, which he would not remember, were documented in a variety of media. She was especially fond of a photo of him fresh from the bath, standing with a towel in his hand and looking like the sculpture of David. She sent it to her parents and shared it with friends as well. The innocent lines of his frame already showed clear signs of a masculine musculature and build. Often she would call him teasingly, in Japanese, "Mama's little David." As if he understood, every time she said that, he would laugh in childish glee.

For Ken's second New Year's Eve, Richard wanted to attend the countdown celebration in Times Square, but Yoko was against the idea, as a suspicious vehicle had just been found on the street there. Her main reason was that it was below freezing with snow on the ground, and she didn't want Ken to catch cold. She also confessed that the specter of car bomb terrorism still terrified her.

"Don't worry about it. You're fine." For the first time, Richard sounded impatient with her PTSD symptoms.

After spending an entire day of vacation in the house, he seemed to have suddenly run out of other topics, and so he started talking about his work, a subject he usually avoided with her. The Federal Housing Finance Agency was going to institute proceedings against a financial institution that he advised, and as a result, he was swamped with work. They had done nothing illegal, and the products had been fully explained. The situations that had arisen were unfortunate, but within the scope of his work as a scholar, he wanted Yoko to understand that he bore no responsibility.

Reserving judgment, she said only, "Are you okay with that?"

Richard suddenly blew up, less at her words than at what he saw in her eyes. They were not blaming him, but looking straight into him as if to penetrate his essence. Resentment triggered a hostility that quickly enveloped his other feelings for her, spreading beyond his control.

"What the hell's wrong with you! How can you talk that way, now that we've got Ken to raise, and we need to stick together more than ever before?"

"Of course I want to support you. Believe me, I do. But don't the life choices you make as Ken's father matter?"

"I'll say it one more time. I'm an academic. I have no way of knowing what goes on in the real world. I'm no journalist, either. I take a neutral position and offer objective theories, that's all."

"As long as you're getting paid for it, people won't see you as neutral."

"I'm caught in a tough situation, and instead of sticking up for me, you're making it worse. Good grief. When you came back from Iraq suffering from PTSD, I supported you all the way. I don't like to say this, but do you have any idea how nerve-racking it was for me, putting up with your unstable mental condition while trying to get my work done? I'm not asking you to thank me. I'm saying when two people love each other, that's how it should be. You're a wife and a mother. Do you have to act like a journalist in your own home?"

"I'm not putting you or your work down. But I would like to know how you see your ethical responsibility, as a scholar. Your responsibility for the outcome—is it zero? I know you care about Ken, but if you saw a child his age crying on TV because he'd lost his house, wouldn't you feel bad?"

"Of course I would. And that would be his *parents'* responsibility. You want me to go to prison because of my work? Would that make you feel better? If I have no future as a scholar, what happens to Ken? I'm a firm believer in self-help. People should lift themselves out of poverty. Now you'll say I'm too conservative, but this country was founded on the ideal of self-help. Not that I expect a foreigner like you to understand."

"It's Spencerism, historically speaking. Hardly new, and not unique to America, either."

"What?"

"Never mind. Go on."

"My family prides itself on being self-reliant. Capitalism is reaching the breaking point. When the waves get high, it's all about making sure you survive. Let me tell you this: in my life, nothing matters as much to me as my family. Sure, I feel sorry for people undergoing hardship. But what can I do? One person has almost no power. Did your going to Iraq solve anything?"

"That wasn't the same as doing nothing—however little it might have helped. It's the same with your work."

"But what if you hadn't gone? What if I hadn't done what I did? The result would be the same. In the end, somebody else would have done the same thing!"

"I disagree. Just as your work is important to you, mine is to me. You're questioning the meaning of how I've lived my life. In that context, I'm asking how you yourself feel. Are you content to just shrug off what happened?"

"Now you're being inconsistent. Are you worried about my feelings? Weren't you just accusing me of not fulfilling my social responsibility?"

"It's both. But I'm not accusing you of anything. I'm asking you to explain."

"Listen. You were doing the right thing, so after you came back from Iraq, I was there for you, wasn't I? All the more so because I love you. I want you to treat me the same way. We're family, so even if I did something wrong, I'd want you to stand by me to the bitter end."

"And I would. Of course. But that wouldn't be the same as approving of what you did, would it?"

"There's a coldness in you, Yoko. I've always felt it. You're cold. That's why I've been unsure whether you would be there for me if I were really in trouble. You're independent. Fine. It's probably got something to do with how you were brought up. You'd have been the same, *whomever* you married. That I can deal with, but for Ken's sake, I wish you'd be a mother who's always there, ready to embrace him in warm, forgiving love, rather than a coldhearted mother who's always in the right."

Yoko was unconvinced by Richard's arguments, but his final words cut her to the core. His emphasis on "*whomever* you married" was a clear reference to Makino. The effect on her was far greater than he could have anticipated.

Words from Makino's breakup email came back to her: "You've done nothing wrong." Words strangely in concert with Helen's sneer at her "idealism" and Richard's snide dig at her "independence." Makino had gone on, "But ever since meeting you, I've been unable to concentrate on my music." He, too, had found himself "really in trouble" and unable to trust her to stand by him in his distress. The nature of Richard's work might not be the only problem. She didn't think of herself as leading a selfish, sanctimonious life. But she couldn't refute her husband's assertion that she was too cold to know the happiness of loving and being loved.

One day during a February snowstorm, Richard looked at Yoko with deep seriousness and told her about his relationship with Helen. Looking at her as she took this in silently and without rancor, he added that he wanted a divorce.

ᕼ

Concerts by the new duo, Satoshi Makino and Fumiaki Takechi, were planned in eight places around the country, beginning in Saitama in spring 2010 and continuing through the summer. It was Takechi's first concert in some time, and his excitement was evident not only in his conversation but also in the blog that he updated as conscientiously as a diary.

Since that first discussion in Taipei, they'd had only seven months to prepare. Makino hadn't played for a year and a half, and so he felt he should proceed cautiously, taking a good year before making a comeback. After his marriage to Sanae, a young male staff member named Igarashi had taken charge of the Kinoshita Music office. The company president was also directly involved in Makino's comeback, and Noda from Globe was present at every meeting. After he was shown the schedule, Makino had strenuously objected to the shortness of the preparation time; he felt he was only being realistic, but it seemed that every time he opened his mouth, the word "can't" came out, until finally he got sick of hearing himself talk.

Today he started in again: "If I were a jazz guitarist, say, someone who ad-libbed onstage, it'd be different. But I'm from the world of classical music. I can't make adjustments while I'm playing. A figure skater having an off day can downgrade his performance from a triple axel to a double, but I can't do anything like that. You've got to understand."

The staff fell silent, unable to argue. Makino, too, was quiet, his lips pursed and his arms folded, but then to their utter surprise, he suddenly sighed. "Strike that. Let's do it. As planned."

For a while afterward, he continued to grumble, but even so, he seemed more like his old self, always joking around with the staff. Surely when he took the stage again, he would captivate the audience with another of his perfect performances. His joking seemed a good omen.

Eighteen months was a hiatus longer than Makino or any of the performers he knew had ever experienced.

Sofue, who was to be admitted to a nursing home at last, said he wanted to go see an art deco exhibition at the Teien Art Museum in the former residence of Prince Asaka. Makino decided to tell him about his plans while accompanying him there. Sofue had still not recovered his full powers of speech, and after viewing the exhibit, Makino did all the talking as they wandered through the spacious garden attached to the museum.

"When you see art deco in Paris, it's lavish and alluring—why the heck is it so unimpressive and dowdy over here? Today's exhibit wasn't bad, but even so . . . Do you suppose it's because the medium is wood?" Makino went on in his usual fashion while Sofue listened, nodding and grunting in agreement as he looked with keen appreciation at the trees just starting to turn autumn colors. Only his eyes expressed his feelings.

After strolling for some forty minutes, they reached a bench by the pond and sat down. For a while they silently took in the scenery. The sky was a clear blue. There was a slight chill in the air, but no wind; the pampas grass never stirred.

Makino talked about practicing the guitar again in preparation for his tour with Takechi. Sofue's expression softened. He said only, "Very good," nearly biting his lip in the process.

"I let my playing slide for so long, it's rough getting back into shape. I'm sure I played better than this when I first started studying with you! Back then I never would have guessed that anything like this lay in store for me." He laughed, but then glanced back at Sofue and was startled to find him in tears. The unparalyzed right half of his face twitched, while the left half remained expressionless.

Makino had heard from Kana more than once how distressed her father was that his former student no longer played. Not wanting to put Makino under any pressure, he had apparently given her strict instructions to say nothing. It bothered Sofue to no end that Makino was helping with his care, yet without his assistance, the burden would fall on his daughter, who also had a toddler and an infant to care for. Aware of his teacher's conflicted feelings, Makino had made light of the situation: "You have so many students nowadays, I've been jealous. I'm happy to monopolize you for a change."

Sanae, too, had pitched in, helping out not only with Sofue's care but with babysitting and grocery shopping. Such uncomplaining solicitude endeared her to Makino.

Sofue tucked in his chin and managed to exercise some control over the trembling of the right half of his face before reaching with his lame left hand for a handkerchief, which fell on the ground. Makino picked it up, brushed off the dirt and small leaves, and handed it back to him. Sofue took it in his right hand and only gripped it in his lap, making no attempt to wipe away his tears.

His posture was good and he looked hale and hearty; from a distance, he gave no sign of illness. Despite suffering inconveniences that were painful to see, not once had Sofue ever gotten emotional with him or Sanae, or even with his daughter. Makino realized with new clarity what a truly fine man his teacher was.

"Anyway," Makino went on, "compared with your rehabilitation, what I've done is nothing. During your surgery, I was prepared for the worst. But look at all the progress you've made. I really admire what you've accomplished."

Memories of the night Sofue had collapsed went through his mind—and memories of Yoko. He hadn't been wrong to remain at Sofue's side that night. Yoko had naturally understood, and they had gotten together the next day or the day after, and today she was here alongside him, pleasing Sofue with some eye-opening insight into the art deco exhibition—might not a world like that exist somewhere, a world where all that was true and his whole being was steeped in happiness? A world where they were together as a matter of course and the idea that they might have slipped by each other that night, never to meet again, was inconceivable. Somehow, he had gotten a raw deal and ended up in this dreary world instead. Makino stared at the tree branches and blue sky reflected on the surface of the pond like photographic images and indulged briefly in this fantasy.

Sofue turned to Makino. "Take it slow," he said, the words less an admonishment than an entreaty.

Makino looked around, thinking he had been asked to do something, but quickly realized Sofue was speaking about the guitar. "Yes, well, that may not be possible. But I won't be impatient." He paused. "While I was away from the guitar, those words of the French philosopher Alain that you used to quote came back to me often: 'That which is not esteemed will be forgotten. This is one of the most beautiful laws of humanity.' Maybe my remembering those words is a sign of my own anxiety. But for a performer, it's a hard truth. Lately I've seen rising talent with my own eyes and asked myself what in my playing might inspire esteem. I need to set my sights higher as I engage with the music, but it's no easy thing."

Sofue looked stern, the right half of his face twisted in regret. With great care, he spoke more than he had in a long time. "I may have told you that too often. Someone with your vast ability—you should be freer. Put away what I said as a childhood memory."

Makino was stunned. For a moment he could say nothing. Then, with a slight smile, he said, "Thank you, sir. My respect for you will never lessen. But yes, I'll take it slow."

Sofue shook his head slightly. Then, as if there was one more thing he simply had to say, he added, "Take good care of Sanae. She is irreplaceable in your life."

Makino felt shaken. Had Sofue read his mind about Yoko a moment ago? He pursed his lips and nodded. As if talking to himself, he said, "I know. I will."

The day he began practicing again, as if to wipe away every vestige of hesitation, Makino carefully performed the unique set of exercises he had done for years before every performance. He relaxed his whole body, not only his arms, remaining conscious of his breathing. During the long interim when the loss of his fingernails had prevented him from playing the guitar, he had taught those exercises to Sofue's pupils.

Finally, after closing his eyes for a short time and bringing his breathing under control, he reached for his guitar. It was a Fleta, the guitar he had most often played in his late thirties, and when he picked it up by the neck, he felt the darkened inner room of his body flood with light.

Ever since childhood, he had adhered to the custom of beginning a practice session by going over scales at considerable length, but today, after strumming a bit, he went right into the Villa-Lobos Etude no. 1, following that with Etude no. 3. Now grimacing, now bending his head pensively as he played, he looked up at the ceiling and laughed silently once he made it to the end. Then he looked down at his hands, chagrined to realize that he was winded so quickly.

He was in terrible shape. But at least the unbearable agony of being unable to play the instrument before his eyes was over. With a sense of relief, he looked back on the painful place he had been until now. *Never again,* he thought.

His fingertips were hot and sore where the strings had rubbed against them, but inside he felt a welling of somewhat sheepish joy. He had been afraid that his fingers would have forgotten how to move, but they had known just what to do, filling him with respect not so much for his own body as for the human body in general. Of course, his achievement was on the level of having crossed a muddy field end to end without a pratfall. From now until he could perform onstage again, the way seemed endless, but oddly enough he did not feel gloomy at the prospect. He had made a start. Thinking of all he had lost, he felt as if a weight had been lifted, a sensation that was part defiance and part new confidence that all would come out right in the end.

"I felt refreshed," he would say later in interviews. This came off sounding rather disagreeably self-effacing, and yet it was exactly how he felt.

From that day on, for three straight months Makino put himself through intensive training, practicing roughly ten hours a day. Most of that time, he spent going over the basics, laying out a plan that was as rational and comprehensive as if he were writing a music practice book. His approach to the music itself was simply to play for all he was worth.

He accompanied Sofue to his rehabilitation sessions and frequently talked with the specialist about the relationship between the human body and brain: the existence of two kinds of memory, for example—declarative memory, the repository of information about facts and events, and nondeclarative memory, the repository of information about physical skills—or how signals from the brain are transmitted through nerves to the fingertips. The doctor hadn't known anything about either Sofue or Makino, but as he became better acquainted with them, he grew interested and had them autograph their CDs. From then on, his explanations of rehabilitation would often use the analogy of performing on a musical instrument.

When he played, Makino did not have such things in mind. He formed only a vague impression of established neuroscience theories, but it made sense to him that artistic expression should involve not merely declarative memory but the effect of motor skills on nondeclarative memory. The difficulty lay in getting the two kinds of memory to work together and influence one another to achieve overall unity.

The melodies he played lacked their former suppleness, and the harmonies were dim and quick to disintegrate—why? What had happened inside him during those months of inactivity? There was no point in trying to think about the problem in abstractions; he wasn't even sure if it was right to separate the two issues. At any rate, not having his fingers work properly was out of the question, and so he practiced not only scales but also highly musical passages from his repertory that showcased essential techniques, going over them again and again.

In the end, the do-or-die plan paid off. Three months later, his fingers moved with a facility that he himself found amazing. His overall coordination was smooth, and he was able to practice for hours at a stretch without discomfort. He not only recovered his former performing skills but took the opportunity to reconsider the fingering of his left hand and the fingerpicking technique of his right, creating a simpler and lighter playing style.

He played through the entire set of the Villa-Lobos etudes and felt that he was gliding with more ease across the pages, as if he had upgraded to a new car. Of course, not everything improved with ease. Technically he still felt a bit shaky, and sometimes he would feel ebullient after practicing only to lose heart again the next day. Still, he was incomparably better than when he had first started, and one way or another, the level of his playing was steadily rising.

Makino reevaluated himself objectively: What kind of guitarist was he, anyway? As far as the motor skills required for a performance were concerned, he had outstanding natural ability; things came easily to him. He enjoyed practicing. By nature, he couldn't bear the anxiety of failing to make an effort. All of which explained why reviews critical of his supposed lack of musicality never failed to open by stating, "His technique is certainly transcendent, and one must admire the devotion he applies to perfecting his skills, but . . ." Nothing annoyed him more than such criticism. When he was younger, he would become defensive and pour oil on the flames by offering rebuttals: "To say that poor playing is more musical and more human takes a low view of music and humanity alike."

As he recalled such episodes from the past, his preparation for the comeback entered its fourth month. Now he devoted his time to polishing his main repertory, piece by piece. He curbed his long hours of practicing to read up intensively on Bach, principally *The Art of the Fugue,* and then took time to read several books that he had purchased after seeing them in Yoko's apartment. René Char's symbolist poetry, until then vaguely known to him through the music of Pierre Boulez, he found absorbing. The anthology filled with abstruse, aphoristic lines was soon marked with underlines and margin notes.

"Clarity of vision is the closest wound to the sun." He was captivated by this mysterious line from Char's poetic wartime journal, *Leaves of Hypnos*. The words went through him like a ray of light and left a strong, indelible impression. They struck him as the keenest criticism yet of his playing. They seemed to resonate with Sofue's laconic comment—"You should be freer"—but while he understood this intuitively, when he tried to put it into words, the meaning eluded him.

Why hadn't he read this book back when he and Yoko used to talk on Skype? He was regretful. He wanted to talk to her. There were so many things he wanted to talk to her about.

When rehearsals for their concert got underway, Takechi marveled: "It's amazing how you could recover your playing in such a short time. Seriously. You're something else, Makino! Are you sure you never practiced at all during that time away from the stage?"

Makino himself trembled to think that if he had waited any longer to embark on a comeback, another concert appearance might have been forever out of reach. "Well, it hasn't been easy," he said. "I'm glad to have you with me." He meant it, and yet their collaboration didn't quite come together.

They each brought in pieces they wanted to play, which they intended to narrow down through rehearsals, and there were also several works arranged expressly for them. But Makino couldn't get used to Takechi's arrangements. Also, Takechi's three new compositions struck him as solid but uninteresting, an impression that was reflected in his playing. A piece either had what he called flair, or it didn't. If asked, he couldn't have explained what he meant without tautology: flair was flair, and that was that.

The more he saw of Takechi, the more he felt that he was a fine fellow, and he trusted the precision of his playing, although he also sensed that this very precision was holding him back musically.

There was no reason to be less than up-front, so in a tactful way he suggested changes to two pieces as they rehearsed, and a third, the adagio of Ravel's Piano Concerto in G, he took over and completely rewrote. It was a long piece with colorful orchestration, so performing it on two guitars was unreasonable to begin with. At one point, Makino was ready to give up: "I like it too, but don't you think it drags on a bit?" But as Takechi was set on doing it, Makino rearranged the piece so that his friend would stand out, including giving him the entire opening piano part as a solo.

As the day of the performance drew near, Makino spoke less and less. Never before had he had trouble sleeping, but now he increasingly lay awake, and he developed the bad habit of getting up in the middle of the night and going to the living room on the fourth floor to watch a movie. In the morning, Sanae would come up from the bedroom on the floor below to find him on the sofa, a frown on his face, wrapped in a sleep so light he seemed about to awaken at any moment. The morning of the actual concert, Makino's first in two and a half years, she found him sleeping like that with the television turned low, and gently covered him with a light blanket.

Needless to say, no one was more thrilled than she at Makino's musical comeback. How she had waited for this day over the past thirty months! She had resolved to devote herself to him and had stayed close by his side, not only because she loved him but as a way of making up for her "sin."

For days after she sent that false email to Yoko, Sanae had been in despair, filled with dread that Makino would soon find out what a shabby and despicable thing she had done. Once, he had telephoned

221

her to ask if there had been any word from Yoko on her cellphone. With no need to lie, she had simply said no. Eventually, unbelievably, it appeared that the pathetic lie she had fabricated would go unexposed, and more—it would alter reality just the way she had hoped and dreamed it would. The details were unclear to her, but from that night on, Makino and Yoko had ceased to be lovers.

The evil miracle she had pulled off spooked her. Surely the day would come when Makino would find out the truth. That anxiety never entirely left her, but as one month went by with no repercussions, then two, she realized that the wrong she had done was being steadily wiped out of existence. No one had found out, nor would they. She gave guilt a sidelong glance but reached out instead for relief, eager to breathe easy again.

After breaking up with Yoko, Makino had not immediately come to love Sanae.

Fired up by Noda at Globe, he concentrated on recording *What a Wonderful World*, amusing the staff during breaks with funny stories as usual, yet somehow his heart wasn't in it. When his nerves relaxed, his features took on the heavy cast of someone waiting—until he came to himself with a start and shook off the mood with a sudden display of empty cheer.

Seeing him like this day after day, Sanae could only pray that time would pass quickly. She felt sorry for him, as if his woes had nothing whatever to do with her, and sometimes she was ashamed of her lack of humanity. Of course she deserved to suffer; the pain she felt was for her a form of atonement.

Unsure what she could do for Makino, she threw herself into the *What a Wonderful World* project and took to doing odd jobs at Sofue's guitar school; she also helped with his nursing care and babysitting the little ones.

Makino, though concerned, never stopped her from making these efforts, and accepted her kindness until finally he worried that she was taking on too heavy a burden. She earned his trust and became close to him because, rather than waiting on him, she was devoted to Sofue.

He had felt a growing dissatisfaction with her as his manager when his feelings for Yoko were deepening, but that had now vanished. At one point he handed her a key to his place and entrusted her with handling things there while he was away.

At such times, she would set foot in his empty rooms and sense something she'd never felt around him before—the lingering impression of other women's physical presences. More than one, she thought. There would be a scarcely detectible perfume in the air, or the living room would seem too tidy for a man living alone. When her sensitive nerves picked up such traces of other women in his life, she was taken aback, yet she felt none of the fierce jealousy and sense of inferiority that had tormented her when he was seeing Yoko. Perhaps it was because these other affairs were brief and casual. With no reason to agonize that anyone else might steal Makino's heart, Sanae took comfort in the belief that she, whom he had scarcely ever touched, was now closest to him of all.

Later, the sight of Makino's disease-ravaged hands—the nails crumbled away, the skin peeling—made her think sometimes that her suspicions might be misplaced. What woman, unless she was deeply in love, would want to be caressed by such hands?

What she had done to Yoko was an anomaly. She would never do such a horrible thing to anyone else out of blind jealousy. As any objective observer could see, Makino had lost his passionate commitment to his performing career at that time. Someone had had to realize that Yoko was not a good influence on him, and that role had fallen to her. Having come up with this desperate rationale for her behavior, she told herself that now she owed it to Makino to see that he returned to the stage.

After six months of Sanae's devoted patience, Makino could no longer doubt the meaning of her unwavering support. At first he banished the thought as preposterous, but then he looked around and realized that he was the only one apparently unaware of her feelings for him.

It was possible that she loved him and had for a long time. The odd way in which she had always looked askance at Yoko finally made sense to him. Strangely enough, he was able to imagine being married to Sanae precisely because he had never once thought of her in a romantic way. He never expected to love anyone again the way he had loved Yoko. Such a rash notion might seem more suited to a young boy whose heart had just been broken for the first time, but in truth, it grew slowly out of a quiet resignation that had surfaced once he turned forty, a resignation that was the exact opposite of childish ignorance.

Based on his quarter century or so of life in and out of love, he couldn't help thinking there might be someone else like Yoko and that she might yet appear in his life; but the idea made him ill, and he quickly banished it.

If loving again were indeed possible, it would have to be love of a completely different sort. Something more suited to him as he was now, something more realistic and, ultimately, more significant.

The dreariness of life without playing his guitar was also wearing on him. When had his life taken this bizarre turn? He needed to get himself back on track. Now was the time to do it, and at his side was a woman willing to do anything to help. She was considerably younger than him, and traces of their relationship as musician and manager remained, but she already had begun loving him—and this at the nadir of his life. Makino thought he could probably love her too, or rather, that he ought to take the positive feelings he had for her now as love. Not seek in her what he had found with Yoko, but forget all that—forget that Yoko had ever been.

When Makino made a declaration of love and proposed to her, Sanae's joy was beyond comparison. And yet, although this was exactly what she had dreamed of for so long, when he put it into words, she found herself locked into disbelief. She couldn't be this lucky. Surely others would also find this turn of events hard to believe. It could only seem reasonable if they knew she had gained his love by dishonest means.

She didn't really feel very apologetic toward Yoko. Nor did she feel guilty about having ruined Makino's love for her. But she anguished over knowing herself unworthy of the enormous trust Makino placed in her, Sanae. He now loved Sanae Mitani! But the Sanae Mitani he loved was not the real her. He didn't love the Sanae who had shamelessly wrenched him from his beloved but the Sanae who, not in atonement for her sin but out of a pure heart, devoted herself to him and to his teacher and his teacher's family. Above all, she feared being found out. Her awareness of continually deceiving him fed her growing self-loathing.

In the end, she had to go back to the justification that had occurred to her on the night of her crime—the concept of an aggregate of sin. No one in the world lived a perfectly blameless life. Everybody sinned; the only question was the total weight of one's sin. This approach, like points deducted from your driver's license for various traffic offenses, became her mental support. She hadn't committed very many sins in her life as a whole, nor was she likely to after this. She undoubtedly had far to go before she was over her lifetime quota. In the totality of her days on earth, that particular sin had occupied only a fraction of a second. Something had gotten into her, that's all. Did that have anything to do with her essence as a human being? If she went on to live a good life, a life better than most, couldn't that one small lapse be overlooked? In so thinking, was she really all that different from the Sanae Mitani that Makino loved?

Sanae had never expected that Makino's difficulties with his music would worsen after he broke up with Yoko and that he would give up performing altogether.

Even after his hands healed and the nails grew back, he made no move to pick up his guitar. Naturally, she asked him about it, and he said only, "I need a little time." To distract himself, he met with people he didn't usually see and took solitary trips. When, late in the fall, he announced that he was about to head off on a trip to the Sea of Japan, she raised a fuss and felt a terrible foreboding. This made him shake his head in exasperation.

She watched over him as he struggled with loneliness, perturbed to think that the weight of the wrong she had done, which she herself should have borne, had, with the wave of some magic wand, fallen instead on her husband. So when Makino began practicing again for his collaboration with Takechi, she rejoiced, feeling that she had been granted forgiveness.

Makino awoke at the sound of Sanae opening and closing the refrigerator door.

"Sorry! Did I wake you?"

"What time is it? So late already?" He looked out the window at the bright sky and yawned. Then he stretched and blinked to see if he had recovered from his exhaustion. "I'll make some toast." He popped two slices of bread in the toaster and drank some Perrier from the refrigerator.

Toward dawn, he had dozed off watching the film *Apollo 13*. Now a certain line spoken by a television news commentator kept going through his mind: "In order to enter the atmosphere safely, the crew must aim for a corridor just two and a half degrees wide. If they're too steep, they'll incinerate in the steadily thickening air. If they're too shallow, they'll ricochet off the atmosphere like a rock skipping off a pond." The image of the Apollo capsule reentering Earth's atmosphere reminded Makino of the night of his breakup with Yoko. Perhaps their intended reunion in Tokyo had been something like that.

Their love had been reckless. To reach fulfillment, their feelings for one another had needed to pass through a corridor just two and a half degrees wide. Instead of burning up on reentry, they had ricocheted like a pair of rocks "skipping off a pond," losing for all time any chance of coming together.

Though the scale of the analogy was too grand for a mere breakup, Makino did not dismiss it lightly, either. The maximum is the minimum—within such a mystical-sounding contradiction lay a hidden gateway to understanding.

While looking at the view of Earth enjoyed from the moon by the Apollo astronauts, Makino had calculated the chances of his encountering Yoko on that vast planet. They were vanishingly small, beyond human power to coordinate, and yet love made such a random encounter seem inevitable. He thought back over the few days between when they failed to meet on the night of Sofue's emergency to when their separation became final, then over the nine months they had known each other, back to the time more than twenty years ago when she had first heard him play as a high school student in Paris, and then all the way back to the time some forty years ago when their respective parents had met and made love and they each had been born and started to grow . . . Staring at the image of Earth floating in dark space, he had idly pondered the passage of time.

A coincidence could not in itself be either good or evil. And yet, if somewhere along the line any little thing had been different, the configuration of the world today might not be the same; he and Yoko might never have met or even existed to begin with.

He thought again of how desperately he had loved Yoko. When he wasn't able to meet her as planned, he had told her his feelings in words as strong as he could make them. And she hadn't answered his emails.

227

He remembered waiting for her alone in Haneda Airport. Was there something more he could have done? Late at night, when lack of sleep led him into such rash reflections, he felt more than ever how much in love with her he still was. He felt that way no doubt because he was recovering his self-confidence as a musician and because, as a result, he was nervous.

Someday he wanted Yoko to hear him play again. For the first time since their separation, the thought came to him. He was happy to find himself back in that frame of mind. At the same time, he wanted to tell her about his present anxieties. He wanted to share them with her, and no one else.

"I smell something burning. Everything okay?"

Sanae's words brought him back to himself, and he hastily turned off the toaster. The toast was black. "Argh, I did it again."

"How many minutes do you usually set it for?"

"I don't know."

"What?"

"I turn it to around five minutes and just take it out when it feels right."

"I've never heard of anyone doing that! With this toaster, four minutes is plenty. That way, even if you leave the toast in longer, the toaster will turn off and it won't burn." She sounded aghast. Since the time she had begun to work as his manager, she had been aware of his shortcomings, and, since their marriage, she had taken to telling stories about them to make people laugh, the way he used to do.

Leaving his cellphone in the taxi that night and then calling Sanae because he didn't know how to deal with the problem had been a typical such blunder. But she never joked about that one.

With some chagrin, Makino joined in Sanae's laughter and went to fetch a pair of cooking chopsticks to remove the charred toast. Then, looking at her hands as she cracked eggs, he said, "Have you lost weight?" When she looked back at him, he thought her face, too, looked thinner.

Sanae looked flustered, but soon smiled. She shut off the fire under the frying pan and turned to face him. "I'm pregnant. I went to the hospital, and they said I'm three months along."

Makino's eyes widened. "When did you find out?"

"About a week ago. You were focused on getting ready for the concert, so I wanted to wait and tell you after the first day, but . . . oops. I spilled the beans."

"I'm sorry for not noticing."

"How could you? It doesn't show yet. Are you happy?"

"Of course I am! Just surprised, that's all. So that's it. Well, I'm glad."

"Then give us a hug, baby and me."

Makino embraced Sanae with much sympathy, aware that she had been apprehensive about breaking the news. He sensed his life taking another step forward. His feelings for Yoko had resurfaced powerfully the night before, but now, he told himself, he must let them go once and for all.

Sanae's arms around him were slightly tensed, as if to protect her abdomen. He must make a success of today's concert, not just for himself as a musician but for their coming life together.

8

The Truth

The settlement of Richard and Yoko's divorce took place in the customary American way, with lawyers from each side meeting in court.

Yoko understood Richard's wish to split up and consented to bringing their short married life of less than three years to an end. She hadn't ever imagined getting divorced, but once she found out about Helen, it all made sense. Helen wasn't merely a passing fling; he planned on marrying her. Yoko was of course upset on learning this, but she didn't blame Richard for his betrayal. Her primary concern was maintaining parental rights to Ken.

Richard explained that in the American system, parental responsibility continued to be shared even after divorce. Barring special circumstances such as domestic violence, it was unthinkable that one parent alone could have sole custody of a child. Yoko looked into this herself, and discussions with her lawyer yielded the same response.

"Lawyers' fees pile up," said Richard. "It's ridiculous to waste one or two years settling something that can be done in months. I don't want to impose an unreasonable burden on you. Let's be practical."

He admitted his guilt in being unfaithful but wasn't going to be a pushover. He asked Yoko—whom he had so often criticized for being cold—to make a judgment based on reason, not emotion, so they could settle everything swiftly and peaceably. From the first, he was willing to make concessions regarding the division of property, but concerning custody of Ken, he insisted on fairness.

Ken was now a toddler, able at last to run around the room without falling over. He was tickled when Yoko played peekaboo with him, hiding behind a door and then sticking her head out. Ken quickly copied this, finding hiding places, poking his little head out, and yelling peekaboo in Japanese: *"Ba!"*

He spoke English to Richard, Japanese to Yoko. When he saw an elephant on television, he would comment in Japanese, "Elephant big!" When she asked him if he liked elephants, he immediately said, "Scary," although he didn't seem particularly scared; that seemed to be the only response he could come up with.

Yoko was not drawn to social media, and she could never understand why people needed to post pictures online of everything they ate; but watching Ken—who would turn to her and cry "Look, look!" no matter what he was doing or what he had found to surprise him—she came to realize that the desire to share must be an innate human trait.

But Ken did not want just anybody, the nameless throngs, to look. He wanted her, his mother, to look, she believed. And she wanted to look. At bedtime he would always ask for her, and when she went to pick him up at day care, the expression on his face when he came running was only for her.

It saddened her to think the time she spent with him would now be halved. Her heart ached to imagine him roaming through Richard and Helen's house looking for her. When they walked down the street, he would clutch her hand tighter every time something scared him. Helen had never given birth; at such times, would she be able to comfort him?

But Ken was still only eighteen months old. However much he missed her at first, he would soon grow attached to Helen too. If for some reason she lost custody and couldn't see him again, he would lose all memory of her and grow up thinking of Helen as his real mother— while wondering how he came to have Asian features. He would still no

231

doubt grow up to be a fine person, a testament to the laudable strength inherent in human beings. She herself had made it safely to adulthood despite having had no father, then a "new" father when her mother remarried. She continued to worry that Ken would miss her. But she was also saddened by the fear that he might not.

As the divorce talks moved ahead, Richard regained his calm. This was the Richard that she knew from their long history. It troubled her to think that their life together had been such a disappointment to him, but then, looking back, she felt as if she herself had been living someone else's life, rarely smiling. More than their inability to love each other wholeheartedly, their greatest misfortune lay in their inability to love themselves—the selves they became around each other.

In the lawsuit brought against the bank that Richard worked for as a financial advisor, he himself was not accused of any unlawful activity, whatever his ethical responsibility may have been, and he continued teaching at the university as if nothing had happened.

The custody issue was finally resolved toward the end of May. According to her lawyer, everything went remarkably smoothly, and because the child was still small, some flexibility was built into the arrangements. For the time being, Richard would have Ken four days a week at the start of each month, from Sunday through Wednesday, and she would have him the remaining three; in the second half of the month, they would switch. Year-round, and during summer and winter holidays, each parent would have charge of him exactly half the time. The arrangement was harder on Yoko, who was all alone in New York, than it was on Richard, who was now living with Helen near his sister, Claire, and her family, but that couldn't be helped.

Yoko was surprised by Claire's icy attitude toward her once the divorce was finalized. Richard's parents also turned cold. The change was perhaps only natural, but its sudden onset made her look back wistfully on the tenderness they had shown her formerly.

Before either Richard or Yoko had set up new living arrangements, they took turns looking after Ken in the house in Chelsea, and Richard continued paying the rent. Soon Yoko found a small place for herself a short walk away in Greenwich Village, while Richard and Helen took spacious rooms in Tribeca.

On the Sunday when she would turn Ken over to Richard and Helen for the first time, she packed Ken's clothes and diapers and told Richard about his favorite toys; then the three of them went for a morning walk on the nearby High Line, an elevated linear park built on a long-abandoned spur of the West Side Line. Since its opening the year before, the newly reconfigured park had become a favorite gathering spot, popular with residents and tourists alike. Remnants of the old train tracks and ties were all around, and on either side of the winding path, 210 varieties of plant species provided rich greenery.

It was a sunny, brisk morning. With the Hudson River on their right, they headed south from West Twentieth Street toward the Meatpacking District. Richard, though a longtime resident of Manhattan, craned his neck to look curiously down at the street below: "What a view!" Looking at high-rise buildings in the distance, he murmured, "Oh, that must be . . . yeah, yeah," reorienting himself, and peered with discreet curiosity through the third-floor windows of buildings close at hand.

Yoko was also fond of the High Line and often walked along it with Ken to go shopping at the Chelsea Market. At first she'd worn him in a baby carrier, then pushed him in a stroller; today he was scampering around, sometimes veering into the path of joggers. Every time this happened, she ran after him, calling his name.

She and Richard both felt a bit nostalgic. It was strange to think they would still be seeing each other regularly even after this. Richard had little to say, but with clear eyes he told her, "You know, I bet we'll get along better now that we're divorced."

Yoko was quiet for a few moments, looking at Ken as he walked along with his hand in hers, and then she smiled. "Maybe so."

Since the marriage had produced Ken, she could not believe it had been a mistake. But if Richard hadn't come to the airport that day, if she hadn't been so exhausted, she would almost certainly have seen Makino again to talk things over. The thought had occurred to her now and then, although she forbade herself from dwelling on it. But now that she was divorced, the significance of that possibility appeared to her in a new light.

Ken tugged hard on her arm, pulling her off balance, and his unexpected strength brought another smile to her face. Her little boy didn't know anything yet. He would have to figure it all out as he went along. What sort of mother would he think she'd been when he grew up?

She hadn't seen Helen since that evening at the party, but the bad impression cast a shadow in her mind. Growing up with Helen and Richard, Ken was likely to acquire values at odds with her own. What thoughts would develop within him as he went back and forth, spending half the week with each parent? Eventually, he would be able to understand the situation, but until then he would be confused and unsure what to believe. She and Richard were likely to clash over his education.

This much was certain: right now, Richard was able to offer a far more stable home environment than she was. She wanted to find new work, but what? She had some hard thinking to do.

"I wish you all the luck in the world," Richard said with unquestionable sincerity.

Yoko, while pondering the meaning of that ordinary word "luck," smiled back at him. "Same here. I hope all goes well with Helen."

※

About a week after the divorce went through and she had begun living alone, Yoko heard from Philip. He was back with the Baghdad bureau and, after six weeks of work, was currently in Paris for two weeks of R&R. After a brief report on what had been going on in his life, he wrote this:

I have some sad news. Jalila's parents were murdered in Iraq. As you know, she'd been wanting to bring them to Paris to live with her, but time ran out. There are no words. Iraq is even more chaotic than when you were here. The withdrawal of American forces will soon be done, but it amounts to a complete rout. Things are getting worse every day, with no sign of improvement anytime soon. The government crackdown on the Sunnis is relentless. It's depressing to think of the retaliation that will follow.

Yoko covered her eyes with her hands and shook her head. "How awful . . ."

The email continued:

Jalila is in despair. I saw her just a while ago, and after so many hardships, she's about lost her sense of purpose. She mentioned she was out of touch with you. When you can, I wish you'd drop her a line. She misses the time when she was living here with you. She's worried about your health too.

I hope you're enjoying life in New York. How's your little boy? I haven't seen you in a long time now, but when I'm in Baghdad, I think back to when you were there. If you come back to Paris, the three of us should have dinner—you, me, and Jalila. I found a nice restaurant that serves Iraqi cuisine.

After coming to New York, she'd kept in touch with Jalila at first, but several times over the past year she had written to her with no reply. With Ken to look after, and her own growing sense of emptiness, she feared her communications had been brief and perfunctory. She could imagine the difficulties Jalila must be facing, and she knew that, to others' eyes, her own life must seem steeped in happiness; the gap had made conversations with Jalila painful at times. Orsa, the friend whom Philip had introduced her to, was friendly and trustworthy, but her work at a travel agency kept her busy and she couldn't always keep close tabs on Jalila. Yoko had last spoken to her on Skype in February, just before Richard confessed his infidelity. Snow had been falling heavily, and in the hush, the disjointed conversation had been almost unendurable. Jalila had been in low spirits, and Yoko had tried to offer encouragement, frustrated at her inability to do anything to help. Ken had awoken crying, putting an end to the conversation. After that came the divorce furor, and their communication had never resumed.

Before she spoke directly to Jalila, Yoko wanted a better sense of what was going on, so she reached out to Philip on Skype. When her PTSD symptoms were severe, she had purposely avoided the news from Iraq, so she had a pile of questions. Besides Jalila, she wanted to hear the latest about the other Iraqis on the bureau staff. At every name she brought up, Philip shook his head, grim faced. After a while, she couldn't go on, and fell silent. Then they talked in general terms about the political situation. She was immersed in the conversation for nearly an hour—something that hadn't happened since she came to New York.

After a while, the topic turned to what she had been doing lately, and she admitted that she was now divorced.

Philip looked surprised, but quickly said, "Congratulations on starting a new life." He lit a cigarette and took a drag on it before going on. "You know, I was sure you were going to marry that Japanese guitarist. You listened to his music constantly in Baghdad. I know you were engaged to Richard at the time, but engagements are easily broken. Come to think of it, didn't you put in to be transferred to Tokyo?"

She cast her eyes down, smiling faintly, and then swept her hair back up with one hand as she replied. "I was in love with him. I've never loved anyone as much as I loved him. But he dumped me."

Philip frowned in disbelief. "What a loser." He sighed and then, after a moment's thought, nodded to himself. "Come back to Paris. Everyone misses you."

"I'd like to, but my son is here."

"I'm still single, you know." He looked straight at her with an expression that might or might not have been serious.

"Oh, are you proposing? I'll consider it if you give up smoking."

"You're saying that because you think I won't do it." Smiling, he stubbed out his cigarette.

Yoko looked at him fondly. "You're the same as ever, despite all the work you do."

"You're the one who hasn't changed. Charming as always. When you left Iraq, I was worried about your health. I'm partly responsible. Maybe I threw your life off course."

Before he was done speaking, Yoko dismissed the idea. "I don't blame anyone for what happened, including myself. Other people have taken my place, and while there may be some things I wish I had done differently, I feel as if my experience can serve as a textbook case showing how the system needs to be improved. I have only the greatest respect for you, Philip. It means a lot, having this long chat with you just when I'm in the middle of trying to figure out what to do with my life."

Philip turned pale, as if her words had forced him to take an objective look at his own life. He seemed on the verge of saying something. Something in his eyes was different; this wasn't the Philip she knew. The look on his face gave her the impression that he was capable of living a very different life.

After a few moments, the words that came out of his mouth were perfectly ordinary words of farewell. But the tone of his voice lingered long in her heart.

The next day, she talked to Jalila, again over Skype. Jalila's French had improved, and when Yoko said so, she seemed pleased; yet she looked drained, her eyes worn out from crying. With her parents gone, murdered, she was struggling to understand why she alone should have survived. Why had she fled the country alone? When her father decided to remain in Iraq, why hadn't she been able to dissuade him?

Her degree from the University of Baghdad had proved to be of no use in finding a job, and so she was working now as a cashier in a supermarket in Saint-Denis, just outside Paris. Yoko had suggested to a friend who designed websites that Jalila could be his assistant, but nothing had come of it.

She was fortunate to be alive, Jalila tried to believe, but the question remained: Why her? She had done nothing to deserve such good fortune.

From her experience with PTSD, Yoko knew how important it was to draw close to someone in pain. That simple act of reaching out brought comfort to anyone in emotional turmoil. But also, Jalila needed to step back and take an objective look at her situation, to understand that the emotions she was experiencing were a known quantity and by no means unique to her. Above all, she mustn't suffer in isolation.

So Yoko talked about survivor's guilt, how in wars, natural disasters, or accidents involving many deaths, those who narrowly escaped with their lives would, instead of rejoicing, be tortured by guilt and sometimes end by killing themselves in despair. US soldiers returning from Iraq and Afghanistan often suffered from the syndrome, but Yoko avoided mentioning this—Jalila's disillusionment with the United States was more intense than ever—and instead gave the example of survivors of the Holocaust and the bombings of Hiroshima and Nagasaki.

For the first time, she shared that her own mother had been in Nagasaki at the time of the bombing. Shocked at this revelation, Jalila expressed deep sympathy. Her mother, Yoko said, felt guilty not just about having survived the bombing but about having fled the city afterward. Unreasonable as it might seem, experiencing the happiness that the dead and others would never know made survivors feel guilty.

"Even if they never actually stood by while someone died or killed someone in combat—even without such graphic experiences—just knowing that they survived and others did not is a source of torment. They think there must be some reason why they alone are still alive, and not being able to find that reason weighs on them. My experience doesn't come close to yours, but I do understand a little."

Jalila wiped tears away as she listened. "Is that why your PTSD got worse when you were in love with Makino? Was it because you were afraid to be happy?"

Yoko was momentarily speechless, but she quickly denied it: "No, my case was different. I had adjusted to life in Baghdad, so when I came back to Paris, I had trouble returning to normal life—"

She broke off, wondering if Jalila hadn't nailed the source of her trouble. Here she was lecturing Jalila about survivor's guilt, and she had never once thought it might apply to herself. Perhaps she had been unconsciously avoiding the realization. After Makino's fateful email, she should at least have answered his telephone calls and spoken to him, but she had just had that horrible flashback, and she was in such a nervous state that she couldn't speak to him, all because . . . For the first time, it occurred to her that her desire to wipe out all memory of her experience in Iraq had had the opposite effect, setting off alarm bells in her psyche and keeping those memories fresh. The self that was happily in love with Makino had wanted to deny and eradicate the self that had been terrorized in Iraq. As a result, that other self had risen up to torment her. Wasn't that it? If the two sides of her had stayed in mortal combat, she, too, might well have been driven to thoughts of suicide.

Her doctor had never interpreted her symptoms as possibly suicidal. But Makino had said it straight out: "If you ever killed yourself, Yoko, I'd kill myself too." The words had sounded preposterous, but had her distress made him say it? Did he still remember having made that promise?

"Well, I don't know," she admitted. "Maybe that was part of it too. After all, I was just back from Iraq, having barely escaped from the bombing, and—" She stopped. Jalila's words had begun to change her perceptions. And yet she did not go so far as to think her symptoms had subsided after marrying Richard precisely *because* the marriage was unhappy.

In the course of sharing these thoughts with Jalila, Yoko confessed that she had just gotten a divorce. Jalila could hardly believe her ears and pressed her for details.

The conversation seemed likely to stretch on and on. They had already been talking for two hours. Yoko proposed that they continue the following week, talking the way they used to, while cooking together over Skype. The unexpected invitation brought a sparkle to Jalila's eyes. They agreed to each come up with two dishes to make and email each other lists of ingredients.

Yoko wanted to visit Paris soon, but before that, she decided to send Jalila a box of gifts—clothes and food, including basic necessities and a few luxury items as well. While planning what to send, she checked Makino's Amazon page for the first time in three years. For a while after Yoko's marriage, Amazon would recommend his CDs to her based on her purchase history, but in time those recommendations had ceased. It was as if the algorithm had heard rumors of the end of their affair. For the first time, she realized that Makino had not put out a single new CD since late 2007.

Korenaga had told her about Makino's musical slump, and Makino had hinted at it himself in that infamous email. Still, it was a shock to find that his music had been silenced for so long.

Worried, she googled him. His Wikipedia page hadn't been updated, but on the first page of results, she found the website of a magazine devoted to classical music with an interview about a new concert tour he was undertaking. In the photograph he seemed a little plumper than she remembered. His smile was cheery and he looked full of life. She felt emotions surge through her.

The interviewer began by referring to the two-year hiatus in his performing career, but all Makino had to say was "I'd done nothing but play the guitar since the age of three—nothing but music, music, music. I needed a break." Yoko's journalistic instincts, and her knowledge of Makino's personality, told her that he would have said much more, probably in his usual joking manner. The rest of his remarks must have been edited out. Could he by any chance have touched on his relationship with her?

He had formed a new duo. She didn't know the other guitarist, but she could tell from the contents of the article how fired up Makino was. She was sorry that his life had been on hold. However, that meant he wasn't as distant as she had feared. And now he was moving forward . . . as was she. If they were both starting new lives at the same time, perhaps somewhere, somehow, they could meet again as friends.

She purchased the *What a Wonderful World: Beautiful American Songs* CD and the one with the live recording of the *Concierto de Aranjuez*, which he had played the night they first met. She got two of each, intending to give one set to Jalila, but later, after they arrived, she hesitated. Given the current situation in Iraq, the title of the first album seemed sadly ironic.

Makino himself had written the commentary. As she looked at the credits, she caught her breath at one line in small print, written in English: "This album is dedicated to my dear Iraqi friend Jalila and to her kindhearted and beautiful friend."

Ж

"People think that only the future can be changed, but in fact, the future is continually changing the past. The past can and does change. It's exquisitely sensitive and delicately balanced."

That's what Makino had said to her that first night, over dinner. Yoko listened to his recording of the *Concierto de Aranjuez* while she gazed at the dedication on the other album jacket and pondered what it meant. The words had to have been written a month or two after their breakup. Had he changed his past with these words? Turned a bitter aftertaste into a cheerful sadness as protection against heartbreak? There was no law against it. He, too, had to move forward with his life.

Perhaps she should just be happy at this demonstration of thoughtfulness from an old friend, without trying to read too much into it. Indeed, as a fan of his music, she could not have been more pleased. If she saw him again now, would he say something to make her laugh while reaching out as naturally as could be to shake her hand?

What was there to hold against him? They had been on opposite sides of the world, about to rush helter-skelter into an ill-advised marriage, and he had had the good sense to put a stop to it. Nothing strange about that, if you looked at the situation that way. Still, leaving aside the reference to her, was it all right for him to use Jalila's name so freely? She pondered this, unable to connect this action to the consideration always shown by the Makino she knew.

Or had he intended to convey some deeper meaning?

Afraid to cause herself more pain by indulging in foolish speculation, Yoko nevertheless asked herself: What might Makino have written in the follow-up emails to that first, devastating one? By erasing them unread, she herself had strangled the life out of their relationship.

True, she hadn't been herself. If she had seen him after that severe episode of PTSD, she probably would have been incapable of coherent conversation, just as she had feared. Once all the emails from him were gone, a dark dizziness had taken over her days. Yet even as she sank deeper into sadness, some part of her had been relieved, had breathed more freely. Back then Makino had been precious to her, but at the same time, he had been a source of enormous suffering.

During the summer vacation after her divorce, Yoko flew with Ken to Nagasaki to spend time with her mother. Her mother had flown to New York to help when Ken was born, but this was his first trip to Japan. She and Richard each had him for a full two weeks that summer.

The summer of 2010 was fiercely hot; the Japan Meteorological Agency declared it the hottest summer in a century. Ken wanted to play on the wooden swing her mother had bought online and put up in the garden for him, but the seat was burning hot, and he had to wait till the cool of evening. He liked sleeping on the rush mat and would take long, jet-lagged naps on it in a room cooled beforehand with the air conditioner, waking up with the pattern of the mat imprinted on his cheek.

Before the divorce, Ken had spent more time with her than with Richard, so he had begun to babble in Japanese. But now that he was spending half of every week with Richard and beginning to speak haltingly to the other children at day care, his English was outpacing his Japanese. And by now, many of the English words he knew would be ones he had picked up from Helen.

When she handed Ken over to his father, he often clung to her and said in Japanese, "I want Mama!" How he spent his time with them she didn't know, for Richard said very little about it. In any case, a week after coming to Nagasaki, Ken would say over and over in a loud voice, with so much energy that they were exhausted, "Grandma, how come no swing? Not yet?"

"He's adorable," said her mother. "He reminds me of you at that age. Bilingual children are slow to speak. He walks well, and he's not even two yet. He's growing up fast."

"Richard says the same thing every time he sees him. The doting father. I think it's better for both of us that we're leading separate lives now, but I'm afraid we're going to have disagreements about Ken's education. He already wants to start him on all sorts of lessons."

At the end of July, the three of them flew together to Tokyo. Her mother was going to visit a friend in Yokohama, and Yoko and Ken were going to spend three days in the city.

"What are you going to do?" her mother asked at the airport.

Protective of Ken's health, Yoko had included extra time in Tokyo just in case it was needed. Fortunately, Ken was fine, and her mother volunteered to babysit if Yoko had plans.

Yoko was debating whether or not to attend Makino's concert. Ever since reading about the new duo's concert tour, she had been considering whether she should go. Originally, eight concerts had been planned around the country, but the response had been so enthusiastic that an additional four were scheduled. The one in Tokyo was August 2. She had arranged the plane tickets so she'd be able to attend.

Advance tickets were sold out; she would have to get in line for a same-day ticket. She might not even be able to get in. All she wanted to do, she told herself, was listen to him play, like any fan. After the concert, he would autograph CDs sold on the spot. She had a vague notion that if she could talk to him as an old friend for a minute or two while he signed her CD, then perhaps her past, too, would change.

She decided to go buy a ticket and asked her mother to look after Ken. Her mother seemed to sense something was in the air, but refrained from asking questions. "You run along and have fun. I'm thrilled I get to have Ken all to myself!"

Yoko had planned to set out early from the hotel, but it took longer than expected to get Ken set with everything he needed till that night. Not only that, he realized he was being left behind and started bawling, so by the time she arrived at the concert hall in Yoyogi, it was past the time when same-day tickets went on sale.

It was another sizzling day, and she was perspiring as she hurried to the ticket counter. She was dressed casually in a striped shirt, the collar opened wide, and a knee-length white cotton skirt, but she had taken extra time with her makeup. She'd been wearing her hair short but recently decided to let it grow long again.

Seeing no line at the ticket counter, she feared the worst, but as it turned out, there were two seats left. "Wonderful! I'll take one."

She was relieved that her plan had worked out, but now it hit her that soon she would be in Makino's presence again. She felt rather overwhelmed. There on the ticket was his name: Satoshi Makino.

As she turned away, she saw a pregnant woman standing just behind her. She started to slip past, happy that there was still one ticket available for the woman, and then heard her name called. She looked up in surprise, and when she saw who it was, her body tensed.

"It's Sanae Makino," said the other woman. "Remember me? We met once before, at Suntory Hall. Back then I was still Makino's manager, working under my maiden name, Mitani. We've been married two and a half years now."

Yoko had no words. Of their own accord, her eyes went to the other woman's belly.

"I'm six months along. Finally."

"Well, congratulations. Boy or girl?"

"It's a girl."

As she looked at Sanae's smiling face, memories came back of that evening in the Spanish restaurant. They hadn't met since then, but it was definitely her. There was no mistaking that face.

"Did you buy a ticket to today's concert?" asked Sanae.

"Yes. I was in Nagasaki visiting my mother and happened to see an ad for it."

"I heard you got married and moved to New York."

Yoko paused slightly. "That's right."

"Is your child here too?"

"Yes, my mother's watching him today."

245

"He must be the cutest thing! Children who are half Japanese and half something else always are. Oh, that's right, you're half Japanese too, aren't you? Well anyway, we're both happily married now, aren't we?"

Yoko sensed a kind of nervous strain in Sanae's smile, a touch of fear. What had Makino told her?

"He's in rehearsal now," Sanae went on.

"Yes, I figured he would be."

"He's given strict orders not to let anyone in."

"Of course. I wouldn't dream of imposing."

"Shall we go somewhere for coffee? It's been such a long time."

Yoko hesitated. "Oh, I don't know. I was just on my way somewhere."

"There's something I have to tell you."

This was unexpected. "Me?"

Sanae nodded, still smiling. The neckline of her thin gray dress was stained with perspiration. Cicadas were chirring in the trees along the street.

Yoko checked her watch. "All right, then. If it won't take long."

There was a Starbucks at the entrance to the shopping arcade on the way to the station. Perhaps because of the heat, it was fairly crowded for a weekday afternoon.

Sanae and Yoko went up to the counter, placed their orders, and sat down. Yoko ordered iced coffee. Sanae bought cookies and a brownie in addition to her iced latte, and set them invitingly in the center of the table. She also went and got glasses of water for them both. Yoko thanked her and set the glass alongside her coffee, feeling that Sanae was being a bit too solicitous.

When they were seated across from each other, neither one spoke at first. Across from her was a woman carrying Makino's child. Yoko thought how much she had once yearned to have his child. But he had loved someone else, and still did. It hit her with force that she was probably too old to get pregnant again. Increasingly uncomfortable, she finally broke the silence.

"What was it you wanted to tell me?"

Sanae had been struggling to find the right way to begin. Now, urged by Yoko, she smiled and looked at her, their eyes meeting. "You know," she said, "for junior and senior high school I went to a private Christian school."

This was so unexpected that Yoko could only murmur, "I see."

"Are you a Christian, Yoko?"

"No, I'm not."

"I don't really understand Christianity all that well, but we had to read the Bible in school. I especially remember the story about Mary and Martha. Do you know it? When Jesus comes to their house, Martha, the older sister, works hard to show him hospitality, while all Mary does is sit and listen to him talk. So Martha gets irritated and complains to Jesus. 'Tell my sister to help out,' she says. And instead of taking her side, Jesus says *Mary* is the one doing the right thing!"

"Martha, Martha, you are worried and distracted by many things; there is need of only one thing. Mary has chosen the better part, which will not be taken away from her." Yoko quoted Jesus's words, savoring them as she spoke.

"Wow! Did you memorize the whole Bible?"

"Hardly. That passage, yes, because it's so problematic."

"Still, to be able to reel it off like that . . ."

She paused. "So what does it mean? Don't you think it's strange?"

Yoko had no idea what Sanae was driving at. She wished she would get to the point. Otherwise she might have to make up some excuse and leave.

Cradling the iced latte, Sanae's hand was wet from the moisture condensing on the outside of the cup.

"Well," Yoko said, "it's difficult. The life of action toward God versus the life of contemplation—"

"I think Mary knew exactly what she was doing. She let her sister do all the work getting things ready, and all *she* did was sit with Jesus. She was mocking her sister! Why didn't Jesus see what a little sneak she was?"

Sanae's naivete did not rub Yoko the wrong way. She had taken to her the night they first met, and even now, the woman's ability to identify with the Bible story and talk about it with passion and a total lack of pedantry was, in its way, admirable. Meister Eckhart's curious interpretation of the passage came to mind, an interpretation hinging on Martha's virginity, which was nowhere mentioned in the text. He praised the godly virgin in general as one who is pure and has relinquished all things, yet, not stopping there, he further extolled the nobility of the spirit that receives Jesus as a woman should, by giving birth, "bearing Jesus again in God's paternal heart"—giving back to God what has been received from God, namely the Son. That mystical vision fluttered before her in the image of the pregnant woman facing her.

Was it possible for her to love Sanae as Makino's wife? Her inability to be happy about Sanae's pregnancy showed there was something wrong with her. Acceptance, she knew, was the only path to happiness for her.

"You could be right," she said.

"What do you think, Yoko? I'd really like to know."

"What do I think?"

"Yes. Tell me."

"Well, let's see. I look at it a little differently. I mean, it is a question of faith, isn't it? Jesus is the Son of God, after all. No ordinary guest. It's understandable that Mary would choose to sit at his side. She probably felt she could do nothing else."

"What about Martha, doing all the work? Don't you feel sorry for her?"

"Yes, but until Martha scolded her sister, Jesus didn't say anything about how busy she was, did he? I think his comment about Mary's 'better part' that 'will not be taken away from her' was meant to allay Martha's anxiety over her sister's choice."

"Oh. But Martha would have wanted to do the same thing, don't you think? Just sit at Jesus's feet. But if she did, who would wait on him and show him proper hospitality? Isn't that why she resisted the urge and kept running around instead? I don't think she really wanted Mary to get up and help her at all. She just wanted Jesus to know how she felt."

"Maybe, but again, it comes down to a question of faith. Say that, one day out of the blue, God speaks to you. You feel his presence very near. That's a precious moment, one cut off from normal time. In that moment, all you can do is sit quietly and listen to his voice. I'll bet Jesus understood Martha very well. In her desire to serve God, she was distancing herself from him, missing out on that precious moment."

"So you're on Mary's side?"

"I don't see it as taking sides, I—"

"Until now, everybody's been on Martha's side, me included. What if Jesus weren't divine, what if he were just an ordinary person? Somebody would have to show hospitality to him, wouldn't they?"

"If Jesus were an ordinary human being, then instead of criticizing Mary to their guest, Martha ought to have spoken directly to her sister—'Hey, sis, how about a little help?' or 'What do you say we trade places for a while, okay?'" Yoko injected some humor, keen to bring this pointless theological discussion to an end. Even though she herself lacked faith—or rather, precisely because a number of times in her life she had been strongly drawn toward faith but had never taken that leap—she naturally saw the story as being all about that. As Sanae showed no sign of backing down, she asked point-blank, "Is this what you wanted to talk to me about?"

The question seemed to untie Sanae's tongue. Everything she had been unable to express was contained in her next words: "I don't want you to come to today's concert. Please stay away. I'll pay you for the price of the ticket."

Yoko's head swam. After a pause, she said, "I'm just a fan of his music. Do I need permission?" She inclined her head in puzzlement, accompanying the movement with a smile, not only to keep the conversation from becoming prickly but to conceal that her feelings for Makino went beyond being "just a fan." The decision to hide her feelings was not conscious. However, in her heart of hearts, she would have had to say that she held out hope that something would develop from an encounter with him today. Sanae sensed that something had passed between Makino and Yoko that still posed a threat. And just like that, Yoko realized that Sanae was right to be wary.

"I don't want you in the concert hall. If he sees you there, he won't be able to focus on his music. That's the trouble."

"It's all right. My seat is way in the back. He and I haven't seen each other in quite a long time, and anyway—"

"But I know it."

"What?"

"I know that, wherever you sat, he would see you. He absolutely would."

Yoko could think of no reply.

"You don't know it, but the two of us had a lot of trouble getting to this point. Makino couldn't touch the guitar for a year and a half. He struggled and suffered. Then he practiced like a demon to make up for it and finally—*finally*—here we are. He's still in a precarious state. There's no telling when he might end up right back at square one. Please don't upset him. Please! Don't make all his effort come to nothing. Don't ruin all I've done for him. You may think you're his Mary, but let me tell you, what he needs is a Martha, someone who can handle all the nitty-gritty details in his life. It's way more than just having good chemistry with him or enjoying talking to him or anything else so abstract . . . After all this time, why did you have to show up again?"

Watching Sanae work herself into a fit of anger, Yoko was reminded of Richard's comment: "You're cold." Richard above all had been looking for a Mary, hadn't he? Someone who would sit at his feet and drink in his words. She could never be that person, and yet she hadn't been a devoted Martha to him, either. Could she have been a Mary to Makino, as Sanae seemed to think? Would he then have been unable to come out of his slump? But hadn't Eckhart taught that, as time passed, Mary would progress from the "sweet solace and joy" she found at Jesus's feet and, for the sake of attaining the eternal bliss that Martha possessed, let go of all else and enter into a life of service?

All of this passed through Yoko's mind in a long moment, and then she concluded that she should not entertain such thoughts. It wasn't a question of faith, and Makino wasn't Jesus. She had loved Makino, that's all. But obviously, the love Sanae had always felt for him was something like religious faith. And out of the turbulence of that love, a new life had emerged, a life that Sanae was even now carrying within her.

Yoko stayed silent, unable to speak.

Perhaps it was true—perhaps she shouldn't go to Makino's concert. Little by little, she sensed that her feelings for him, which had been intensifying since her divorce, were changing into pain.

The long silence led to an unexpected development.

Yoko had been looking down, and when she raised her eyes, Sanae started in again: "You've done nothing wrong. But from the time he started seeing you, Makino was unable to concentrate on his music."

Yoko turned pale. She stared at Sanae with astonishment. Fresh suspicion took root within her, and in a flash, her memories of that rainy night took on a different coloration. Words from Makino that for three years she had tried to forget, words that had finally started to fade, now echoed in her mind: "You've done nothing wrong. But from the time I started seeing you, I've been unable to concentrate on my music." But the voice saying those words now belonged not to Makino but to Sanae, sitting here across from her.

Sanae did not immediately notice the change in Yoko. "I'm afraid the same thing could happen all over again," she said, before finally falling silent with a distrustful air. Then, as if reading Yoko's mind, she raised a hand toward her mouth; the hand froze in midair, then clenched into a fist.

"It was you, wasn't it?" said Yoko.

Sanae bit her lip.

"You sent that email, didn't you?"

Under Yoko's penetrating stare, Sanae's expression was a patent admission of guilt. When she didn't attempt to deny it, Yoko closed her eyes. A tremor crossed her brow. To stop herself from slipping away from reality, she gave her head a slight shake.

Sanae watched as if in a trance. And then, seemingly unable to stop herself, she began to recount everything that had happened that day, keeping nothing back. She described seeing Yoko at the south exit of Shinjuku Station. She said she had sent only the one email, that she'd had nothing to do with any further exchanges between them. And she defended what she had done.

"I'm sorry, really I am. But if I hadn't done that, I truly believe Makino still wouldn't be able to play the guitar. You have a wonderful life. But if he were taken from me, what would I have? Nothing! Whatever happens, I want to stay by his side. Even if our relationship is based on something fundamentally wrong. Living according to what's right isn't my goal. My only purpose in life is him, my husband! So I beg of you, stay away from the concert today. Stay out of his life. He and I have a life together now—him, me, and the baby that's on the way."

Yoko said not a word while Sanae talked. In silence, she forgave Sanae the unthinking impulsiveness that would go on wounding her, Yoko, like a dull sword. No violent hatred filled her; rather, she felt hollow. Somewhere in the back of her mind, one word echoed: *Why?*

252

Knowing it was pointless to ask aloud, she repeated the word like a prayer.

Sanae's cowardly resolution gave her a special air of superiority. Yoko was repulsed by that defiance and her willingness to commit outrages in the name of love. With a pang, she felt that she herself was incapable of such self-abasement for love. But Makino had loved her for herself. Perhaps Sanae was getting back at her for having been loved by him without any need for subterfuge.

Once more she asked herself: *Why?* The question wasn't directed at Sanae but at something ill defined and momentous.

After Sanae finished, Yoko couldn't speak. When she took her eyes from Sanae's face and looked down at the tabletop, she did not reach for the now-watery coffee but for the glass of water. Sanae flinched, as if expecting to have the contents tossed at her. Sensing this, Yoko tilted the glass and studied the edge of the water, rounded by surface tension. Then she looked back at Sanae with a disconsolate expression.

"And are you happy now?" she asked in a low voice.

The answer was swift. "Yes. Very."

Yoko stared, searching Sanae's face, then dropped her eyes to Sanae's belly. She looked up again and nodded. She did not ask, "And Makino?" Opening her purse, she took out the ticket she had purchased an hour before and laid it on the table.

Surprised, Sanae waited for her to say something. Then she hastily got out her wallet.

Yoko stopped her. "Treasure your happiness." She spoke quietly, without a trace of irony, and even sounded cordial, before she got up and walked out the door.

When she arrived back at the hotel earlier than planned, her mother and Ken were still out. Alone in the room, she fell onto the bed made up with fresh sheets and sobbed her heart out.

※

Makino and Takechi wrapped up their successful tour in Koriyama. As time went on, Makino had gradually hit his stride. He was careful to achieve balance with Takechi, working with his partner's distinctive style and actively encouraging him; after a performance, they would get together and go over any passages that had bothered them.

The adagio from Ravel's Piano Concerto in G came at the end of the first half. Makino had hoped that it would let Takechi shine, but during intermission, people often talked rather about Makino's supple skill.

Toward the beginning of the tour, Takechi had come across a blog that slammed their duo mercilessly, and it gnawed at him. Against his better judgment, Makino had read the piece too, and it made him furious. Most of the potshots were aimed at him. Hearing that he was making a comeback, the blogger had gone to hear him play, full of expectation, but found no trace of his former genius. He felt sorry for him, he said. Takechi's playing was insipid and forgettable, but in his current state, Makino could probably do no better for a partner. And so on.

He'd laughed it off. "Amazing how you dig stuff like this up, Takechi. Thanks to you, I read it too, and now I'll be upset for a while. But it's just one man's opinion, so let it go. Plenty of other people liked the concert just fine." Despite his seeming casualness, inside he felt a nudge of fear: What if his musical ability were to desert him again?

A week later, just when he had begun to forget the whole episode, Noda told him something that set him back on his heels: "You know who wrote that piece? It was Okajima, the guy from Jupiter."

Noda had known about the blog for some time, but not who wrote it. The blogger was a great classical music fan whose writing, though often hostile to Makino, Noda found informative. He looked it over periodically and noticed that some of the content sounded familiar; the author also wrote Amazon reviews under the same handle. Noda did a little digging and realized that this was the same person who had trashed Makino's *What a Wonderful World* album in a single-star review.

This, too, was of course merely "one man's opinion." But then, Noda happened to stop by Okajima's desk and saw the blog's administration screen on his computer. Unable to remain quiet, he had confronted Okajima on the spot. There was no law against a company employee using a private website to bad-mouth one of their own musicians—but Okajima had previously gone out of his way to show the excoriating review to Noda and had expressed hot indignation right alongside him.

"So what's the big idea, Okajima?" Noda demanded. "Are you trying to settle a score with Makino and me?"

Okajima had turned red but otherwise ignored the tongue-lashing. He didn't speak to anyone for the rest of the day and resigned the next.

Makino listened, thunderstruck, and when he heard this news, he let out a deep sigh. He had heard that Okajima was unhappy about being sidelined at Globe, but there was nothing he could do about it. He doubted that Okajima's trashing of the album was based entirely on resentment, but either way the incident left a bad aftertaste. To comfort Takechi, he explained what had gone on. Takechi's comment was charitable: "He didn't need to quit over something like that." He seemed relieved.

Before going onstage, Makino insisted on having half an hour to himself. His pre-performance jitters were worse than before, but now he tried not to take that fear lightly.

Each member of the audience contributed a small amount of silence to the performance, the space of a single seat. A single cough could destroy it, but they managed to cover for each other and maintain the general silence from beginning to end. They willingly abandoned sound and entrusted it to the two performers.

Makino was moved by the thought of the people waiting to hear his music. Since his comeback, he hadn't given a single recital, and at concerts he hadn't played any solos, but he sensed it was only a matter of time. He owed much of the change to Takechi's steady support.

The program included pieces familiar to guitar fans, such as Debussy's "Clair de Lune," arranged by Julian Bream and John Williams; Leo Brouwer's Tríptico; and Astor Piazzolla's Tango Suite, as well as pop songs such as "A Dream Goes On Forever" by Todd Rundgren, which was also part of the *What a Wonderful World* album. On the last day of the tour, Makino had the most confidence in the final number on the program, his own arrangement of the fourth movement of Mozart's String Quartet no. 17—"The Hunt." It was a piece seldom adapted for a guitar duo. He liked the fine counterpoint in the opening section, but he'd had a hard time getting the arrangement just right. Certain passages had left Takechi scratching his head, but throughout the tour, Makino had kept touching up the arrangement and now he at last had a final draft.

The Mozart received a huge ovation. Ten months after ending his long silence on the guitar, Makino felt confident that he had weathered the crisis. At the autograph session afterward, several people even commented admiringly on his air of vitality. That in itself was unusual; he couldn't remember such a thing having ever happened before.

He left the concert hall and went back to the hotel, where he joined the closing party with staff members who had come all the way from Tokyo. The celebration went on till around midnight. By then Sanae had already gone back to their room. He and Noda hung around in the hotel bar till one in the morning, talking shop, but suddenly they remembered that the hot spring bath closed at two and rushed off to get there in time. In the spacious bath, there was only one other person. The town was in a valley, and the bath looked out on thickly forested slopes. Makino took his time soaking in the outdoor hot spring, enjoying the tranquility. As the alcohol in his system took effect, he fell into a light drunkenness that thankfully allowed him to avoid thinking.

Wearing a thin cotton *yukata* robe, Makino headed back to his room and came across Takechi, sitting in a massage chair in the dimly lit corridor. He bought two bottles of water from a vending machine and sat down in the chair next to his.

Takechi looked up and grunted in greeting. His hair was already dry, so he must have come out of the bath quite some time ago. Makino held out a bottle of water, and with a friendly grin, Takechi accepted it and took a swig.

"Thanks. I was thirsty."

"How's the massage? Feel good?"

"Yeah, these chairs have come a long way. They work you over from head to foot. Ever tried one?"

"Nah. Once, I had a bad experience with a chiropractor, and the next day I couldn't stand up. That stuff can be murder. If you're not careful, you'll end up flat on your back."

"What was it, muscle pain from the chiropractor's massage?"

"Something like that, but really bad."

"The human body is a mystery."

"You can say that again. Look at me. I ended up losing a year and a half of my life."

Makino sank back into the chair and reclined the backrest. The cool of the leather felt good against his flushed skin. "Maybe I'll try the spine straightening program," he said. It cost 200 yen for ten minutes. The chair went into action, the noise reverberating in the quiet. He murmured his appreciation.

Beside him, Takechi sat up and took a sip of water. "Maki-chan, whatever happened to the daughter of the *Coins of Happiness* director? You never see her anymore?"

Makino opened his eyes and looked at the ceiling, then over at Takechi without turning his head. "Why?"

"The other day Korenaga came to one of the concerts, and when I played the theme from *Coins of Happiness*, we ended up talking about her. Yoko, wasn't that her name?"

"Yeah. We lost touch. What's she up to?"

"Married and living in New York, apparently, with a little boy named Ken."

"She's a mother."

"So it seems. Korenaga said she hadn't heard from her much lately, either. I remember for a while there, every time I saw you, you'd go on about Yoko."

"I would?"

"Oh yeah. All the time. Praised her to the skies. She sounded too good to be true."

Makino laughed, mocking himself, his eyes on the now closed and silent game corner. "Maybe so. She was a rare one, all right. We kind of drifted apart."

The massage chair came to a stop, and all was quiet again. Makino brought the backrest upright and drank some water.

Takechi seemed to have heard something more from Korenaga, but sensing that Makino didn't want to talk about Yoko, he tactfully changed the subject. "Anyway, the tour was really fun for me. Sad to think it's all over."

Makino agreed with a smile. "Let's do it again sometime. I had a good time too."

"The thing is . . . I thought of announcing it publicly today, but the truth is I'm planning to call it quits with the guitar."

Makino turned to face him. "What do you mean?"

"My dad's a Buddhist altar craftsman up in Yamagata. My brother was supposed to succeed him, but for one reason or another, that's not going to happen. So Dad wants me to come back."

"A Buddhist altar craftsman? Wow. That must be an amazing world. It's such detailed work, with spirituality at the heart of it. But can someone past forty still master those skills?"

"I used to help out when I was a kid. I love the guitar, but I love that work too, and I'm going to devote myself to it from now on."

Makino remembered that after his parents died and he had to empty out the family home, he hadn't known what to do with the altar. He hadn't thrown it away, but now it was shut up in a closet in his practice room, untouched. *Times are hard for musicians, but Buddhist altar craftsmen must be having an even tougher time,* he thought, though he didn't say so out loud. He could guess what a difficult decision this must have been.

"Couldn't you do both? I don't see why you should have to give up the guitar for good."

"I suppose I could take in pupils, but I'll have to clip my nails, so it wouldn't really work. I had a hard time making up my mind, but going on tour with you, having this great experience, helped me decide." He looked wistfully at the nails on his right hand. "I'm glad I could share a stage with you at the end, Maki-chan. During the performance today, I was remembering how we met at the Tokyo International Guitar Competition way back when."

"Yeah, I remember that."

"Sofue was always going on about you—what a prodigy you were. How even though you were still in junior high, you could play everything by Sor."

"Sor only wrote sixty-three works for guitar."

"Yeah, but you were a kid! I never heard of anyone else that age pulling it off."

Makino shrugged and gave a crooked smile. "I was a hick from Okayama. I figured that, even if I made a splash at home, when I went to Tokyo, there were bound to be all kinds of people better than me. Plus I figured guitarists in France and Spain knew things I couldn't even

259

imagine. I was always insecure. I practiced like a demon, and not just to play better. It was an obsession."

Takechi listened as if deeply impressed. "I never imagined anything like that. I never practiced like that, either. I've gotta hand it to you."

"Yeah, but when I finally went to Paris, the students in the École Normale said they'd never played the complete works of Sor. Admitted it without the least embarrassment. You could have knocked me over. I thought Sofue had pulled a fast one on me. And also, maybe my insecurity's got something to do with the guitar itself. No matter how much we practice, pianists just look down their noses at us, like, 'Really? That's all?'"

"True. I remember the first time I saw you, everybody else was poring over their music, getting ready for the big moment, and darned if you weren't reading a novel! Carpentier's *The Lost Steps*."

"That's right, that's the one. What a memory!"

"Afterward, I bought the book, but I never could get through it, which only increased my awe of you."

"That's a dense book. I only read it because Sofue told me that to be a guitarist, I needed to do more than play the guitar all the time, I needed to read up on the countries of people like Brouwer and Villa-Lobos, learn about their backgrounds. I went to the biggest bookstore in my hometown and they said that was a novel about Cuba, so I bought it."

"Sofue never gave me any advice like that. But man, I gotta tell you, seeing you read that book before the competition really intimidated me."

Makino smiled. "Then my strategy succeeded."

Takechi blinked, then grinned as he realized Makino was teasing. "Then when I heard you play in the competition, I was blown away. After that you won the Paris International Guitar Competition too, and your career took off like a rocket . . ." Still wearing a smile, he stared at Makino with evident strain.

Makino sensed what was coming.

"For a long time, I really didn't like you, Maki-chan. Your very existence got under my skin. I used to wish you would drop dead, go fall off a cliff or something. Just the thought of you was painful. I was jealous. No joke. Jealous not just of your talent but of the way everyone loved your talent."

Makino looked away, pretending to adjust the hem of his robe. He smiled awkwardly and nodded. He'd had to listen to sudden confessions like this before.

"So when you invited me to fill in for you at the concert in Taiwan, I had mixed feelings. When I heard you couldn't play, I wasn't *happy*, but I did feel a kind of relief. Not much of a friend, am I?"

"Oh, now . . . Don't put yourself down."

"But when you invited me to form a duo with you, I was psyched. Playing with you every day has been a revelation. Now I see why the guitar loves you so much."

"The guitar?"

"You and I both play the guitar, only it's got a completely different attitude toward me." Takechi chuckled. Then he added, "I also sense what you must have gone through all that time when you couldn't play."

Makino felt increasingly uncomfortable and was striving to keep his expression calm. "Age has something to do with it. For both of us. This may sound presumptuous, but when John Williams formed Sky, he was around forty. To paraphrase Master Shinran, if even a maestro can be saved, how much more so a mediocre talent."

"You think so? I always liked Sky."

"Not me. But I get it, why John Williams would want to do something like that. At around forty, I did things like change my guitar to a Smallman, and for a while there I lost my bearings, but thanks to that experience, I was able to revamp my playing from the bottom up. I've come to think it was a necessary process. Wait a few years, Takechi, and you may have a change of heart."

"You could be right." Takechi smiled in seeming agreement.

Then they stepped into the elevator and went back to their respective rooms.

When they parted, they shook hands. That handshake, more than the one they shared the next day in Tokyo Station, lingered long in Makino's memory.

⋈

Six weeks later, Makino was a guest artist in a concert by a Belgian theremin performer at the Blue Note jazz club in Minami-Aoyama. It was a joint performance, Makino providing accompaniment for vocalizations of works by Rachmaninoff, Ravel, Villa-Lobos, and others. The star was a handsome young man whom Globe was currently pushing. Makino accepted the gig out of curiosity and found it fairly enjoyable.

After the second performance that night, he stayed for a drink, and by the time he got home, it was past midnight. With her due date looming, Sanae usually went to bed early, but for once she was still up, sitting on the living room sofa with a vacant air. Her eyes were red from crying.

"What's wrong?" said Makino, setting down his guitar.

Sanae silently held out a postcard. Her hand was trembling.

Makino scanned the text and let out an exclamation that sounded almost angry. It announced the death of guitarist Fumiaki Takechi. He had died two weeks before, just a month after the final concert in Koriyama.

"I was really surprised, and when I called to express my condolences, his mother picked up. She said he died in an accident."

"An accident? What kind?"

"She just said it was an accident."

Makino reread the card. He turned it over and examined the other side, then looked again at the words "passed away" as if contemplating whether they might have some other, unknown meaning. The funeral had been restricted to close relatives. Makino nodded wordlessly and handed the card back to Sanae.

"I wanted to at least offer some incense for him, and I asked when I could drop by, but his mother said they're all still coming to grips with what happened and it would be better if I stayed away for now. I'll take care of things here if you want to go."

"No thanks. I'll pass."

At his unsympathetic tone, Sanae looked puzzled. "His mother sounded awfully grief stricken. I'm sure it would mean a lot to her if you went."

"I'll go, but not right now. Since she asked for some privacy, I'd best leave her alone for a while."

He went upstairs to deposit his guitar in the practice room. Then he sat down on the sofa and let his head fall, dazed.

Takechi's death was almost surely no accident, he thought, feeling sympathy for his friend's mother. He remembered his final conversation with Takechi in the hot spring hotel. Was there something more he should have said? When Takechi had said he wanted to quit the guitar, instead of being understanding, should he have strongly objected and encouraged him to go on? Had he shown a bad attitude toward Takechi during their joint performance? Why hadn't he noticed anything? When had Takechi begun having suicidal thoughts? He had been inhabiting a world without Takechi for two weeks already, never knowing. His thoughts whirled. Just as his life was on the upswing, now this heavy blow . . .

The motive probably wasn't simple. There were undoubtedly things he didn't know. Even so, he couldn't help blaming himself for his friend's death. And he had no one with whom he could share his feelings.

Makino did not distance himself from the guitar all over again because of Takechi's sudden death. Rather, he began accepting recital offers and preparing to appear solo. Takechi had emphasized the difference in their abilities, but Makino now felt fortunate that he had never had a similar "accident" during his long hiatus.

While the sad news prodded Makino into action, it sent shock waves through Sanae. Knowing nothing of what Takechi had said that night in the hotel, she took his death as literally accidental. Makino did nothing to disabuse her of this idea. A cold uneasiness took hold of her. How could someone so honest and good have had his life taken so young, while she went on living a peaceful life? Surely Takechi had never done anything as horrible as what she had done. And yet instead of being forced to pay for her sin, by some miracle she found her fondest wishes coming true: Makino loved her, and she was about to give birth to his child.

She lived with a sense of strangeness.

Whether one was happy or unhappy, the question always remained: *Why me?* And in the absence of a clear answer, one couldn't help wondering, *Do I deserve this?* Ever since they'd married, Makino had been nothing but tender toward her. It was a side of him she had never known when she was his manager; back then he had acted more like himself, she thought. He trusted her implicitly, and now and then showed her some special kindness, as if afraid he wasn't being appreciative enough. But when he was involved with Yoko, he had given her, Sanae, short shrift; surely that indicated his true feelings. She found him hard to read. The thought that he might not love her after all terrified her.

The baby was a girl, the doctor said, and not in breech position; everything pointed toward a normal birth. Sanae felt blessed. All the paraphernalia needed to welcome a baby into the world was ready: towels, tiny undershirts, baby clothes, bottles, diapers, toys, a crib, a stroller, a baby carrier, a car seat . . . Their lives had been steadily invaded by pastel pink and a soft white the color of whipped cream. Even though he was already drowning in CDs, Makino had bought special music for infants, and he had gotten someone to give him an infant play mat.

But through all this happiness, there was a pervading sense of strangeness.

They had agreed that Makino would pick the name for a boy, Sanae for a girl, so the task fell to her. She couldn't think of a good name right away, and that ordinary, exciting dilemma faced by any new parent got tangled up with her sense of guilt, making her restless and impatient. She bought three books on how to name your baby and looked at all the suggestions—including those for boys—but nowhere did she find the one name that would be right for *their* child. She didn't even find one that seemed close.

Finally, she had a disturbing dream. Her daughter was getting ready to enter nursery school. All the children had red ribbons pinned to their chests, and Sanae was carrying her child, filling out the necessary forms. Makino stood by, talking to someone. When she told the receptionist the child's name—what it was, she couldn't remember afterward—the woman ran her finger down the list and looked for it, but it wasn't there. The head of the school was called in, and they searched up and down for the name with no luck. Panicky now, Sanae said the name over and over. At some point the baby had reentered her womb; she could feel its nervousness spreading inside her. This was all the parent's fault, beyond question. Finally, the receptionist said with a quizzical look, "How very odd. Are you sure you gave her the right name? Are you really qualified to name this child?"

This peculiar dream seemed more real to Sanae than any of the signs of happiness surrounding her. This must be punishment for the wrong she had done. Women sometimes—not often, but sometimes—died in childbirth. If that happened to her, she would end her life a hopeless, shameless wretch, unable to do enough good deeds to counterbalance the wrong she had done.

The usual hormonal imbalances of pregnancy exacerbated her painful feelings of self-recrimination. She looked back with bewilderment on what she had said to Yoko: "Living according to what's right isn't my goal. My only purpose in life is him, my husband!" Clearly that had been going too far. She didn't normally think that way. The words had burst out under pressure from Yoko.

Yoko always pressured her, questioned her. About what? About her essence as a human being. Whenever she thought about Yoko, Sanae felt a devastating sense of inferiority. She had only spoken to Yoko once before their conversation in the Starbucks, four years ago; Yoko had been nice then about her inability to follow parts of their conversation.

Standing in line behind Yoko at the ticket counter, she had recognized her instantly and called out without hesitation. Since Yoko was two years older than Makino, that would make her forty-four, but she was no less beautiful than when Sanae had seen her in Shinjuku Station that time: she had an unmistakable presence.

Throughout their conversation, Sanae had been desperate. As they talked, she had felt with foreboding that Yoko might take Makino from her. After blurting out the truth, she had looked at Yoko's stricken face and thought again how lovely it was, but she had also both feared and hoped that Yoko might become enraged or dissolve in tears.

That hadn't happened. Yoko had never lost her composure for a moment, had only looked at Sanae with eyes of deep melancholy. Eyes that seemed to Sanae filled with pity, almost like the eyes of Mary as she looked up at Martha from her spot at Jesus's feet.

"And are you happy now?" Yoko had asked. The one question, above all others, that she didn't want to be asked. Was it really Yoko who had asked that question? She wondered now. It seemed to her that the cry of her own heart was mingled in her memories.

※

After Takechi's death, Makino heard from Korenaga, formerly of Jupiter, for the first time in three and a half years. They met in a café in Shibuya and talked for an hour or so. They were able to speak without tension because they were discussing the cache of Takechi's unpublished recordings she had in her possession. Makino promised to find a way to publish the material, and she thanked him. She felt bad about never having been able to release a solo album of Takechi's music.

Makino told her a little about his final conversation with Takechi in the hot spring resort. She seemed to know the cause of his death, and as Makino talked, her eyes filled with tears. To change the subject, he said something about Yoko. Korenaga hadn't heard from her lately and knew nothing about the divorce, but she told him how over the moon Yoko had been around the time of Ken's birth. She also mentioned Yoko's struggle with PTSD before her marriage to Richard.

"She didn't tell anyone about it, just suffered on her own. I never knew anything until after she was married. She said she thought that without Richard's support, it would've been worse. She's a strong person, so it must have been pretty bad."

Makino frowned. "When was this?"

"After she came back from Iraq. Right around the time you changed record companies. I guess you weren't in touch. Anyway, she had a rough time. And she was looking after an Iraqi refugee at the time, a woman . . ."

Makino nodded vaguely and looked away. Korenaga apparently hadn't seen or heard about the dedication on *What a Wonderful World*.

"Something wrong?" she asked.

"No."

At that time, they had been talking on Skype nearly every day. Why had she kept her illness from him? Was that behind the sudden change in her attitude after she came to Tokyo? Had she silently been protesting, "You rush to be with your teacher the moment he falls ill, so why can't you see my pain?"

He thought back to the mysterious reply he had received to his email the following day. In response to his suggestion that they meet, she had written, "I'm sorry. I can't go on anymore," and broken off

267

all communication. The words had read like a direct translation from the French. Had she perhaps been ill at that very time? Was that why she had rushed to Nagasaki to be with her mother? But if so, he could only wish she had confided in him. Why hadn't she? Was it because she wanted to ensure he gave Sofue priority?

So it wasn't only Takechi. He also hadn't picked up on the suffering of the woman he adored. Makino was sick with regret. He felt his memories shifting colors. He longed to apologize to Yoko. His heart broke at the thought of the suffering she must have endured by herself in Paris. What he couldn't understand was why she had never sought his help. He was forced to doubt their love itself. He could only turn to his increasingly fragile memories of her and sadly ask, *Why?*

More than three years after Makino's breakup with Yoko, a flushed, weary Sanae said she needed to tell him something. She looked stricken, and so he immediately worried that something had happened to the baby. His expression of fatherly concern was the final incentive she needed to unburden herself of the truth.

"Remember the night Sofue-sensei had his stroke? There was a big rainstorm, and you forgot your cellphone in the taxi, and I went to get it . . . Well, actually . . ."

His wife's unexpected confession left him stunned. She told the story in bits and pieces, and here and there he asked a question, until he finally had a clear picture of just what had happened that night. And Yoko's health had been poor . . . although Sanae apparently didn't know this.

Yoko had definitely sought help. Until then, she had kept her suffering completely hidden from him, but by the time of their reunion, she had been desperate. And he had shut her out, for no good reason, as far as she could tell. She must have been blindsided. Remembering the series of miscommunications, he was nearly beside himself. What had happened was utterly stupid, but that made him feel even more torn. How hurt she must have been! But she had accepted that out-of-the-blue announcement that they part company. Now he had no doubt it was because she loved him. That's the kind of person she was.

Now it all made sense—not just Yoko's mysterious change of heart, but also his wife's slavish devotion to him. Imagining the guilt Sanae must have felt, he thought pityingly of how she had stuck uncomplaining by his side while he was a mess. For two and a half years, she had supported him emotionally and financially while handling all the details of his daily life. He owed her an enormous debt; there was no denying it.

Yoko's face rose fleetingly to his mind, but it was overpowered by the stronger memories of his two and a half years of marriage to Sanae. Knowing Sanae as well as he did, he could all too well imagine the desperation that had led her to send off that false email. Even though she had deceived him, Makino felt no surge of ill will. That's how much his feelings for his wife had deepened. Ironically, her confession brought that home.

"Why tell me now?"

She meant to say that she had seen Yoko, but what came out of her mouth was something else. She had been thinking about confessing ever since the news of Takechi's death, she said.

Makino nodded understandingly, but he was not entirely satisfied. "Are you sure it isn't because you figured now I wouldn't leave you, with the baby coming?"

Sanae widened her eyes and shook her head, but no words came.

For a long while Makino said nothing, his eyes downcast, and then he looked at Sanae. "Why didn't you just go on saying nothing? I think that would have been better."

She seemed to find a sliver of hope in his words. "I'm sorry," she said.

As he watched, the imploring look on her face slowly took on signs of liberation and relief. He looked at the two coffee cups on the table and then at the crib in the corner, overflowing with brand-new baby clothes and toys. If she hadn't lied, this marriage, this life, would never have come about. Was this reality bad? The two and a half years that needn't have been—were they leading to a future that ought not to be? "Take good care of Sanae," Sofue had said. "She is irreplaceable in your life." Had something in the determined cheerfulness with which she nursed him suggested to the old man that a confession of this sort might be forthcoming?

After a while, he said, "I understand what you told me. Anyway, right now the important thing for you to do is rest and give the baby top priority."

Sanae nodded, and spent the rest of the day shut in the bedroom crying.

On October 14, a baby girl weighing a little over six pounds was born to the Makinos. Two weeks later, Sanae named her daughter Yuki, written with characters for "gentle" and "hope."

※

After her vacation in Japan with Ken that summer, Yoko felt that her life had reached a turning point.

After several months of wondering what to do, she took and passed the examination to join an international human rights watchdog NGO headquartered in New York City. In late October she would start work in their Geneva office, which focused on refugees. Her job was to investigate the human rights status of refugees in every country in the European Union and pressure the United Nations and the various governments to improve the situation. The NGO itself had a long history, but her department was fairly new. Her contract specified that she would be stationed in Geneva but spend half of each month working at the headquarters in New York.

When her PTSD symptoms were severe, she had sought only to distance herself from her memories of her experience in Iraq, but now that she had confidence in her health, she was eager to make herself useful again. If she stayed in New York, she would be unable to see Ken half the time anyway. Rather than dwell on that fact and feel miserable, she wanted to turn the situation to her advantage in some way. Clinching her decision was the murder of Jalila's parents and the difficulties Jalila was facing trying to make a life in Paris. Beyond reaching out personally to her friend, she wanted to do something to improve the system itself.

She had also been inspired by her conversation with Philip, who was now back in Baghdad. He had reminded her of the sort of people she felt comfortable with and wanted to be around from now on. Surrounding herself with such colleagues and engaging in meaningful work was the best escape from her current ennui.

Her determination was strengthened by the clash in values she had experienced with Richard. What would Ken think of her life choices? She couldn't deny Helen's role in his life, but she wanted him to grow up knowing that his mother had a different way of thinking.

When she proposed dividing Ken's care so that they each had him for two weeks at a stretch, Richard objected at first. Through his attorney, he claimed that it was a violation of their settlement. A week later, however, he came around to her way of thinking. She had no doubt that he meant it when he said that he wanted to support her independence out of "friendship," but at the same time, she sensed that he had decided her peripatetic way of life could end up increasing his time with his son.

Yoko's conversation with Sanae in Tokyo also factored heavily into her decision to take the new job. She didn't think she had purchased the concert ticket with ulterior motives, yet Sanae's keen eyes had picked up on a certain underlying expectation whose existence she could not, in retrospect, deny. She had never known herself to be so irresolute, so unwilling to accept reality. That showed how much Makino had meant to her, but at the same time it showed that she'd been stuck in the past, that there was nothing pushing her toward the future.

She was contemptuous of what Sanae had done, but rather than burning with resentment, she felt life's emptiness. As a journalist, she had interviewed many people in far more impossible circumstances, those who had endured far more severe hardships. She shared the same planet with them, and yet their situations were so different. True, that way of thinking could lead to a certain shallowness in one's emotional life; compared to a war zone, any life experience could be dismissed as "not *that* bad." And now her involvement with war zones would be deepening. Still, she couldn't stop grieving over what had happened.

One thing nagged at her: Did Makino know the truth? Did he know about Sanae's email, and about her own collapse that day? If not, she wanted to clear up the misunderstanding. But to what end? Probably she should just forget the whole drama. The sight of Sanae's baby bump came back to her. That child had done no wrong. Wouldn't it be best to let Makino enjoy fatherhood? Wasn't this all the more true because she herself had been unable to enjoy an uninterrupted relationship with either her father or her son? Saying nothing was the final duty demanded by her love for Makino, she told herself, and tried to believe it.

Before leaving for Geneva, Yoko went to see her father in Los Angeles. She had taken Ken to see him once when he was a newborn, and after that, they had met in New York; she had gotten the impression that her father didn't think much of Richard.

They agreed to meet in her Santa Monica hotel and walk from there to a nearby restaurant. In the morning, she went jogging for an hour along the boardwalk, and then swam in the pool. She had spent very little time on the West Coast, but now as she lay stretched out by the pool looking up through palm fronds at the blue sky, she had the strange, unreal feeling that if she and Richard had lived here, their marriage might have turned out differently.

Her father was dressed as usual in a black shirt and a panama hat that went well with his beard. He looked fit and healthy, but his shoulder-length hair, which he wore straight back from his forehead and behind his ears, had gone completely white.

Yoko knew that her mother had first been attracted to Solich for his looks, not just his personality and talent. His features had a severity that made people nervous, but when he spoke in his deep voice, the genial crow's-feet around his eyes charmed listeners. Yoko thought he had only grown handsomer with age. Was that because she had spent so little time under the same roof with him while growing up, or did mother and daughter have similar taste in men? His expressive eyes suggested a deeply contemplative nature.

He was as taciturn as ever—all the more reason she remembered long afterward the way his smile broadened in seeming relief when he spotted her in the hotel, and his big hug. They lunched on a sunny terrace, and as they ate, Yoko talked about her divorce, her trip to Nagasaki with Ken, and her new job. Solich listened attentively and asked questions, especially about the new job.

"Will you do on-site surveys of refugee camps in the Middle East and North Africa?"

"Not primarily. I'll receive the reports from inspectors, scrutinize them, and make recommendations to the UN and to the various governments. But it's a small department, so there probably will be times when I'll have to go myself. I won't be gathering information on a variety of topics and reporting them widely to the public, as I did as a journalist. Now I want to focus on the refugee issue and be involved in drafting measures to deal with it. Reporting is of course important, but it has its limits. Jalila has been a big influence on me."

273

Solich sipped some red wine. "You're a warmhearted person, Yoko. I'm afraid neither your mother nor I can take credit for that. It must be nurture, not nature."

Yoko scoffed. "I was divorced for the exact opposite reason. My husband told me I was cold. It's nice to have parents. They always take a favorable view of their children."

"I worry about the hardships you may suffer because of your kind heart."

"You don't need to worry about that."

Solich set his glass down with a rather solemn face and then looked up at her. They were near the seaside, but traffic was heavy on the street in front of them, drowning out the voices at the other tables.

"Facts are facts," he said. "In today's world, probably nothing is more important than verifying the truth of information. News that's fake or biased can change the fate of a country, or a person, for the worse. You used to write critical pieces, but Yugoslavia's 'ethnic cleansing' was the fault of the media as well as the politicians. There are people with no interest in getting the truth out. They'll stoop to anything. I'm proud of you, but I worry too."

"Thank you, Dad, but I'll be fine. Working with refugees isn't like going to the front lines—places that were just bombed, say—to report on the damage. It's not as dangerous as you think, and believe me, I think a lot about my own safety in the choices I make. I'm too conservative, if anything. I have Ken to think of now, and I can't take unnecessary chances."

"I'm not questioning your common sense. The question is what brought you here today, not yesterday or tomorrow but *today*? What made you be present here and now? In *Death in Venice*, Aschenbach thinks he's pursuing Tadzio, but in fact he's the pursuee."

"Well, in that case, I have no means of avoiding my fate anyway, do I?" She said this lightly, in good humor, but ever since her brush with death in Baghdad, she had been having similar thoughts. "Your films all deal with the question of predestination. What about now? Are you still pessimistic about free will?"

Solich dabbed at his mouth with his napkin, leaving some of his steak uneaten. After thinking a moment, he looked fixedly at Yoko. Though they had never lived together, his mannerisms and hers were very much alike. Her mother had marveled at it just this summer.

"Free will is necessary to have hope for the future. People need to believe that there is something they can do to make a difference. Right? But at the same time, free will increases their remorse over the past. They feel there must have been *something* they could have done. Sometimes, a belief in destiny is comforting."

Deep in her father's eyes, Yoko saw great strength. "Right. I see that. So the present is the incongruous juncture of the past and the future." Her father must be thinking of the bloody wars that had torn his native Yugoslavia apart, but what rose immediately to her mind was a far smaller, more intimate memory of something too insignificant to call a tragedy.

Her breakup with Makino hadn't been inevitable after all. There had been any number of ways to prevent it, none of them very difficult. This realization increased her misery. She had wanted to get in touch with him, and obviously she should have. Yet she couldn't and hadn't.

All this time, she had told herself she needed to respect Makino's feelings. "I'm sure you'll understand," he had written. What else did she want him to say? She should have tried harder, yes, but at the time, she was on prescription drugs for a mental state that made such an effort impossible. Ever since learning the truth from Sanae, she had felt her calm resignation shattered by the thought that there must have been something she could have done.

"I'm thinking of making a new film," Solich said. "Quitting teaching at the film school."

"How wonderful!" Her eyes shone. It had been a long time since she'd seen one of her father's films.

"But the script isn't coming along. As I'm sure you know, there are two kinds of tragedy: classical, which concerns fate, and modern, which concerns character. Right?"

"Yes."

"Oedipus killed his father and married his mother because that was his fate. He had no choice. But Othello's offense grew out of his passionate nature. If he hadn't been so simpleminded and quick to fly off the handle, he never would have killed Desdemona over a mere handkerchief. Of course, it was more complicated than that, but you get the point."

"Sure."

"Lately it seems to me that we're back in the era of classical tragedy centered on fate. Hollywood is surprisingly sensitive to such change. Unlike my films, which are more novelistic, Hollywood movies tend to be lyrical sagas describing the exploits of a hero. Think of *The Matrix*, or any number of others."

Yoko leaned back and crossed her arms. She thought of several examples and nodded. "Richard and I often talked about that. How the vast systems put in place through globalization are designed to minimize human uncertainty and absorb it as a predictable factor, focusing on the continuous smooth functioning of the entire system. Even conflict is accepted as a given. But then what happens to the possibility of individuals influencing society, causing great change, whether for good or for bad?"

"What do you think?"

She hesitated. "I don't know. I'm torn. I have a feeling I contradict myself, depending on the circumstances. If no one acts, society won't function, but the mechanization of society means that people don't have to think and act for themselves. If cars are driverless, everything people in cars do becomes unnecessary, superfluous—or errors that the system is preprogrammed to deal with. The internet makes it possible to talk face-to-face with people far away, but there's plenty of room for abuse too. Abuse is just a foreseeable glitch in a system where communication is an end in itself, and whether that means someone gets hurt, or two people are separated forever, doesn't affect the system. A person could go mad trying to figure out who to blame or thank for their unhappiness or happiness. Including me . . ."

After lunch, before Yoko returned to her hotel, she and her father went for a walk down Ocean Avenue. After life in New York, where skyscrapers cut off her view of the sky whether she looked up or straight ahead, the sheer expanse of sky over the sea was refreshing.

A drowsy white light fell upon the palms and fig trees. Her eyes on the shadow she cast on the grass, she discovered that it was not simply black, but composed of myriad colors.

Solich wore his light jacket slung over his right shoulder and his hat pushed down on his head so it wouldn't blow away. The enormous beach was crowded with afternoon sunbathers. The water must have been cold, for apart from surfers, most people were content merely to get their feet wet.

Yoko stood next to her father and watched for a while as the waves lapped the shore. "Dad, you may have answered this before, but could I ask you one thing?"

Solich nodded. Her tone made him brace himself.

"During the nine years between *Morning Sun in Dalmatia* and *Coins of Happiness*, what were you doing? I mean, after you divorced Mother and went away, leaving me behind."

"Didn't she tell you anything?"

"Nothing. But she doesn't bear you any grudge."

Eyes ahead, Solich squinted as if the sun were too bright. "I was in danger."

Shocked, she looked up at him. "Why? From whom or what?"

His eyes seemed to be responding to the diffuse thoughts inspired by his memories. "President Tito was a film buff. He gave *Morning Sun* high praise. Didn't like the script for my second film. He wanted me to make partisan films like *The Battle of Neretva*. Glorify the partisans as the genesis of the founding of Yugoslavia. But back then—think what it was like there around 1970—a nationalist Croatian Spring movement arose in Zagreb, shaking up Yugoslavian unitarism. It was inevitable. I considered myself far more of a Yugoslavian than a Croatian, but I could see that, in the long run, the suppression of Croatian nationalism would lead to a bad result, especially since there was friction with Serbia. The last thing I wanted was for my film to be used against the nationalist movement."

"The party threatened you?"

"There was some danger of arrest, but that wasn't the real trouble. I had to make my second film outside the country. Moved to Brussels. But among the backers was a far-right group under the impression, because of my clash with Tito, that I was a Croatian nationalist. Tito took the final scene of *Morning Sun*, where the main character's body lies sprawled on the earth, as a poetic homage to the sacrifices of the partisans. But the nationalists saw that character as a Croatian, and they, too, were profoundly moved. So much so that they decided to fund my second film. Then, once shooting started, they discovered that the film wasn't what they wanted it to be. The producer was partly to blame. Who knows what he told them in order to get their funding. That's probably why it all got so complicated. You see, I wasn't in danger just for ideological or political reasons. Money was involved too. The ones who came after me—who branded me a traitor—were Mafia types."

Yoko let out a long breath. "And then?"

"I was afraid there would be repercussions for you and your mother. I couldn't rely on the police, and after moving a couple of times, I talked it over with her. Whether she could stay married to me if it meant living in hiding."

"And . . . what did she say?"

Looking down, Solich adjusted his hat. "She said no. She didn't want to put you in any more danger. She wanted to bring you up in a proper environment, she said. I agreed, so that was that. For safety's sake, I expunged you both from my record. But it was for the best. Because for the next four years, I lived underground."

Yoko bit her lip to keep it from trembling and gave a series of short nods. Solich put an arm around her shoulder.

"Inside, your mother kept blaming herself. But the reason she never told you is probably because she didn't want to frighten you."

"Yes . . ."

"On the few occasions when I was able to slip away to see you, you couldn't speak English, and we couldn't talk. I was always going to tell you, after you grew up."

Yoko leaned against her father, wiped her eyes with one hand, and pulled her black sunglasses down from the top of her head to cover her eyes. Solich hugged her tighter to calm her trembling.

"Do you regret it now?"

"The important thing to remember is that I always loved you both. I'm sure it's hard for you to understand, but that's why I cut myself off from you—because I loved you. And see what a fine young woman you've grown into. Your mother has led a quiet life too. No, I don't think it was a mistake."

Yoko shook her head. "But I never got to live with you growing up," she murmured. Then she smiled, as tears ran down her cheeks. "What wasn't a mistake is . . . right now. This moment that has completely rewritten my past." Yoko thought back to the night of her first encounter with Makino, as if—through all the days and months between—he had been speaking of this moment yet to come.

Solich nodded. He did not try to put the rest of his thoughts into words, but instead yielded himself to the sound of the waves.

9

At the End of the Matinee

For Satoshi Makino and Yoko Komine, 2011 was a year when the forces of repulsion and attraction operated in equal measure.

After Sanae's confession, Makino's feelings for his wife were bound up in layers of contradiction. He felt cold wrath and mournful sympathy, aloof contempt and deep pity. He was suspicious of her every word and gesture and more understanding than ever before. Along with a disgust that urged him more than once to leave her, he felt a comfortable, familiar love more deserving of the name "affection." The unconditional trust that Sofue and his daughter Kana placed in Sanae grated on him, yet if anyone had attacked her for her wicked behavior, he would undoubtedly have defended her in a fury. He stood ready to protect his wife against all comers.

Excitement over the birth of his daughter made Makino forget his negative emotions for a while. Seeing Sanae in labor, however wrongheaded her tenacious love for him might be—or all the more so because it *was* so wrongheaded and tenacious—he thought her heroic. The process of childbirth made him appreciate the purely biological side of life. Although unaware of how this had changed him, he was instinctively affected by it. He held his wife's hand, brought his face close to hers, and murmured words of gratitude.

The fragility of his newborn child moved Makino profoundly. She was completely helpless and dependent on them; without their care, she would not survive. Those thoughts in turn evoked wonder at the elaborate workings of the human body.

The baby filled Makino's life with all sorts of new sounds. There was her crying, of course, but also her soft breathing as she slept, mixed with faint little noises; the rustle of her bedclothes and the creaking of the crib; CD lullabies and squeaky toys; Sanae's cooing, maternal voice . . . All those sounds were now part of his daily life. If he were to "perform" John Cage's famous *4'33"* composition now, the instrumentation would be utterly different from the year before.

Sometimes when he was practicing, he would get up to check on Yuki in sudden concern. Besides her sleeping face, he loved to look at her hands—hands that had yet to know the feel of so many things in this world. His own hands must have been the same when he was born. His father had dreamed of making him a guitarist; what had he felt as he looked at his tiny hands? And now, forty years later, *these* were his hands. Flexing them, he would marvel anew that he lived by making music with them.

At night, Makino fed Yuki so Sanae could get some rest. Sanae worried about his lack of sleep, but he loved that half hour with his daughter. It was midwinter, so he wrapped her in a baby blanket before setting her on his lap. He held the bottle in one hand and used his guitar footrest to straighten his back and stabilize himself. If he forced her to drink too much, she balked, but once he got the hang of it, she drank well without spitting up. He was proficient at burping her afterward too. Handling a baby was a little like playing a musical instrument.

As he felt the baby's nearly seven pounds, her softness, and the faint warmth she gave off, he strongly rejected any idea that her birth might have been a mistake. Yet, if he had stayed with Yoko, this child would not exist. Looking at her face as she slept, he wanted her to grow up secure in the knowledge that she was the product of genuine love between her parents. The idea that the father who held her in his arms cherished a woman other than her mother she would surely find unforgivable.

Sanae's parents came from Fukuoka for a visit, and her mother stayed on for a while to help with the housework and childcare. When Sanae and he were first married, his in-laws had been reserved around him, and during his long slump, they had been disturbed—her father especially had been disapproving—but now that Yuki had come along, they all made an effort to warm up to each other.

While Sanae was nursing the baby, Sanae's mother came to Makino and told him earnestly that she had always worried that her daughter was too hasty and self-willed to be the wife of an artist, but now she was thrilled with the birth of this beautiful granddaughter. She beamed.

He knew he ought to forgive his wife. If her action produced happiness, why should he reject the cause? Anyway, he absolutely had not settled for Sanae because he had lost Yoko. Their life together was founded on mutual love. Knowing that the past was fragile and liable to change at a moment's notice, he strove not to alter it, to leave things as they were.

After the Tohoku earthquake of March 11, Makino's devotion to his family was intensified many times over. On that day, he was at home, practicing on the second floor; Sanae had gone out with Yuki to register her for a day care that would begin in April. For the first time in a while, he played his Friederich guitar and then leaned it against the music stand. The next moment, he felt a strong rolling motion. The Friederich toppled over, cracking the soundboard. He lunged for his beloved Fleta and protected it with his body. It was unhurt.

He jumped up, clambered over the piles of books that had fallen from the tilted bookshelves, and tried to reach Sanae on the phone but couldn't get through. He raced over to the day care center and found them both safe, though the place was a shambles. With every after-shock, someone's voice called out evacuation orders.

Thereafter he was glued to the television, watching images of damage from the tsunami; he secured supplies of food and water and worried about reports of damage to a nuclear reactor. Friends from overseas sent a flood of messages inquiring about their safety; what was he still doing in Tokyo, they wanted to know. Makino couldn't tell if evacuation was really necessary.

He'd been scheduled to give a recital in Yokohama in early April, his first in four years, and long discussions were held about whether to cancel.

Two weeks after the disaster, Sanae's exhaustion reached the breaking point. For Yuki's sake rather than her own, she combed the internet for information on the location of radioactive substances in Tokyo and food contamination, but she ended up more confused than ever. Since she was at her wits' end, Makino decided to give in to her parents' pleading to have her and the baby stay with them in Fukuoka for the time being. He went along and spent a couple of days in their home in the district of Hakata. The absence of aftershocks was a distinct relief. The atmosphere downtown was lively, unlike the depressing state of Tokyo, where all the neon lights had been extinguished to save electricity.

Then, alone at home in Tokyo, Makino immersed himself in the unaccustomed and welcome silence, but he was lonely. Marriage and fatherhood had changed him. He watched television more than usual, following the repeated images of the tsunami and coverage of the victims as well as the minute-by-minute reports on the changing status of the nuclear disaster. He couldn't focus on his music. He spent hours on the computer gathering information. The Japanese character *kizuna*, "human bonds," was everywhere, having taken on special meaning in the face of devastating loss, and its ubiquity induced a manic state that left him, too, exhausted.

He decided to go ahead with the concert even though aftershocks were continuing. Sanae was against it, worried that he would be subject to criticism; but thinking of the profound pain he himself had recently endured, he decided to assert his conviction that now more than ever, the world needed music. Tickets sold out, but how many people would actually show up was anybody's guess. He spent a long time discussing with the sponsors what to do if it became necessary to evacuate the concert hall.

Like other artists with scheduled events around that time, he was bound to come under fire whether he went ahead with the concert or not. He announced that all proceeds would be donated to areas hit by the disaster, but criticism was harsher than he had expected. Some found staging a concert disrespectful; some said it showed a lack of common sense, as the next big quake could come at any moment; others decried the waste of scarce electricity; and still others lambasted his offer to donate the proceeds as hypocritical, a mere publicity stunt. Being attacked for doing what he thought was right would ordinarily have made Makino mad, but the disaster had unnerved him, and he questioned his own judgment.

When the day finally came, a long line formed at the ticket counter.

Makino found it at once sobering and uplifting to perform a comeback concert under these trying circumstances. To begin with, he had to overcome his own anxiety. On top of that, he had to respect the absolute silence of the dead and also share the myriad silences that each of the fortunate living would carry with them, fashioning it all into music. Those who came would be refugees from a shattered, noisy existence undeserving of the name "life."

Thanks to the calisthenics that he had started doing after Takechi's death, he had shed some weight, and his face had regained its wiry strength. He was fit, and yet for the first time in his life, he vomited backstage from nerves.

After being interviewed by two Japanese newspapers and a CNN reporter doing a feature on Japan, he retired to his dressing room and, guitar in hand, thought of Takechi, who had died never knowing of the Tohoku triple disaster—the earthquake, the tsunami, and the breakdown of the nuclear reactor. That simple fact gripped his mind. Takechi lay quietly at rest, oblivious to the nation's shock, grief, and anguish, and there was no way to tell him. Unable to find any meaning in this, Makino's thoughts circled endlessly around that inscrutable fact. He missed the sound of Takechi's voice . . . Soon he realized that Takechi's spirit had helped him get through the interval before his performance.

When he went onstage and looked out at the faces of the people filling the seats, he felt a thousand emotions. He looked up slightly, smiled, and bowed his head. The applause seemed to contain an undercurrent of sympathy for his complicated state of mind.

The program contained old and new pieces in equal numbers. Makino played smoothly and surely to the end. The act of playing was what mattered today, he reminded himself. Midway through the second half, he played the adagio movement of the Ravel Piano Concerto in G in a revamped arrangement for solo guitar. For his first encore, he played *The Cathedral* by Barrios, to meet audience expectations, and for his second, he played Villa-Lobos's "Gavotte-Choro" for the first time since he'd played it in Paris for Jalila, just after she'd fled Iraq. He didn't speak a word into the microphone. After numerous curtain calls, he bowed and left the stage for the last time, finally confident that going through with the concert had been the right choice.

Afterward, he spent some time alone in his dressing room and came to a conclusion: now was the time to tackle Bach again. During the years when his career had been on hold, he had thought constantly of this, and after the disaster, something Yoko had once said came back to him: "I really felt that, yes, this is music from after the Thirty Years'

War." She had felt the inevitability of Bach's music arising in the wake of that bloody war that decimated the German population—a realization that had come home to her while listening in Baghdad to a recording of the suites for unaccompanied cello that he, Makino, had made in his twenties. This knowledge gave him strength to resist the waves of helplessness that came over him after the disaster.

In the year that followed, Makino was as determined as ever to protect his family, but as a guitarist, he often had Yoko on his mind.

Toward the end of 2010, Yoko went to work in Geneva. The first two months were difficult. She was unused to the job of human rights overseer and to the NGO, and flying back and forth between Geneva and New York every two weeks was more grueling than she had thought it would be. She had trouble settling into a rhythm. The freezing temperatures didn't help. Still, the skyscrapers and noise of New York were a good foil for the quiet Swiss lakeside, as she had anticipated.

As she grew more accustomed to her work, she found time for extras like reunions with Swiss friends from her teenage years. She went to see her old school, and as she walked by the lake and through the old part of town, she felt a resurgence of the emotions she had experienced more than half a lifetime ago. She liked nothing more than sitting in the little library in the house where Jean-Jacques Rousseau was born, now a museum, and reading rare old books.

Her work consisted of dealing with issues such as the forced transport of Roma refugees and the housing problems of Middle Eastern refugees in France, the latter a topic she had some personal knowledge of. After Tunisia's Jasmine Revolution, she paid close attention as such upheavals began spreading in a chain reaction across North Africa toward the Middle East. She didn't visit the places in question herself but reviewed others' reports and made policy recommendations. When the United Nations Human Rights Council was in session, she went nearly every day and gave speeches before representatives of member nations, the drafts of which had to be written in a formal, nonjournalistic style.

The work was hard, but with time, her sense of fulfillment grew. Her increased confidence made her life with Ken in New York that much more rewarding.

Yoko learned of the Tohoku triple disaster while she was in Geneva. She immediately contacted the NGO staff in Japan as well as her mother in Nagasaki and friends in Tokyo. Everyone was safe. Approximately two months later, her mother started going back and forth to Fukushima, the site of the nuclear accident, as a volunteer relief worker. As she learned more, Yoko found that Japanese-language coverage of the disaster was somewhat misleading and, for the first time in her life, began writing an anonymous blog, translating informative articles from English, French, and German newspapers and television reports. She was aware that this was a violation of copyright law, but she felt justified during such an emergency and was prepared to delete the blog if anyone objected.

Passing on false information would only create more confusion, so she was scrupulous in her selections; her posts on the nuclear disaster in particular were frequently quoted and stirred up considerable debate. In barely a month, Yoko's blog became famous, with each post garnering thousands of shares. Entitled *Overseas Coverage of the Great East Japan Earthquake*, her anonymous blog was referred to more often than any other such site that sprang up.

Worried about Makino's safety, Yoko googled his name. She was concerned not just about him but about his child and the child's mother, Sanae. She prayed as a matter of course that all three of them would weather the crisis safely, but assured herself that Sanae would be sure to think first of the well-being of her husband and baby. Yoko was rather surprised at herself for her response, yet it felt natural. Her only concern was whether Sanae could handle the stress.

She learned that Makino was safe by coming across articles bashing his decision to carry on with a concert. The decision, which she was sure he had agonized over, seemed characteristic of him. She empathized with what he must be going through. In her blog, she introduced an article from RFP—the French news agency where she used to work—with friendly coverage of a Tokyo concert and added an unusually long note defending musicians who had become the target of criticism. She touched on Makino's Yokohama concert in passing.

When the manager of Kinoshita Music showed him the post, Makino was greatly encouraged. Usually, the blog took up exclusively disaster-related articles, and this detour prompted lively speculation about the blogger's identity. Knowing that someone understood him was of great comfort to Makino; he never dreamed it was Yoko.

Nor did Yoko have any way of knowing whether or not he had read her note.

Makino's new album, *The Complete Set of Bach's Unaccompanied Cello Suites*, was released in early February 2012. The old version, which Yoko had been so fond of, was considered representative of Makino's playing and often featured in magazine specials on classical music as a "must-listen." Makino, however, found special meaning in reprising the performance after the disaster.

The recording took place over a three-day period in London's Abbey Road Studios, and Makino was closely involved in the postproduction, for which the studio was famed. The recording company had chosen Abbey Road. While Makino did not feel particularly strongly about the Beatles, he enjoyed working in that studio, which was also renowned for its classical recordings. When the album came out, he was rather abashed to see it advertised as "recorded in the famous Abbey Road Studios!"

Still, he was pleased with the result. The CD was released simultaneously in Japan and abroad, and to his relief, the critics liked it. Many wrote of feeling "saved" by the music—a word one seldom encountered in reviews. Reporters asked about his long slump and the birth of his child. They also posed questions about the impact of the disaster, but he limited himself to simple expressions of his feelings. Although a year had passed, recovery from the damage inflicted by the tsunami, as well as the handling of the nuclear disaster, was ongoing, and the scale of the effort was too big to express in words.

It was a difficult time to be selling anything, but to Makino's surprise his album was named Editor's Choice by a prestigious magazine and awarded a gold prize by the French music magazine *Diapason*. Furthermore, a CNN special entitled "The Tohoku Disaster: One Year On" showed images of his Yokohama concert as well as the new Bach recording. Boosted by this publicity, as well as Noda's promotional project—posting sheet music from *What a Wonderful World* and offering lessons online to guitar aficionados around the world—the Bach recording became one of *Billboard*'s top-ten bestselling classical albums.

Makino was scheduled to perform in Cuba and Brazil in 2012, but with the success of the Bach album, another performance was added in New York City's Merkin Concert Hall. The recently renovated thirty-year-old hall, with seating for 450, had a reputation for near-perfect acoustics. Tickets sales were robust, and apparently not all the purchasers were Japanese. Little did Makino know that among them was Yoko Komine.

While working on the recording in London, Makino had caught a glimpse of Yoko on television. Watching the BBC news in his hotel room before going out for dinner, he saw a report on the deliberations of the UN Human Rights Council over the Assad regime's suppression of protests in Syria. Then, for a few seconds, there was Yoko delivering a speech in English with her name and title at the bottom of the screen, followed by a brief interview out in the corridor.

Makino froze while buttoning his shirt, his eyes fixed on the screen. His breath caught and he sat down on the bed, watching her. Dressed in a suit, she had her hair swept up, showing off her slender neck to good advantage. She spoke in her low-pitched voice, with the same intellectual manner he remembered so well; the look in her eyes was impassioned.

More than four years had gone by. She looked a bit older, to be sure, but she was full of life. Memories of the many nights they had spoken over Skype flooded him. He missed that time. Her life had certainly moved on. She would never know how much she had inspired his music after the disaster. Perhaps somewhere she had heard his new rendering of Bach, but seeing with his own eyes how busy she now was, and in view of the awkward way they had broken up, it seemed unlikely.

For the first time since the breakup, he googled her name and checked the website of the NGO she now worked for. It was headquartered in Geneva, which meant she no longer lived in New York. CNN had given her surname as "Komine," her maiden name; what about her husband, the American economist, and their child? Korenaga had reported that Yoko was happily married, and Makino had no reason to doubt that. It never occurred to him that she might be divorced.

Still, having glimpsed her on television, he spent the night before his recording session wishing fervently that he might somehow see her in real life. Ever since the disaster, he had lived with the lurking fear that sudden death might strike again at any time, and so he had forced himself to face the future resolutely. Now his bottled-up yearnings overflowed. All he could think was how much he wanted to see Yoko again and talk with her to his heart's content.

Makino's New York recital was set for the second Saturday in May 2012, at one in the afternoon in Merkin Concert Hall. Tickets sold out a week beforehand.

He talked over the program with the sponsors and decided to focus the first half on the works of Leo Brouwer and other twentieth-century composers, such as Villa-Lobos and Toru Takemitsu. In the second half, he would perform three of Bach's cello suites. For his encores, he said he would play pieces from the *What a Wonderful World* album "as the mood strikes me."

Once the New York performance was scheduled, Makino couldn't help remembering that New York was where Yoko used to live. Had she still been living there, he wondered whether he would have tried to get in touch with her. Until that moment, he had strenuously avoided thinking of doing such a thing. All he had to go on was her old mailing address at RFP, but Korenaga would probably know her current one.

As he went on about his daily life with Sanae and Yuki, Makino felt guilty about his desire to see Yoko. He wanted to unconditionally commit himself to Yuki's life; if he couldn't do that, he would be a worthless human being. *Too much time has gone by,* he told himself over and over, irritated at himself for clinging to the past.

The sight of Yoko living a life filled with meaning and zest made him happy and proud, and it also made him feel that he had best keep away. Still unaware of the encounter between her and Sanae, he longed to dispel the misunderstanding of that night in Tokyo. He wanted her to know how much he had loved and needed her then.

But really, what difference would it make after all this time? He was trapped by the reality of life in the moment. They each had moved on to fulfilling new lives with their own separate, intense emotions.

Certainly, the past could be changed. But could you change the past without also changing the present? Wouldn't Yoko chastise him with the same words he had said to Sanae? "Why didn't you just go on saying nothing? I think that would have been better."

Makino set out alone on the long trip to New York and Central and South America, accompanied by neither Sanae and Yuki nor anyone from Kinoshita or Globe. He had asked the sponsors to arrange for a room in New York where he could practice, and he was staying in a midtown hotel.

Before dinner on the day of his arrival, he went for a walk in Chelsea. Korenaga had told him that this was where Yoko used to live. Every time he spotted a woman with Asian features or passed a woman and child, he realized that somewhere inside he was searching for her. At a red light, he told himself to cut it out. He had no business seeing her. And anyway, she wasn't even here . . .

And so, on the day of the performance, he took the stage not knowing that Yoko was seated in the back of the hall on the first floor.

Yoko purchased *The Complete Set of Bach's Unaccompanied Cello Suites* soon after it came out, but she was so enamored of the earlier version, which she felt gave full play to Makino's genius, that she couldn't bring herself to open it. This new album marked an end to his silence as a recording artist, and it had come out less than a year after the Tohoku disaster. With that in mind, she finally listened to it, and as she did so, felt shame for having held back.

She almost forgot that she had once loved and been loved by him, so enchanted was she by his presence as a musician. She felt a special reverence for him as someone of her own generation, and was moved in ways she couldn't express. This was simply fine music; that's all there was to it. If only she could congratulate him. And if Sanae's support had made this possible, she wanted to congratulate her too.

Not long after she began to work in Geneva, Yoko had been introduced by a friend to the chef of a famous restaurant who became romantically interested in her. A Swiss divorcé, he was a bit older than she, and his restaurant soon became one of her favorite haunts. Every time she went there, they would get into long conversations, and he invited her to parties at his place featuring home-cooked meals. Twice they went out for dinner together. The idea of starting a relationship with him was tantalizing, but she was so busy that, in the end, it came to nothing. Still, after five years of being torn between Makino and Richard, she was pleasantly surprised to sense the possibility of a different love in her life. Her memories of Makino seemed to recede even more. She got along well with her new colleagues, and apart from missing Ken when she was away, she enjoyed her single life. Still, there were times when she felt lonely.

When she found out about Makino's upcoming concert at Merkin Concert Hall, she checked her schedule and realized she would be in New York then. She purchased a ticket. Unlike that time when she had run into Sanae in Tokyo, now she had fulfilling work to do. Going to the concert would be a way of drawing a curtain on the past, once and for all. She put off deciding whether to leave without seeing him or simply greet him as an old friend.

𝄡

On the day of the concert, the sky was so blue that people setting out on their morning errands looked up and stared, open mouthed.

Makino had slept well, and he felt good. Rehearsal went without a hitch. When the concert hall staff heard him play for the first time, they were impressed, enthusiastically shedding their skepticism. Makino himself felt confident, but since he had no prior experience performing in the United States, he couldn't predict how the audience might respond. In chatting with the staff, he told an anecdote in his usual comical way: he had stepped into the hotel elevator just as a guy all sweaty from the gym got off, leaving behind a pungent odor, and when a woman got on at the next floor, she had assumed the smell came from him, much to his dismay. Surprised at his droll humor, the staff burst out laughing. He felt himself relaxing.

Alone in his dressing room, Makino filed a rough place on one nail while he looked over the sheet music. This was how he had to get through the silence before the performance.

Meanwhile, Yoko, whose New York apartment was fairly near Makino's hotel, was having a simple brunch and looking through her large window at the piercing blue sky. Richard would be handing Ken over to her the next day. As she put on makeup in the quiet room, she studied herself in the mirror. It had been five years since she'd seen Makino. She couldn't decide what to wear, but finally put on a white Chloé dress and set out with a light jacket around her shoulders. She didn't want to stand out, which was also why she had chosen a first-floor seat toward the back. But then again, she wondered if she should have chosen a more striking outfit, since she might see him after the concert.

By the time she arrived at the hall, the seats were already filling up. People were chatting as they waited, apparently eager to hear Makino play, and here and there she caught snatches of Japanese. Sitting on either side of her were Americans who didn't seem to know much about Makino but came because they liked his CDs.

Soon it was curtain time. The lights went down and the stage lit up. After one or two last coughs, there was silence.

The door at one side of the stage opened, and Yoko's pulse began to race. There was a burst of applause. A moment later, Makino appeared, wearing a black shirt and pants. He walked to the center of the stage with his eyes downcast and glanced at the audience before sitting down. Yoko swallowed hard, watching his every move as he adjusted his footrest and settled his guitar on his lap. Makino was here. Not in memory, but right here, so close she could have run up to him. It took a few moments for this reality to sink in.

The program opened with Brouwer's famous three-part *The Black Decameron*, followed by works by Villa-Lobos, Toru Takemitsu, and Rodrigo, the first half ending with Brouwer's Sonata for Guitar. The moment part one of *The Black Decameron*, "The Warrior's Harp," began, with its highly charged rhythms and mystical double-octave leaps, the hall was transformed. As the recursive melody gradually intensified, the sustained notes rang straight out to the farthest corners of the hall, unhindered. Those familiar with the music and those hearing it for the first time were similarly amazed by the powerful sound.

With each succeeding piece, Makino portrayed a fresh musicscape, conveyed with such variety of expression it was hard to believe the sounds all emerged from the same instrument. Going beyond the faultless, almost too-perfect world of his former style, he now seemed to allow the music freedom to dance, watching over it and then, with consummate skill, guiding it to fresh heights. This was the new style he had achieved after working his way through the long slump.

Each round of applause increased in intensity. Finally, after his rendition of the dynamic third movement of Brouwer's Sonata, some listeners were so excited that, even though the concert was only half over, they sprang to their feet with shouts of "Bravo!" Makino seemed surprised; he took a few steps forward from his chair and stood transfixed for several seconds. Then, regaining his composure, he bowed and left the stage.

Yoko sipped coffee alone in the lobby during the intermission, listening to snippets of excited conversation around her. Even here in New York, Makino had succeeded in capturing the hearts of his listeners. She remembered the first time she had heard him play, long ago in Paris. Snobbish devotees of classical guitar, skeptical of the "boy genius"— and a Japanese boy, to boot!—had begun chattering with irrepressible excitement after the first half of the program. She fondly remembered the mixed emotions his playing had aroused in her, how she had been almost envious of his talent.

A faint clatter as she returned her coffee cup to its saucer told her that her hand was trembling. "His gift is like a paper airplane that God folded and let fly just for fun." That had been her first impression of Makino's music. In its solitary flight, that paper airplane was soaring high over new vistas—and now that she knew not only the beauty of its line of flight but also the sensitive quivering of the tip slicing cleanly through the air, the music stirred her more profoundly than ever before.

All this time she had kept her memories of him from five years before stored carefully away, but he himself had moved on to a world far beyond her reach. He was remote, and she was just another listener, not at all special. Telling herself this helped to melt the tense stiffness inside her, but it also made her unutterably sad. Makino did not seem to have noticed her.

She particularly wanted to hear the Bach half of the program, but what if he did see her and lost focus, spoiling this concert that promised to be such a success? Perhaps she had better leave during the intermission. By now she was more or less convinced that what Sanae had said was true: her existence had been a distraction to Makino. Thinking she should at least congratulate him, she took out a notebook and started to write a letter, but midway through, she tore the page out and crumpled it into a ball.

An announcement rang out: the second half was about to begin. She looked back and forth between the entrance to the hall and the building exit. It was truly beautiful weather outside. She stood hesitating until hardly anyone else was around. And then, still filled with misgivings, she made her way back to her seat.

Makino reappeared on the stage, now wearing a crisp white shirt. Because she felt so distant from him, it should have been a simple matter to draw a curtain on the past once and for all, as she had planned. But now, seeing him in the flesh, feelings that she had thought long since gone came rushing to the surface, throwing her off balance.

He had chosen three of Bach's cello suites: the representative Suite no. 1, the infamously difficult Suite no. 5, and finally Suite no. 3, which had been one of the most beloved pieces in the classical guitar canon ever since Segovia's recording was released in 1961.

When the music began, Yoko stared at Makino, his head turned down as if engaged in solitary contemplation. The guitar never moved, seemingly suspended in air. Makino's playing was known for its clarity, and today, perhaps because of the fine acoustics, the timbre was round and lucid. Compared to the concert's first half, which had highlighted Brouwer's "hyper-Romanticism," Makino's playing was now more architectural, and the harmonic cross sections shone like a polished mirror. The vibrant sound glimmered with what might be called a detached tenderness. By turns deep and light, the music wove a multitude of sounds and visions into an exquisite tapestry.

Yoko closed her eyes and recalled Makino's performance of *Concierto de Aranjuez* five and a half years before, in Suntory Hall. Their subsequent conversation and smiles. The lingering, longing looks they had exchanged through the taxi window at the moment of parting . . . Then came a jumbled succession of memory scraps in no particular order: the day in Paris when Makino had declared his love for her, her married life with Richard, the terrorist bombing in Iraq, Skype conversations with Makino, Jalila's phone call from the Paris airport, the rainy night sky seen from her bed in that Tokyo hotel, Ken's birth, her confrontation with Sanae, the profile of her mother chatting while she drove in Nagasaki, her father's embrace in Santa Monica . . .

Her heart was torn by memories of all the time that had passed since she had met Makino. She felt tears swell behind her eyelids but fiercely resisted the impulse to cry. *How can this be?* she asked herself yet again. How could it be that they had ended up leading separate lives?

The question seemed to emerge from Makino's performance itself. In Bach's seemingly infinite formal experimentation, Makino had found an exceedingly modest expression of doubt and given it quiet, strong resonance, the assured performance of his twenties giving way to an insecurity of far greater depth. His music posed questions bursting with awe and originality, echoed by responses containing mystical magnitude, affirmation, and consolation.

Yoko understood exactly where Makino was. She knew what territory he had reached as a musician and what he sought to express. She was profoundly moved that all he wanted to say took the form of this resounding music. The Prelude no. 3 that she had listened to daily in Iraq was infused with new light. A brighter, calmer, warmer light . . .

She mustn't see him. She had to accept that it was too late. She thought of her childhood longing for her absent father and of the loneliness Ken was now enduring. She thought of the child born to Sanae and Makino. And she reveled in the life-affirming wondrousness of Makino's music. That affirmation mustn't be destroyed. She had come here, after all, to mark the end of a certain period of her life . . . And yet she wanted to hold on to his love at least for the duration of this concert. Though she had been with him only three times, he was the love of her life.

The music soared on. Oh, that this moment might last forever, might never end.

The second half of the concert, unlike the first, was marked by a delicate, soul-satisfying exaltation. The audience's faces, eyes fixed on Makino, shone with a slightly tormented luminosity. Some people, instead of swaying or tapping in time to the music, mouthed silent words, secrets known only to themselves.

When he finished playing the final Gigue movement, Makino received a standing ovation. Yoko, too, was on her feet, clapping hard while burning the scene into her memory.

Makino looked around the auditorium, clearly deeply moved, and bowed. He left the stage and then returned for an encore, playing "Visions" and "What a Wonderful World." He looked much relieved. The audience, thoroughly satisfied, was also more relaxed now and seemed almost ready to sing along. The couple sitting next to Yoko did in fact mouth the words under their breath as he played.

Before his final encore, Makino took the microphone in hand and addressed the audience in English. After expressing his appreciation, he said, "I have never performed here before, but the acoustics are wonderful, and I have really enjoyed this afternoon. Central Park is nearby, and you know, it's such a beautiful day that I think I'll go for a stroll around the pond after the concert."

The audience greeted this unexpected announcement with smiles and applause. Yoko looked steadily at the expression on his face.

After a pause, Makino looked in the direction of the rear first-floor seats and said, "And now, at the end of the matinee, I will play one more melody—a very special melody—for you."

Yoko stopped smiling and caught her breath. Makino was looking straight at her. There could be no doubt: this next encore was for her alone.

He took his seat, positioned his guitar, and sat motionless for a few seconds. Then he began to play the famous theme from Jerko Solich's *Coins of Happiness*. The moment she heard the opening arpeggios, tears spilled over and ran down her cheeks.

X

After the performance, Makino went for a walk alone in Central Park, admiring the green leaves of the trees lit up by the soft afternoon sunlight. The tide of his euphoria had ebbed, taking with it a big piece of himself, and he savored the quiet tranquility.

He didn't know his way around New York, and the park was so huge he might have gotten lost if not for the cluster of high-rise buildings that towered in the distance on the Upper East Side, helping him get his bearings. Families were out enjoying the weekend, and picnickers and sunbathers dotted the grass.

He had become aware of Yoko's presence in the audience after finishing the last piece in the first half of the program. When he stood up to acknowledge the unexpected applause, he had spotted her sitting in the shadowy back of the theater. For an instant he had stood frozen, feeling as if time had stopped.

When he returned to the stage, the first thing he'd done was to make sure she was still there. More than anyone else, he wanted *her* to hear his new Bach. He felt a flood of joy, and at the same time, out of the tangled skein of memories that had come back to him during the intermission, he vividly recalled that night five years before in her Paris *appartement* when for a sublime ten minutes he had played for Jalila. He sat on his chair in the same frame of mind as on that night, picked up his guitar, and closed his eyes. And then, plunging alone into the vast sea of silence, he began the prelude to Bach's Cello Suite no. 1.

The sound of a distant police siren reverberated across the sky and faded away. Sensing a change in the sunlight, Makino hurried along. Fragments of the *Duino Elegies* poem quoted in *Coins of Happiness* revolved in his mind:

> *Angel! If somewhere there were a plaza we know nothing of, . . . might not a pair of lovers, who in this world never succeeded in mastering the acrobatics of love, tremblingly display those high-flying, daring figures . . . ? Surely they*

300

would not fail again . . . standing on the once-more silent
carpet, those lovers wreathed now in true smiles.

He came to the edge of the pond, which reflected the deep green all around, and in his eagerness and anxiety kept changing his grip on the handle of his guitar case. He walked along, his eyes searching wide across the space before him. Just off the path curving gently around the pond, he saw a bench in a shady spot straight ahead.

He stood still. Watching the desultory play of the afternoon light on the surface of the pond was a woman, seated alone on the bench. She slowly turned her face toward him.

He looked at her and smiled. Yoko started to respond, but it was all she could do to maintain her composure. She stood up, purse in hand, and turned again to face him. He was already walking toward her. His figure grew bigger as she watched. With reddened eyes, she finally smiled too. Five and a half years had passed since the smiles they exchanged the night they first met.

ACKNOWLEDGMENTS

This book could not have been written without the cooperation of many people, for which I am deeply grateful. Classical guitarist Shin-ichi Fukuda in particular made himself available from the very beginning, when the novel was still in the planning stage, and I am greatly in his debt. Guitarists Daisuke Suzuki and Yasuji Ohagi also gave me advice.

Concerning Rilke's *Duino Elegies*, I did the translation myself (using the text *Werke in drei Bänden* by Rainer Maria Rilke, Horst Nalewski, ed., Leipzig: Insel-Verlag, 1978) under the supervision of the German literary scholar Yoshikazu Takemine. I of course am alone responsible for any infelicities.

In addition, the following associations and individuals gave me valuable input: the Japan Association for Refugees, the Association of Nagasaki Hibakusha and Their Testimonies, Jean-Marc Mojon, Robert Campbell, and Kanae Doi, Japanese representative to Human Rights Watch, the international nongovernmental organization.

Finally, in the course of gathering information about Iraq, I had the unparalleled chance to sit down with the late freelance journalist Kenji Goto for long talks about his experiences covering global conflict. My description of Jalila's refugee experience is largely drawn from his

December 11, 2004, report in the *Independent Press* entitled "Pari no Irakujin josei" (An Iraqi woman in Paris). It pains me more than I can say that I can never deliver this book to Goto, who was eagerly looking forward to its completion. On January 30, 2015, he was executed by Islamic State militants. Rest in peace.

ABOUT THE AUTHOR

Photo © Mikiya Takimoto

Keiichiro Hirano is an award-winning and bestselling novelist whose debut novel, *The Eclipse*, won the prestigious Akutagawa Prize in 1998, when he was a twenty-three-year-old university student. A cultural envoy to Paris appointed by Japan's Ministry of Cultural Affairs, Hirano has lectured throughout Europe. Widely read in France, China, Korea, Taiwan, Italy, and Egypt, Hirano's novels include the Watanabe Junichi Literary Prize–winning novel *At the End of the Matinee*—a runaway bestseller in Japan—and the critically acclaimed and Yomiuri Prize for Literature–winning *A Man*. His short fiction has appeared in the *Columbia Anthology of Modern Japanese Literature*. For more information, visit http://en.k-hirano.com and follow Hirano on Twitter at @hiranok_en.

ABOUT THE TRANSLATOR

Photo © 2014 Toyota Horiguchi

Juliet Winters Carpenter is a veteran translator and professor emerita of Doshisha Women's College of Liberal Arts in Kyoto. Her first translated novel, *Secret Rendezvous* by Kobo Abe, received the 1980 Japan-US Friendship Commission Prize for the Translation of Japanese Literature. In 2014, *A True Novel* by Minae Mizumura received the same award as well as the American Translators Association Lewis Galantière Award. The audio edition of her translation of Shion Miura's bestselling novel *The Great Passage* won an Earphones Award. Carpenter's other recent translations include *An I-Novel* by Minae Mizumura and *Pax Tokugawana: The Cultural Flowering of Japan, 1603–1853* by Toru Haga. She lives on Whidbey Island in Washington.